SISTERS PUL

"I'm going to buy sheep of my own," Katie announced, "and build up a flock so that when I leave here I'll have something." She didn't look down at the feedsack, but Rebecca did.

"It's time to go," she said, stooping to pick it up. "Are you sure you'll be all right here?"

"Yes. It's the only chance you've got."

Rebecca reached out and then crushed Katie in an embrace. Her heart ached and her eyes stung with tears. How long would it be until they were reunited? Katie would be alone now, and she was pitifully small to stand against Amos's wrath. It would burst across this valley like a thunderstorm. And yet there was steel in this girl. Rebecca could feel it, and that made her ashamed of her own doubts and fears.

"Good-bye," she whispered. "May God protect you until we are together again."

"Go on!" Katie choked. "Run and never come back to these people."

Rebecca tore herself away and stumbled into the night, feeling more hurt and alone than she ever had in her life.

WIND RIVER

GARY McCARTHY

LEISURE BOOKS NEW YORK CITY

For Katie Greene,
who also has an indomitable spirit.

A LEISURE BOOK®

April 1998

Published by

Dorchester Publishing Co., Inc.
276 Fifth Avenue
New York, NY 10001

ISBN 0-8439-4377-7

Chapter One

The slim young woman lowered her head and leaned forward, straining at the shafts of the Mormon handcart, her bare toes biting into the warm, red dust of Utah's Echo Canyon. For a moment, the cart would not budge. Her breath came in short desperate bursts, and her arms and shoulder muscles corded. Maybe, she thought, this is finally the end.

But the cart broke its inertia. The wooden wheels, long since worn dry of grease, protested sharply, and the cart rolled onward, following the deep ruts of the emigrant trail.

Rebecca Prescott, seventeen years old, tried not to think of the heat, a heat so intense it felt as though a stove lid had slammed down on the world. She kept her blue-green eyes riveted on the ground; she was barefoot and could ill afford to step on a horseshoe nail, a sharp piece of twisted metal, or a shard of glittering glass.

The Mormons had given her shoes, but they hadn't fitted and had blistered her ankles until perspiration burned like stinging nettles. She'd traded the shoes for five pounds of cornmeal and a pound of sugar. Now the food and her strength were both gone. Rebecca dared not think of their situation but instead reasoned that if her father ever got over his fever and could walk, perhaps they could trade the handcart for food and some cloth so that she might sew a dress for herself and one for little Katie. She did not want to go back home to Springfield, Illinois in rags. Yes, Micah had failed again—in the Gold Rush country of California and then on the Comstock Lode of Nevada. He'd failed again, as he always had—

only this time they'd lost Beth from pneumonia. As far as Rebecca was concerned, he'd killed her mother. And now, as he lay unconscious while she and Katie pulled and pushed the hated handcart, Micah was killing them, too.

She loathed him for that, and if she'd had the courage, she would have left him with the Mormons and continued on to Springfield, where they still knew people who cared—people who lived with some dignity and whose homes had windows and board floors; people who ate with knives and forks and not with their unwashed fingers.

As each agonizing step brought her closer to her own kind of people, closer to home, Rebecca told herself that this terrible canyon, with its red rock walls, must surely be the devil's own gateway out of a desert hell. This canyon was her final test; she knew that it would finally deliver them into the cool, high grasslands of Wyoming. She remembered their journey out to the West and how they'd admired the swift pronghorn antelope with their pure white rumps and large, ever watchful eyes. Back then the Prescotts had been a real family, touched and almost enchanted with the grandeur of the American West as it had unfolded across the window of the rocking stagecoach. What an adventure it had seemed! But soon they'd come to the Utah and then Nevada deserts, and the wonder of it all just evaporated in the choking heat and dust.

This *was* the final test. And now the air was so hot it burned her throat and left her gasping and dazed. At least they wouldn't die of thirst, for there was a stream running along the canyon's floor, a stream clogged with willows, cottonwoods, and grass. The water was good and ran pure, as though cauterized against the sun-baked rocks.

The stream danced in sunlight, gurgled and laughed and enticed her to rest, to bathe in its coolness, to lie up under the trees, shielded from the fiery sun. But she paused only a moment. Hunger rode her with its whip hand, and Rebecca thought she and Katie would die if they didn't eat soon. Perhaps, she told herself, by late afternoon we will be out of this canyon and be among the antelope again, and I shall steel myself and then kill one to eat. Or possibly we will find a family with a little extra food and they will invite us to share a meal.

Unlike her father, Rebecca would accept any charity now. She would smile and pretend she didn't notice the bold, hungry eyes and how the men stared at her. If she were to believe their words, and even those of her departed mother, she would have to concede that she was beautiful. Slightly taller than average, she had a heart-shaped face with very high cheekbones, large blue-green eyes with dark, gracefully shaped eyebrows, and a wide, generous mouth. Though she tried to protect her face with a drooping slouch hat, the sun's reflection had given her skin a tawny golden color. Her neck was long and slender, much more suited to necklaces than to the rough homespun collars she always wore, and her honey-colored hair was long and thick. Her mother had fretted that Rebecca's beauty could be a trial for her, a cross to bear. Rebecca didn't know about that; so far, happiness had been as elusive as her father's dreams.

"Rebecca," Katie begged, "can't we stop to rest? Father looks to be burning alive."

"Just a little farther," she whispered. "Just to those rocks up ahead. By that fallen tree."

Katie sighed with disappointment, for the tree was still far away. Rebecca pulled even harder. Katie was just a slip of a girl, not nearly strong enough for this ordeal. A feisty, willowy little trooper, she never complained. Rebecca admired her courage, her blind trust first in Micah, now in her sister. There had been times these past few weeks when that trust had made all the difference between quitting and going on. Katie was the real fighter; she wasn't going to be tall or pretty, but instead God had endowed her with an inner strength and a perseverance that Rebecca truly envied. Katie was a happy girl; nothing really discouraged her, even when she'd looked into the face of tragedy on that rainy Sierra morning when they'd buried their mother in the rich, dark soil flanking the Stanislaus River.

Rebecca's mouth hardened with bitterness at the memory. She wished Micah had been the one they'd read the Bible over. It would have been justice. It was he who'd dragged them from Illinois into the awful years of poverty, who'd kept them scrambling from one gold camp to another, only to fail again and again, ever poorer, ever more locked into an endless downward spiral of despair. Did the marriage vows mean a woman had to forsake everything—her home, her friends, the simple, decent pleasures and small rewards of a lifetime of virtue and dedication—for an egotistical fool of a husband? Micah spun his dreams as a spider spun its web, and the dreams were just as fragile and not nearly so fine. At first his dreams were spellbinding. How well she remembered listening to him by the light of their hearth fire! But as she grew older she came to see that he was a man of words, and that words could not feed and clothe a family. Beth had never seen the real man she'd married, and perhaps that was God's mercy.

"Rebecca! We're at the rocks. You promised."

They came to a halt. Rebecca released the shafts, then unwound the rags from her palms and turned to look at her father. She could not escape a moment of pity; he had aged so these past few weeks. Most of his hair was now white, though the red dust gave it a mousy brown appearance. He'd lost the fat that he'd always worn around his waist even while his family grew thin. With luck or family connections, he might have been a successful politician. Words! My Lord, he was full of them! They were the only things that he really loved and that came easy to him. He'd grown up in Ohio and had been weaned on the impassioned sermons of his fire-and-brimstone preacher father. Rebecca didn't know why he hadn't taken up the call himself; maybe because he'd always lacked self-discipline. Micah couldn't stick with anything for long. Opportunities had come to him, but not the miraculous good fortune that he'd always courted. Micah could dance and he could sing; he could even be an enthralling orator. And yet . . . and yet for all those talents and his considerable charm, Lady Luck had spurned him, never to provide that one golden chance in life that can lead to worldly riches.

He was like the glass Christmas ornament she'd had as a child and still remembered vividly. It was faceted and dazzling with color when twirled before the firelight, but once stationary, the magic was gone, the colors not so pretty nor sparkling, and the facets themselves indistinct figures with a dull sameness. She had fought her disappointment and raised the glass back up to the firelight, only to see that the ornament was cracked and hollow. Ever since that Christmas, Rebecca had always distrusted anything that gave the eye an illusion of bright, flashy perfection.

Thinking about him and seeing his red wind-burned and sunburned face, Rebecca felt ashamed, and to atone for the uncharitable thoughts, she made herself dampen a cloth from the stream and wipe the dirt and sweat from her father's face before she allowed herself to drink. She then walked over and sat beside Katie and slowly, luxuriously tested the water with her sore and swollen feet. She stretched full out and gazed up through the branches of the cottonwood trees and saw an eagle. It floated effortlessly, and the sun made its great wings shine.

"Look at him," Rebecca sighed. "He floats above the earth where it's cool and he can see the face of the world curve from sundown to sunup. And if he had a mind, he could probably fly to Springfield by tomorrow. And here we are, crawling along like . . . like insects."

Katie giggled. "Insects? Oh, come on! We're not *that* bad off."

"Almost. We're out of food."

"We'll find some. Could be fish in here even." Katie peered at the water, saw only minnows. "Besides, didn't they tell us there was a stage station in Echo Canyon?"

Rebecca brightened. "I forgot! That's right. It's supposed to be at the eastern end."

"This can't go on forever. We're climbing, and once we get out of here it will be cooler."

"I hope so. I never want to see another desert again." Rebecca wearily climbed to her feet. "We'd better go on now. Give father some more water. I'll refill the canteens."

Katie looked at Micah. Worry marred her usually pleasant face. "Do you think he'll be all right?"

"I don't know. See his lips move? Perhaps he and God are talking it over now. Our father always did think he had special gifts."

"Rebecca! That's a terrible thing to say. You've got to forgive him or there will be a mark on your soul."

Rebecca didn't answer. Katie was only fourteen, and she was far too young to understand how things had been before they'd sold everything to come out West. Katie was lucky. She didn't remember how Beth had looked then, so happy that her laughter was almost musical. It would do no good to tell her sister how their mother once had possessed a real zest for life and not even Micah's early string of failures had been able to change her. Beth had always been full of hope, never doubting her husband, encouraging him to find his dreams. Right to the very end of her days, she had sworn that her husband would succeed if only they had faith in him just a little longer. Well, a little longer never came. Instead, Beth had been laid to rest in a pauper's grave, and her marker would rot within a year. She would be gone as if she'd never existed, except in the hearts of her daughters.

They moved out of the shade of the cottonwoods, and the heat hit her like a body blow. Ahead the heat waves shimmered up the canyon walls, and far to the south Rebecca saw an enormous mushroom-shaped cloud billowing toward heaven. Under that cloud it might be raining warm water on the plains, and she fervently wished she were there to tilt her face upward and let the sky wash not only the red dust away but also the hatred she felt for Micah.

"There!" Katie gasped much later. "Isn't that a stage station?"

Rebecca lifted her head and glanced at it. "I think so.

It's still far away, though. Let's keep moving."

When they finally did stagger into the station yard, Rebecca called out, but there was no answer. "It seems deserted," she said, trying to beat down her sense of disappointment.

"Everything is in order." Katie glanced about warily. "I can just feel that something is wrong here."

Rebecca had the same sensation. She stepped out of the handcart shafts, then gathered up Micah's cap-and-ball rifle, a rifle she knew how to use if necessary. She handed Katie an old flintlock pistol that neither of them trusted, but it looked fearsome. "Let's not use either of these relics unless we just have to."

"We ought to get out of here," Katie said.

"We need food now." They both glanced at some scrawny, molting chickens over at the far end of the yard. They looked faster than desert roadrunners. They'd be near impossible to catch before dark, but they might at least have a few eggs hidden in the grass.

"Anyone home?" Rebecca yelled, hearing her voice echo into silence.

Cocking the big rifle, she walked over to peer into a small rock-and-mud lean-to. Obviously it was the blacksmith shop; she could see an anvil and forge and a neat array of black-smithing tools hung along the back wall. Whoever worked in here was an orderly man. She backed out and moved cautiously toward the station itself. It was also made of rock but was much larger, perhaps the size of three freight wagons pulled up beside one another. Built into the side of the canyon, it was skirted by a well-worn path around one side that brought one up onto the thick sod roof, which was littered with cigarette butts. The inhabitants of the station had obviously enjoyed sitting up there and smoking. The front of the station was formidable-looking and consisted of big rocks and mortar. The door was constructed of split logs, as was the shutter over a small window under which were two little gunports. It was a fortress, designed to resist an Indian attack and to withstand a siege. Rebecca could see no sign of Indians. The hoofprints in the yard were all of shod horses. She moved closer.

"Maybe someone is dead in there," Katie whispered nervously.

Rebecca had already considered that possibility. "Then we have to find out. And besides, if there's any food inside, he won't be needing it."

"I'm afraid of this gun," Katie said. "Father told me it could blow up in your face."

"Let's trade, then. You stand back from the door while I push it open."

With the big pistol like a rock in her hand, Rebecca approached the log door. She made sure that Katie had the rifle up to her shoulder, then she placed her foot against the door and shoved it hard. Sunlight washed through the doorway and showed them a man lying face-down on the dirt floor. His right pants leg was covered with dried blood, and his fist clenched a gun.

Rebecca dropped her pistol and fell to his side. "He's breathing!" she exclaimed, managing to roll him over. "Quickly, bring me some water!"

He was a tall, angular man with a lean face covered with whisker stubble. Although he was probably only in his early twenties, there were already deep squint lines at the corners of his eyes. He was square-jawed, with a scar over one eye and another faint one down along the prominence of his cheekbone. A rugged-looking man, he reminded her of so many of the breed of lonely cowboys and outpost tenders she'd seen these past few months. As she studied his face, he suddenly opened his eyes. "Miss," he said in a scratchy voice, "if you ain't an angel and I ain't in heaven, then don't say anything."

She pushed herself away from him. "This is Echo Canyon, and you've been shot."

He levered himself up on one elbow, pain making the color seep from his face. "Yes," he grunted.

"Who did it?"

"I don't know. I got out of bed at daybreak to go feed the horses, and as soon as I stepped out the door, someone bushwacked me. I dragged myself inside, barred the door, and prepared to fight. Whoever it was just took my horses, and there was nothing I could do to stop them. I tried, though. I unbarred the door and was ready to go out in a blaze of gunfire like a true and loyal employee of the Wells Fargo Company, but by then they were gone. Guess I passed out I was so disgusted with myself."

"It certainly wasn't your fault."

"That's not the way the folks who pay me will feel about it. Make no mistake. I'm out of a job, even out of my own horse." He gritted his teeth. "Damn it! The things a man has to go through to get saved by a pretty girl!"

She couldn't help laughing this time, and it made his mouth form a wide smile. "Who you traveling with?"

"My father and sister. Father is running a fever. Katie is coming back now with water for you."

He nodded. "Suppose you could help me to my bunk?"

The man was all muscle and bone, and as he leaned to take the weight off his injured leg, she smelled horse, leather, and gunpowder, each strong, like the man himself.

He was quite tall, and as he gripped the doorframe for support and looked down on her, he said, "I'll try not to put too much weight on you."

Rebecca avoided his eyes. She had never held a man before—except Micah. "I'm stronger than I appear. Are you ready?"

"Yep."

They swayed and shuffled across the hard dirt floor, bodies close, breath coming in bursts. They rested once, halfway across, when she thought he might pass out again, then made it the rest of the way to his bunk, where he sank down with a groan.

Katie appeared with the water, and he drank deeply, his eyes expressing his gratitude. There were quick introductions—the man's name was Bryce Sherman—then an awkward silence. Rebecca used it to study the dim interior of the station. It was Spartan and, like the blacksmith shop, very orderly. What furniture he had was crude, fashioned from rough logs—a pair of bunk beds, a table on which some harness was being repaired, no chairs but instead simple benches, and a cookstove that appeared ready to collapse. Along the back wall were several barrels, which Rebecca supposed contained flour and other staples, as well as a long shelf of canned goods that she tried not to stare at with famished eyes.

But most of all she was aware of a blessed coolness. The dim interior of the station, protected by the thick sod roof and rock walls, at once reminded her of a much loved root cellar where she'd played all one sweltering midwestern summer as a child.

"I'd better go get our father and bring him in here. The sun is still pretty awful," she said.

"Wish I could help you," Bryce said, "but I can't. You can lay him on the other bunk over there."

Outside, the air seemed all the hotter. They pushed the Mormon handcart right up to the door and pulled their father out and dragged him across the floor, then rolled him onto the bed. His eyes fluttered open and his mouth worked silently.

"He looks bad," Bryce said. "What ails him?"

"It's a fever. He's weak, and sometimes he comes awake and his mind is clear and other times he's like this. I think being inside where it's cool will help."

"So would food, I'll bet. I've got crackers, flour, dried figs, and lots of beans and salt pork. If you look around outside, you might even find an egg or two."

He didn't need to say any more. Katie got the stove going, and despite the heat it gave off, no one complained. In short order, Rebecca made pancakes, stacks of them, and she fried the pork in a batter of chopped figs, crackers, and eggs. It was delicious.

"Miss Prescott," he said to Rebecca when they were finished, "have you ever dug a bullet out of a man before?"

The tin plate in her lap spilled to the floor. "No." She glanced at his leg. "I don't think I could."

"You have to," he said almost matter-of-factly. "If you don't, this leg will fester and I'll lose it for sure."

"But you need a doctor! Surely the best thing to do would be to wait for the next stage and—"

"That won't be for another five days." He rubbed his face. "I'm sorry. I have no right to ask it of you. But you're going to have to dig the bullet out."

Rebecca saw him reach into his pocket, and then he tossed her a big jackknife, saying, "It's the sharpest blade I own."

"You could bleed to death," she told him, clenching the knife. "I could cut a vein or an artery and then there'd be nothing in the world I could do to stop the bleeding. Only a doctor knows where the blood vessels are in the upper part of your leg."

"The closest settlement is Temple City, and they probably don't even have a doctor," Bryce argued. "After that, it's all the way to Salt Lake City, and it would be too late."

"How far is Temple City? I can walk fast and—"

"Listen to me. My leg is on fire now. I've seen enough bullet wounds to know that this one goes nearly to the bone. I'll lose my leg if it's not taken care of today."

"Rebecca," Katie said quietly, "I'll help you. We have to do it."

"I'll need hot water and some rags." She opened the jackknife. "It's dirty."

"I'm sorry. Never expected it to be used on me. Over there on that wall peg is my extra shirt. I just washed it, so it's clean. You can use it for rags."

"Hate to ruin a good shirt."

"I'll buy another. You can't do that with a leg."

Rebecca put on water to boil while she tore up the shirt. She could feel him watching her, probably trying to decide if she was strong-willed enough to do this without fainting. Well, that was a darned good question and one she was asking herself.

"Rebecca?"

"Yes?"

"There's a jug of whiskey over there behind that saddle. I think I'd best have me some. Maybe you could use one too—to steady your hand," he added quickly.

"No, thank you." She met his eyes when she gave him the jug. "You had better tell me what to do while you can."

17

Bryce took a long pull on the jug. He coughed, and his eyes filled with tears. "Awful stuff," he grated. "But what you'll have to do first is to cut away the pants leg and clean it up a little so you can see what it looks like."

She didn't want to see it. "Then what?"

"Then take the blade of that knife and poke down inside the hole until you feel the lead ball. When you feel the scrape of it, you have to fish it out." He tried a grin that just didn't work. "That's all. There's doctors everywhere out in this country, and most of them never had any more of an education than you're going to get."

"The water is ready," Katie said, interrupting a long silence.

Rebecca washed the knife. Her hands were shaking, and she hoped he didn't notice. "Even if I get it out, I still want to go for a doctor. He might have medicine, for you and our father. Now, where exactly is this Temple City?"

"Due north. Ten, fifteen miles. It's resting in a big valley surrounded by low hills. In the daytime you can see the Mormon church steeple for miles. I sure wish you wouldn't go there."

"Why not? We've walked all the way from California. Fifteen miles is nothing to be concerned about."

"There's more to it than that. A lot more that you'd have to know. There's a cloud hanging over those people. They're not to be trusted, and—"

"Shh!" Rebecca hissed angrily. "I know Mormons. They saved our lives just weeks ago in Salt Lake City. So whatever you were going to say, I don't want to hear about it. Not now. Not when I'm facing this."

Bryce glanced down at her hands and saw the tremors she was trying to hide. He nodded, then upended the bottle of whiskey and drank savagely until it funneled out of the corners of his mouth and he began to cough. When he spoke, his voice grated like the axle of Rebecca's handcart. "Best dig it out now, then. Do it quick."

Rebecca's eyes met Katie's, and she hoped her own color was better than her sister's. Katie looked ready to swoon. Rebecca forced herself to study the wound, and now, while she still could, she stuck the blade deep into the angry, puckered flesh of his leg.

His spine arched like a bow. His eyes dilated, and his lips drew back from his teeth as an animal cry filled his throat. Katie fell across his chest and struggled to hold him still. She squeezed his neck, and there were big tears in her eyes and her expression was torn with anguish for his pain and suffering.

Rebecca had jerked the knife from his wound, and now, as she heard her sister's choking sobs, she realized that she must not quit again, no matter what happened, if she were going to finish. With fresh determination she again slowly pushed the blade into the bullet hole, and, ignoring everything else, she willed herself to think of the knife as an extension of her own fingers, a living thing that she could and must control. She began to probe deeper and deeper as the blade vanished into a dark, welling pool of blood. Good, she thought, let it bleed well to release the poisons inside.

She felt Bryce arch again. The blade was buried almost to its wooden handle, and now it hung motionless until she felt him relax. Then suddenly the leg muscles went limp.

"Rebecca, he's fainted!"

"Thanks be to God," she sighed, and a moment later she felt the steel, now so very much a part of herself, scrape something. Bone? No, too loose and not solid enough. This *had* to be the lead ball, the thing she must coax and somehow draw from deep in his body.

Katie was mopping Rebecca's brow, keeping the salt from her eyes. The rag she used felt cool, and it lifted rather than diminished the level of her concentration and focused all her senses on the bullet. She could feel it, close her eyes and almost see it. The bullet would not be either round or cylindrical in shape. The force of impact would have flattened and misshapened the soft lead. That would make it easier to remove, give her flat sides and jagged edges to hook the blade into. Rebecca began to gently pick and twist at the lead, praying all the time that she did not chip any of it away to start an infection.

Forceps. She dreamed of a surgeon's forceps. This seemed to be taking forever. What if Bryce suddenly awoke and—

"Rebecca, is it coming?" Katie was mopping her face dry again.

"Yes. I'm sure of it. But it's taking forever!"

"Don't give up. It'll be over soon. You can do it. I know you can, as well as anyone could."

Rebecca felt a surge of renewed confidence, then realized that Bryce was losing too much blood and that the bullet was too slow in coming out. Something new had to be done, and so she did the only thing that came to mind—she made herself slide her forefinger down along the cutting edge of the blade until she could feel the lead with the tip of her fingernail. Rebecca's heart was pounding in her ears, but she still managed to hook the fingernail under the metal. Squeezing it against the point of the knife blade, she began to draw it out.

When the ugly, twisted bullet slid into view, Rebecca was seized by a wave of exhilaration so powerful it almost swept her away. She had to lean on the bed for support, and she had a crazy impulse to throw her head back and shout with joy. Instead she choked out, "I think he'll be fine now, Katie. Just fine."

Katie took her arm and helped her to a chair. She knelt down before Rebecca and her eyes were shining with pride and admiration. "Of course he will," she whispered. "You saved him, Rebecca. Just sit here and rest for a minute while I try to stop the bleeding."

This time Rebecca let her little sister make the decisions. As soon as Katie was gone, however, she arose to see how their father was doing.

He sensed her presence, and his eyes fluttered open. "Did you dig it out?" he asked in a voice surprisingly clear.

"Yes."

"I want something to eat and drink. It's time you attended your own instead of a stranger. I smell food. Shouldn't have to ask for it."

His face was petulant and pasty. He reminded her of

a sickly, spoiled child, and Rebecca couldn't stand the sight of him for another instant.

"Come back here!" he cried shrilly.

But she couldn't. Out the door she raced into the cool night air. Rebecca drank deeply of it. She felt the light-headedness of the growing surge of nausea that had been rising inside vanish. Now her mind and senses grew crystal clear, as clear and clean of worry as the first, brave evening star now appearing. She *had* done it! Saved a man's leg and maybe even his life!

Rebecca felt wonderful. She leaned against their Mormon handcart and watched the sunset fade into the western horizon and ring big cotton clouds like a necklace of rose petals. The air was already growing cooler, and it would be dark within minutes. Somewhere nearby a coyote howled, and its high, lonesome serenade bounced around in the canyon unanswered. Despite her exhilaration, Rebecca was unspeakably weary. The grueling journey and the surgery had left her physically and mentally exhausted.

"He's sleeping now," Katie said, stepping outside to join her.

"And the bleeding?"

"It's stopped. A little has soaked into the bandages, but not much. Rebecca?"

"What?"

Katie linked their arms. "You were just wonderful in there. I couldn't believe you were my very own sister. You ought to be a doctor."

"It's a man's profession. They don't let women go to medical school." She gazed intently upward toward the north rim. In the fading light she quickly charted a path that would take her up and over. She was a good climber, and there would be a three-quarter moon to guide her up the wall. If her strength lasted, she'd be fine.

"You're leaving us now." It wasn't a question.

"I have to. For him and for father."

"Are you afraid of those Mormons?"

"Yes."

Katie's thin arms reached out and wrapped themselves

around her. "If anything happened to you, I'd die."

"No, you wouldn't. You'd do fine. Staying here with two sick men is really the hard job. I'm just going for a walk." She had to unlock Katie's clasped hands from around her waist. "We're going to make it," she said. "All of us."

Then she quickly kissed her sister on the cheek and hurried away into the failing light.

Chapter Two

Rebecca pressed her back to the canyon wall and slowly sank into a trembling crouch. Her lungs were burning and her legs shook violently. Yet the top of the rim was not much higher, and she knew she was going to make it. Two hours earlier she'd stumbled upon an old game trail and had followed it ever higher until the north rim of Echo Canyon loomed just above. Her face was badly scratched, as were her arms and legs, for the game trail had angled up steeply through heavy brush.

She waited until her breathing returned to normal and the cool wind had dried the perspiration on her face. Directly below was the stage station, but she couldn't see it clearly. Rebecca pushed away from the wall, once again thankful for the moonlight. Carefully she moved ever higher, always aware that one false step could result in a rock twisting underfoot and a serious, even fatal, fall. This time she was determined to crest the rim before stopping again, and after what seemed like hours, she finally crawled the last few yards up onto the tableland.

She twisted around on her hands and knees and felt a cool breeze, which gave her enough strength to stand. The view in any direction was magnificent. Overhead the moon glowed as warm and comforting as an old friend, and its light bathed the landscape in silver and shadow. She could see the stream mirrored like a glistening thread as it traversed Echo Canyon. To the west were the mountains beyond which lay the Great Salt Lake Basin. To the east, rolling like a dark green sea, was the Bridger Basin of Wyoming. But to the north—to the north lay a

Mormon settlement that Bryce thought cursed and to which she must go for help.

Rebecca glanced up, took a bearing on the North Star, and began to walk in that same long, swinging stride that had brought her all the way from Gold Rush California, where her mother now lay at rest. Somehow she knew that if Temple City were a place where women and children lived together it couldn't be as cruel as the mining camps she remembered so well. And if there was a doctor among these people, then he would come to help, for, above all, he was sworn to save lives.

Sunrise found her asleep on one of the low hilltops that overlooked an immense valley. Rebecca awoke covered with dew, and when she pushed herself up into a sitting position, she looked out to see the hills, wet and sparkling like a blanket of diamonds. It was breathtaking, and as the sun detached itself from the lands to the east, the diamonds began to fade and the green, green grass of summer rose to the warmth.

Her eyes searched northward, and a smile lifted the corners of her mouth as she noted with approval the low, grassy hills, perfect for sheep or cattle. There were heavy stands of timber, especially along the streams, which raced down from the higher mountains into a vast parklike valley that stretched as far as the eye could see northward and was at least twenty miles wide. And in its center Rebecca saw glinting sunlight reflected off the tin roofs and glass windowpanes of what she knew must be Temple City.

Barking dogs split the silence, and Rebecca realized that a young man with a rifle and a woman in a dress and flat hat were standing off to her left, gazing at her. In her early forties, the woman already had deep squint lines in an otherwise pretty face. Behind them stood a rough log cabin, and beyond that was a meadow full of grazing sheep. They were Mormon shepherds.

Rebecca raised her hand in greeting as the dogs came bounding forward. The larger of the pair, a beautiful black male with a white collar, growled at her.

"I mean you no harm," she said, standing quietly without showing fear as her mother had taught her.

The dogs began wagging their plumed tails. Rebecca petted them and waited as the shepherds came to investigate.

"Who are you?" the woman asked quietly. It was a direct question, but not at all challenging. The youth next to her had her same even good looks, pale blue eyes, and fair complexion. Rebecca knew without asking that he was her son.

"Miss, are you all right?" the woman asked worriedly. "You look pretty tired and all scratched up. Can we help?"

"Yes." She felt a rush of gratitude. After what Bryce had said about these people . . .

"Whatever is wrong is going to be all right. I don't know how you got here, but you're safe now."

Rebecca forced a smile. "I know that. It's not me I'm worried about." And then she told them why.

When she'd finished, they wasted no time. Mrs. Anna Ludlow did, however, insist that Rebecca wash quickly and put on one of her dresses, because Rebecca's own was hanging from her like rags.

"Jude will take you to see his father. Amos is the leader of our settlement, and it is from him that you must seek help."

"Is there a doctor in town?" Rebecca asked, praying the answer was yes.

"I'm afraid not, but several of our women are very knowledgeable about medicine, especially in the use of herbs to break a fever or to draw poison from a bullet wound. We've learned from bitter experience."

Jude saddled their horses as Rebecca hurried out of the small shepherd's cabin. "Will you be coming into town tonight?" she asked Anna.

"Oh, no. My place is here from spring to fall. Here with my sheep."

"But doesn't your . . ." She bit off the question.

Anna smiled. "Don't be embarrassed. Yes, I think he does miss me, but we are a large family, and Amos has several wives."

GARY McCARTHY

She felt her face warm. "I didn't mean to ask that."

"It was a normal question," the woman said. "Now hurry. Tell Amos exactly what you told me. He is a hard man, but not without some compassion. Jude?"

"Yes."

"Speak on behalf of these people."

"I will."

They rode away at a gallop. Rebecca hadn't been on a horse for years, and it felt wonderful to race across the valley floor, the horses jumping small canals and an occasional prairie dog hole. The morning sun was still rising, and lovely white and yellow daisies sprayed the grassy fields with color. Rebecca glanced sideways at the young man beside her. He was solidly built, more square than angular. His dark hair was brushed back under his hat brim and over his ears, his chin was pointed, and his mouth was generous. She hoped that the father was as kind as the son and wife appeared to be.

As they moved down into the valley, they began to pass farm after farm. Most of the houses were long, white, single-storied buildings that reminded her of stables because they had many doors. The fancier ones were encircled by low, shady verandas. Rebecca saw a number of women on some of them; they appeared to be sewing and often waved a piece of material in greeting. As Rebecca and Jude neared the town itself, the homes became closer together and had gardens of potatoes, onions, cabbages, and masses of tomatoes. There were flowers, too, great beds of them planted around the porches and near the lawns. What struck Rebecca most forcibly was the order and cleanliness. There were no rank weeks to be seen, no trash piles, but instead manicured lawns, lovely tree-lined streets, and fine homes, some two-storied with balconies. Rebecca saw dozens of children; they seemed to be playing everywhere, and they appeared to be exceptionally healthy.

They slowed their horses and entered a street of business establishments.

"This is it," Jude said, waving to a youth of his own age

26

who stared at Rebecca with more than passing interest. She realized that her arrival was generating considerable attention.

"They're not used to strangers," Jude explained. "Especially young women strangers."

Rebecca felt acutely self-conscious, aware that Mrs. Ludlow's dress was a little too short and revealed her bare ankles, which she was now glad she'd taken the time to wash. "Is your father in some business here?"

"He owns the only lumber mill and a couple of thousand sheep," Jude said, not able to disguise his pride.

They dismounted in front of the only brick-faced building on the street. It had two stories, white shutters and doors, a shining brass lock and handles on the front door, and the name AMOS T. LUDLOW painted in gold lettering across the window.

"Come on inside," Jude said, helping her dismount and tying up their horses.

She was overcome with doubt as they approached this impressive building. It didn't help when she glanced down at Anna's borrowed dress, which was too small. She desperately wished she had some shoes to wear. My God, she thought with anguish, I look like a beggar.

Jude seemed to guess the cause of her sudden hesitation. "If you'll excuse me for saying so, you are a remarkably pretty woman, even in my mother's old dress."

She smiled, appreciating his kindness. "Thank you. But right now I feel tired and ugly."

"My father won't think so," Jude said. "Let's get this done."

Inside, Jude swept through an outer office, ignoring the protest of a wizened clerk who sat perched on a stool over a pile of ledgers.

"Father," he said, pushing open an inner office door of polished mahogany, "I'm sorry to disturb you but—"

"Then don't," an impatient man growled.

Rebecca, hearing the tone of his voice, almost whirled and ran. She would have, had Jude not taken her arm and led her into the office. It was richly appointed, everything in wood and leather, heavy and impressive, like the

27

man who glared at her across the desk. Amos Ludlow
had been about to say more, but when he saw her his
mouth snapped shut and he laid down his quill and rose
from his chair.

In that moment, Rebecca saw a bull of a man in a black
suit, vest, tie, gold watch and chain. His thick black hair
was dusted with silver, giving him a distinction that a
younger man might envy. Not tall, he was powerful-
looking, and the hump of his broad shoulders topped a
chest as big around as a rain barrel. He wore a full beard
the tip of which was the color of platinum. Rebecca had
seen pictures of Ulysses S. Grant; Amos Ludlow was that
kind of impressive figure. Only the uniform was missing.

"Well," he said, lowering his voice. "Whom do I have
the pleasure of meeting?"

"Her name is Miss Rebecca Prescott. She needs our
help."

Amos's bushy eyebrows arched with curiosity. "Jude,
you will be good enough to wait outside while I speak
privately with Miss Prescott."

Rebecca almost protested. There was something predatory about Amos Ludlow; his eyes were not content to
remain above her neckline.

Jude tried to object. "I think—"

"Outside." It was a flat, hard command.

Jude stiffened, then whirled to leave Rebecca alone
with his father.

"Please sit down." He indicated a chair across from his
desk. "Now," he said, taking his own chair and leaning
forward, "before you begin, I must ask you one question.
Are you a saint?"

She blinked in confusion.

"Apparently not," he said tolerantly. "We, the members
of the Church of Jesus Christ of Latter Day Saints, are
saints. This was foretold to our martyred prophet, Joseph
Smith, when he was visited by God and Jesus Christ, who
commissioned him to be the one to restore the true
Church of Christ on the earth."

"I see." She did not see at all.

"Good! Our heritage, our beliefs, are founded on the

truth, and you would do well to study them in our Book of Mormon."

"Please, Mr. Ludlow. I'm sure you mean well, but right now I am seeking not truth but a doctor for two men who are seriously ill and needing help in Echo Canyon."

"Who are they, and what's wrong with them?"

"One is my father. He is sick—probably from bad water." Rebecca had no intention of telling Amos Ludlow that the other man was Bryce Sherman. "The second man works for the stage company. He was shot in the leg two days ago by horse thieves. I managed to remove the bullet, but I've no medicine to stop an infection or blood poisoning."

"I suppose neither is a saint," Amos said gravely.

"No, but they're good men and need your mercy. They would be willing to listen to your word of truth," Rebecca said quickly, sensing that he was going to deny her help, "just as I would be, in gratitude for your concern and kindness. So would Katie."

"Katie? Who is she?"

"My younger sister. She is only fourteen."

"Have you and your sister yet been baptized?"

"As small children. Why do you ask?"

"We believe in baptism by immersion, but only for those children who have reached the age of accountability for their actions. So it would seem that, by our standards, your baptisms were invalid."

Rebecca had to fight to control her temper. "Will you help us?" she managed to ask in a tight voice.

"If you all will come to live among us and attend our church so that you might know the truth and you agree to obey our rules without argument and to work for your keep, then, yes, we will help."

His price was high indeed. Still, it had to be paid. Rebecca curtly nodded in agreement. "Very well, but we don't expect to stay long; we have our own beliefs, our own lives to pursue."

"To waste in sin and ignorance," he said bluntly. "We offer you eternal salvation and everlasting joy in the Celestial Kingdom."

"It is unfair to think all others should be denied what you say awaits."

"Life is unfair. We know that better than anyone. Now," he said, "you are asking us to help you, to leave our work and travel at some risk. There have been Indian attacks on the stage line. In return, I demand that you promise to stay here until you have been taught the truth according to our beliefs. Do you agree?"

"I have very little alternative but to agree."

"Miss Prescott," he said patiently, "the Lord has a plan for all of us. Difficulties arise because we do not see the plan unless forced to do so. Perhaps it is His will that has brought you to us in need."

He reached across the desk and, before she quite realized it, enfolded her hands in his own; then he turned them over for his inspection. They both saw the thick, ugly calluses that layered her palms. He brushed them gently with the edge of his thumb, saying, "It has been a long time since I've seen these on a woman."

She withdrew her hand from his, unsure of how to react to the surprising emotion in his voice. "Thank you, sir. Could we leave for Echo Canyon very soon?"

"We will depart at once. And while we're gone, you will stay at my home to eat and rest."

"I can't do that. I have to go with you. It is my father and sister in Echo Canyon."

He was obviously annoyed. "You must learn that a woman has to do as she's told. I'll make an exception in this case, but not again."

Rebecca said nothing. She just turned and let him follow her to the door. It would do no good whatsoever to explain to him that she refused to accept the idea that a woman had to blindly acquiesce to a man's wishes when they were contrary to her own. Amos Ludlow would be shocked to know that, and even more shocked to know that she believed in the cause of woman suffrage, which was being led by a few courageous women back East. No, she thought, allowing herself to be escorted to the door, let him think what he chooses.

*　　*　　*

Katie had been awake most of the night and had fallen asleep only when she believed that Bryce and her father were slumbering peacefully. Around midnight Micah's fever had broken, and within an hour he was on his feet, weak, but clear enough of mind to start complaining. Bryce's leg wound hadn't reopened, and he was sleeping well.

When Katie awoke it was full morning. She glanced over to see her father snoring, but was shocked to see that Bryce was gone. Katie was out of bed in a moment, angry and fearful. What a fool the man was! Didn't he realize the danger of reopening the wound? Damn him! If he bled to death she'd never forgive herself—or him. Half asleep, half dressed, she stumbled out of the station, the sun blinding her for a moment.

Where was that man! Angry and alarmed, she shielded her eyes and frantically glanced about. The yard was empty! She began racing around, first to the blacksmith shop, then over by the corrals, then up the hillside and . . . "Well, goddamn you!" she cried, grinding to a halt. "What are you doing up *there*!"

He pushed his hat back from his eyes and sat up. As she watched with mounting anger, he slowly dangled his good leg off the roof, and then he looked down at her and smiled lazily. "I was just soaking up the warmth of another nice morning. Something wrong?"

"Something wrong! You almost caused my heart to burst with worry. Didn't you see me scrambling all over this place?"

"Nope," he said. "My eyes were under the hat 'cause of the bright sun."

He was so calm and so much healthier-looking that Katie's anger seeped away in a hurry. "At least," she groused, "your leg isn't bleeding. It's a wonder, too, given that you got up there by yourself."

"Oh," he scoffed, as though he'd completely forgotten the wound. "It looks fine. Changed the bandages myself this morning. No sign of poison. Going to be a real scorcher again today. Best keep the windows and door closed so it will stay cool inside."

31

Katie went up and sat down beside him. The man was impossible, and yet she found him captivating. "How long have you been living here?"

" 'Bout a year, this time. Saw it first in 1860. It was fall. These cottonwoods and aspen," he said, pointing, "were gold. I was about eighteen and had starved myself down to a hundred and thirty pounds so I could ride for the Pony Express."

"You must have loved it." She wanted to hear more, know more about him, and she hoped he'd speak to her not as a girl but as a young woman.

"Yes," he said, his face relaxing as his mind drifted back, "I did. The Pony was probably the greatest outfit I'll ever be a part of. Just to join, you had to swear on the Bible not to cuss or drink. It was hard, but worth it, because I rode with men like Pony Bob Haslam, Erastus Smith, William Cody, and others that no one will ever remember. We carried *history*, not mail."

"Were you ever attacked by Indians?"

"Sure! We all were. In Nebraska it was the Sioux; in Wyoming, mostly the Cheyenne; and in the deserts of Utah and Nevada, the Paiutes and Gosiutes shut us down cold for a few weeks. But they *never* got our *mochilas*. The only thing that beat us are those damned telegraph poles you see strung across this country."

Katie frowned. "I've heard it said that the railroad is coming. Will that do away with the stagecoach?"

He sighed sorrowfully. "It will. I'll be out of a job within two years if they're on schedule. I understand they're already across the Missouri and laying track in Nebraska. Out in California the Central Pacific is hiring Chinese to drive rail over the Sierras. Ask me, it'll be a race worth watching."

"Why just watch?" The question popped out of her mouth unbidden.

"You saying I ought to lay track?" He studied her with interest.

"No, only that . . ." She tried to put it into words. "Only that if the railroad is coming, you seem like a man who ought to be helping to build it. That's all."

That seemed to flatter him. "Maybe." He laced his fingers behind his head and stretched out on the earthen roof. "The truth of it is, I don't much like progress. Don't like those damned old telegraph poles and wires. They look like gallows. And the railroad, well, I've never seen one, but from what I hear they're noisy as hell, stink, and throw smoke and ash all over creation. The Indians call 'em iron horses, but a horse has heart; an engine is just a danged old smoking tin can."

Katie didn't agree. She'd ridden one in California and seen the Virginia and Truckee line at work on the Comstock Lode. "They're the future, Bryce. You can't fight it. Rebecca told me so."

He cocked one of his eyebrows with amusement. "You appear to put a lot of stock in what Rebecca thinks. Sooner or later you're going to have to start forming your own ideas."

"Those *are* my ideas!" She was hurt and offended. "Rebecca and I don't agree on everything. Rebecca thinks a woman ought to decide on things. I say if she's married she ought to let her husband have the final word. My sister once listened to one of those woman suffragists and agreed with her! I never could."

"Well, good," he said. "Those kind of people got no business out here in the West, and your sister ought to have sense enough not to listen to them."

"Rebecca's headstrong, but she's also smart," Katie said.

"No offense. Just glad you do think for yourself." He was grinning at her. "You know something?"

She blushed. "What?"

"You're kind of cute. Must have about a thousand freckles."

Katie swallowed noisily and looked away. She was confused and wanted to hit him one minute, hug him the next.

"Katie?" He sat up. "I meant no disrespect."

"I know." She squirmed uncomfortably.

"I think we'd better go back inside now," he said quietly. "I got enough sun, and if your father wakes up and

33

finds us missing, he's going to have quite a start."

She didn't want to go, but he was already pushing himself erect. She took his arm and looked up at him. "I love Rebecca. But I've an independent mind. I *am* my own woman, Bryce. I'm fourteen years old."

He shook his head. "You're still a girl. Out here, women age way too fast anyway. Don't rush your life."

He tottered off balance and Katie grabbed him around the waist, feeling emotions she'd never known could exist. She desperately wanted to tell him he was wrong. Well, half wrong anyway. She wasn't really a grown woman, but the way she was feeling about Bryce Sherman wasn't being a girl either. It was awful, being something halfway between.

Rebecca was the first one into the rock station house, and she was overjoyed to find them all recovering. There was much to say, but before she even had a chance, Amos Ludlow stepped into the doorway, his thick body blocking out the sunlight. He cleared his throat, and when Rebecca turned around, she saw that his eyes were locked on Bryce. As he strode forward, his voice shook with fury. "Brother Sherman. I should have guessed."

Whatever Rebecca had been about to say was forgotten. She watched Bryce, noticed his eyes shutter. "Amos, you're the last man I'd have expected to help Gentiles."

Banter was not the Mormon leader's style. "You should have stayed with us or returned to Salt Lake City. You could have been someone, instead of . . ." He glanced around the spare rock dugout and didn't need to say anything more.

"How many wives do you have now?" Bryce asked with malicious delight.

Ludlow's eyes flashed. "You still haven't learned your manners, have you?"

"Nope. But I do know this: You'll never have enough wives as long as you can climb in and out of a bed."

"Damn you and your filthy mind! You're taking the next stagecoach east. Time has softened neither your

tongue nor your heart. You are a fool and a sinner. I'll
be whipped before I'll help you!"

"No, you'll be double damned. A stagecoach ride to
Cheyenne or even Salt Lake City might kill me. Do you
want my death added to the others?"

"Shut up!"

"I won't leave him," Katie said. "Not here alone."

Rebecca glanced at her sister. "That's right. We won't
let him stay here unattended." She turned to Amos and
the Mormons who'd crowded inside. "You take us all and
I swear we'll live by your rules as long as we're your
guests. Father, do you agree?"

Micah just nodded. He looked poorly and was staring
at Bryce and Amos Ludlow.

Amos's big fists were clenched. After a moment he said,
"We've come this far, we'll go through with it." Then he
whirled and bulled his way outside, swearing, "I hope he
bleeds to death in the handcart!"

Bryce lay on a pile of straw in the Mormon handcart.
The day was growing short. They'd have to take a long,
circuitous route back to Temple City, and it was time to
get moving.

"Mount up," Amos ordered the dozen men under his
command. "Ed, you ride behind, leading the handcart
horse. Let's move out. Miss Prescott, the horse you rode
here will pull the cart, so you'll have to ride double behind me. Jude will double with your sister. Your father
looks strong enough to ride double too. Any more than
one body on that cart will collapse it."

"I could walk," she said, not wanting to ride with him.

"Miss Prescott, don't test me. You've already done
enough walking. I've learned you are strong-willed; don't
be mulish."

She glared at him, shoved her foot into his empty stirrup, and swung up behind. Amos led off, and the others
followed. Rebecca heard the handcart begin to protest
loudly under Bryce's weight as it followed them back
across the hard miles over which she and Katie had
toiled only two days earlier. It was more than discour-

aging, but she had no choice. When they finally were out of the canyon, it was dark and they turned north. Then, with the creaking wagon scaring the night creatures and grating all their nerves as raw as the wooden hub, they lined out across the hills toward Temple City.

"We'll make it fine now. It will be good to see home," Amos said around midnight.

When she didn't answer, he added, "Miss Prescott, how much do you really know about our people?"

"Very little." Please, she thought, not tonight. Not a lesson tonight!

"You will learn a great deal about us in the weeks ahead. Watch closely and you'll see a happier, more industrious community than you have ever supposed could exist. We are a family. However, I'm afraid that you and your sister will be separated. You'll stay in my household while—"

She instinctively rebelled. "Mr. Ludlow, my father and Bryce Sherman are men and will make their own decisions, but I will not agree to being separated from Katie."

She felt him stiffen with anger. She didn't care. If they couldn't provide for her and Katie in one household, then she was for leaving immediately.

"Miss Prescott, you are a grown woman. You can't always be with your sister. Before long you'll go with a husband. That is the way of it."

"I may never marry," she announced, wanting to shock him. "Upon our return to Springfield, Illinois, I intend to seek employment, not a husband."

"A spinster?" He was obviously appalled.

"You say that as though it were a curse," Rebecca protested. "My aunt never married and was a very happy woman. She taught school and lived to be eighty. She died content, and her final advice to me was to stay single. She said if she'd had to care for a man, she'd not have lived past fifty."

"The woman led a barren life!" Amos railed in disgust.

"Barren! Why, my dear Aunt Gwynneth was loved and respected by hundreds of students. She shaped their minds and gave them the key to knowledge." Rebecca's anger was hot now. "On the other hand, I watched my mother's sufferings, and I will not endure living with a fool or a tyrant. And furthermore, I resent your words!"

Rebecca could stand no more of this man. She jumped from his horse and landed on her feet. She would crawl to Temple City before riding with Amos Ludlow.

"Miss Prescott, get back up here!" he thundered.

With the starry heavens as his backdrop, Amos Ludlow's voice shook with unquestioned authority.

Rebecca's resolve cracked yet did not crumble. "I will not!"

"You are a very willful young woman. Even a mulish one!"

Everyone had stopped. Rebecca stood alone, quaking but defiant. "I don't care what you think of me."

Amos lashed his horse and rode on. A moment later the Mormon handcart rolled by, and Bryce said, "That's telling the old tyrant! Would you like to ride along with me?"

"The cart would collapse." Besides, it wasn't respectable to lie down beside a young man, even if they were being escorted by a crowd of stern Mormons.

"If it collapses," he said, "they'll find another. Come on up. You're staggering."

"No!" she snapped in exasperation, fed up with men who kept telling her what to do. Rebecca grabbed the side of the handcart and stumbled along in the darkness.

"You'll never make it," he said quietly after a mile had passed.

"I will if you just talk to me so that I stay awake. You owe me that much, Bryce Sherman!"

He rolled over on one side. The straw crunched so invitingly Rebecca wanted to weep.

"All right. I'll talk now while we have the chance. I'll tell you a thing or two about these people that will keep you awake."

"I'm listening." But she wasn't really. She was so exhausted she could concentrate on nothing more than keeping her feet moving.

"Have you ever heard of the Mountain Meadows Massacre?" he asked, glancing ahead to make certain no one could overhear.

The tone of his voice jerked her into a state of alertness she hadn't thought possible. "Any reason I should have?"

"Every reason." He paused so long that Rebecca thought he might have decided not to continue.

"Listen," he said finally. "It's going to be a long night, so I might as well start from the beginning."

"It's easy to see that you and Mr. Ludlow are enemies," Rebecca said. "Is that what this is all about?"

"That, and a lot more. You see, I was once one of the people."

"You?" It seemed impossible. He was so . . . so different from them. There was no reverence in Bryce, no respect for anything. Only defiance and a tough fatalism that he seemed almost proud to exhibit.

"Hard to believe myself whenever I think about it, which isn't often. But as a kid I was filled with hatred for the Gentiles, who'd driven us out of Missouri. That was where they killed my father and some elders and then threw their bodies down our water wells."

Bryce's face twisted until it was a hard, unforgiving mask. "But that wasn't good enough for 'em. They finally hounded us north to a place in Illinois called Nauvoo. For a while they left us in peace, and we built another city with nothing but our bare hands and faith in God. The Gentiles were just waiting for us to finish. We should have known better. No sooner were we done than they came at us just like before; different people, same hating faces and curses. When, we fought back, they threw our prophet, Joseph Smith, in jail. We tried to protect him, but . . ." His voice died.

Rebecca reached out and touched his arm. "They killed him, didn't they?" She knew full well they had.

"Yeah. Him and his brother. Shot 'em down like caged animals. That pretty much broke us. I wanted to stand and fight, but the grown-ups, the elders, they scattered and ran for their lives. We were driven like rabbits before a prairie fire, and we ran blindly, without hope. I can still picture it, a blizzard before us, the hellish orange glow of our homes burning to the sky. I was sure we would die in the snow and ice of that winter. We had almost no food, little clothing or supplies. It seemed even to the bravest among us that it was the end."

"But it wasn't. You did make it to the Great Salt Lake."

He grimaced with self-loathing, as though he blamed himself for having survived. "I made it, and so did some of the others, but so many of us died. My mother starved to death. She was frozen solid when she was lowered into the grave, and she couldn't have weighed sixty pounds. We'd all have died if it hadn't have been for Brigham Young. He saved us. I don't know how he drove us through those times, but he did. I've seen him strip the bark off trees and eat it same as the rest of us. Brigham was starving too, but there was a fire, a belief in him that wouldn't die, refused to quit. Somehow he made us believe too."

Rebecca tried to imagine how horrifying that journey must have been. She and Katie had suffered, but they'd never been so desperate as to eat the bark of trees.

"Brigham Young," Bryce said with solemn conviction, "is one of the greatest prophets in history."

"You can say that, having left their church?"

"Yes, and I'll tell you why. Once it was certain that we were going to found the city of our dreams in Salt Lake, Brigham began to order the strongest of his people to go out and preach our faith, to claim other lands and spread what he believed to be the true word to all the people of America, and the entire world. We were called missionaries. Yet some of us who had no talent for preaching were expected to go along to help those that did and to work for the good of our church. We were asked to labor in the wilderness in order to increase our material wealth for the betterment of all."

"How?"

Bryce shrugged. "Well, I was sent down to southwest Utah to help mine iron."

"But you don't sound as if you wanted to go."

"I did not. Mining is hard, crippling work, and I had my friends in Salt Lake City. And a girl I was courting in a manner that was entirely pure and innocent."

He almost smiled with the memory. It made his face soften, and he showed a rare touch of boyishness.

"Besides," he continued, his face growing serious once again, "I had to give up my job as an apprentice gunsmith. I liked guns even back then, and it gave me the chance to handle them all I wanted. I figured I'd likely need to use them down in the iron country."

"Indians?" They were the most obvious danger on the frontier.

"You bet. Brigham sent us into a country where we were badly outnumbered and the Indians weren't friendly. We lived day by day, certain we'd wake up to an attack and knowing we couldn't stop it if it came. There were just too many of them to fight."

"I'm surprised Mr. Young didn't recall you, especially the women and children."

"They did a lot of frettin' and praying. More and more wagon trains were passing through the Indian lands, and things were getting worse all the time. Finally it all came to a head the day a group from Arkansas and Missouri arrived."

"What did they do?"

"Plenty. They were tall, hard-eyed fellows, and quite a few of them wore Bowie knives and all manner of guns stuck into their belts and boot tops. A good many were pure mean, and they were bragging that they'd had a part in the killing of Joseph Smith. Some of the worst paraded drunk up and down our streets, calling our women whores and swearing they'd stay and help the United States Army come and drive us into the wilderness."

Bryce shook his head as if he could make the memory disappear. "Those people hated Indians. They poisoned an ox down near Corn Creek and gave it to them, hoping to poison the tribe. I'm not saying they were all like that, but their leaders were a tough, hard bunch."

"Trying to poison the Indians with a gift was a despicable thing for them to do!"

"They paid for it." Bryce had to clear his throat. "The Indians swore vengeance. Demanded we help them kill everyone on the wagon train. They made it very clear that if we refused to help, they'd kill us, too."

Rebecca had a sick feeling that was growing by the second, coming up from her stomach and filling her with a terrible dread.

He's turned his face away. "So . . . so we said we'd help. We found the wagon train already under siege by some of the more eager bucks. Whites and Indians alike had already died, and it was clear we weren't going to be able to change the Indians' minds. We did what we had to do to save ourselves."

"You betrayed them?" Rebecca was appalled.

"Yes. We went into their camp and promised that if they'd hand over their weapons, we'd see them safely through our country."

"I can't belive they'd trust you!"

His voice grew hard. "They were desperate, Rebecca! They gave us their weapons and let us divide them up and take the women and children away in one group, the menfolk in another. They . . . they were confused; some sensed the trap but were outshouted and overruled."

Rebecca gripped the side of the cart and dug her fingernails into its worn, rotting fiber.

Bryce had forgotten her. He was reliving his nightmare and was gazing fixedly up at the heavens as if trying to explain it all over again to God that he might rid himself of the guilt, the memory. "Someone yelled, 'Halt!' and that was the signal to open fire on the men. We were each supposed to kill the Gentile standing closest."

Bryce's head rolled back and forth on the straw as he wrestled with his demons of despair. "The guns were booming. Men screamed and ran for their lives. The one I was supposed to shoot was not much older than I was, and he fell down on his knees and begged for his life and he was crying and choking, and I'll never forget that I just threw my gun to him and took off running. I streaked past a knot of those Missouri men just as the Indians jumped them by surprise and started shooting them full of arrows and taking scalps before they were even dead. I went over a hilltop and barreled right into where they were slaughtering the women and children."

The words were tearing out of him now. He was writhing in torment and drenched with sweat though the night was cool. Rebecca was numb and just let him finish.

"I yelled for the Indians to stop, and I saw some of my own people with blood on themselves and that's when I threw up. Then I found a horse and almost rode it to death trying to get away from that place."

But you never have, Rebecca thought. And you probably never will. "How many were slaughtered?"

"Over a hundred," he said in a haunted voice that cracked. "Only a few of the smallest children were spared."

She ground her teeth together. He was waiting for her to say something—anything. Rebecca couldn't, so she just stumbled on in silence, glaring at the dark riders from Temple City and hating them, each and every one.

Chapter Three

Rebecca stood waiting for Bryce and watching an approaching snowstorm come rolling south toward their valley. It was hard to believe they'd been here since last summer. At first she had found each day in the Ludlow household unbearably tedious. She and Katie could not talk easily with Amos Ludlow's four wives, and the constant prayers and readings from the Book of Mormon had driven her to distraction. The perfect order she'd observed on the first day in Temple City extended from the streets into the homes. Each of Amos's wives and her children occupied separate upstairs quarters of their own that had several small partitioned cubicles for sleeping. When the children became old enough, they were expected to move downstairs into a communal sleeping arrangement much like a military barracks. Every room in the big, sprawling house contained a fireplace, and because the winters were severe, it took a small army of workers just to keep the household in firewood.

In keeping with a policy of nonfavoritism, the quarters were of identical size, yet no two were exactly alike, and there was a good deal of envy, because some were more pleasant than others in the wintertime, or had a better view of the front street or nicer furniture. When Amos was present there was tranquility, for he ruled his household in stern silence, but when he left for his office there was plenty of wrangling among the wives and children.

To Rebecca's way of thinking, polygamy itself was responsible for the inevitable spats, fits of jealousy, and bursts of temper. Despite them, the work got done with surprising efficiency. These people weren't lazy and seemed to thrive on hard work. Every quarter was scrubbed and cleaned until it shone, and then the wives and older daughters would attack the communal parlors, kitchen, laundry, and other rooms with a zeal that bordered on fanaticism.

The regimen did not vary from day to day. At five in the morning the wives arose and were expected to have an enormous breakfast on the table forty-five minutes later. It was no simple task, and it was one in which Rebecca and Katie were expected to participate fully. With Amos glaring down at them from the head of a massive table, his wives and eleven children said their thanksgiving prayers, and then the clatter of knives and forks on plates created a veritable din and the table itself was a blur of flying arms and elbows. The cleanup itself took half the morning.

Micah, with his peculiar sensibilities, would have been appalled. He'd taught his daughters the refinements of table manners, which they soon dropped in order not to be left hungry while the platters were scraped clean. Rebecca was glad that her father had left during that first week to live with Temple City's harnessmaker. She didn't often see him anymore, but when she did, it was obvious that he was more content than he'd been in years. He'd regained his strength and now seemed almost at peace with himself, a fact that made Rebecca a bit resentful. Had it not been for him, she and Katie wouldn't be here; they'd be in Springfield.

Where was he, anyway? The approaching storm would soon make it necessary for her to return to the Ludlow household. Bryce had whispered something to her on the streets about their leaving soon. How soon? Not in a blizzard they wouldn't, not even if it would erase their tracks and delay pursuit. And pursue them Amos would. Rebecca had no more illusions about her status among the people of Temple City: she and Katie were expected to become Mormon wives whether it was their choosing or not. Oh, Amos hadn't exactly said so, but the look in his eyes told Rebecca all she needed to know about his intentions. She would be Vida's successor for his favor, the new wife, youngest and prettiest.

Rebecca ground her teeth together. She would not let that happen under any circumstances, and if it meant flirting with Bryce, then flirt she would. He was their only chance for escape before next spring, and she had no intention of waiting that long.

The temperature fell rapidly. She had to go any minute; Katie would already be worrying about her. Poor Katie, to whom she'd had to lie in order to meet Bryce and who was hopelessly in love with a man who cared very little for her. It deeply saddened Rebecca every time she thought about Katie's feelings for Bryce. He was not especially kind or gentle and, in fact, was probably rather cruel—for reasons she supposed reached back to his early Mormon childhood, the tragic loss of his parents, and then Vida's marriage to Amos Ludlow, a man he hated.

Rebecca blew warm breath into her cupped hands and rubbed them briskly together. Where was that man? The wall of the storm was only a few miles away. She stared at it with fascination. From ground to sky, blue-gray and swirling, it rushed forward obliterating farms, trees, hilltops, and everything in its path. It was almost time to run.

A branch snapped behind her and Bryce emerged from the forest nearly out of breath. His cheeks were pink and his dark hair plastered wetly under his wool hat. He looked to be in magnificent condition, the picture of manhood.

"Sorry I'm late."

"We haven't much time," she said, glancing at the approaching storm. In a way, she was almost relieved that this was to be the briefest of meetings. The last time she'd met him alone he'd tried to kiss her, and now she was uneasy in his presence, unsure of his true intentions.

"What did you want, Bryce?"

"Always so businesslike," he said, trying to make it sound light but unable to hide his real disappointment.

"I'll be missed if I'm not back soon. They'll be alarmed

GARY McCARTHY

in the face of this snowstorm, and they might even send
out searchers."

"Let them worry," he snapped. "Rebecca, if you
wanted, I could get us horses right now. It would be so
easy to steal a few when everyone is inside. We could
have them in ten minutes and outrun this storm even if
it chased us clear down to the Green River country."

Rebecca blinked. He was serious! Actually hoping
she'd say yes. "And what about Katie? The girl who just
lives for your smile? Or my father?"

"You don't give a damn for Micah," he challenged.

It wasn't quite true, but close enough that she put no
strength to her words. "I don't love him like a father,
Bryce, but that doesn't mean I'll just leave him, either."

"If you tell him about our plans, he might tell the Mormons."

"He would never do such a thing."

"Can you be sure?"

She couldn't. "No," she admitted. "But Katie swears he
can be trusted, and she understands Micah far better
than I. Bryce, I have to go now." There was a look in his
eyes that made her take a quick backstep.

"Why are you so afraid of me?" he cried. "I'd never hurt
you."

"What about my sister? Will you hurt her? Why did
you kiss her that night?"

His face dropped, and his shoulders settled with resignation. "I don't know," he said. "But it isn't my fault
that she fell in love with me."

Rebecca had no intention of arguing the point in a
snowstorm. She began to walk, and Bryce fell in step.
The storm was almost upon them, and the trees were
bending before the wind, their tops whipping like green
flags.

"Is Amos still"—he was shouting to be heard—"is
Amos still bothering you?"

"I stay away from him."

That seemed to satisfy Bryce. The rest of the trip to
town was made in silence as they hurried before the
wind. The streets of Temple City were deserted, the shops

46

and offices barred and shuttered. At the place where they parted, Bryce took her arm and yelled, "It isn't my fault about Katie!"

Snow had began to fall. It covered his shoulders and cap, glistened wetly on his long, dark lashes. In that moment she wanted to believe him, and so she just nodded. He smiled broadly, and when he lifted his arms to hold her, Rebecca ducked and ran down the empty streets toward Amos' house.

In the swirling wind and snow his voice somehow reached out to her, clear and with power: "We're leaving, Rebecca. ALL OF US. AND SOON!"

"Soon" came unexpectedly early. During a warm spell four weeks later, as she and Katie hurried down the street after a late-afternoon church gathering at the community hall, Bryce stepped out of the shadows. "Don't stop walking. Just slip in behind me and follow along this wall to the alley."

"Where are we going?" Katie whispered with excitement.

"Away from here."

"Oh, Bryce, I knew you'd help. But we can't leave our father. He's back at the hall. I'll go for him."

Bryce looked at Rebecca; his meaning was clear. She said, "He doesn't want to come, Katie. He's happy here, happier than he's ever been in his life."

Protest boiled up in Katie's eyes, but they were moving into the dark, shadowy alley; Rebecca made herself look ahead toward three horses that Bryce had saddled and ready, plus a fourth animal loaded with a pack and supplies. The full realization that they were finally leaving almost took her breath away.

"This one," Bryce said quickly, "is mine. These other three I borrowed from Amos Ludlow."

"You stole them?" Katie's mouth fell open, and she stared at him in near disbelief. "Bryce, you have to return them! The Mormons will track us down, and you'll be hanged for a horse thief. It's not worth it for us to get away like this."

"They've got to catch us first," Bryce said grimly. "Besides, I've been slaving fourteen hours a day in one of their logging camps for damn little money. I figure these animals kind of even the score. Let's mount up!"

Katie grabbed Rebecca's arm. "We can't let him do this," she pleaded. "Don't you see? This is exactly the kind of thing Amos wants Bryce to do so he'll face the gallows."

"We have to go," Rebecca said raggedly. "If we're ever to get away from this place we have to go now."

"At the risk of his life!"

"It's my choice," Bryce said angrily. "Now, mount up!"

Katie wouldn't let go of Rebecca's arm. Rebecca had to pry her sister's fingers loose. "Amos wants me to marry him. I have to leave now, Katie. You . . . you don't understand what it would do to me if I had to marry Amos."

Katie admitted defeat. "All right," she murmured. "I'll go with you, but—"

The hard and terminal sound of a bullet being levered into the chamber of a Winchester choked off Katie's next words. "Freeze!" a cold voice ordered. "Or you're a dead horse thief."

"Jude Ludlow," Bryce said in a voice gone old as he raised his hands. "You've been watching me ever since I arrived. I should have known you were just waiting for this moment."

Obviously proud of himself, Jude smiled. "I'm going to give you a chance not to meet the hangman."

"What for? Rebecca?"

"Hell no," Jude said. "Katie is the one I favor."

There was a long moment of strained silence.

"She's just a kid," Bryce said with disgust.

"How can you say that!" Katie cried. "You kissed me."

Bryce colored deeply, and stammered, "What do you want of me?"

Jude kept the Winchester right on his chest. "All right, you asked, and I'm going to tell you. I want to leave Temple City and ride some country with you. I want to drink red-eye whiskey and stand in a saloon with a glass of it in my hand and watch the hurdy-gurdy girls dance, and

I want hot coffee to ease my hangover the next morning. I'd enjoy smoking a cigar or chewing one if smoking made me sick, and I want to learn how to play faro and stud poker. Can you understand what I'm telling you?"

"Sure I do," Bryce said, relaxing but still keeping his hands up around his shoulders. "You're feeling just the way I did seven, eight years ago. You're being chewed alive. You want to sow your oats and ride the damn wind!" He chuckled softly, perhaps in memory of wilder days not so long past. "Jude, you want to be another ring-tailed roarer and a high plains drifter. Damn betcha, I understand! It's natural, and I even admire you for wanting to do it."

"I *knew* you'd understand!" Jude said with a wide smile. He looked as though he was ready to do a dance step right in the alley. "And that's exactly why I'm here now and why we have to leave these ladies until we can come back for them."

"The women are coming," Bryce said coldly. "And I'm no goddamn nursemaid."

"Nursemaid or dead horse thief," Jude spat in fury. "Which is it you want to be?" He pressed his cheek to the rifle and began to pull the trigger.

"Jude, no!" Katie shouted. "Don't. Rebecca and I can wait. We'll be happy to wait! Isn't that true, Rebecca?"

Rebecca managed to nod her head. "We'll still be here. It's not worth your dying for," she whispered as Amos's big leering face appeared like a vision so real she began to tremble.

Bryce cursed, but he knew Jude wasn't bluffing. And as long as he protected Jude he would be welcomed back. But if anything happened to Amos Ludlow's son, Bryce would be a wanted man.

"I'll be returning for both of you."

Rebecca nodded again, but she was afraid it would be too late.

Spring faded into the early heat of summer. The days folded upon one another like the pale petals of a rose. Rebecca moved through them trancelike, as if walking

GARY McCARTHY

in a shadowy time; she could not bear to think or feel too deeply.

"We will marry in July," Amos Ludlow had proclaimed.

"No. I would rather die."

"*You* will not. Bryce Sherman will. I have an order for his arrest. Brigham Young himself has given me approval to place a bounty. It is for a thousand dollars—dead or alive. Marry me or I'll issue it."

"You hate him that much?" She knew that he did. She knew also that he would do as he said, and afterward would force her into marriage anyway.

"He has taken away my son and led him into damnation. If I let him, he would also take you straight to hell."

I'm already there, she thought miserably. "If you call off the bounty . . . if you do that, I will marry you. But I could never stay in your house with your other wives. I just couldn't."

"Will you give me children?" He loomed over her. "I want them."

"Only . . . only if you destroy the warrant and promise never to harm Bryce in any way." If she refused, she knew Bryce was as good as dead.

"Agreed!" Now he smiled, reaching out to touch her. "You shall have a cabin by the long meadow."

It was on the first day of July that Amos Ludlow stood up at the head of the great table and addressed his wives and children.

"My family, I have an announcement for you this evening. I will wed Miss Rebecca Prescott in our home tomorrow."

No one breathed or made a sound except Katie, who moaned in anguish.

Amos ignored her. "So there is cause for joy among us as we share this food. I have bought a cabin for Rebecca, who, like Anna, will tend our flocks until fall. I will stay there with her for a week before returning to this house. I think, now, congratulations are in order."

The wives congratulated Amos and Rebecca and then looked down at their plates and ate in silence.

"How did you do it!" Katie shouted at him. "How? She would never consent to marry you of her own free will!"

"Silence!" he roared. He measured her up and down. "*You* are becoming a woman, *Miss* Prescott."

The implication was chilling. Katie trembled. When she turned to Rebecca for support, her sister was gone.

Rebecca stood by a tree. Her eyes were fixed on a distant mountain, and her voice was steady but resigned. "Katie, I would rather die, but there is no choice. He's placed a bounty on Bryce for horse stealing. He'll be shot on sight when he returns if I don't marry Ludlow."

"But when Bryce discovers—"

"He mustn't! You must never tell Bryce why I married."

"Can't you run away? Rebecca, you mustn't do this!" Katie couldn't believe this was happening to her sister. Not to Rebecca!

"No. I am watched constantly. That is why I'm going to live with Anna and help take care of the sheep. Anna understands. She will help me to endure. In time, she may even help me escape."

"Belonging to someone like Amos Ludlow will kill you."

"A woman *never* belongs to any man," Rebecca reminded her sharply. "Besides, I'll escape before the sheep are driven off this mountain. They will, of course, hunt me. Mormons believe a marriage carries on forever in heaven."

"I'm going away with you."

"I'd counted on it. We will run far away. They'll never find us."

"Will Bryce? Rebecca, I have to see him again."

Rebecca stared into the distance. She wanted to tell Katie that Bryce was not the man for her, but she couldn't. "He'll find you."

Katie nodded. Her eyes were wet. "What about you? How can you marry Amos?"

"If I refused, Bryce would surely die, and Amos would find another way. Maybe something even worse."

"Nothing in the world," Katie choked, "could be worse than this."

The wedding ceremony was a simple, hurried affair, and the celebration afterward was strained. Even the children, who generally were so well behaved, seemed sullen and argumentative. They fought until Amos thundered at them to go to their rooms and not come out until he and Rebecca had departed.

The carriage was brought around by the liveryman, a sad-faced fellow with great moon eyes behind thick spectacles. "Well, Amos," he said, "you always did get the prettiest women and the fastest horses."

It was meant to be a compliment, but the other wives clearly were offended. Katie understood. They were jealous and resentful because Rebecca would now take Vida Ellen's place as the favorite and showpiece. Amos's favor was temporary. Mormon husbands were taught never to show any preferences, but while that was worthy advice, it was totally unrealistic. Not even a saint could keep from being partial to a pretty woman as opposed to a plain one, a happy wife who rarely complained to a stern, nagging one.

Rebecca's face was rigid. She seemed not among them as she was helped into the carriage.

"Good-bye," Katie whispered.

Rebecca nodded stiffly, and it was plain she was concentrating with all her strength simply to retain some control.

"God bless you, Rebecca!"

Amos Ludlow eased himself into the buggy seat. He'd put on considerable weight over the winter. It showed in his belly and jowls. He glanced down at Katie. "Smile, young lady. Your sister and I have been joined together in holy marriage by God. It is a bond that will last forever."

No, it won't! she thought bitterly. It'll last until Bryce returns to kill you.

"Git up, horse!" he yelled, cutting the animal sharply across the rump.

Katie stood in the rock driveway and watched until the carriage was out of sight. When she turned around, the wives were still there and they were watching *her*. And it was the same look they'd once reserved for Rebecca.

Katie whirled and ran down the street. The realization that she was alone drove into her like a dull knife. She ran and ran until she was standing high on a hillside above Temple City. She knelt in the grass and prayed. Dear Lord, I do not approve of whatever You are doing this for. Dear Jesus, are You so busy tending souls in their middle level You've no time to watch out for us while we're still alive?

There was no answer. There never was when she really needed one. Fighting back her anger and the urge to quit speaking to God, since He never listened, Katie made herself pray the only prayer she had any faith in at all.

The Lord is my shepherd; I shall not want. . . .

Rebecca was paralyzed with dread. She stood rooted, staring at the wall of the cabin. Glistening drops of golden pitch oozed from fresh-cut wood.

"Do you like it?" Ludlow asked quietly. "I've been out here twice in the past month making sure that everything is in perfect order. It cost me over a hundred dollars to fix it up and have that window put in so you'd have a view of the mountains and your sheep."

Like a sleepwalker, she moved over to the window. From her cabin the land fell away gently down to a broad meadow with a creek. There were thick stands of aspen, cottonwood, and willow, and a family of beaver had dammed up the water flow to create a huge natural watering hole where she could swim.

He placed his big hand on her arm. "On hot summer days we can bathe together in those cool waters. No one could see us, not even from the ridges. Anna will bring a small flock of sheep over next week when I've gone. She will teach you how to tend a flock and care for it."

"Let me see the newspaper again," she told him quickly, breaking from his grip. Knowing she'd saved a life was the only thing that kept her sane.

"Damn it!" he shouted. "I've already shown it to you!"

"Again! I told you I wanted it." There was an ax outside. If he was lying, she'd use it on him before he could take her.

He stormed over to his baggage and emptied his clothing on the bed until he found the month-old Salt Lake City newspaper.

"Here! Memorize the damned thing and never speak to me of Bryce Sherman again!"

Rebecca picked up the newspaper. She stared down at the small, second-page notice. She didn't need to memorize it, because she already had. It said, "Be it known that Brother Amos Ludlow of Temple City has dropped the reward and all charges against one Bryce Sherman. The charges were filed in error, and the man is absolved of the charge of horse theft."

"Rebecca?" He cupped her face in his hands. Shook her. "Rebecca, it is time."

The newspaper fell to the ground. His hands fumbled at her buttons and the lacings of her undergarments. Rebecca did not fight him. Almost trancelike, she let him strip her clothing away and lead her over to the rough wooden bed. She didn't watch him peel off his shirt and pants as desire flooded over his reason.

"Mrs. Ludlow," he said thickly as he eased her down. "You will soon learn that I know all the ways of pleasuring my wives. And you *will* be pleasured, Rebecca. I will not leave until you tell me I pleasure you."

She gasped, and stiffened with pain as he moved into her. This seemed to excite him greatly. Soon his powerful body bent and convulsed, then shuddered as he filled her with his seed.

He moaned with raw animal pleasure and then panted, "By God, I hope you don't take to smelling like a sheep this summer! Even that couldn't keep me away from this cabin. But you won't, will you?"

Her eyes were shut tightly, and tears bled from their corners. "No," she choked into his ear.

He pushed himself up on his elbows and stared at her face and breasts. "You are more beautiful to me than any of them ever were, Rebecca. You can have whatever you want, if it is in my power to give it to you. Name it."

Her eyes opened. She did not dare tell him she wanted only to go away. Or even to die.

Chapter Four

She had watched her new husband ride away and heard him call, "I'll be back with the shearing crews in two weeks!"

"And I'll be gone from this valley," she'd sworn.

Rebecca walked slowly down to the stream, and though it was still early morning and the air was cool, she peeled off her clothing and stepped into the cold water. She would wash away the smell of him if it took until dark. And she *would* find a way to escape before he returned, because she could not bear to let him touch her again. Not that he was cruel; in fact, much the opposite. Now that he'd won her in marriage, he seemed almost compassionate. After their first bout of lovemaking, he had really tried to pleasure her, and finally she'd lied just to rid him of his guilt.

But how could she feel anything but bitterness toward a man who'd forced her into marriage by threatening another's life? It didn't matter that he was convinced she would someday thank him for giving her the comforts he could afford in this life and a place with him in heaven during the next.

Rebecca scrubbed her skin vigorously with fine sand until it was pink. Then she climbed out of the stream, slowly dressed, and began to walk toward the flock of sheep. Her job was to stay with them until late afternoon, then begin to herd them down toward the bedding ground before dark. Anna was to bring her a sheep dog to help her drive the sheep and to guard them at night from coyotes.

As she neared the flock, Rebecca had to smile at the

lambs, who danced and bleated and followed their mothers about. The lambs were frightened, timid little creatures, and most were less than three weeks old. Some were black-faced crossbred sheep, but most were a French breed called Rambouillet, a dual-purpose breed, she'd learned, good for both meat and wool and with enough foraging ability to gain weight even down in the dry sagebrush country outside Salt Lake City.

Amos didn't like sheep at all. To him, they were foul-smelling, stupid, and noisy. They drew flies, ticks, and coyotes. They also made him nearly as much money as his far more troublesome logging business.

Rebecca had already learned some of the rudiments of the sheep business. There were three major yearly activities, each ushered in by a changing season. In the winter the ewes were bred down in the low country so they would lamb early in the spring. The lambing was the most critical time of all. A two-year-old ewe having her first lamb very often would refuse to allow it to nurse and would have to be caught and hobbled or even tied up until she finally gave in and accepted her offspring. Even delivering a lamb could be an ordeal. Sometimes the shepherd had to reach up into the ewe and drag the lamb out of her womb.

In midsummer the men of Temple City would do the shearing. It was a happy occasion. The women sewed big sacks for the wool and cooked for days. The men would have shearing contests, and there would be a great deal of excitement as thousands of sheep were gathered into the huge shearing pens. Amos had explained that each family in the valley owned at least a few hundred of the animals, and just sorting them and keeping the wool bags marked and their weights recorded was a complex job. Wool was a cash crop, and the people of Temple City relied upon it for a significant part of their livelihood.

Rebecca studied her flock. Yes, they were in need of shearing. They looked hot, and when she saw the lambs pushing their faces under all that wool to nurse, she thought of how she would be trapped forever if she already carried the seed of a child that Amos had worked so feverishly to plant inside her. The very thought of being pregnant by Amos Ludlow made her weak and sick with dread. *That* was the reason she dared not let him visit her even once again. He was a vital man, and she knew he would impregnate her soon.

But escape, she'd quickly learned, would be far more difficult than simply running away. There were at least six flocks being tended in this valley, and one neglected for even a few hours would quickly scatter and attract attention. Rebecca would be discovered missing, pursued, then overtaken; Amos had provided her with everything but a horse.

Her first thought had been to seek Anna's help. After long, agonizing deliberation Rebecca knew that she could not, because as punishment Amos might never trust Anna with the flocks again and would force her to live in Temple City with his other wives. It would kill Anna, rob her of the outdoor life and her "woollies" she so loved to tend. Rebecca couldn't do that.

The bark of a dog caused her to turn to see a small figure plodding along the dirt road from Temple City. The figure grew larger and larger until Rebecca cried, "Katie!"

"You can still laugh," Katie said a little later. "I wondered if you ever would again."

Rebecca smiled but avoided her sister's eyes as they trudged back toward the flock. "How did you get Amos to allow you to come visit?"

"I told him it would make you happy and . . . grateful," Katie added with obvious embarrassment.

"Clever. Did he let you come to stay awhile?"

"Yes." Katie's eyes danced with unconcealed delight. "Rebecca, I can stay right up to shearing time."

"I can't believe it!"

"It's true," Katie said. "Rebecca, I think we ought to go away. *Now*. Not wait until Bryce and Jude return. That could be a year or more."

It was true, and if she stayed, she knew she'd bear Amos's child by then. "I agree with you," Rebecca said. "But look about us. Any way you turn, you'll see distant flocks, and every day they are moving to find the best grass. I couldn't be more closely watched if I were in Temple City. I noticed that Amos made you walk all the way out here. We could never escape on foot."

"Why not?" Katie didn't understand. "If we go right after dark, we could be at the Echo Canyon station by midnight, and then—"

"Then what? Both stages run in the daytime. They'd come for us long before that."

"It would be kidnapping."

"Would it?" Rebecca shook her head. "Is it wrong for a man to claim his wife? No, and I couldn't ask some poor station tender to risk his life or even to leave his job to take me to Fort Bridger, which is the nearest Army post. Besides, if I abandoned these sheep for a single night, the coyotes would slaughter dozens of the new-born lambs."

"Then what can you do?" Katie slumped with disappointment.

"I haven't quite decided. All I know is that we have to find some way out of here before he returns. Katie, I can't live through . . . through that again!"

Katie heard the anguish and desperation in her sister's voice. After a long moment her shoulders lifted with determination. She had made a decision that would profoundly affect both their lives in the months ahead. "I want you to teach me everything you know about these sheep. Right now."

"I could do it in five minutes. But why?"

"Because tonight you are leaving and I'm going to take your place tending this flock. With luck no one will realize you're gone for days."

"No!"

"You must, Rebecca. I can face Amos. You can't."

"Katie, I could never leave you here alone. Just forget the whole idea." She would *never* abandon her sister.

"Both of us staying isn't going to help. Besides, I'm in no danger from Amos or Jude. I'm only fourteen, Rebecca."

"Mormons have wed fourteen-year-old girls."

Katie shook her head violently. "Not against their will. I haven't joined their church, but I've become their friend. Actually, I *like* them. Yes, there are a few like Amos, but most are good people who'd never allow Amos or Jude to wed me if I begged him not to."

"Katie, I'd be afraid for you."

"Bryce is freed of all charges, but when he returns someone will have to tell him about . . . about everything. Try to explain what happened. I want to be the one."

"It would only make him even more bitter. He'd try to kill Amos for sure."

"What can I tell him?"

"Anything but the truth. Tell him . . . tell him I was promised a large dowry."

"He'd not believe that."

"Make him believe it! You must!"

"Then how do I explain your running away?"

She shook her head dejectedly. "I don't know, Katie. I just don't know. Think of something."

"I'll try." She wanted to change the subject. "I told Pa about the wedding."

At the mention of her father, Rebecca's eyes flashed with anger. "What did he say?"

"He was surprised, then pleased. He said he wished he had been there, but then it happened so quickly. Did you know that he's going to join their church?"

"He wants another wife, damn him!"

"I suppose that's true and part of it. But not all. Rebecca, he really believes in the Book of Mormon. He told me these people are going to give him a little lot in town and help him build a house before winter."

"They've bought him even cheaper than I'd expected."

"He loves you, Rebecca. He honestly wants you to be happy. He just doesn't understand."

"I don't believe it."

"It's true. When I told him you'd up and married, he was so happy you'd gotten someone as important as Mr. Ludlow."

Rebecca's fists knotted. "He never even suspected the

truth, did he? If it hadn't been for him, we'd still be together in Springfield."

"Maybe we were meant to come west. Maybe there's a reason."

Rebecca's head jerked up. "A reason? What possible reason? To suffer in the cold and lose Mother, then to almost die of thirst in the Nevada desert?"

"No, but—"

"And to end up here! Me, forced to marry a man I detest, to be bred by him like one of his farm animals and then expected to bear his children?" Rebecca choked back a sound in her throat. "I'm done with men, Katie. Finished. I should never have forgotten Aunt Gwynneth's advice. From now until I die, I will never let another man take my heart—or my body."

Katie sat numbly beside her sister. What she really wanted to do was throw her arms around Rebecca and cry—but she couldn't. Not now. For the first time, she realized that Rebecca needed *her*.

"Hello," a voice called.

It was Anna Ludlow riding up on her sheep horse.

"Say nothing about tonight," Rebecca warned. "If she knows, Amos would treat her harshly, and the dear woman really loves him."

"I brought you a friend and helpmate," Anna said, dismounting. "One of the best old sheep dogs in the country."

It was a large male, gray-muzzled and a little stiff in the hindquarters, but still powerful and alert in appearance. His coat was long and shiny, black with a proud white mane. His tail was a white-tipped banner; it curved over his back and danced as he moved. One ear was up, the other half-cocked. There was a smile on his face and intelligence in his brown eyes.

"Girls, this is Rebel."

"He's beautiful!" Katie exclaimed. "Where did you get him?"

"There's an old man named Mr. Archer down the valley. His health is poor and he's slowly cutting down on his flock. I told him Rebel would be well treated and worked only in the summer. He gave him to me knowing you'll need a good steady dog with no bad habits."

Katie bent and patted the dog. Its thick coat was surprisingly soft. The floppy ear was torn ragged, and his face was tooth-scarred. "Is he a fighter?"

"Only against coyotes. Rebel is smart enough to drive them off the sheep but not go chasing after a pack of them in the dark. Once the coyotes realize there's no one around with a rifle, they'll turn on a dog and kill him. I've lost a good many young ones that way."

Rebecca said, "He looks very wise."

"He is. Come on, I'll show you. Stay close and just watch my arm signals."

They approached the flock, and, seeing Rebel, the sheep were instantly alert. Anna gave a sharp whistle and Rebel turned to see her arm point south. The dog gave a happy bark and went to work. He moved in and the sheep hurried away. He raced forward, then doubled back, his tail swishing with obvious delight. When a ewe tried to break away, Rebel was after her in an instant, teeth flashing, though he didn't nip hard enough even to break flesh. In less than two minutes he had eight hundred ewes going south at a good steady walk.

Anna whistled again. This time her arm made a sweeping motion toward the west and Rebel slid to a stop, barked sharply, and then raced around the flock, turning them to the left.

"He's so quick!" Katie said. "He runs like a young dog."

"He's never wasted his energy, that's why. Notice how he gets them moving, then stays back? He doesn't want to excite the sheep. Actually, he shouldn't bark at all, but Archer said he enjoys his work so much that he never had the heart to scold him for an occasional yip. He responds to whistle, voice, and, most important, just to your arm signals."

Anna demonstrated by making a circling motion, explaining, "A thousand head of bleating sheep can't be outshouted all day or you'd soon lose your voice. Also, if there was a strong windstorm in the trees or we were near a river, he'd never hear you. You find a dog that constantly watches for your signals as well as the flock, you've a good one. Rebel is that kind of dog."

They watched as Rebel began to circle the sheep into a milling band. Then the dog trotted slowly around them at a respectful distance and sat. His head moved from Anna to the sheep and back.

"He's a prince," Anna said with unconcealed admiration. "You see how he leaves the flock alone now? Young dogs work the sheep too hard. It's the shepherd's job to fatten his flock, and an overeager pup will quickly wear off weight—and profit. Rebel is firm but patient. He's almost as good as my Louie. Maybe even better."

Anna glanced up at the sun. "Going to be dark before I get back if I don't start now." She climbed back on her horse, untied a sack, and pitched it down to Rebecca. "Meat for Rebel. It ought to last until the shearers come."

She started to leave but had one final piece of advice. "What you don't know, Rebel will show you. Treat him kindly, but don't try to make him a pet. Cats are pets. Dogs are meant to work."

With that she was gone. Rebel, meanwhile, kept circling the herd, looking from sheep to the vanishing Anna to Katie and Rebecca. Katie had few doubts the dog was awaiting a signal. He barked sharply.

Anna Ludlow twisted around in her saddle. She was a half mile away, but even at that distance they all saw her raise both arms and firmly bring them down. Rebel collapsed in a furry heap, tongue hanging out of the side of his mouth. He gratefully laid his chin on his paws and relaxed to watch his new charges.

"Thanks!" Katie yelled, waving to Anna.

"No!" Rebecca cried. "Stop waving!"

Rebel had seen her and was on his feet in an instant, leaping one way then the next in abject confusion.

"Down!" Katie cried, feeling awful because of the dog's erratic action. Together she and her sister made the downward motion again and again.

Rebel cocked his head, then sank back to the grass. He looked disgusted.

"What happens if a bee flies by my ear and I want to

swat it?" Katie asked. "Rebel will go crazy."

"I don't know," Rebecca said. "Run behind a tree, I guess. Let's get back to the bedground. Give him the signal."

Katie wasn't sure, but she raised her arm and pointed toward their distant cabin. And Rebel gave her another chance.

They stood in the twilight and watched the sun plunge into the sharp, snow-tipped peaks of the Wasatch Mountains. The ewes had finished settling down, and their lambs were nestled in close at their sides, while Rebel trotted around the flock once more.

Rebecca lingered, a small feedsack of clothing and belongings at her feet.

"Do you have any money?" Katie asked.

"No. But I'm sure I can earn enough in Fort Bridger to buy a ticket east. It will take some time perhaps, but I'll do it." She hoped she sounded confident.

"Are you going back to Springfield?"

Rebecca pondered the question. At first it seemed the only logical thing to do. She had aunts and uncles there and friends who would take her in until she could find steady employment. Yet the thought of returning alone, penniless and in disgrace, was unbearable. She couldn't hide anything from them, none of it. Not the way her mother had died and how she hated Micah. Not about leaving Katie like this, and not even about her marriage. A marriage that was legal and forever binding. Amos Ludlow would never consent to have the vows nullified.

"I couldn't face them," she admitted. "Someday, perhaps, but not now. And not without you."

"Then where will you go?"

"I don't know. Maybe Boston or New York. Someplace far away, until I can think clearly. I'll write as soon as I'm settled. And I'll send you money. You'll need money."

"How? They'll know it's you. Amos will hear of it and—"

"It doesn't matter!" Rebecca lowered her voice. "Katie, once I'm far away, it's over. Amos wouldn't dare come east for me. And he's no thief. You'll get your money."

"I'm going to buy sheep of my own," Katie announced, "and build up a flock so that when I leave here I'll have something." She didn't look down at the feedsack, but Rebecca did.

"It's time to go," she said, stooping to pick it up. "Are you sure you'll be all right here?"

"Yes. It's the only chance you've got, and Rebel will take care of the sheep."

Rebecca reached out and then crushed Katie in an embrace. Her heart ached and her eyes stung with tears. How long would it be until they were reunited? Katie would be alone now, and she was pitifully small to stand against Amos's wrath. It would burst across this valley like a thunderstorm. And yet there was steel in this girl. Rebecca could feel it, and that made her ashamed of her own doubts and fears.

"Good-bye," she whispered. "May God protect you until we are together again."

"Go on!" Katie choked. "Run and never come back to these people."

Rebecca tore herself away and stumbled into the night, feeling more hurt and alone than she ever had in her life.

"I can't take you any farther," the driver had said. "Company orders say we're to help people get to safety. You'll be safe enough at the fort."

Rebecca had nodded gratefully. She had no intention of explaining how desperate her circumstances really were, nor that she was an escaped wife of one of Utah's most powerful polygamists.

"Have you no luggage, miss?"

Rebecca shook her head. The driver glanced toward the station tender, who just shrugged. She'd told him only that she needed to catch the first eastbound stage. He'd wanted to know more, probably even suspected she was running away from Temple City but knew better than to ask. Still, as she took the driver's arm and was about to be helped up into the coach, the tender said, "Ma'am?"

"Yes?"

"If someone should come looking for you, should I tell 'em you went east or west?"

Rebecca's voice was steady. "I think you know the answer to that. I'll be in your debt."

He was a surly old man, small, leathery-faced, and bandy-legged. For the first time, he grinned at her. "That's what I thought. Good luck."

"Thank you."

She stepped up into the coach, aware that her stockings showed above her ankles and that they were torn and dirty. The past few days had been tense, and she felt wrung out from worry. The dark interior of the coach was like a sanctuary. She stumbled forward and might have fallen if a man hadn't caught her arm and helped her into the seat.

"I'm sorry."

"Don't be," the Army officer who faced her said. "You look, if you'll excuse me, as though you could use some rest."

He was quite handsome in his double-breasted frock coat of dark blue cloth, and he was also a little drunk. She watched as he deliberately pulled a silver flask from his inside pocket and extended it with a gallant flourish.

"No, thank you."

He shrugged with an air of exaggerated indifference. "I thought not, but it would have been poor manners on my part not at least to offer. I'll do the honors for both of us."

Rebecca turned her attention up toward the canyon walls, half expecting to see Amos Ludlow and a band of angry Mormons bearing down on her, determined to capture her and enforce their marriage vows. Oh, how she wished to leave this place! Not until they were completely out of Utah Territory and inside the walls of Fort Bridger would she feel safe.

"You look very worried, miss," he said, taking her arm.

Rebecca stiffened. "Let go of me, sir!"

"In a moment. Please understand that I am a doctor, and it is my professional opinion that you may faint at any moment. Your breathing is too fast, your color pale, and your skin damp. You are highly agitated, and your pulse is . . . racing wildly at over one hundred."

She pulled her arm free. "I'll be fine!"

"My name is Captain Devlin Woodson the Second. And yours?"

She hesitated.

"Have you forgotten your own name?" he asked. "Let me help you think of one."

"That won't be necessary," she said. "My name is Miss Rebecca . . . Holt, and, if you will pardon my saying so, I wish we would leave."

"Expecting some kind of trouble that I should know about? Let's see, I do have a gun around here somewhere. Unbuckled the blamed thing because it's so cumbersome."

He'd filled the seat beside him with what she supposed was a medical pack and boxes of supplies. At his feet was a leather case, and that was where he finally located his gun. "Here it is! I believe it's even loaded."

"Don't take it out of the holster. You won't be needing it. I promise."

He studied her. He had a wide forehead and curly brown hair. His nose was slightly aquiline, and his mouth posed in a lopsided grin. His best features were his luxuriant mustache and a rugged square chin. He was neither tall nor short but quite trim, and despite being tipsy, he sat as erect as a statesman, as though to slump would be foreign to his breeding.

He put the gun away. "I believe you—about the gun— not your name."

"It matters not to me. What are we waiting for?"

He pushed back the leather side curtain and craned his neck out the window. "An unruly horse. But don't worry, they will soon club the dumb beast into submission and we'll be on our merry way."

Rebecca's mind was filled with agitation. Had they found Katie and the sheep? What if they were waiting in ambush at the eastern end of Echo Canyon? They could block it. And what then? Surely the driver and this . . . this drunken doctor would not help her. Rebecca's eyes dropped to the gun. If they were waiting to reclaim her, she was going to take that gun from its holster and shoot the first man who tried to drag her from this coach.

"Surely you're not thinking of robbing *me*, are you?"

Rebecca glanced up. He'd followed her gaze. The question was so ridiculous she laughed aloud.

"Then why were you eyeing my gun? Are you being pursued, young woman? Are you—could my wildest fantasy be coming true—a beautiful damsel in distress?"

He was drunk, but very bright. Rebecca decided to steer the questioning to her own advantage. "Are you living in Fort Bridger?"

"Existing, yes. There is a distinction. Actually, it's a beautiful place to be in the summertime. It sits low among the rolling hills on Black's Fork, a superb trout fishing river. It goes right through our parade ground."

The way he said it, Rebecca thought he didn't enjoy fishing.

"And if one likes to hunt or trap like old Jim Bridger, it's a paradise."

"But you don't."

"No," he said definitely. "I don't enjoy any of those things. I am a frontier misfit. A graduate officer from West Point who has seen the follies of killing and now seeks only to heal. I could not begin to tell you how many men I led to their deaths at Shilo and Bull Run. It was madness, and I almost went mad. Would have if I hadn't . . . Do you object to me telling you all this?"

"No, not at all."

"Good. My story is blessedly brief. I deserted the Union Army and raced back to Delaware and medical school. My father is also a doctor. He expected more of me than the others. Graded my papers far too critically, but I still managed to top my class."

"Why weren't you arrested for desertion?"

He looked sheepish. "My father is rather prominent, and I swore to finish school and reenlist as a medical officer. My intent was, and still is, to save as many lives as I'd wasted."

He paused, took a quick drink, sighed, then leaned his

head back and stared at the roof of the coach. "Confession really is good for the soul, and now I begin to see why the Irish masses tell everything to their priests. You are my captive priestess, and this is our confessional."

"This is a stagecoach, and I think you've had enough to drink," she said sternly. "Stop it now or I shall ask you to be quiet."

"Oh, will you now?" His eyebrows arched. "A fine priestess you are. Have I spoken a single vulgarity or even made a vague proposition? Have I offended you in any way whatsoever?"

"No," she said quietly. "But if you keep drinking, you may. Please stop."

He uncapped his flask, took a farewell drink, and poured the rest of it out the window just as the coach lurched forward.

"Thank heaven," she breathed as they surged ahead. Rebecca felt the iron-rimmed wheels slide across rock as the coach skidded out of the yard and hit the rutted road east.

Devlin Woodson said, "If this is to be a real confession, I have to confess that I was responsible for the deaths of eighty-six men in the war. As of yet, I've saved only thirty-one, including Indians, so, as you can see, I am still fifty-five down."

Rebecca stared out the window. She couldn't see any sign of riders yet. Hope grew brighter.

"Miss Holt, I am returning from Nevada, where a small massacre occurred and I was able to save four more lives. With any luck, a few more skirmishes perhaps, I think I'll have it all squared up before I'm thirty-five."

Rebecca had never met anyone quite like this. He was an educated young man doing the right thing for all the wrong reasons. "Will you feel absolved of your guilt?"

"I don't know." He relaxed, looked away for a moment, and then reached down and picked up his gun and holster. With steely deliberation he unbuttoned his coat and drew the sash and holster around the emerald green medical officer's sash about his waist. He rebuttoned his coat, then the collar, though the air was warm. His eyes never left her face.

"What are those called?" she asked, pointing to the golden fringes on his shoulders.

He flicked them with a forefinger. "These are called epaulettes, and they designate an officer's rank. The longer these fringes, the higher the rank. These two silver bars tell everyone I'm a captain."

"That's nice."

"Not really, but it is respectable. And this silver wreath with the Old English letters MS means that I am in the medical service. In the military, rank is everything. It is all quite orderly."

She glanced out the window again. They were almost out of the canyon. Just another mile or two.

"If they are waiting," Devlin said very distinctly, "I will use this gun on them."

She twisted around. Saw the heavy pistol resting on his lap, and noted that his face was quite serious.

"I couldn't have you interfere," she said. "You have a mission to save fifty-five lives. I'm but one."

"I have another mission now." His gaze was penetrating.

"And that is?"

"To see you remain at Fort Bridger."

She waited until they shot out the eastern portal of Echo Canyon and were sailing across open prairie before she turned back to face him. "Your mission to save fifty-five lives is gallant. Don't confuse it with thoughts of me—for I have a very selfish mission, and that is to go east as soon as possible."

"The fall colors are magnificent around Fort Bridger," he told her.

"Then I hope you enjoy them, Captain Woodson. As for me, I will see them in New England."

He started to speak, thought better of it, and turned toward the window. A sideways glance told Rebecca he was smiling faintly, and that strong jaw of his had a set look of determination. All in all, she decided, he was a very unusual man.

Chapter Five

Even before she arrived, Rebecca learned all about the colorful Fort Bridger from Captain Devlin Woodson II. It had been established by Jim Bridger, the famous guide, mountain man, and fur trader in 1842 as a small Indian trading post. There'd been just a few rough log cabins and Indian lodges. But Bridger had chosen the site well; and his trading post had prospered, first in dealing with the Utes and Shoshonis, then later with the increasingly heavy flow of westbound immigrants along the Oregon Trail. In 1858 the Mormons had bought the fort, but they were soon forced to relinquish it to the U.S. Army and had pushed on to Salt Lake City. It was now a prominent trading center and military outpost. While many army forts in the West were crude tent or adobe camps, Fort Bridger was considered both picturesque and comfortable, with its well cared for grounds and solid log homes and outbuildings.

"Is Mr. Bridger still at the fort?" Rebecca asked, watching a herd of antelope graze on the rolling grassy hills.

"No, Bridger left to retire on a Missouri farm. I advised it because of his health and failing eyesight. Jim Bridger is missed here. I never knew anyone who could tell tales the way he can. It was hard to figure out truth from fiction, and sometimes I'm not sure he remembers which is which himself. But he loves this country. When he started to go blind, it almost broke his heart. He couldn't see the distant mountains that he knows better than any white man alive. But he is a shrewd bargainer, and when he sold his trading post to the Mormons for eight thousand dollars, he didn't bother to say that he had no legal

71

claim to the property. He apparently mentioned something about an old Mexican grant, but there wasn't any.
That's why they had to abandon the place when the Army
threatened to chase them off."

"I imagine the Mormons were furious."

"They still are. Brigham Young has petitioned Congress for redress, but he'll never see a penny of his
money. I imagine Jim Bridger decided it would be
healthier to put a few miles between himself and the
Mormons."

Rebecca glanced up to see him watching her closely.
He said. "You'd agree on that, wouldn't you, Miss Holt?"

She ignored him, because her denial would sound false
and only confirm his suspicions.

"Miss Holt, I know it's none of my business, but—"

"You're correct," she said in a clipped voice. "It isn't."

"*But*," he pressed on, "when we reach the fort, there
will be many questions, which you seem unwilling or unable to answer. I just thought that perhaps together we
might conjure up some convincing lies."

Rebecca glared at him with open disapproval. "Those
questions are no one's business except my own."

"Not entirely true. You see, I couldn't help but overhear
you tell the driver you are without funds."

She colored with indignation. "And you intend to take
advantage of that bit of information!"

"Not at all. My dear woman, I've even been debating
about lending you the stage fare out of this wilderness."

"Why?"

"To win your undying gratitude, of course. Unfortunately, that emotion would do me precious little good if
you were several thousand miles away."

"I would do you no more good if I am stuck in Fort
Bridger." She sighed. "Please understand, Captain, I just
want to be left in peace. I've nothing against you."

"That's gratifying but offers little satisfaction. How
about if I offer you a job?"

"Doing what?" she asked suspiciously.

"Assisting me at the infirmary with sick call and various wounds. Once a month or so I have a surgery or

amputation to perform, and those who survive need constant nursing care."

"Are you serious?"

"You mean you doubt that any of my operative patients recover?"

"Of course not. You know that's not what I meant. Tell me, what could you pay?"

"That would depend," he said. "If you insist on leaving the moment you have a few dollars and can reach the next military post, which would be Fort Laramie, then it would hardly be worth training you as an assistant. On the other hand, if you were to agree to spend, say, a year . . ."

"A year! That's impossible!"

"Nine months, then," he said hastily.

"I want to be a teacher." She thought of Bryce and how she'd dug the bullet from his leg. It had been one of the most thrilling and important moments of her life. Scary, but immensely rewarding. And now she had the opportunity to learn medicine from a real doctor. The offer had immense appeal.

"I think you'd be a superb assistant," he said as if guessing her thoughts. "If you help me, I'll promise you ten dollars at the end of every month. That's almost as much as a private earns in this man's Army. You won't match the offer. There are a dozen wives of enlisted men on this post trying to hold down laundress jobs who would almost kill to be my assistant."

Rebecca could tell by his expression that he wasn't exaggerating. She weighed the offer carefully. There was a risk of being discovered by the Mormons, yet it seemed small. She knew that the Army and the Mormons were not friendly and that a few years ago a war between them had barely been averted. Also, by remaining in Wyoming she would be close to Katie and could send her a few dollars each month. If she were frugal, at the end of nine months they might both have enough saved to buy tickets eastward. Yes, she thought, perhaps this was a godsend—if she could control Captain Woodson's ardor. It could be Katie's salvation and her own. She had to try.

"All right, Captain. I'll stay for nine months."

His face lit up like an excited schoolboy's. "That's marvelous! This calls for a celebration!" He reached into his bag, fumbled around for a moment, and dragged out another bottle of whiskey. Uncorking it, he said, "You must at least join me in a toast."

She didn't want one, but he was so pleased she hadn't the heart to refuse. "Just a sip."

"Fine. It will put the color back into your cheeks." He extended the bottle toward her.

She accepted it gingerly, took a swallow, and gasped, "It's terrible! How do you stand it?"

"Acquired taste. After a few drinks, you will be amazed at how good it becomes. Try again."

She did, but it tasted just as bad, and she pushed the bottle back at him. Her eyes were watering; her stomach and throat burned.

He drank deeply, then corked the bottle and tucked it away. A second quick search through his bag produced another bottle, and he held it out to her.

"No more, Doctor," she protested. Even two swallows had made her feel light-headed.

"It's a syrup I made of cloves and licorice for your breath. You can't arrive smelling of whiskey. They wouldn't forgive me."

So she drank, though *it* tasted awful too. Almost at once she felt an overwhelming lassitude; her eyelids began to droop, and she fell asleep.

"Miss Holt," he was saying. "Wake up. We've arrived, and your accommodations are ready at Judge and Mrs. Carter's home."

She couldn't seem to clear the fog from her brain. Still half asleep, she let him carry her across the parade ground and into a house to set her down on a bed.

"She has been under a severe strain," Devlin was saying. "And presently her health is not good."

"Then she shall remain our guest as long as she desires."

"Thank you, Judge Carter. Mrs. Carter."

Rebecca forced her eyes open to see a gentle, matronly woman with gray hair and a warm smile say, "We'll take care of her, Devlin. Don't you worry. But shame on you, for not telling us your cousin was arriving from Sacramento to help you!"

Rebecca shook her head. Cousin? Sacramento? She wanted to tell these people that it was all a lie, but she was so tired she decided it could wait until tomorrow.

That night she slept deeply. For the first time in months her dreams were peaceful instead of fearful. Amos Ludlow's face did not appear before her, only Katie's. Once Rebecca heard her say, "You were wonderful, better than a real doctor even. You should be one, Rebecca. You should!"

Captain Woodson was in her dreams, and he was laughing, and she wasn't sure whether or not she should laugh with him. But mostly she felt safe and protected. She hadn't felt that way in a dream since her mother had died. Rebecca nestled down in the deep feather mattress between clean cotton sheets and felt very, very good.

The sun was high and filtering through the muslin fabric of her bedroom curtains when a soft but insistent voice woke her.

"Rebecca. Rebecca, wake up. It's almost noon."

Her eyes opened. Captain Woodson was seated beside her bed. He took her pulse. Then, as she came fully awake and was about to tell him she wouldn't tolerate lying to these people, he popped a thermometer into her mouth and said, "Your color is much improved this morning."

Rebecca glared at him.

"But not your disposition, I see."

He seemed to leave the thermometer in far longer than was necessary, and as he watched her, he scribbled something in a notebook, thought about it, then wrote a few more lines and tore the pages out and showed it to her.

It read: "Please don't be angry with me for giving you an acceptable background. Without it, the circumstances would have made it unrespectable."

GARY McCARTHY

She looked up at him and removed the thermometer. "Sooner or later these people will discover the truth. They're your friends. How can you lie to them?"

"It wasn't easy." He glanced at the thermometer and put it carefully away. "Rebecca, I promise I'll tell them soon. But for now I'm ordering you to stay in bed and rest for a few days. You are exhausted, underweight, and generally run down. As for the story about being my cousin, it was the only one I could think of that would keep tongues from wagging around here. You are going to cause one hell of a stir at Fort Bridger."

"Then perhaps I should just go?"

"How, on foot? Or perhaps with some passerby?"

"But I'm not your cousin!"

"Fine," he said with an edge on his voice. "Then who *are* you? Not Miss Holt, I'd bet!"

When Rebecca averted her face, his voice softened. "I'm sorry, Rebecca. Your past is your own business, but you needed one or you'd have had to explain why you showed up in Echo Canyon alone and penniless. And you don't appear eager to do that."

"Captain," Rebecca swallowed dryly. "You have lied to your friends, given me a place to stay and a job. And I know why. And"—it was oh, so difficult, but Rebecca had to say it—"and I will not repay you by becoming your mistress."

"That's fine," he said in a stony voice. "I'd have been surprised and disappointed if you had."

"I wish I could believe that," she murmured.

"You can."

Outside, a thundering voice bellowed, "Attention! Forward, march!" And a hundred boots hit the rocky ground like one. "Your left! Your left! Your left, right, left!"

Captain Woodson watched her with amusement. "Company drill," he explained. "Two hours every morning and afternoon, weather permitting. Same for the cavalry. It's ceaseless. After a while you won't even hear it."

"Tell me about this family."

"You will love them all. Judge William Carter is a transplanted Virginia gentleman who raises the finest pure-

76

bred merino sheep in America. His wife, Mary, is a jewel, and without their friendship, I think . . ."

Whatever he'd been about to say, he'd decided not to follow it through. "Enjoy your rest. It will be brief, because I do need your help. You'll find the judge's library to be the finest in Wyoming Territory." He grinned mischievously. "You can read, can't you?"

"Certainly!"

"Thank heaven," he sighed. "I could never love an illiterate."

"Get out of here," she told him.

He patted her hand. "Bed rest. Lots of it. I'll be by to see you twice a day. Any more often and the men would begin to suspect my interests were more than professional. As it is, the entire post is dying of curiosity."

"What if the stagecoach driver tells them about my turning up in Echo Canyon?"

"He won't. I bought him off with the promise of a bottle of whiskey every time he passes through."

"You think of everything, don't you, Captain?"

"Not everything." He winked. "I've gotten you in bed, but that's only half the solution, isn't it?"

She gasped in outrage and swung at him, but he leapt back out of range, laughing. "I'm sorry. One of my great shortcomings is candor. But in truth, I'm a gentleman and a man of honor. I would *never* compromise a decent woman's reputation."

After he departed, Rebecca was visited by Mary Carter and her six children. It was quite a family, and she couldn't help but note the pride Mrs. Carter took in showing off her four girls and two boys.

"You'll learn quickly enough about life on an Army post," the judge's wife promised. "Since you're young and pretty, I'm afraid our sick calls are going to be the most popular event of the day around here."

"I hope I'm not a bother."

"Oh, you will be, but we'll all enjoy it." She laughed. "I would offer you only one piece of advice, and that is not to become too interested in any enlisted man. There are some fine, handsome young men among them, but their poor wives are considered 'camp followers' by Army regulations. Do you know why that term originated?" Mary Carter shook her head and her round, gentle face wore an expression of genuine compassion.

"No."

"Well, I think you can easily guess what kind of women follow camps of men. It's an insult to these good wives, and most of them have a miserable time trying to raise a family on the pay their husbands receive."

"I have no intention of marrying anyone—ever," Rebecca stated flatly.

Mrs. Carter must have thought she was joking until she looked at Rebecca. And then she knew she meant it.

A few days later Captain Woodson left her alone in his cluttered office while he passed through the infirmary to attend the morning sick call. He had just finished showing her all the neatly labeled medicine bottles, the surgical instruments, the bandages, splints, and bottles of solution, and now she knew a few moments of doubt and apprehension. She couldn't for the life of her remember what he'd said about any of them! Surely he didn't expect her to recall what medicines did what in addition to his nearly two hour lecture on the skeletal, circulatory, and digestive systems. Why, he'd smothered her with words and terms that sounded like a foreign language and hadn't given her so much as a moment even to ask a question! Now, realizing she'd been too embarrassed to admit her ignorance and confusion, she felt used and cheated. She wasn't stupid; far from it. He'd simply given her way too much, way too fast.

Rebecca shook her head as if to clear her thoughts. It was funny, but ever since she'd removed that bullet from Bryce's leg she'd fantasized about what it would be like to be a real doctor. Devlin was the first she'd met, not counting all the men who'd just learned by trial and error or from reading some almanac or the labels on medicine bottles. But now, after the lecture, she felt overwhelmed by her own ignorance and the complexity of the human body. It was one thing to dig a bullet out of a leg, an entirely different thing to know which medicine to use for what ailment. And what if you made a mistake? What if you gave some poor soldier expectorant when what he really required was an emetic? He'd wind up spitting himself to death instead of vomiting up stomach poison. And cathartics—were they supposed to clean out a person's system, or were they used to replace lost blood? Rebecca groaned with frustration. She couldn't remember anything!

She slumped down at his paper-strewn desk and gazed dispiritedly at the piles of medical journals, notes, and correspondence. Noting a half-filled jar of arrowheads and bits of lead, she realized at once that they'd all been removed by the Army physician during his stay here at Fort Bridger. Why, there must have been two dozen! She closed her eyes; how glad she was that she'd been able to resist the urge to tell Devlin about her own little surgery. She'd have hated to be patronized, and Devlin was too much the gentleman to have acted otherwise.

Brisk footsteps across a hard wood floor brought Rebecca out of her reverie. Devlin was returning from the parade ground. Sick call was over, and here she'd been squandering time wallowing in self-pity. Rebecca spied a broom and began to sweep furiously just as the door opened.

"What on earth are you doing?"

She glanced up as if surprised. "Sweeping." It seemed obvious enough.

Devlin scowled menacingly. "Miss Holt, I did not employ you to sweep my floors. I have Army privates to do my housekeeping. They need the exercise. You do not!"

She propped the broom back up against the wall. "Then what am I supposed to do? I don't know anything." The words began to tumble out of her mouth. "I didn't even comprehend a fraction of your lecture. I don't mind doing the housekeeping, or I can mend blankets or wash bedding or—"

"Stop it!" he said angrily. "Is that all you really want? Just something to do in exchange for a few dollars? Something that requires no skill, no thought, no training, just muscle and a mind weak enough to endure the numbing monotony?"

She saw that he was furious and filled with contempt. A vein throbbed at his temple, and his eyes were pinning her for an answer.

She whirled away from him, feeling her own anger flashing toward the surface. This had been a mistake. All of it. She would leave this fort even if it meant walking to Illinois. What right did this man have to berate and insult her? To lord his knowledge and medical skill over her the way he'd done for two solid hours? None. He had absolutely no right whatsoever.

"I've asked you a question, Miss Holt. Someone as beautiful and filled with life and adventure as you deserves more than drudgery, but you must use your abilities to rise above the ordinary." His voice assumed a kinder tone. "Dear woman, please say that you agree."

She spun around to face him, and her cheeks were hot. "Yes, I wholeheartedly agree, *Doctor*. However, you have deliberately chosen to make me feel stupid by throwing so many new words around that I'm completely confused and demoralized. A moment ago I was feeling stupid, but now . . . now I think *you* were the one who was stupid. Or were you just trying to impress? To tell me everything you learned at that important eastern university over the course of four years?"

His eyes widened. He let out a low whistle, and then he broke into a smile and clapped his hands lustily, shouting, "Bravo! Nicely done, Rebecca. I love your spirit. Please, never lose it."

She was suddenly thrown off stride. "Do you mean it?" This man's temperment was as capricious as the prairie winds.

"Of course I do. You were absolutely correct. I *was* trying to build myself up in your lovely eyes. It was shameless, sophomoric, and completely egotistical." He clasped her hands between his own and kissed them with a flourish that left her quite unsettled. "Will you find it in your heart somehow to forgive me?"

The appeal was exaggerated, even theatrical. But that

was Devlin, and she knew that he was overacting to hide the very real sincerity of his plea, and that if she did not forgive him, he would probably drop to his knees and make a complete fool out of both of them. He was utterly impossible, and she hadn't the power to stay angry with him for even another second. Rebecca sighed. "I'll forgive you, but I don't think I'll ever remotely understand you."

He smiled handsomely. "Then don't try, because no one really understands anyone else. People are too complex, and one of the greatest mistakes we as humans repeatedly make is to assume others use the same thought processes as ourselves."

"Are we each that mysterious?"

"I think so. As for myself, I've totally given up on trying to understand my fellow man—or woman."

"I thought you, a doctor, an educated man, would want to know the answer to everything."

"Who can claim to understand himself? And without that, how can we go into the minds of others?"

"You really surprise me," Rebecca said. "I've never met anyone who talked as you do."

"I am a closet philosopher, one without the pure intellect to advance the science, yet with enough keen perception to see the flaws in it."

"Is it true," she asked eagerly, "that knowledge is like an unquenchable thirst, that the more you drink of it, the more you desire?"

He loosened his military tie and let it hang askew. In his dark blue uniform with the gold braidwork, he looked exceedingly handsome. "To a point, knowledge is like the thirst. I've read many of the greatest philosophers from Socrates through Aquinas and Immanuel Kant. Some of the most brilliant I couldn't even follow through their reasoning. Only one thing really kept poking me in the brain, one truth among all the words and convoluted logic."

"And that was?"

Devlin chuckled boyishly. "And that was that none of them agreed on much of anything."

"Are you going to tell me next, then, that since there is

81

no true agreement among the greatest minds of civilization, there is no real truth?"

"Yes! Exactly."

"That's ridiculous!" she cried. "Religion aside, for the moment, if you see or hear or touch a thing, it's real. A rock, for instance, is definitely a rock."

His eyes narrowed playfully. "Maybe. What about a pond?"

"The same."

"Then what of the desert mirage? The optical illusion, the tricks our minds play, the very image we carry of ourselves?"

"What are you talking about?"

"Simply this: Are we the person we believe ourselves to be, or the one our enemies believe? Or our friends? Look in the mirror, Rebecca. Write your description on paper, and compare it with my description or that of any ten people. All will be different, all true to the observer. Is reality, then, only in the mind of the individual?"

Before Rebecca could form an answer, he was continuing, caught up in the excitement of his ideas. "What separates us from all the lower animals is our ability to accept things in the abstract—beauty, honor, devotion, the very idea of our own mortality. If I really love you, can you honestly say my love is any less real than a simple rock?"

"I think I understood you better when you were drunk."

"I labor under the same illusion," he said. "But that aside, let's be serious. Stay with me and I'll teach you enough about medicine and philosophy that you'll not be overwhelmed by anyone ever again. And furthermore, I'll stretch the limits of your own considerable intellect as well as prove that my love is *more* real than a rock."

She cocked an upraised eyebrow at him. "Why don't you show me your infirmary and explain my nursing duties?"

"I'm afraid," he said with an air of resignation, "that you have a rather disagreeable streak of practical responsibility."

It was her turn to smile now. "Yes, I do. And in the months to come, Captain Woodson, you might just also benefit in some ways."

He chose not to argue the point and started toward the infirmary. Rebecca followed, thinking how lucky she really was to have met such a person. Despite the arrogance and cynicism that crept into his conversation, there seemed to be a good deal of doubt in him, and that made him very, very human. Being a physician probably was a daily reminder of how little we understand about ourselves, about anything. Devlin apparently had come to believe that education and even brilliance were not the keys to the deepest of human mysteries. Was that being fatalistic, or realistic?

Rebecca halted beside him in the barrackslike infirmary. He glanced at her with a troubled expression, perhaps wondering if he'd said too much or too little. Rebecca's fingers reached out and brushed his sleeve. "Captain Woodson," she murmured, "thank you for this work and the chance to learn so much from you."

His head lifted, and he seemed to grow taller. "I'm a damn fine man and physician," he said, with none of the banter that was so typical of him, "and I think I might be just good enough to finally deserve a woman like you."

In the days that followed, Rebecca was never again to see Devlin attempt to put on a show of his education and knowledge. When news spread that a young and beautiful and unmarried woman was "the doc's cousin and new helper," the number of soldiers who fell out for sick call swelled to such exaggerated proportions that even the enlisted men had to struggle to hide their sheepish grins.

Devlin was prepared. He confronted the malingerers with a bucket of quinine water and a large box of Ayer's Cathartic Pill and announced to the assembly, "All right, soldiers, those of you who aren't sick now sure as hell will be when I've dosed you this morning, and those of you who are sick will, unfortunately, fold over and die."

More than forty enlisted men and a shameful number

of junior officers made a dramatic recovery and begged to be dismissed at once.

Only one man remained, a thin, wavering private standing on one foot. "What about you?" Devlin asked quietly.

"Broken foot, Captain, sir."

Devlin and Rebecca assisted him inside at once.

"What happened?" Devlin eased him down on a bunk while Rebecca slipped off his untied boot only with the greatest difficulty. "It's badly swollen," she said.

"Tell me about it, Private," Devlin ordered, bending down to remove a bloody sock and examine the foot.

"Happened about five this morning. Got trapped in a stall and then kicked and tromped on by a horse at feeding time."

"Four hours ago!"

"Yes, sir."

The boy was beginning to shake now, possibly as much from Devlin's outburst as the injury.

"You should have come to me at once. The swelling is so bad now that I won't be able to tell if the bones are broken. Can you move your toes?"

"I'll try, sir."

The toes did move, and the tension in Devlin lessened. "Now, arch your foot if you can."

The boy tried, and the only thing that happened was that he almost fainted.

"Broken foot," Devlin announced with resignation. "He'll be off his feet for a month at least. "Soldier, do you want an honorable discharge?"

"Sir?"

The kid clearly did not understand, and neither did Rebecca.

"I said, do you want out of the United States Army? If you do, I can give you authorization to muster out as soon as you're fit to travel."

The boy swung his head toward Rebecca as if seeking some kind of help. She lowered her eyes and heard him say, "No sir! I'm in this man's Army because I want to be. I want to make it a career, sir."

"Are you certain? You understand the life of an enlisted man. Low pay, tough, dirty work, long hours, and damn little thanks."

He swallowed noisily. "It's the best I'll ever see. I got no home, nothin' to go anywhere for. Here I'm fed, clothed, and I got me some of the finest buddies a man could ever hope to know. You kick me out if you've a mind to, Captain, but I won't quit this outfit."

"Devlin?" She had no idea what this was all about. Why was he forcing such a question at a time like this?

"Miss Holt," he said, "a fracture of the foot often never heals entirely. A soldier has to be able to march and sometimes even run carrying a full pack over terrain a goat would avoid. For miles. His life depends upon that ability, and this man knows it. Am I correct, soldier?"

"Yes, sir." The answer was barely audible.

Devlin patted the man on the shoulder. "Cheer up, boy. I'm going to do my best to set this foot, and then only time will tell if it heals well enough not to cause pain or keep you from remaining in the United States Army."

"Thank you, sir."

"Miss Holt, please bring a basin of warm water and clean up that foot. There's a deep and nasty cut over his heel, and that will have to be sutured and bandaged. With the way this foot is so distended, I'm not even going to attempt to align any bones today. We'll just wait and see."

Ten minutes later she had finished cleaning the foot and was watching Devlin complete the final suturing. His technique was so smooth and adept that she'd been amazed at how quickly it had all gone. Rebecca had used the scissors to assist him, and then bandaged the foot and ankle following his exact instructions.

"Nicely done," he said, rising. "You have excellent hands."

"Thank you." The compliment filled her with pride. "I . . . I never thought I'd see flesh sutured up that way with hardly any discomfort to the patient."

"He was in plenty of discomfort. You can be certain of that. If he'd just had the wound, he'd have howled like a

Comanche. I'm only admitting this to you now so that the next time I suture you don't think I've lost my touch."

"I see. Could you . . ." She was too uncomfortable with her request to finish it.

"Could I what? Out with it."

"All right. Could you teach me how to suture like that?"

His smile evaporated. "Why, that really is the physician's role."

"I'm sorry," she said quickly. "Of course it is. I shouldn't have asked. I could never do it half as well as you anyway."

He avoided comment, but an hour later he was as cheerful as ever and Rebecca resolved never again to ask to do something that he believed was a doctor's work. Even so, she could still watch him, and perhaps alone in her room at night she could attempt a few sutures just in case she were ever needed to help in an emergency. With God's protection, that situation would never arise; Fort Bridger needed Captain Woodson far too badly to lose him, even for a short time.

To Rebecca it seemed he was the most important man at the entire fort. They were all very lucky to have him. Very lucky.

Each day that had passed after Rebecca's flight from the great Utah valley had given Katie a deeper sense of triumph but also a growing knot of apprehension. It was almost a week now, and Rebecca would be so far away she'd never be found. There was another thing that gave her great pride, and that was that Micah had obviously kept the secret. Rebecca's absence was still undiscovered.

Good for you, Father, Katie thought every evening as she returned to Rebecca's cabin in the meadow with Amos Ludlow's flock. Let Amos explode in fury at the deception that had deprived him of his latest and most prized acquisition. Too bad they couldn't have spirited Rebecca to freedom before the marriage and its loathsome consummation. Katie hadn't even been able to look at the bed where they'd lain, much less sleep in it. She'd stripped it of blankets, and she used the floor at night; if she'd had a little more courage she'd have smashed the bed up and used it as firewood. But that, she'd decided, would be rubbing salt into the wound, and she still had to live in this valley until Bryce returned.

It was at breakfast one morning that Rebel's excited yips and barks warned her that a familiar guest was approaching her cabin. Katie peered through the curtains and saw Amos. He was trotting up the road.

She let the curtains fall back into place. The waiting was over.

She was afraid. She remembered just how powerful and ruthless this man could be, and how, the eve of the wedding, he'd made it clear that she was old enough to suffer a similar fate. Katie backed up to the fireplace, then reached out and clenched the poker in case she had to defend herself against his rage. She needed a gun, but it was too late to think of that now.

The door banged open. "Rebecca!"

She took a deep breath. It would take a few moments for his eyes to adjust to the poor light, and she wanted no words to be uttered by this man that were not meant for her ears.

"Mr. Ludlow, it's me, Katie. My sister isn't here."

His face went stony. He swiveled his shaggy head about on the thick trunk of his neck and surveyed every corner of the room. Satisfied that Rebecca was indeed absent, he growled, "Where is she, out with the flocks already?"

"No, I am tending your flocks now. Rebecca has gone away forever." The word "forever" had almost choked her, but she'd had to get it out.

Amos had already turned and was moving through the doorway when the impact of that final word caught and froze him in mid-stride. His powerful arms shot out, and he grabbed both sides of the doorframe and slowly turned on her as he reset the grip of his mighty hands. Spread-eagled against the blue sky, arms upraised, his immense, thick legs knotted like tree stumps, Katie thought he looked big and stout enough to rip the door-

GARY McCARTHY

way and the entire log wall apart and bring the roof
crashing down to bury her.

"Where!" he roared, still hanging against the blue box
of sunlight. "Where did she go!"

"She . . . she's just gone, that's all! Far away, Mr. Ludlow. So far you could never find her." Katie was more
scared than she'd ever been in her life, but she was more
glad, too. She hated this man, and she couldn't keep from
letting him know it.

He released the doorframe and took a step forward.
He was breathing hard, and though his face was in
shadow and she could not see his eyes, she knew they
would be murderous. "I'll find her, you little bitch. You
think you've tricked me, but I'll show you and her. You'll
pay. You have earned the wrath of God himself by coming between the holy union of a man and his heavenly
wife. God *will* punish you!"

Katie almost began to giggle, so great was her relief.
She wasn't at all worried about God's punishment at this
moment, not with Amos Ludlow towering in the doorway. "I'll take my chances with Him over you any day,"
she said boldly.

He stared at her for a long time. Then he relaxed, and
when he spoke, his voice was more sad than angry. "You
poor, poor thing. You have been deceived by your own
sister. It is Rebecca's sin, not yours. *She* will suffer in the
fires of hell if she does not return to me as my wife." He
moved forward. "Where is the Bible? I have left a Bible
here for your comfort and wisdom. Where is it, Katie?
We will see what God has to say about this thing and
then you will understand."

"I don't need to see the Bible!" she cried. "What you
did to her was wrong, Mr. Ludlow. Wrong and sinful."

He opened the bottom drawer of a small, scarred bu-
reau; she knew he'd found the Bible. He thumbed the
pages, saying, "She has cursed me as well as herself, Katie. I loved her above all the others, and now the Lord
has seen fit to strike me a blow for my vain foolishness.
But he will punish your sister far, far more fearsomely
for breaking the marriage vow. Her only hope of salva-

88

tion rests in her return. That is why I must find her quickly. Before she goes the way of the devil and wallows in sin."

He glanced up from the Bible. His eyes were pleading with her now. "For the salvation of her soul, Katie, where is your sister? Where can I find her?"

She had an almost irresistible compulsion to tell him, but she did not. "I'm afraid I can't tell you that. I don't know, anyhow. Give up on her, Mr. Ludlow. She is just gone."

Like a brick afire, the Bible leapt from his hands, and he bellowed with hurt and fury. Katie saw his huge fist come slashing in toward her face. She tried to throw herself backwards but was far too late. Her own cry of terror died in her throat as a bright orange ball of fire mushroomed like a flame behind her eyes. She heard a roaring like a hurricane through the trees and knew that she was spinning downward faster and faster. When she struck the floor, there was no pain, only a sick sensation of being pulled inside out until she thought she was coming apart into little pieces that would never fit together again.

And then the roaring fell to a moaning sound that she thought would never end.

Chapter Six

Rebecca's confidence and medical knowledge grew rapidly with every passing week. Devlin was a born educator, a skilled, thoughtful man who delighted in explaining to her the practice and theory of medicine with the aid of diagrams and university notes and books.

No question was too trivial, and on the rare occasions when he wasn't certain of his facts, he and Rebecca would dig them out of some ponderous medical tome and then enjoy the discovery like a couple of children uncovering small treasures. It was at such times that Rebecca found herself being drawn to him by a force she did not even try to fathom.

It wasn't love. Oh, no, she would never, *could* never, fall in love and hope for marriage and perhaps even children. Not with Amos Ludlow and the shameful secret of her past in Temple City. In the eyes of the Mormon Church and the law, she was already a married woman. As such, she could never go back, nor could she move forward into the respectability of a loving marriage with a man like Captain Woodson.

Sometimes the reality of her predicament and the thought that she would never be able to fall in love and lead a normal life was almost too much for Rebecca. At these times she would slip into fits of melancholy that would sadden Devlin. Over and over he attempted to break through and discover the secret of her past, for he was certain it contained the cause of her sorrow. He alternately pleaded, cajoled, and then tried to outwit her into making some slip of the tongue that would give him the clue he so desperately needed. But Rebecca never allowed herself a completely unguarded moment, even though there were many times when all she wanted to do was confess to Devlin and plead for his help.

But that would ruin everything, so she resigned herself to being Devlin's friend and doing the good work they did together in the infirmary. Rebecca believed she could find enough happiness in his friendship to give her life stability and rewards; Devlin felt otherwise. Confused, exasperated by her dark moods and the struggle he saw within, he often used whiskey as a balm and escape. When this happened Rebecca would be seized with guilt, yet unable to change anything for the better unless that meant going away, never to return. She took long, solitary walks on the meadows and hillsides to find some peace of mind in the beauty all about the fort. She prayed, too, and her prayers were always for Katie and Devlin as much as for answers to her own tangled existence.

Mary Carter gave her a diary one day with the explanation that "when you have to leave us someday, you might want to have a book full of memories of Fort Bridger and these times together. You may not realize it, young lady, but you are living a very exciting life compared to most young city women."

Rebecca had thanked her and began to write enthusiastically about her days and the special moments she prized with Devlin, such as when he'd finally consented to let her tie off a small blood vessel during a minor surgery. Devlin still had a strong opinion of exactly what her limits were to be, and had she allowed herself to, she might have felt some annoyance at this professional exclusion, which at times seemed inconsistent and even arbitrary.

Sensing her exasperation one day, he said, "Rebecca, I know you don't understand why I won't allow you to perform this technique, even though you could probably do it almost as well as myself."

She'd said nothing, but her eyes must have shown that she agreed.

"There are reasons, and they center on the fact that

even the simplest surgery can go wrong. You must know instantly what to do if you are going to save your patient's life."

"At times," Rebecca said, "it almost seems as if you only want me to learn just so much and then no more."

"That's ridiculous! Listen, already your knowledge and ability are far superior to most of the so-called doctors who hang out their shingles and practice medicine in western towns. Blood-letters! Leech-keepers! They often do far more injury than harm. But *you*, Rebecca, you are becoming a very skilled person indeed."

His assessment and admission of her knowledge and talent gave her a tremendous amount of satisfaction, so much that she'd written a full page of gushy nonsense that night in her diary—for Katie.

Katie was always on her mind. What had happened when Amos had discovered he'd been tricked? Had he been as furious as she imagined, or had he realized that it would be foolish to search for her? She spent hours writing in her diary, describing the fort itself, the buildings, the men and their families, the sounds, the smells, and the beauties of nature so close at hand. One of the tributaries of the Green River sparkled through the parade ground and was a favorite place for the children to catch frogs and swim on warm summer afternoons. When the day's work was finished, small groups of men and their families and friends would picnic along its banks, enjoying the shade of the cottonwoods and dense willow thickets while the children played games of hide and seek. There were wild roses too, thousands, of a deep vermilion that made one want to wish that summer would never end. But there were also mosquitoes, horseflies, and brutally hot days when the air was a blast furnace under a fiery sun.

Rebecca suffered these trials as did all the others at Fort Bridger. She worked early in the day and late in the afternoon and tried to nap at midday. Actually, she'd adapted well to Army life. As Captain Woodson's cousin, she was accorded almost the same status as an officer's wife. She was, however, disturbed by the rigid Army caste system, which separated the officers from the enlisted men and divided their women in the same way. It was painful to see how the officers held themselves in such high esteem while their men were treated so shabbily. When out on patrol, an enlisted man was not even allowed to speak with an officer—communication was through the first sergeant. At Fort Bridger, officers' wives exchanged pleasantries with their lower-class counterparts, but little more. The two groups of women were not permitted to socialize, a fact that angered Rebecca.

"It's not an entirely stupid rule," Devlin had explained. "If a man has to give men orders every day, he can't allow friendships to interfere."

"But the wives and children! What about them?" Rebecca had demanded in exasperation. "Why should there be two choral groups? Two quilting clubs and two separate picnics and parties for the holidays! I like most of the women here, no matter who they happen to be married to, and I refuse to let your silly rules tell me who I can be friends with and who I cannot! And what really infuriates me," she continued, warming to her subject, "is how the children learn so young that they are either inferior or superior, depending on their father's rank. It is wrong, *Captain*!"

He hadn't argued that point, because he readily agreed. Yet he'd pointed out that an officer could not order men into battle at dawn when he had played poker and drunk whiskey with them at night. Furthermore, if one's wife was friendly with an enlisted man's wife, disciplining him or cutting his pay would affect both families.

Rebecca could understand that, yet it seemed to her that military life was such a sacrifice that it would not hurt to encourage social events for everyone. After all, Fort Bridger was a lonely place to spend years, and while the men had their own motives for joining and staying in the Army, the only reason for the women to endure the monotony and isolation was to keep their families together. No wonder so many men quit when their hitches were up or simply deserted the post at the first opportunity. In the month since she'd arrived, Rebecca had witnessed five men, unsuccessful deserters, dressed in drab, ill-fitting clothes, struggling about the compound, chopping weeds and dragging a twenty-five-pound ball and chain. Devlin constantly had to treat their swollen and bloody ankles. These men were in torment and would not be drummed out of the Army until their cruel sentences were completed. Given the prospect of this punishment, a deserter often preferred to shoot it out rather than face capture. Military justice, it seemed to Rebecca, was terribly harsh. To miss roll call in the morning was to lose a month's pay or to endure two weeks in the guardhouse. A soldier found drunk would be strung up by the wrists or thumbs to dangle on the very tips of his toes. By noon his legs would begin to spasm and he would be in screaming agony. Finally he would be cut down and then force-marched ten miles with a fifty-pound log chained to his back. It broke men's spirit. It broke Rebecca's heart.

Army regulations recommended the death penalty for no less than twelve offenses, including desertion under fire, striking an officer, or sleeping while on guard duty, even within the fort itself.

"I have," Devlin had confided, "known men on extended patrols, pushed beyond their endurance, to light matches to their fingers in order to stay awake during their guard. I have treated their burns on the mornings after."

Rebecca was appalled. "I don't see how you can remain in the Army after seeing the brutality."

"Brutality? I was in the Civil War, remember. Anyway, I am here because this is where I'm needed. Most of the Army posts don't even have qualified doctors, which is why I was returning through Utah when we met in Echo Canyon. There'd been a battle, and I was the closest physician available. Unfortunately, most of the wounded had already become infected." He'd shaken his head. "I told you the other reason. I can save more lives here in one year than I could in ten working back in Washington, D.C., assuming my father's practice."

Rebecca respected him for that. He'd never come right

out and said it, but by piecing together conversations, she'd learned that he was from a very wealthy and prominent medical family. Two of his brothers taught at Harvard and Cornell. Devlin frequently received letters from them, and for days his mood would be subdued, his nights alcohol-soaked. Rebecca decided that he missed his family very much and that he was not well suited to life on the frontier. Once she had asked him if he planned to make the Army a permanent career. His laughter had not been pleasant.

"Let me tell you something about military tactics and how I feel about the U.S. Army's policy toward the Indian."

"I don't think I want to hear about it, Captain."

He was insistent. "You really ought to be enlightened. After all, when you go back east you'll be quite a rarity, once people discover that you have lived on an Army outpost among the soldiers and savages. They'll ask if we are winning the fight against the Indians. Tell them yes. But also tell them how." He stared moodily out the window, not really watching the cavalry drill on the parade ground. "It's like this, Rebecca. When I was a young cadet at West Point, the Army's strategy against the Indian was one of simple pursuit. We were taught to gallop after them across the plains, blowing bugles, waving banners, and generally making a fearsome racket and a terrifying sight with our polished sabers. It was an utterly ineffective way to fight Indians. We lost hundreds of men, because, you see, the Indians could usually outfight, outmaneuver, and, if all else failed, outrun the more encumbered soldiers. By the early 1860s, the military minds in Washington realized that the best method of eradicating the plains Indians was to wait until wintertime, when the blizzards cover their hunting grounds and prevent them from escaping our traps. Now we attack their winter camps, and even if some do escape, we burn their lodges and winter food supply and slaughter their weak horses. Without horses or food, they must surrender quickly or perish. Many warriors choose death. The squaws and children who are strong enough often straggle onto our reservations—those who don't freeze to death making the journey."

Rebecca shook her head. The image of suffering women and children made her shiver.

Devlin yanked out his pocket watch. "It's time for us to visit Mrs. Lacy. She's due to have her baby any day now."

They left his small, cluttered office and entered the infirmary. It was a drab, narrow room, whitewashed and lined on one side with four stripped bunks and folded military blankets. Across the aisle was a partition that shielded the surgery from view. Two more hospital beds were there, always held ready for emergencies. The entire room smelled of lye and carbolic acid. The captain was a demon for cleanliness.

"Wait a minute," he said. "First Sergeant McConnell is due in with a dislocated elbow. Give him a glass of 'relaxant' and tell him to wait. I'll be back soon and pop the joint into place. It helps if he is at ease. Dislocations are very painful. Give him all he wants to drink."

Rebecca nodded, a little disappointed at not getting to see Mrs. Lacy. She was the wife of a young corporal, and this was her first child. Devlin had promised Rebecca she could help with the delivery.

Twenty minutes later the door rattled open and in shuffled the first sergeant, his face pale and his arm belted tightly to his chest. He was a short, powerful man with a bulldog face and a shock of gray hair. His nose was crooked, his eyebrows black and unruly. He had a belligerent jawline and no-nonsense black eyes that were bloodshot from dust, whiskey, or lack of sleep. At Fort Bridger, J. D. McConnell was accorded the respect of every man from the commanding officer on down. He had a reputation for meting out discipline with his battered fists.

"Where's the captain?" he growled impatiently.

Rebecca brought him a chair. "He had to go see Mrs. Lacy and asked me to make you comfortable until he returns."

"Make me comfortable!" McConnell fairly shouted.

"Ha!" He ignored the chair and began to pace. "How can I be comfortable when my shoulder feels like someone ripped it off and then sewed it on upside down?"

She had no answer. Besides, he didn't expect one. "Captain Woodson said I could give you some relaxant." Everyone on the post knew it was little more than grain alcohol, as were most of the more popular tonics and medicinals.

Sergeant McConnell brightened. "Then let's get it out!"

She poured the first sergeant a generous dose, and he tossed it off and banged the cup down for more. Rebecca poured again. He drained the cupful and motioned for yet another. After dispatching that with similar alacrity, he finally sat down and absently polished the tops of his boots on the back of his pants, then yanked out a corncob pipe and sucked on it even though it was empty.

"You ever dislocated anything, miss?"

"No, but once I broke my arm."

"That's nothin'," he scoffed. "Broken bones don't hurt much. I've had dozens busted. My nose three times. The captain, he fixed it once. Sure hope he hurries back. How about some more of that relaxant? I still ain't entirely relaxed."

She poured. His disposition was improving by the minute.

"So you're his cousin, huh?"

She nodded. He didn't look convinced, but evidently decided to keep still about it. "Well, I suppose you've heard of me," he began.

"Yes. Captain Woodson says that out on patrol fighting Indians, your judgment is second to none."

The thick eyebrows rose. "Well, bless his whiskey-loving heart! He *is* a good man. Smart, too. Did he ever tell you about the time we were attacked by a hundred or so Sioux up on Muddy Creek?"

"No. He doesn't talk much about the patrols."

"He doesn't?" McConnel deflated a little.

"No."

"Humph. Well, I know a time or two he's had some trouble with some of the senior officers when he's wanted

97

to doctor an Indian. We don't have enough medicine to do that sort of thing. Ought to end their misery and be done with it. That's better than they'd do for ours."

Rebecca frowned. Devlin hadn't mentioned this source of trouble, but she believed it. The captain was no Indian lover, but he'd not be able to see anyone suffer.

McConnell quit pulling on the corncob. "This elbow of mine is aching again. Best have another cup. Don't know what I'll do when the captain ain't around to help me pull it back into place again. Happens every few months, and I wouldn't let another man touch it. Some of my men would sure as the dickens like to, though!" He chuckled to himself and knuckled his fighter's nose.

"Is Captain Woodson going someplace?" Rebecca asked.

The first sergeant sipped relaxant and eyed her thoughtfully before answering. "He's going to an early grave, and that's for certain."

Rebecca stiffened. "Why do you say that?" she demanded impatiently.

"Well, danged me for opening my mouth, but you being his cousin or something, maybe you could talk some sense into him. You see, it was like what happened at Muddy Creek that I started to tell you about. We was jumped in the creek and four or five of us was blown right out of the saddles. Lieutenant Brooks, he was in charge, and he didn't have much experience. He lost control and started yelling. It was a mess, and I was glad when the lieutenant took an arrow in the leg and fell. I ordered everyone to hit the brush and fight. I knew we were outnumbered at least four to one. If we'd scattered and run, we'd have been clubbed out of our saddles."

"What about the captain?" Rebecca didn't care about all the grisly details of an ambush. She did . . . yes, she did care about Devlin. Very much more than she dared admit. Besides, he was so badly needed here at this isolated Army outpost.

"Well, I was coming to that, miss. You see, we were under heavy fire. Those Sioux realized they had us pinned down, and they took cover along the opposite bank and set up heavy fire with both arrows and bullets. But do you think that stopped the captain from going out into the creek after that damned cub Lieutenant Brooks?" He jammed the corncob between his yellow teeth. "Hell no, it didn't! I yelled at the doc to stay put, but he raced out there, picked up the lieutenant, and started dragging him back to us."

Rebecca stared at him in wonder. She'd never thought the captain was a coward, but neither had she suspected him of being a hero.

"Too bad for the lieutenant, though," McConnell said. "Indians riddled him three more times before the doc could get him into the bushes." The sergeant took another pull on the pipe. "I tell you that didn't slow Doc down for a moment, though. He went after them others in the water. Damned if he didn't save a couple that sure would have been scalped come nightfall. They gave him a medal for it, but I never seen him wear it. Just like the others."

"Others?"

"Sure, he's done it before, and he'll keep doing it until his luck runs thin. I've tried to keep him down. We got privates that we can sure afford to lose a sight easier than the captain. I've tried to talk to him. So has the judge and our commanding officer. Maybe you ought to. Being of the same blood, maybe you can make him understand."

Rebecca refilled his cup. The bottle was empty now, and she wasn't going to give this man any more without Devlin's permission. What she *was* going to do, though, was have a good long talk with the captain about how this post needed him and how he still owed society those fifty-five lives. Getting himself killed wasn't going to atone for Bull Run or Shilo. Somehow, before winter and the first bitter Indian campaign, she meant to make him believe her.

The first patrol into Indian country had started out almost two weeks earlier. They'd departed right after a November blizzard, and for the last few days terrible winds had howled across the Wyoming plains with a savagery that Rebecca could not have imagined. People at Fort Bridger had told her of winters when the temperature plunged to twenty below zero and it was almost painful to breathe, when packs of wolves howled mournfully under a frozen and brittle moon and the land convulsed with the cold.

But today it was warm. Rebecca and Cynthia Lacy had gone for a walk, eager to scan the northern horizon for the overdue patrol that was the cause of increasing worry among the inhabitants of the fort. As they walked, their breath hung like puff clouds about their faces. Neither spoke until they reached the brow of a high knoll and could observe the rolling sea of snow-clad hills. To the north nothing moved, and the snow reflected upward, causing the sky to assume the color of glacial ice.

"They'll be back soon," Rebecca promised. "Don't worry."

Cynthia Lacy *was* worried. Her eyes were rimmed with dark circles, and she was too thin. Rebecca knew that she had not been able to properly nurse her infant son and that Judge Carter had been giving her tins of canned milk, but they weren't making the baby strong.

"Rebecca, I don't know what I'd do if Edward were killed in an Indian battle." Daughter of a Nebraska minister, Cynthia had met and fallen in love with young Corporal Lacy, never suspecting the lifestyle to which she would be expected to adapt. "I'm so scared I can hardly sleep at night for worrying. When Edward gets back I'm going to ask him to resign when his enlistment is up. We could go to California. It's warm and sunny there year-round, isn't that right? Our baby would grow strong in California, don't you think?"

Rebecca looked at her friend, a girl no older than she but one whose face already carried the shadow of a life of fear and fatigue. "I think that would be a good thing to do, Cindy."

"What is your family like? You've never even said where in California they live."

"I have a sister," Rebecca answered carefully. "My

mother is buried near a town called Placerville. Her grave overlooks a river. It's peaceful."

"And your father?"

Rebecca was silent for a moment. "He's dead too," she said finally.

"I'm sorry. Maybe . . . maybe when you go back to California I can meet your sister and see you again. Neither Edward nor I know anyone out there and—"

"Cindy, look!"

Far, far away, she'd seen a moving speck.

"Is it them?" Cynthia gasped.

"It has to be," Rebecca cried. The two women stood side by side on the crest of the little hill, watching the figures come slowly nearer. Suddenly Rebecca turned to Cindy. "Go back to the fort and tell everyone to start the meals. They'll be famished."

Cynthia didn't want to go, but Rebecca was firm. She could recognize a travois even at this distance, and there were several of them. She didn't want Cynthia Lacy to face what might be the destruction of her world out here in the snow.

Apparently they'd found the enemy waiting. The closer the column came, the more desperate things appeared to Rebecca. She hurried out to meet them, praying silently that not too many soldiers had died or been wounded—especially Captain Woodson or Corporal Lacy.

It seemed an eternity before she reached the struggling band of cavalrymen. First Sergeant McConnel was the leader. He was bent forward, sucking on his pipe, and when she came abreast of him he said, "Miss Holt, our doctor got hisself tomahawked and then frostbitten from doing surgery without gloves."

"Where is he?"

"In the back, on a travois."

"And Corporal Lacy?"

"Nary a scratch on him. Lucky man."

Rebecca hurried away, running over the snow past the line of horsemen bundled up in their buffalo coats. When she saw Devlin lying on the travois her hand flew to her mouth. He wasn't the same man who'd left only two weeks before. His face was bearded and colorless and there was a haunted look in his eyes so real that she had to stifle a cry of alarm. He had a bloody bandage wrapped around his head. Rebecca ran to his side.

"We made some errors," he said, trying to smile up at her. "Did you miss me?"

"Yes," she said. She took his heavily bandaged hands into her own. "Are they bad, Captain?"

He swallowed. A cloud of fear passed across his eyes, and he said, "It's the fingers of my left hand, Rebecca. I don't know if I can save them from gangrene."

She avoided his eyes and nodded with grim understanding. She more than anyone knew how important a surgeon's hands were. The captain's fingers were his profession. Long and sensitive, they could deftly probe a bullet wound or deliver a baby with a gentle competence at which she could only marvel. To lose the ability to perform surgery would be to rob Devlin of his very reason for existence.

"Rebecca," he said quietly as she followed along beside him, "Major Reed has a shattered forearm. I'll have to do surgery if he's to live. Set it up and be sure to warm the room. He's already in shock. Tell McConnell what you need. He'll assign men to give all the help necessary."

"Devlin, you can't operate!"

"I've had plenty of time to think about that. Maybe I can if we tape the instruments to my right hand. I'll have to amputate. Get things ready the moment we arrive at the fort. It may already be too late. Now, go ahead."

She wanted to protest, to tell him it was crazy. He wasn't fit to stand, let alone operate. But when she met his gaze, she realized that nothing she could say would change his mind.

"All right," she whispered. "I'll have everything ready."

The major was delirious when they strapped him down on the table. Devlin ordered her to place a chloroform sponge over the man's nostrils. The chloroform bottle was almost empty. She hoped it would last through the surgery, though she doubted there was any chance of the major pulling through. He was in shock from cold and loss of blood.

"That's enough chloroform," Devlin said. "Now apply the tourniquet about two inches above where that bone is sticking out."

She did so. Though Devlin's right hand wasn't as bad as his left, its fingers were still swollen to twice their size and she had taped the scalpel into his palm.

He leaned heavily against the table, and she saw that he was swaying.

"Private! Get Captain Woodson a chair. Put books under the legs—and hurry!"

He closed his eyes, saying, "If I fall, you must rouse me to finish. Give me some whiskey now."

He had never drunk while doing surgery before. In fact, he'd always managed to abstain for twenty-four hours prior to an operation. But one look at him told her he wouldn't last without the stimulus of alcohol. She brought the bottle, then held it up to his mouth. He drank it like water. The color rose into his cheeks, and he shuddered gratefully.

"That's better. Let's get started."

Just for a moment, the shining blade hung poised over the flesh. Then he made that first deep incision as she began to work furiously to staunch the blood flow with a clamp and carefully prepared lengths of surgical thread.

"Take it easy, Rebecca," he coached. "Relax. Tie this big one. Don't get impatient. Now twist the arm. Tighten the tourniquet. We're hemorrhaging too badly."

The scalpel continued ever deeper, and then suddenly the major's heels began to drum on the table and a scream poured out of his distended mouth.

"No, Rebecca! Tie off that artery. Private, resoak the chloroform sponge and hurry!"

The frightened soldier lunged for the bottle and knocked it spinning. It hit the floor and shattered.

Again the major screamed. Again and again. Rebecca somehow managed to tie off the artery, then she dropped to the floor, trying to soak up enough chloroform to somehow finish this nightmarish surgery. But just as she rose to her feet, there was a rattle in the major's throat and then a shudder passed through his tortured body and he lay suddenly still. Rebecca stared at him, the sponge forgotten in her hand.

Devlin choked, and staggered like a blind man. "Damn it, no! He should have lived!"

"You tried," Rebecca said, taking his arm. "Captain, you can't blame yourself! He was in shock. You've told me the chances of surgery on a patient like that are never good."

Devlin nodded, but there was no conviction in it. Like a sleepwalker, he found his bottle, took a drink and then another. When the surgery was empty and they were finally alone, he stared at her and said, "Well, Rebecca, now it's my turn."

He raised his left hand. "There's no choice," he said with dull finality. "These three middle fingers must go or gangrene will spread up my hand, then my arm. It doesn't take long. You're the only one who can help me."

She shook her head. "Please, I can't. I've never even seen you do an amputation!"

"Then I shall die." He drank again. "To be honest, I don't care so very much. I can't be a surgeon anymore, and you will be leaving. Take away those two things, and even whiskey won't make this world tolerable."

"Stop it!" she yelled. "You don't know what you're saying!"

"Sure I do. I'm saying, without you I've no chance at happiness. And without the full use of my hands I'm little more than a medicine man."

"I won't leave you like this." It was a vow.

"Why not?" He flared. "You want out of here, don't you, Miss Whoever-the-hell-you-are? Then go! Go back to the judge's house and sleep. There's a stage that will come through, barring another blizzard. You know where I keep my money. You're fired."

She took a step forward. Then another. Her eyes locked with his. "I won't let you die," she heard herself telling him. "You of all people know the value of life. You took an oath!"

"To save the lives of others."

"To save lives," she countered. "That damn sure includes your own!"

"I can't do surgery. I need both hands to tie sutures."

"Then I'll continue to help you. We'll work together." Hope cut through the despair in him. He rose to his feet, fighting to stay erect, and staggered toward her. "Don't you understand that I don't want to live without you?"

"Devlin . . ."

"No, listen," he begged. "What are you running from? Yourself? Or to what? Spinsterhood as a teacher? We are saving lives here, Rebecca. Lives! You and me."

He halted and raised his left hand again. "I need you now—and always. Help me, Rebecca. I'll tell you exactly what to do as long as I can bear the pain. Fingers are quick and easy. I'll live, if only I've something to live for. Let me make you happy. Let me help you forget whatever it is you fear. I can do it for you. I swear I can!"

She looked up at him. "You say . . . you say you can make me forget my fears. God help me, but I so desperately want to believe you. Yet I'm not sure that anything I could say or do will make a difference. Devlin, you're a tortured man, bent on destroying yourself with whiskey."

"I'll quit drinking. Devote everything I am to you and to medicine. We'll be a team. Next fall we'll quit the Army when my time is up and I'll take you back to Washington. I'll never be a great surgeon now, but I could be a fine professor. We could both teach if you wanted."

"You'd let me do that? Even if your family disapproved?"

"Hell, yes! I'd let you do anything but love someone else. That would kill me."

The way he said it made her heart break. Scorching tears sprang to her eyes, and Rebecca put her arms around him and held him very, very close. "I'll marry you if that's what it takes to keep you alive."

"That's exactly what it will take," he grated. "That and a little bit of surgery."

Rebecca steeled herself. She would marry him, and she would amputate his fingers, because, in a way she didn't quite understand, she'd grown to love Captain Devlin Woodson II.

Chapter Seven

Katie had driven her flock of sheep up into the mountain meadows where the grass was richer. It was late August, and down in the valley the air was warm and dry. All the shepherds had migrated upward to the forests and higher ranges they used each year. Katie was perfectly content to live and sleep in the sturdy sheep wagon Amos had provided. The wagon stood beside a sweet spring hidden in a thick grove of aspen that was already beginning to turn the colors of fall.

Autumn came early up near the timberline, and at night Katie would build a warm fire in the cast-iron stove near the entrance of the wagon. There was a woodbox, which she kept full, and under the bed, which took up almost a third of the living space, there was a shelf for canned foods. She had a small folding table between two narrow benches along each side of the wagon, and beneath each bench was more storage space. The bowed wagon hoops supported a taut expanse of heavy canvas that when the little stove was hot, glowed orange in the night.

Katie loved the sheep wagon and far preferred it to the log cabin, which filled her with memories of Rebecca. The sheep wagon was much more cozy and, since it was off the ground, easier to keep clean. Though she would live in it for only a few months, the wagon was designed to be occupied year-round. Katie shuddered to think how cold it would be in the wintertime. Some sheepherders pinned newspapers to the inside of the canvas to help keep in the heat, but more than one had died in a fire

107

when these papers had accidentally fallen onto the hot stove.

Katie lay on the straw mattress and listened to the wind whisper through the chattering aspen leaves. It was a peaceful sound, and it reminded her how much her life had changed in the few years since she and Rebecca were girls sleeping in a tent along the banks of a Sierra Nevada river. It seemed such a long, long time since they'd all been together. Things had been hard then; they'd panned barely enough gold dust to survive, but even so, she'd felt happy and secure believing that her mother and sister would take care of her even if Micah failed. They'd talked a lot about Springfield and how they'd all go home again. Mother had said it would be hard for Micah to go back, that his pride would hardly allow him to return to Illinois as a failure. And they'd all dreaded the terrible Humbolt Sink desert they'd have to cross.

As it turned out, her mother didn't have to make the crossing. Katie was glad that she hadn't suffered that final ordeal before passing away.

An owl hooted from the branches of a nearby tree and then flew on silent wings to begin its hunt. Katie heard a coyote howl, and, outside her door, Rebel growled low in his throat as the flock slept. So far this year she'd lost only four lambs to the coyotes, two of them on the same night. Katie had heard Rebel fighting and had raced out into the darkness. Two quick shots at the moon had sent the coyotes fleeing, but not before the damage had been done. Katie had wept, her heart torn by the sight of the dying lambs, who lay bleeding in the grass. She'd mercifully killed them, and for the rest of the night she'd sat up with her gallant sheep dog and they'd found consolation in each other.

Now Katie only half slept at night, and she knew that Rebel spent much of the dark hours patrolling the edges of the flock. Up near the timberline there was always the chance of being struck by wolves, bears, or mountain lions. Unfortunately, the sheep didn't make her or Rebel's task of protecting them a bit easy. A restless ewe might clamber to its feet, decide to leave the bedground long before dawn, and go off to only she knew where. Katie didn't understand what would prompt such a defenseless creature to abandon its safety and do such a foolish thing, but it would. When that happened, Rebel would be awake instantly and drive the ewe and her obediently following lamb quietly back into the flock. The ewe might become stubborn enough to keep attempting to escape until dawn, when she'd finally fall asleep and then bleat irritably when it was time to move off the bedding ground in search of forage. It had taken only a few days for Katie to decide that sheep were not very intelligent nor even hardy animals. Sometimes one of the beasts just took it into its head to die, and nothing could be done to save it. They would eat poison weeds with relish. The most unbelievable incident so far had been when Katie had found three sheep stuck on their backs and unable to right themselves. Their wool was flattened like pillows along their sides, and, with their little legs waving frantically, they would have died in a few more hours if she hadn't come to their rescue and righted them. Sheepherding, Katie had discovered, was much more demanding than most people realized.

Amos Ludlow and a stranger approached her camp at mid-morning the following day, and Katie's stomach tightened with anxiety. Ever since the day he'd struck her down to lie unconscious for hours, she'd both hated and feared him. But he hadn't carried out his threat to locate Rebecca, because he was too smart to jeopardize everything for one of his wives—even his most prized.

Since that time Amos had just barely tolerated her, probably because she was tending his sheep in return for a few of the older ewes for herself. Katie meant to build her own flock, and with luck she could easily sell them for a good profit when she left Temple City. At least, that was her plan. Her only fear was that Amos had ideas of his own.

The men dismounted and tied their horses. Katie wondered who this new man was. She was even more curious when Amos said sharply, "You wait here, mister. I'll tell you when you can speak to her."

The stranger's eyes shuttered. He looked dangerously angry. "It has to be alone."

The man was middle-aged, hawk-nosed, lean, and tough-looking. His angular jaw was set with determination.

"It will be," Amos said. "Just do as you're told."

Amos came toward the sheep wagon alone. "This man has a message from Bryce to Rebecca. Apparently he and my son are in Virginia City, Nevada. I'd have run him off except I wanted to know about Jude, and he won't tell *me* a damned thing. I told him you are Rebecca. If you tell him you're not, neither of us will learn anything, so you'd better not make me a liar."

"I can't do that!"

Amos roughly took her arm. His grip was quite painful as he led her up near the spring. "Listen," he grated. "I could have sent you packing after your sister, and maybe I should have. Now do as I say!"

Katie twisted free. "Why didn't you send me away?" she demanded.

"Because you may be the only reason Jude comes back," Amos said bitterly. "And if you think that pleases me, think again. Anna begged me to let you stay, because Jude told her he wanted to marry you when you were grown."

Katie shuddered visibly at the thought. Her voice trembled. "Mr. Ludlow, I'll never marry Jude."

"You're damn right you won't, because as soon as he comes back you're leaving this valley! You and your sister have been nothing but misery. Your father told me he feels the same way."

Katie smothered her fury. It would only work to her disadvantage to tell this man that she'd leave with Bryce and her sheep and not a minute before. And the mention of her father brought back a flood of painful memories. He'd never even invited her to his wedding. It was as though she and Rebecca had ceased to exist for him. She didn't understand that and never would.

"Miss Prescott," Amos was saying, "don't you even think of telling this man who you really are. If he ever finds out, it will be from me, not you. He has news of my son, and you'll cooperate and tell me the truth as to where he is and when he's coming back. I have need of him."

Katie glanced at the stranger. He looked ready to ride out and forget the whole thing, he was so impatient. She had to know about Bryce, and if that meant using deception, then she'd do it.

Amos beckoned the stranger forward and left them alone. The man studied her full-length, and Katie had the impression he was faintly disappointed. Yet when he spoke, his tone was polite but low and serious. "Miss, all you've got to do is say so and that Amos Ludlow is a dead man. We take his horse and the two of us will be long gone before these Mormons know the straight of things. I can get you out of this mess and on the Overland Stage."

"I can't," she told him.

"Why not?" He took a thick envelope from the inside of his jacket. "Miss, I'm a close friend of Bryce Sherman, and it's a good thing, too, because there's no less than five hundred dollars in this package."

"Five hundred!" She took the envelope. Her hands were shaking. "Have you counted it?"

" 'Course not! He told me. You see, I owe Bryce, because he once saved my skin. We met in Virginia City, and he made me swear to give you this money personally. He even told me to wait until you could write him a letter so I could post it from Echo Canyon."

"He's in Virginia City?"

"No, he's on his way to Colorado. That Jude fella he was with kept saying he wanted to drift on up to a new mining town named Leadville. Supposed to be even richer than the Comstock."

"How is Jude?" Katie glanced over at Amos. He was watching them closely, straining to hear.

"You can tell that fella that his son is no better mannered than he is," the man said. "I swear I don't know why Bryce fools with the kid. He's going to get them both killed. In fact, he got into a mess of a gunfight in Virginia City, and that's why they lit out at night for that strike in Colorado Territory with Jude Ludlow so drunk he was tied across his saddle with a gag in his mouth. But don't tell his father that."

"Don't worry," Katie promised. "I won't. But I'll have to tell him something good."

The man frowned and thought hard about it. "You tell him his boy is making a lot of money—so was Bryce, or I guess he'd never have been able to send you this five hundred dollars. You know, you're younger than I'd expected, Miss Rebecca. I'd pictured you different, after listening to Bryce run on about you and him planning to marry."

Katie stretched to her fullest height. "I'm old enough."

His eyes lowered for just a fraction of a second. "Yeah," he concluded. "I guess you probably are, but just barely."

Katie flushed. "I believe I'll start that letter. But where will you send it?"

"To the Miner's Hotel in Leadville, Colorado. I got a cousin who's staying there, and I asked Bryce to look him up for me."

"All right." Katie took a smudged sheet of folded paper from the envelope. Across the top were scribbled these few words: "Dear Rebecca, I want you to save this money for us. It is safer with you. Tell Dave Bender thanks for delivering it, and I'll be seeing his cousin in Leadville soon enough. I love you, Bryce."

Katie's eyes stung for a moment. What she wouldn't give to have him say or write those last words to her! She turned away so that neither of the men could see her face. Beside her, Rebel sensed her pain and whimpered softly as she tried to gather her strength and write a letter that she would sign with Rebecca's name. The enormity of this dishonesty almost paralyzed her with guilt, yet there was no choice if she ever expected to see Bryce again.

"I hope you can read and write," Bender said, " 'cause, Miss Rebecca, I can't help you at all."

"I can." Katie found a pencil under the money he'd

sent. Bryce had thought of everything. And now she was going to do her best to deceive him.

Dave Bender took her letter and rode away, but not before promising to come back and help her, and to deliver any more letters that Bryce might send.

"What did he say about Jude?" Amos asked hurriedly.

Katie told him, though she left out the part about his drinking, not so much to spare the man anguish as to avoid any excuse for the rekindling of his anger.

"Did he say when they were coming back?"

She shook her head. Katie saw the disappointment on his thick, ruggedly handsome face. Yes, he was ruthless when in quest of something like Rebecca, but he had loved her, just as he loved Jude and wanted him back safe.

Katie's voice softened. "Don't worry. He'll return. He said . . . he said Jude was in good health."

"I hope so." Amos brightened a little, then mounted his horse. "You got a bundle of money, I see." He paused. "I could claim that as mine, you know. It was sent to my wife."

"It was sent to *Miss* Prescott, and I'm the only Miss Prescott here."

Katie studied Amos Ludlow's broad face carefully. "The instructions that came with this money are to save it for Bryce. I intend to do that."

Amos was taking her measure as well. "We have nothing between us but enmity, Miss Prescott, and you consider me an evil man. But I'm no thief, not even when it comes to dealing with a man like Bryce Sherman. How do you intend to safeguard his money?"

"I'll buy sheep. Some of yours, if the price is right."

He thought on it. "Three dollars each would be fair."

It was high, but Katie wasn't in any bargaining position. "Only if you let me winter them with your own if Jude and Bryce aren't back by that time."

"Three twenty-five each and you can take your pick. No one else in Temple City will deal with you if I won't."

It was true. Katie tried to keep the emotion out of her

voice. "All right, I'll buy one hundred fifty."

"Then it's a deal." He took her money. "It beats me how you think you're going to get them out of this valley by yourself."

"That's my problem." Katie turned toward the sheep wagon. "I'll be right back with paper and ink. I'll be wanting a bill of sale, just like the others."

He almost smiled. "Of course. You have a head for business, I think. Too bad Jude doesn't. Maybe you could help him."

It was a jab designed to spur her anger, but Katie ignored it. Later, after she'd gotten the bill of sale, and hidden it, she carefully selected her own ewes out of the flock. She already knew enough to choose the best. That evening she pulled out the note that Bryce had written to Rebecca and reread it. She felt so lost and forsaken she almost broke down and wept. How deeply she missed her mother and sister! How she ached to go back to those childhood days in Illinois when life had seemed so full and happy! Now she was alone, and she had taken money from the only man alive that she cared about. She knew she could make a profit with the sheep and repay Bryce with interest by the end of next year. Over and over she told herself that he would be proud of her, not angry. But when she stared at his note, Katie knew with certainty that he wouldn't be proud at all; he'd be furious and, yes, heartsick with disappointment, because she was not and never would be Rebecca.

"I love *you*, Rebel," she whispered, hugging her only friend. "You and Bryce and Rebecca."

The following April, Katie and Anna Ludlow sat on the tailgate of a supply wagon and watched Temple City recede into the distance. It was a warm, blustery day in April, and high up in the Wasatch Mountains they were experiencing a Chinook, an unseasonably pleasant, warm wind. Katie loved it, and as they jounced along toward the sheep camps, she basked in the balmy dry breezes. Reclining on a sack of flour, she listened to the creaking, groaning wagon and studied the huge billowing clouds that lumbered southward across the sky. She knew Anna was just as happy as she was to be returning to sheep camp after a long winter confined in the Ludlow household. The sun felt good on her skin, and as they rolled up into the mountains, they could see that the grass was already sprouting. The Chinook winds had been blowing for four days, and in that short time the country had been magically transformed from a white wilderness into a world bound by a convenant to spawn life. You could feel an awakening—smell it too. The ground was thawing, and the air had an earthy tang to it as their heavily laden wagon churned through mud, spinning big wet globs of it in their wake. All about them water sparkled in little rivulets as the Wasatch Range sweated under its fast-disappearing blanket of snow. If these drying winds continued another twenty-four hours, the last of the brave snow patches down in the summer meadows would bleed away.

"I love the Chinook," Anna sighed. "Without it, this spring magic would take weeks and the grass would never come up bold and fast, as it is doing now. This new grass is sweet, Katie. The young mothers and their babies grow strong quickly on it after the lambing."

"I can hardly wait to see if my ewes are all pregnant." Katie had spent months wondering how well she'd chosen her sheep. With luck, most of them would lamb, nearly doubling her flock. And if the lambs could be kept alive until they were big enough to be weaned, she'd really have something to show Bryce when he returned.

Anna smiled. "Hope that eighty percent of them are and that seventy percent live. At any rate, in another week you should know. The Basque herders left the Salt Lake Basin two weeks ago. They'll be pushing the ewes up very slowly because they are pregnant, but they must arrive before the lambs start to be born on the steep mountainsides. But don't worry, those Basques know sheep better than any people in the world. They handled the breeding, and they know exactly when the lambs are coming. They will be here, Katie. We just have to have our camps ready for them."

Katie nodded. They'd do it and enjoy every moment of

it in this beautiful countryside. Perhaps by the time their sheep arrived the hillsides would be adorned with a carpet of wildflowers—mountain cowslip, shooting star, spurred columbine, Jacob's ladder, and the pretty buttercups—all of them nodding and dancing in the summer wind. They would stretch for miles, so vast and brilliant one might think they were a patchwork quilt made by the angels.

Katie took a deep breath and tasted the sharp, biting fragrance of pine, fir, aspen, and spruce. She wished Bryce could be here to see it with her. Maybe he would come soon. Only weeks ago she'd had another visit from Dave Bender, who was now the station tender in Echo Canyon. There'd almost been trouble, and Amos had warned him not to come back. Katie wasn't sure he'd not try anyway, especially if she were out in the hills with her flock. Bryce had sent Rebecca money again, but there had been no note. Katie felt an immense disappointment at not hearing from him, but she was not sure she wanted to read another love letter meant for Rebecca's eyes. She'd use the money to buy more sheep in the fall. They would all belong to Bryce, of course. He didn't know it, but she was going to make him money.

Katie had tried to envision his reaction a hundred times when he first learned of her sheep buying. Would he see that she had worked hard to double, even triple, the value of his investment? Or would he be so angry at being deceived by her that he would not care, or even listen? It was enough to make her lose sleep.

Katie had applied a bold yellow slash of paint across the shoulders of each ewe she'd purchased last year. One didn't brand sheep with a burning iron like horses or cattle. They were too fragile, their skin much too thin. After shearing, the brands would be repainted, and the paint would remain on the ends of the wool all through another year, faintly perhaps by spring, but nonetheless distinguishing her sheep from those of Amos Ludlow. And soon there would be the lambs to paint also.

"Anna?"

"Yes."

Katie sat up. Before long they would be at her cabin and begin unloading supplies. "Do these Basque people speak English?"

"Not very well, though some of the older ones usually know a little more of the language. In fact, they are great talkers. Most, however, stay to themselves. They are hardworking people, and I think that is why Brigham Young allows them to herd our flocks."

"I want to help them."

Anna frowned. "They prefer you'd not. They have their way of lambing, and if you don't understand it, you'd only annoy them."

"I ought to be able to help with my own sheep," Katie said stubbornly.

Anna could see that there was no use in arguing. Once Katie made up her mind to do something, she was bull-dog stubborn about it. "Do what you must. They are your sheep. Why are you building a herd?"

The question caught her by surprise, but Katie recovered quickly. "I don't plan to stay here in Temple City forever. I thought you knew that."

Anna was still for several minutes. "Yes, I'm afraid I did. But I was hoping you might become one of us."

"I just can't. I've tried, Anna, but it won't happen. When Bryce returns, we're taking the flock and leaving this valley."

"Do you really believe you'll be allowed to do that?"

Katie felt a chill pass through her. "You mean . . ."

"I don't want to speak of it," Anna said abruptly, turning away to leave Katie to her own conclusion.

It was inescapable. Of course they wouldn't be allowed simply to walk away. Katie began to tremble in a hopeless rage. Now, finally, she understood the awful truth—she'd created her own prison! She'd raced headlong into Amos Ludlow's trap. No wonder he'd allowed her to choose the best ewes in his flock—he intended to keep them!

Katie's high spirits plummeted. She was worse than a fool. Overwhelmed with anger and remorse, she would say no more.

*   *   *

The sheep arrived early. Katie barely had time to chase the mice and raccoons out of her sturdy log cabin before she heard the clear tinkle of sheep bells. There was a great rush of excitement then, and Katie and Rebel went out quickly to meet the flocks.

There was a vantage point on a knoll not far from her cabin, and she was out of breath when she reached it. Off in the distance she saw the huge bands of sheep, each kept separate from the others now branching off toward different pastures. Beside her, Rebel yipped with excitement. After the long winter in Temple City he was fat and eager to get back to work. They could both hear the bleating, an all too familiar sound that the animals could make for hours on end. It had almost driven her to distraction until she'd learned to tune it out. Now it was like music.

"Come on, Rebel! Let's go show them the way to the bedground!"

She ran across the green hills with Rebel barking beside her. When they came to the flock, Katie's eyes quickly surveyed the animals and counted the ewes with the yellow shoulders. On some of them the paint was almost gone, but when she reached two hundred, she knew that they'd all arrived safely.

A short, powerful man in his forties detached himself from the flock and came to meet her. He was dark-skinned and had the most luxurious mustache Katie had ever seen. His eyes were as black as his hair, and when he smiled at her, his strong teeth were so white against the mustache that it was almost dazzling.

"Good afternoon." His eyes seemed to miss nothing as, in one quick glance, he surveyed her heaving breast, her strong legs, and the new roundness at her hips.

Katie flushed with embarrassment. She had never seen such boldness and admiration in a man's eyes.

"Good afternoon," she stammered, introducing herself.

His name was Sabino Echavarria, and he was in

charge of the delivering and lambing of Amos's flocks, as he had been for two years.

"Some of them are mine," she blurted.

"Oh. The yellows?"

"Yes."

"They are the very best of the flock. Congratulations. They will all soon be mothers. Our rams, they do good job on your ewes. Eh?"

"They . . . they must have!"

"Good!" He laughed. "I am glad you are so grateful. What have you cooked for my men tonight?"

Katie's face dropped. "No one said I was supposed to cook for you."

His smile remained on his face, but his voice took on an injured tone. "Of course you are! That is part of our deal with Mr. Ludlow."

"Well, it isn't part of *my* deal. If you're hungry, I'll come up with something for tonight, but tomorrow, Mr. Echavarria, you and your men are on your own."

"It is of no importance," he said with an exaggerated shrug. "We will worry about tomorrow, tomorrow. The sheep, they will soon start lambing, and there will be no time to eat anyway."

He was right. The very next day the flock began to lamb, and from that moment on, all the appreciative looks and attention that Katie had been receiving were forgotten. She quickly learned to tell when a ewe was about ready to produce her lamb. An hour or so before the delivery, the ewe's head would suddenly lift. The animal would stop grazing and begin to trot around, bleating to the lamb inside her. If she saw another newborn, she would try to mother it until its own jealous mother butted her away. This could be repeated again and again as the pathetic mother-to-be grew more and more agitated until, finally, she would collapse in a state of hard labor. Katie stood by, shocked into fascinated horror. Was this the way it was for a woman? The ewe looked most uncomfortable. Lying on her side, her great woolly coat hot and greasy, she panted and strained. Her mouth was distended, her eyes wide, as her little body convulsed at ever shortening intervals and with greater and greater intensity. She looked to Katie as though she wanted to die.

Katie searched about for help and was amazed to discover at least a half dozen other ewes on the ground and Mr. Echavarria's men working frantically to see that each delivery was going smoothly.

The ewe at her feet moaned. Even under its great woolen coat, she could see its body contract like a fist.

"Come on!" Katie urged the ewe. "You can do it!"

The poor creature was trying. The contractions were so closely spaced she seemed hardly able to get her breath. Her tongue was hanging out, and she was gasping. Her eyes rolled up, and she looked hideous as her body knotted over and over.

Katie glanced around. The men were working furiously. Not forty feet away she saw one young man fall down onto his knees. Scarcely believing what she was seeing, Katie watched him slip his hands, then his wrists, inside the thrashing ewe. He jammed his legs up against her rump and leaned back and began to pull! Katie's eyes widened. The ewe was going crazy. He was ripping her open! Suddenly the lamb inside of her popped out like a bloody cork. Instantly the man was wiping afterbirth from its face and then climbing to his feet and hurrying to another sheep.

Katie stared at the ewe struggling at her feet. The poor beast was growing weak. It kept beating its head against the earth as though it might knock itself mercifully unconscious. Katie took a deep breath and squatted on the ground, placing her feet against the ewe's rump. She swallowed, reached down, and then steeled herself to bury her hands up inside the hot, rigid body of the ewe.

For a moment she could feel nothing but the powerful uterine muscles squeezing down. The ewe made a terrible sound. With the last of its strength, it began smashing its head up and down again. She saw blood spurting from its nose and then its entire body convulsed. The ewe knotted inside and Katie felt the lamb filling her hands. She grabbed something solid and began to pull. The ewe tried to twist sideways and climb to its feet.

"Lie still!" Katie begged. "Don't give up. It's coming."

She leaned back, pulling harder than ever, but just as she felt it coming, the ewe rattled in its throat and died.

"Oh, no!" she sobbed.

"Keep pulling! Don't stop!"

Her face covered with sweat, her dress and arms soiled with wool and blood, Katie glanced up to see Sabino running toward her. He was yelling frantically.

The ewe's body went limp and Katie threw all her strength into pulling. With a renting of the dead ewe's flesh, the lamb was torn into the world. Katie gasped, rolled over, and cupped away mucus from its mouth and nostrils. It wasn't breathing! The sheepherder dropped beside her and began slapping its side. Not hard, but not easy either. After three or four blows, it gasped and began to breathe.

"You did it, Mr. Echavarria! You saved him!"

He grinned broadly. "No, *you* did it. We will jacket this lamb for a new mother. Quick, I show you."

It took them only minutes to find a stillborn lamb. One look at its poor heartsick mother told Katie that the ewe understood only that it had lost something very precious. Its dead offspring was picked up and taken away from her sight. In a moment Sabino's knife was out and he was slicing away its skin along the rear legs, then along the stomach. He grabbed the pelt on either side and tore it off the dead lamb to the shoulders, then cut down both legs and yanked it free.

"Come on, miss!" he shouted. "I show you this one time, then you do it!"

Katie stilled a protest. The bloody little carcass they'd left on the grass seemed tragic. She could never do that! She watched Sabino shake the pelt right side out and race to the lamb Katie had delivered, tie the pelt on its back, and hurry back to the bereaved ewe. He shoved the lamb's face against her teats. The little baby was an awful sight. Fresh blood was still dripping from the warm jacket it wore. It had two tails. Katie couldn't imagine how any mother could be fooled by such a grisly costume, but after a few nudges and questioning bleats, the ewe was convinced. Tragedy turned to bewilderment and then joy as her bleating took on a different sound. Finally she quieted and began to rumble in her throat. It was like no sound Katie had ever heard before. A sound of deep pleasure and affection.

Katie laughed. "You did it!"

"Of course, miss!" he shouted. "Now you do it next time!"

Katie turned back to the ewe and her adopted lamb. In the crisis moments before, she hadn't noticed that the mother had a yellow patch on her shoulder. With a rush of gratitude, she realized that Sabino Echavarria had given her one more addition to her flock. She knew it had not particularly mattered to him as long as the lamb was saved. But it did to her.

Katie began to run toward her cabin. There was a good sharp butcher knife she could use. If there were to be any more adoptions of jacketed lambs, they might as well be to her ewes, if all else was equal.

Amos Ludlow be damned.

Chapter Eight

"Rebecca!"

Rebecca's head snapped around and her heart froze when she saw Bryce Sherman and, behind him, the angry, accusing face of Jude Ludlow.

It was her worst nightmare because, only a few months earlier, she and Devlin had gotten married. He had resigned from the Army and they intended to work together and build a thriving medical practice in Fort Bridger. Rebecca had intended to tell Devlin about her Mormon marriage, but . . . somehow, she had never quite managed to bring up the subject. Now, however, it appeared that Bryce and Jude would be the ones to reveal her shameful secret.

Bryce reached for her but Devlin, his face a mask of confusion, stepped between them. "What the—"

Rebecca's vision swam, and she struggled to her feet. How could this be happening? What kind of God could raise her to the heights one moment, then destroy her life and those of the two men who loved her in the next?

Bryce reached for her, and Devlin stepped between them. "What the—"

Bryce was the larger, more powerful of the two, and he flung Devlin to the ground. "My God, Rebecca, I never dreamed—"

Suddenly, Jude Ludlow grabbed him from behind and yelled, "Bryce, she's married to my father. I tried to tell you. They were married last year in Temple City."

Jude was not strong enough to restrain Bryce physically, but his words had the effect of a blow.

Devlin had been rising, his fists knotted and fury in his

eyes. Jude's statement stopped him in his tracks.

"Is it true?" he mouthed, the blood draining from his cheeks. His eyes pleaded for denial. "Rebecca?"

But it *was* true. She wanted to explain, but no words came. She saw his face collapsing in his hands, and his shoulders begin to shake as he groaned with a sound that was torn from the deepest part of him.

"Oh, Jesus!" Bryce whispered, his arms falling to hang limp at his sides. "Rebecca, you've just torn out my heart, damn you!"

She didn't answer him as she moved trancelike toward her husband. If only she could explain!

"Get away from me!" he cried, raising his hand to strike her if she came nearer.

Rebecca halted. "I'm sorry, Devlin. I tried, oh, how I tried to explain it to you. But you wouldn't let me. Every time—"

"I don't want to hear any more."

"Well, I do," Bryce gritted. "You've got eight hundred dollars of my money, and I've got these damn letters of yours. I want to swap."

Rebecca had only to glance at them. "They're from Katie. It's her handwriting. She stayed in Temple City waiting for you."

Confusion clouded his features. "Why? Why did she write this kind of letter and sign your name? My God, I've read them so many times they've burned into my memory. They are love letters!"

"She's in love with you. I guess . . . guess she thought if you came back to Temple City that somehow you might fall in love with her."

He groaned and crumpled the letters in his fist. "I thought they were from you. That's why I saved them. Just tell me one thing."

"I'll try."

"Why did you marry Ludlow?"

"You wouldn't understand."

"Hell no, I wouldn't! Tell me anyway. Did that big lusting sonofabitch force you into it?"

She wavered. If she told him the truth, he'd wind up

getting hanged for certain. "I married him of my own free will."

"You're lying!"

Rebecca swallowed. "Bryce," she whispered. "You *must* believe what I've just told you. Stay away from Amos."

Devlin's voice cut between them. "I believe you, Rebecca. I believe you are the greatest heartbreaker since Cleopatra. You're poison. A killer of souls." He took a ragged breath. "My father was right. The only thing that is worthy and endures is science. Strange, isn't it, how one finally sees the truth."

"That isn't the truth!"

"Oh?" He raised his eyebrows questioningly. "And *you* are going to tell me what is?"

When she couldn't answer, he shook his head in pity. "For me the truth is that I am going to get drunk enough to ignore the good people of Fort Bridger and climb on the eastbound stage. I'm going to attempt to stay drunk until I reach Washington, D.C., and if there is anything left of my pickled brain, then I will pursue science with such an intensity that I will never, ever think of you again. I'll discover a cure for . . . what the hell, I'll discover one for heartache! For fools like me. I ought to get rich, if there are five or ten more back there like you."

"Devlin, please!"

"My dear," he said in a voice that quavered with passion. "You have one hour to banish yourself. If I see you after that time, I will undoubtedly be drunk enough to flay you with a horsewhip. Good-bye and good hunting."

Good-bye, she thought, watching him go and, with him, all her dreams for happiness.

Bryce swung her around. "You whore!" he grated. "No, for someone like you, that's a compliment. At least a whore gives you pleasure for your money. All you give is pain."

Rebecca steeled herself, reached way down inside, and found the strength to face her accuser, knowing that she *had* married Amos to protect his life. Knowing that gave her enough dignity to stand up to Bryce.

GARY McCARTHY

"I'm sorry."

" 'Sorry' isn't half good enough. Rebecca, you ought to be horsewhipped, but he wasn't man enough to do it, and I guess I haven't the stomach for it either. But I'll tell you this: I aim to have my money back."

"Then go to Temple City. If Katie received it, the money will be waiting."

"It'd better be. If this was some scheme you and she put together, there's going to be hell to pay."

"She loves you. I wish she didn't."

"No, she don't," Jude gritted. "Let's ride, Bryce. There's nothing here for either of us."

He spurred his horse and galloped away.

"Catch him," Rebecca begged urgently. "You can see he wants Katie for himself. Don't let her be forced into polygamy!"

Bryce smiled cruelly. "After I get my money, he can do anything he wants with her."

"Damn you! Have you forgotten how that girl helped save your life in Echo Canyon?"

The hard cut of his mouth softened ever so slightly. "No, I haven't forgotten," he admitted grudgingly.

"Then be kind to her. Help her escape Temple City. She doesn't belong there. I should never have let her stay."

His expression stiffened once more. "She wrote those letters!" he bellowed, shaking them in her face. "She wrote 'em so I'd keep on sending money."

Rebecca's eyes flashed. "If you believe that, you are a fool twice over, Bryce Sherman. Why don't you go and find out?"

The lean muscles of his jaw relaxed. "I guess I will. Where shall I send her?"

Dutch John's line of freight wagons was soon leaving for the goldfields. Rebecca watched as the wagons stood in readiness. She suddenly decided that was the only place she could wait for Katie.

"Tell her I'll be in South Pass City."

"Yeah," he said bitterly. "You ought to do a real good business there. All right, I'll tell her."

He stepped into the saddle, a tall, hard-faced man

126

who'd aged greatly in the year since she'd parted from him. There were deep worry lines on his brow, and his last traces of boyishness were gone forever.

"Bryce? Katie begged me not to marry Amos. I did anyway, and I've been paying for it every day since. I've ruined my life. Don't let this ruin yours, or hers. Get away from them! And when you do, watch out for Jude Ludlow."

"Jude's got no trouble with me," Bryce grated. "And I've no thought of coming between him and Katie. All I want is my money and to get far away from you, her, and those Mormons."

"Then you won't help her? Bryce, please!"

"Sorry. The bets are off, and the game you've been playing on me is over. You're holding an empty hand, Mrs. Ludlow."

With that, he drove his spurs into the flanks of his horse and rode away.

Rebecca stood alone on the parade ground. Finally she started toward their quarters, trying to gather her thoughts and decide what to do. Devlin had banished her. Banishment. Was anyone banished anymore? No matter. She was, and about all she could do was to grab her valise and start walking. Maybe she could ride with Dutch John and his wagons. If not, she would walk to South Pass City. As she'd walked from California. Only this time she would be alone.

Cynthia Lacy came to her side. "What happened? Something terrible has happened, hasn't it?"

"You didn't hear?" It seemed impossible.

"No. There was a horse race going on and the children were yelling. Besides, I didn't want to hear. I could tell by your faces."

Rebecca kept walking. "It's over, Cindy. Devlin and I are leaving."

"Oh, dear Lord, no! Please don't."

"I'm sorry." She blinked wetly. It seemed that she was saying she was sorry to everyone. "You see, there really is very little choice now. Good-bye."

She left Cynthia and finally reached her quarters. She

didn't expect to see Devlin, but he was waiting. For a moment, as she stood by the open door, she thought she saw forgiveness, but it melted into naked hostility. He lifted a whiskey bottle and drank until he began to choke.

"Out of practice," he coughed.

Rebecca hated to see him do this. It made her angry. "Are you going to drink yourself to death?"

He glowered at her. "I may."

"What about the fifty-five lives you still owe? When we met, you told me they were your purpose for living. Don't they count anymore?"

"What else do you want from me? My blood?"

Rebecca grabbed her valise and began shoving things into it. Clothes, a few pieces of her mother's jewelry, a picture. She hardly even noticed.

"I'd like to think I loved a man with character, Devlin. A man who could bend but wouldn't break. I'd like to think you'll not destroy yourself with self-pity."

"Jesus!" he hollered. "I'd like to see you out of my life!"

The valise was full. Rebecca stared at him with a mixture of love and compassion. There was so much she wanted to say. So much. If he had just looked up at her and shown any willingness to listen. But he just sat there, drinking and hating her.

"Good-bye, Devlin. Before you are too drunk to think, I would suggest you decide what you intend to tell the people of Fort Bridger about us."

He looked up. Obviously he hadn't thought about it yet. But he should. Rebecca knew that such a scandal could haunt his medical career and social standing forever. The word would spread even to Washington.

"Tell them what you like," she continued. "Say I left you for another man. You are better at making up my past than I am."

"Rebecca?"

She froze, felt her heart leap in her chest.

"Yes," she whispered.

"I'll think of something. I won't tell them the kind of woman you really are."

Her eyes stung and she wheeled brokenly away.

"Goodbye, Devlin. And may God help us both."

She lowered her head and started walking.

Cynthia Lacy raced up. "Rebecca, where are you going? *Please*, tell me what happened!"

She avoided the woman's eyes. "I'm leaving him. I'm catching Dutch John's wagon train to South Pass City."

"But why?" she cried. "Rebecca, I thought you loved Devlin. And all of us!"

She shook her head violently. "I hate him. I hate this place. I'm going crazy here. Leave me alone!"

Rebecca beat herself into a run. The valise pounded her thigh, and she tried to blot out everything except gulping the sweet spring air into her burning lungs. On and on she ran until the sound of her heart drummed in her head and her legs cramped and spilled her on a ridge, wanting to die, knowing she would not.

Minutes passed as the sun rolled in crazy circles around the sky and then finally chose a resting place. She sat up and looked back. Fort Bridger appeared peaceful and secure. Smoke drifted up from the cooking fires, and Rebecca watched the children play. There would be no children's laughter in South Pass City. Mining towns were raw, hard places where men worked, fought, and drank themselves into a stupor. She'd been in the California goldfields and the Comstock; this would be no different. The heart of a gold-fevered miner was as unyielding as the rock he battled. She would find no pity, and the certainty of that knowledge made her resolve to survive with what little dignity remained until she was reunited with Katie.

Movement off to the side caught her attention, and she saw two fast-moving horsemen approaching. It was her friend the great Shoshoni leader and his son, Eagle Wing.

Watching them approach, she was forcibly struck by the contrast in their sizes and ages. Even in the midst of her own despair she was moved by what she knew to be their situation and that of all their people. Like it or not, their world was flying apart like the burst of a cannon shell. Washakie understood this. The great sea of buffalo that had been their sustenance for centuries was being decimated even now by the river of whites flowing from the east. When the transcontinental railroad slashed through Wyoming in the next few years, the river would become a torrent and the buffalo would vanish from the plains like snow before the warm Chinook.

Rebecca guessed that was what gave this man such nobility. He *knew*, and yet he was committed to saving what he could for the generations to come. While other tribes seemed to be willing, even eager, to sacrifice themselves in a few glorious years of battle against an enemy they could not hope to defeat, Washakie had chosen a much more difficult road to travel. He'd chosen to be a peacemaker, a friend of the whites, even when they broke their promises and scorned him. Some of his younger warriors had rejected his choice as cowardly, and many of them had died in the Battle of Bear Creek four years earlier.

As she watched the chief and the boy approach, she saw how insignificant her own fate really was. Washakie was gambling for the preservation of an entire race of people; she, meanwhile, was concerned only with her own life and Katie's.

Rebecca felt a little ashamed of herself. She scrubbed the tears from her eyes and stood up to face this man, who carried a crushing load of responsibility for generations yet to be born.

The two riders pulled in their horses and dismounted. Washakie handed his reins to the boy and came forward. As always, he studied her face carefully for several moments before speaking. Rebecca knew he'd see that she'd been crying.

"Why you go, Rebecca?"

She would never lie to him, and yet it was so difficult to explain. "I have been found to be a bad woman, Chief."

He scowled, then shook his head vigorously.

"It's true," she declared. "I have two husbands."

"Two."

She lowered her eyes in shame. "Yes. I was married to a Mormon in Temple City."

Washakie shrugged indifferently. "But he is not here."

"It doesn't matter. It was wrong of me to take two men."

"And is it wrong for me to take three wives, Rebecca?"

"No."

"Then, if you want, I take you as fourth."

This made her smile, in spite of the way she felt. "I am honored, but I cannot."

"Humph." He glanced back at Eagle Wing and frowned in concentration. "Where you go now, Rebecca? Run from husbands?"

"Yes. I am going to South Pass City to wait for my sister."

"Sister run from husbands too?"

"No," she said with a small laugh. "At least, I don't think so. I am going to catch that wagon train." She pointed to it. Dutch John was several miles away.

"Okay. You take present first. This from Eagle Wing."

At a signal, the Shoshoni boy stepped forward and offered her the horsehair reins to his pony. He looked proud enough to burst.

"Thank you," she said with deep emotion. "She is beautiful." And the animal was. Rebecca had no trouble at all displaying her pleasure at the gift. The mare was a soft dun color, very nearly the shade of doeskin, and she had a flowing black mane and tail. She would have been too small for a big man like Washakie, but she was perfect for Rebecca. Her coat shone like polished pecan wood, and Rebecca knew that Eagle Wing had spent many hours currying her for this moment.

Rebecca walked completely around the mare. She picked up each hoof, ran her hands down the smooth forelegs, and even inspected the teeth, as if she knew everything about the judging of a fine horse. She did not, but she had seen the ritual repeated many, many times.

She brushed her hair back. "She is finer than any horse I have ever seen. Better even than the cavalry horses."

"Damn right she is," Washakie said, translating to the boy, who nodded vigorously. "You ride now. Make her run hard."

Rebecca drew a deep breath. There was a blanket strapped to the mare but nothing more, and she was not particularly competent on a horse. Yet there seemed little choice, so she hoisted her skirts and hopped astride the mare, grateful that the animal had stood quietly while she arranged her dress and took her valise from Eagle Wing.

Now that she was ready, she had a sudden urge not to leave. For a moment, as she looked at the Shoshoni and across the rolling hills down toward Fort Bridger, she thought perhaps she should go back and try to say something—anything—to make Devlin forgive her. An hour ago she had been the proud and happy wife of an Army Officer, being feted for her accomplishments of this day. Now . . . now, she was nothing but a shamed woman riding away alone toward God only knew what fate. And yet she couldn't help feeling that Devlin should at least have listened.

"You good woman," Washakie said as if reading her thoughts. "You change your mind, I still take you as fourth wife. You become Shoshoni medicine woman."

She swallowed noisily. "Thank you, Chief." She tore her eyes away from the distant fort. Then she grabbed a hunk of the pony's mane and drubbed her lightly with the valise. Rebecca almost flipped over backward, so powerfully did the mare lunge forward. In four strides she was running at full speed and Rebecca was clinging for her very life. Never had she been on such a horse! She leaned close to the mare's neck and let the wind buffet her face and sweep her past far behind.

"Go on and run!" she urged, glancing up at the Rocky Mountains beyond. "Take me away!"

Dutch John would want some answers, but she wouldn't be giving him any. Rebecca knew she could set bones and suture as well as or better than anyone. She *would* find the strength to hang on in South Pass until Katie arrived from Temple City. She'd also save enough money to buy them tickets for Springfield. Maybe Devlin was going to give up, but she wasn't!

Rebecca had decided that she could face anything. She had nothing left to lose.

Katie dreaded the thought of Sabino Echavarria and his Basque shepherds leaving. In the three weeks since their arrival she had come to feel a kinship with these people as they worked together to have a good lambing season. Out of eight hundred and twelve lambs born, only seventeen had died, four lost to predators and the others either at birth or soon after.

She'd been surprised at the number of two-year-old ewes who had absolutely refused their lambs, no matter how hard the Basques had tried to make them accept them. These poor, motherless orphans were doomed without fresh milk.

"Isn't there anything that can be done for them?" Katie had asked as their bleating became weaker by the hour.

"Sure," Sabino told her. "If you have the strength and patience, you can teach them to drink milk from a pan."

"Then we must do it!"

"They're not worth it, Katie. They have to be fed five times a day. While you are doing that, you may lose even more to coyotes and disease. Besides, there are no mothers left with milk. To double them up, even if the mother accepts this, will cause two lambs to weaken."

But Katie wasn't able to stand the idea of losing the dozen orphans. She had galloped her old sheep-camp horse into Temple City and returned with milk, which was far more plentiful than cash among the Mormons. She rushed out to the flock, noticing that in the short time she'd been away one lamb had died and another seemed too weak to have a chance at survival, even though she pushed its soft muzzle down into the milk.

"Sabino, it's not doing anything!"

He rushed over and tore a small piece of cloth from the hem of her dress.

"What are you doing!"

"Watch," he grunted, wrapping the material around his thumb. "Better to tie it on. Then dip it in the milk and let it soak like this for a second. Now push it up into his mouth."

"He's still not doing anything."

Sabino leaned closer and shook the little lamb roughly. When its eyelids only fluttered, he pinched its ear. Hard. The lamb's eyes popped open. It squealed in pain, and Sabino jammed his thumb into its open mouth and began to stroke its throat.

"There, you see!" he cried. "This little one has life in him yet. Now you do it."

By the time Katie had her thumb in the lamb's mouth, it was really beginning to take an interest in the fresh milk.

"Will he live?" Only a moment before, she had thought this one was definitely lost.

"If you keep your thumb in its mouth for the next week or two, maybe."

Katie's spirits plummeted. There were so many others! How could she. . . .

Sabino dipped his thumb into the pail of milk and wiped it on her nose. "Katie, don't take everything so serious! Two weeks we have been here and you have yet to laugh. This one will live."

Katie smiled with relief. "You're probably right, Sabino," she said, "but you don't know how much I need this flock to grow. If I can save these orphans, I've increased my own lamb crop by nearly a third."

He frowned with open disapproval. "Is it worth your health? You will have to stay awake night and day. You have to eat and sleep. The flock must be tended, and you have only one dog. Old Rebel, he's a pretty good dog for you, but he cannot do it alone."

"Then I'll buy more dogs." It seemed an obvious solution.

"Ha! You think they come cheap? A good dog, he may be worth forty, fifty dollars, and a bad dog is worse than nothing."

"I'll train some."

"Do you know how?"

"No, but I thought you'd tell me before you go."

He laughed outright at that. "I will! But you must remember this: two dogs is good. They eat better, they play and are happier. Three dogs, always in trouble. No good. Besides, they eat too much."

He got up stiffly and walked away. "Three dogs eat more than you do."

That settled the matter. Katie looked forward to purchasing a new dog. She had kept a little of Bryce's money for just such unforeseen expenses. Buying a pup and enough cow's milk for the orphans was going to use up all her cash before summer was over. But by then the orphans would be strong enough to forage for themselves and she'd have a young dog trained to help Rebel. That's when she'd leave this valley. Bryce would help her. These were his sheep too.

The thought of Bryce made her tremble with both dread and excitement. Perhaps Amos would realize that even he couldn't steal her flock. Katie tried to imagine what would happen when Bryce understood the fine profit he could make on these animals. Maybe he'd want to trail them east to Laramie or Cheyenne and sell them. But maybe, by the time they were into Wyoming, he'd understand that this flock could be nurtured and tended and someday parlayed into thousands. They had the seeds of a sheep-raising empire if they wanted it badly enough. Cattlemen started the same way and became rich; there was no reason they couldn't be as successful with sheep. Katie remembered the excitement in California when two men drove a flock of twenty-five thousand sheep from New Mexico to the fertile San Joaquin Valley. The sheepherders had made a fortune selling mutton to the meat-starved forty-niners.

And wasn't there a big gold strike a little more than two hundred miles away, at South Pass City? Why, she and Bryce could make an enormous profit!

These possibilities made Katie lie awake with anticipation and, at times, even smothered the worries that assailed her. Would Amos try to stop them by force? And how, she fretted, would Bryce react upon discovering that Rebecca had married and then fled? Bryce had a fierce temper, she knew. Somehow she had to keep him from doing something reckless.

And finally there was Jude. She hadn't forgotten his parting words. *"You're the one I want."*

Surely he'd not meant it. Katie didn't even want to consider one more obstacle to leaving. Maybe he'd tasted freedom long enough that he wouldn't even return. She hoped he wouldn't. She'd seen what they'd done to Rebecca. They wouldn't do the same to her.

Her thoughts moved back to the present. She had come to accept the loneliness of her life, and it *was* lonely, especially during the long months between spring and autumn when weeks might pass before Amos or Anna visited. True, she really wasn't alone, not with Rebel and her flock, and the valleys and mountain meadows in which she grazed her animals were not especially isolated. This summer, however, was shaping up as particularly dry, and she would probably have to go up into the mountains beyond the sheep wagon to find good forage.

The loud bleating of her orphan lambs pulled Katie out of her reverie. There was no sense in worrying herself to death about the future. Rebecca had fretted herself nearly sick, and it hadn't helped her one bit. Katie vowed, starting back toward her camp, that she would not marry Jude, not for any price. She had Rebel and a flock of good ewes and healthy lambs, and she meant to leave Utah Territory with Bryce if he'd go with her, or alone if he would not.

It was late afternoon, and the day was still and lazy. On a gentle thermal breeze that swirled over the waving grassland, a chicken hawk wheeled against the sun. It was hunting, yet you could tell by its sluggish wing movement that the bird was almost indifferent to its task. Katie, alone since the Basques had departed, lay on a hillside with her hands folded behind her head and allowed her mind to drift like the hawk.

Fresh grass, spring flowers, and the heavy, familiar scent of Rebel teased her nostrils. It was good to let the spring-soaked, tepid earth seep into her back while the sun bathed her face and loosened the limits of her mind until it frolicked in summery daydreams.

This was the only restful time for a shepherd, when the flock dozed on the grass and even her voracious orphan lambs slept peacefully. The interlude might last a quarter of an hour or more, depending on the sheep. If a cloud passed overhead, suddenly cloaking them, the flock might leap to its feet and start milling about in abject fear as though they alone knew the world's end was at hand. Or if the chicken hawk plummeted to catch a fat prairie dog and lifted it squealing in terror, the sheep might roll their eyes at the sky and run.

But at least that made some sense—it was an instinct for survival. Only two days before, she'd watched helplessly while a golden eagle came down from the sky to snatch up a lamb and haul it away in its great talons. Katie would never forget the little creature's bleats as it was carried over the grassy hills to vanish forever.

She'd yelled, and even cursed in fury at the bird while the lamb's mother had wailed in stupid bereavement and immediately begun to search for its offspring among the anxious flock. Long after dark she'd heard the ewe's mournful croaking. How unfair life was that such a mother would lose her baby while other ewes preferred to abandon their little ones.

A butterfly, bright gold brocaded into its wings, danced overhead, and the chicken hawk wheeled toward Montana. Rebel, ever vigilant, pushed himself to his feet and wagged his tail as if telling her that it was time they circled the flock.

"All right," she said, knowing he was right.

Suddenly the dog's ears pricked erect and he barked, something a good sheep dog never does except as a warning. Katie rolled over on one elbow. She saw an approaching rider. Then, her eyes widened and her heart began to pump fast. It was Bryce! She knew it long before she could see the line of his cheekbone, the blunt squareness of his jaw. She knew it by the way he rode and the rack of his wide shoulders, which boxed out a square of blue sky.

Katie jumped up; her legs were unsteady. Absently she brushed dead grass from her dress and smoothed back the errant wisps of hair. She was suddenly afraid to face him. All the dreams that had kept her hopes buoyed since Rebecca went away now seemed like childish fantasies or, even worse, childish deceits.

She was *not* Rebecca—and she trembled that he might hate her for that, if for no other reason.

He grew larger on the land and therefore more threatening.

Rebel smelled her fear. A low rumble filled his throat, and his upper lip curled.

"It's all right," she whispered. "This is the man I . . . I love. The one we've been waiting for. Be still!"

The dog fell into a fretting silence. It kept glancing up at her with its blood-rimmed, chocolate-covered eyes.

A few yards away Bryce reined his horse to a walk. Katie was jolted by his haggard appearance. This man was a stranger, a man who now wore hard worry lines on his face, who sat unsmiling, and whose cold eyes pinned her down like a bug.

She tried to resurrect the romantic image she'd carried tucked away in the deepest, safest part of her mind. She remembered how his lips had curved in a gentle, teasing way she'd come to adore. Now the lips were compressed, the face hard, that of a man who has come too far, too fast, for too long.

He scared her.

"Bryce?"

"It's me, all right."

His voice was like a bucket banging up out of a deep well. She tried to sense a warmth there, but the sound was ice cold.

"Bryce," she repeated stupidly.

He thumbed his dirty brown Stetson back on the pale upper part of his forehead. "They told me you were here. Jude wanted to come, but I wouldn't allow it yet."

"It's not Jude I've waited for." She wanted to say that

it was he, but now that he was here, the words curdled in her mouth.

He considered her for a moment, then he slowly raised a thin leg over his saddle and eased himself to the earth, the way a man might who was bronc-crippled or aged. He was faded-looking, that's what he was, she decided. His clothes had no color, and his skin was not a healthy tan but rather a kind of gray.

Katie took a half step forward, then checked herself, seeing for the first time the pain that was buried deep in his eyes.

He knew. That was it. He knew about Rebecca.

He let the reins fall from his hand and then he groped in his pants pocket and dragged out a wad of letters.

"You write these?"

"Bryce, I—"

"You did, didn't you?" he said disgustedly. "God damn it, what for? To get my money!"

She was rocked by the fury in him and even more by the accusation. When words failed her, she began shaking her head back and forth in protest.

"I want my money, Katie. I don't want you, but I'll take you away from here. From all of 'em."

Hope flamed in her chest. He *did* care. "Thank you," she replied. "I do want to leave."

"Fine. Let's get my money and ride."

"I don't have it," she told him, suddenly fearful once more.

"You got it from Dave Bender, didn't you?"

"Yes."

When his eyes dilated, she rushed on so fast she was almost babbling. "Bryce, there are no banks here. I had to invest your money. I . . . I bought sheep."

"Sheep! You spent my money on sheep?" Anger changed to disbelief.

"You'll thank me, Bryce. Come look. Ours are the ones with the yellow paint brands on their faces. We've an outstanding lamb crop. Oh, Bryce, wait until you see all the little orphans. I—"

His hands snapped down like talons on her shoulder,

GARY McCARTHY

and she gasped in pain as he jerked her around.

"You spent my money on sheep! Goddamn you, Katie! I ought to beat the hell out of you!"

With a deep growl Rebel sank his fangs into Bryce's boot tops. As he whirled to face the dog, Katie broke away. Rebel was crouched, ready to spring, his hackles up and a menacing rumble in his throat that left little doubt that he would attack.

Bryce's hand curled around his gun butt.

"No!" Katie begged.

"Then call him away."

"Rebel. It's all right." She knelt down and wrapped her arms around the dog, hugged him, and felt him trembling just as badly as she was.

Bryce vaulted into his saddle.

"Where are you going?" Suddenly she was afraid of being left behind, that he would leave her to Jude.

"I'm going to visit Amos Ludlow."

"No!" She threw herself at him, grabbed his leg, and cried, "Don't you see? Killing him because of Rebecca will only get you hanged!"

He laughed—a wild, bitter, ironic laugh. "I'm not going to kill him. Least not until I make the bastard buy back those sheep."

The full impact of his words almost took the breath from her. He wanted to sell their flock to Amos! And Amos would give him nothing!

"Wait, please! I've got ideas. You don't know how much profit we can make."

"And I don't give a damn. I hate sheep, and sheepmen. I even hate the smell of the things. Now, let go of me."

Katie twisted her arm through the fenders of his saddle. "If you ride away now, you're going to have to drag me under your horse clear to Temple City," she vowed. "I won't let Amos beat us out of what we've got!"

"What's this 'we' business?" he demanded. "It was my money that bought 'em."

"And my blood and sweat that made 'em grow and multiply!"

Katie tore free of the saddle. To hell with it! She wasn't

140

going to get herself dragged to death over a hardheaded fool. "If you want to sell the ewes I bought with your money and get skinned by Amos, then do it! But not until after weaning time, because their lambs are mine. And I'll be damned if I'm going to make Amos Ludlow any richer!"

Bryce glared down at her, but she would not look away.

"How long till weaning?" he seethed.

"End of summer."

"What am I supposed to do until then?"

"I . . . I don't know. I hadn't thought about splitting the flock."

"I see. Well, what in blazes *had* you thought of? Did you just think I'd sell my horse and saddle, buy a dog, and turn shepherd? I once rode with the Pony Express!"

Katie suddenly realized how wrong she'd been to assume he'd share her dream of a sheep-raising empire. Why should he? He didn't understand them. He hadn't been here when they'd all fought to pull the bloody and gasping lambs into the world or when Sabino had shown her how to jacket the deserted babies.

He was shaking with anger, trying to roll a smoke and making a mess of it as he talked. "I said I rode with the Pony Express. I fought Indians. And I'll be damned if I'll lower myself to trailing along on foot in sheep dust and sheep shit."

"All right," she replied evenly. "You do what you want. But I'll tell you this, Bryce Sherman. A year from now you'll be dead broke, and I'll be worth two thousand dollars."

"Being out here with woollies has addled your brain. I don't believe you."

"Amos Ludlow would. That sawmill you once worked at—why, Amos told me the money he makes from it doesn't begin to compare with his sheep income. If you don't believe that, ride into town and sell your sheep to him for fall delivery."

He lit the cigarette and inhaled deeply. The smoke that curled from his nostrils was almost the color of his hollow cheeks. But now he was in control. "Girl, all I want is my money and to leave this part of the country before I do decide to kill Ludlow. If you want to stay until fall, then good luck. I'm riding with a clear conscience."

He started to rein away.

"Wait!" she begged. "I'll give you two dollars for each of them. That's better than a sixty percent profit."

"I'll take it."

Katie slumped with relief. "Good, but I haven't the money yet. I'll pay you when we get to . . . South Pass City."

He stiffened. The cigarette hung forgotten from the corner of his mouth. "How'd you know that's where your sister is waiting?"

"She's waiting there?" Katie hugged herself with joy. "I didn't know. I thought maybe she was in Springfield."

Anyone could see her happiness and surprise was no act. Bryce studied his hands and smoked, avoiding her eyes until he whispered, "Why'd she do it?"

"Do what?" She knew what he meant but needed time to think.

"Why did she marry Ludlow? Katie, it's tearing my stomach out."

He was almost begging. The man was a physical wreck. There was nothing of the Bryce Sherman she remembered and had loved. He was all gone.

"Please, Katie," he breathed. "Did he make her do it?"

When she couldn't answer, he shook his head as though dazed. "I *can't* believe she loved him. I saw her, you know."

Katie took a step back. Her hand flew to her mouth in surprise. "When?"

"Last week in Fort Bridger. Jude and I didn't expect it. Rebecca was married to an Army doctor." He said it like a curse.

Katie's hands dropped lifeless to her sides. She stared in disbelief at this man as if to divine the real truth. He was wrong. "Rebecca would never let herself be married twice."

"But she did, god damn it!" He piled off of his horse

and grabbed her roughly. "Katie, I loved her. I . . . I thought she was beginning to love me too. Then . . . there has to be some reason." His mouth grew hard. "I think it was Ludlow. He forced her to marry him. He ruined her."

He was very near the breaking point, and she knew that she had to tell him the truth. "Bryce, Rebecca married Amos so that you wouldn't be charged and convicted for the theft of those horses you and Jude rode away with. She saved you from the hangman."

Bryce threw his head back and sucked air through his open mouth. He stood rooted in some terrible inner battle until at last his body relaxed and his jaw muscles corded with decision. "Thank you," he grated. "That's all I needed to know."

He swung into the saddle and reined his horse toward Temple City.

"Bryce, no!" she shouted.

But he didn't hear her now. "My God," Katie moaned as she sprinted for the corral and her own animal. "I did it. He's going to kill Amos Ludlow!"

Chapter Nine

Her old sheep horse was blowing hard and flecked with foam by the time she reached Temple City. She'd expected to find Bryce on the way to the gallows and Amos probably shot, but instead she galloped into town just in time to see them brawling like wild men.

Katie reined in her horse and stared helplessly. The townsmen yelled encouragement to Amos as he clubbed Bryce and sent him reeling along the storefronts. He grabbed Bryce by the collar and spun him about, only to take a vicious uppercut to the jaw. The crowd fell silent, but Amos just shook his head, then lowered it. Bryce tried to sidestep him but lost his balance, and when Amos drove his head into his stomach, they both flew off the boardwalk and leveled a hitching rail. It snapped like a shot, splintering the dry pinewood like a matchstick.

Katie whipped her horse toward the two combatants. They were both bleeding and battered, yet obviously neither was ready to quit. She had never seen men fight so viciously. They struggled erect and began to hammer each other again. She found herself both appalled at the savagery and, at the same time, strangely fascinated. Amos was clearly the heavier and more powerful, yet it seemed to her that Bryce was winning. He was quicker, and though his blows lacked the impact, they were landing far more steadily, and there was an intensity in his eyes that was frightening to see. Katie had the impression that Amos could not whip him, that Bryce would fight until the death if need be.

They stood toe to toe, and then Amos took a small backstep, and then another. He was gasping for breath, and his face was covered with purple blotches where Bryce's fists had landed. His starched collar was torn half off, and his shirt was blood-spattered. When he threw a punch, he lunged off balance, and then Bryce was on him like a swarm of hornets.

Amos covered his face and Bryce sank his fist in the man's stomach. Amos dropped his hands and Bryce drove his shoulder up and under a winging uppercut. When it connected, there was a sickening popping noise and Amos hollered and shielded his broken nose.

Katie looked away, telling herself Amos had this coming. Yet she wished to God the beating would end.

A man whooped, "Now you got him! Stomp him good, Amos!"

Katie's head lifted. Bryce was down! She watched as he tried to stand. Amos drew back his leg and kicked for the face.

"Look out!" she cried.

Her warning was unnecessary. At the last instant, Bryce rolled. The boot whistled inches above his head. Before Amos could recover, Bryce grabbed his heel and twisted hard. They both fell, and Katie lost sight of them for a moment as they rolled about, fighting for a dominant position.

Bryce was on his feet now, but he was swaying with fatigue. She saw him beckon the other man to rise, and then Amos was being helped up. For a moment they each just stood there, fighting for breath, hating each other. Then Bryce attacked.

His fists were a blur. He seemed like a whirlwind of destruction as he landed punch after punch until Amos was staggering like a drunk and his face was a bloody mask. And still Bryce kept hitting him.

"That's enough, Bryce!" Jude yelled.

Katie located him in the crowd, and it was like seeing a total stranger. Like Bryce, he was leaner. He wore a mustache and a bright orange silk scarf at his neck. Katie thought he looked dangerous, not at all like these stolid Mormons. He seemed a cross between a gunfighter and a riverboat gambler.

"No more, Bryce," he said, grabbing him by the shoulder.

Bryce batted Jude's hand away. His eyes were wild; he was possessed by the single-minded purpose of beating Amos senseless. He couldn't stop. Katie saw Amos actually lift off the ground when Bryce whipped a booming right uppercut that landed just under the breastbone. Amos screamed silently. He folded at the waist as if someone had taken a pair of scissors and snipped his spinal cord. Bryce sledged him behind the ear and he collapsed in the dirt.

That's when Jude cursed and pistol-whipped Bryce. Katie was off her horse and at Bryce's side in a moment.

"You didn't need to do that!" she cried.

Jude reached down and grabbed the unconscious Bryce under the arms. He lifted him up and over his shoulder, saying, "Come on, Katie. Let's get him out of here. Bring me his horse."

She was stunned, yet his voice and the faces of the people around them told her this was no time for conversation.

Jude studied her. Something dark and powerful was trying to fight its way out from behind his eyes. Whatever it was, he seemed finally to control it, for he bent low and grated, "I can save his life only if you help me, Katie. Now, are you going to help me get him out of here?"

A man blocked Jude's path. He turned and shouted, "All you men, don't just stand there. My father needs a doctor. Find him! Take Amos to our house. Hurry now!"

One of them stooped to grab Amos and then everyone was trying to help. Jude wasn't a big man, yet he was strong enough to get Bryce draped and tied across his saddle.

"Let's ride," he said, grabbing his own horse and swinging into leather. "Come on!"

Katie was astonished that no one tried to stop them. But these were peaceful men, more given to holding a shovel than a gun. And without Amos to stir them up and lead them, they were content to avoid trouble. As they galloped out of town, Katie felt wave after wave of gratitude toward Jude. "You did it!" she shouted.

He laughed, and it was as she remembered. A good laugh—full, throaty, and uninhibited. "Yeah, but I'll catch hell tonight!"

Katie was surprised to learn he was going back. She could see that he was different now.

They continued to ride until her horse began to stumble with fatigue. Jude pointed toward a thick stand of cottonwood trees by the river. "We'll rest there."

The grove was cool and restful. They laid Bryce beside the river, and she saw that he was beginning to come around.

Jude was nervous. "I'd better go back to town and see how my father is," he said. "If you're planning to leave, you'd better do it now."

"I'll have to get my sheep first," Katie said.

Jude shook his head. "No time. When my father wakes up, all hell is going to break loose. You won't get another chance."

"I've done nothing wrong," she said stubbornly. "And . . . and, no! I won't be driven from here without what is rightfully mine!"

"Then you're a bigger fool than he is, and you deserve each other," he said bitterly. "If you try driving sheep, any sheep, from this valley, we will hunt you down."

"Do it if you must," Katie said. "But our blood will be on your hands. Your father may be able to justify murder, but you can't."

"Stop it!" His eyes pleaded. "Don't you understand I'm trying to help?"

Katie knew he was. "Yes, but those sheep are *mine*. I've pulled some of those lambs into this world, and I've doctored and milk-fed others just to keep them alive. They're all I have, Jude. I don't want to leave here like Rebecca."

"You're not like her at all," he said fiercely. "You are ten, a hundred times the woman she'll ever be."

Katie saw no point in arguing.

"So long, Katie. Tell Bryce he owes me." Jude started for his horse.

"Jude?"

Her voice stopped him with a foot in the stirrup.
"Yeah?"

"You could help us," she heard herself telling him. "I'd give you half my lamb crop."

He mounted wearily. "No thanks. I'm my father's oldest son. Someday I'll own all the sheep I'll ever want."

"And all the wives?" The moment she said it, Katie was ashamed. He'd tried to help them, and her question was unkind. "I'm sorry."

"Don't be, Katie. You would be enough woman for me. If you stay in this valley, I'll come courting."

"I'm not leaving without my sheep, and I'm not marrying you either," she said stubbornly.

He grinned. With a slow wink, he said, "Don't bet on that. I'll be seeing you soon."

She watched him ride away. Her mind was in a turmoil. She would not leave without Rebel and her sheep, yet she couldn't remain to be courted by Jude. All her silly dreams about Bryce were just that—silly dreams. He was a stranger to her. She'd built up some romantic image that lay shattered at her feet. And he hadn't even been grateful. He hated the sheep.

Katie was confused. Desolation slipped down upon her like a cloak. She stretched out on the grass and waited. Overhead a gentle breeze riffled the tall cottonwoods and made little puffs of cotton sail to land on the river to be spun away by cold currents toward an unknown destination perhaps hundreds of miles away. But somewhere, Katie thought, one of these cottonwood seeds would wash up on fertile soil. Next spring, if the water level was just so and the temperature and sunlight warmed and coaxed Mother Earth, the seed might send out feeble roots while its grass-thin trunk reached for the sky.

Katie watched the little flotilla of cotton riding and bouncing happily downstream. Theirs was an adventure, the stuff of life. Each year the journey would be repeated a million times over, and though very few of this little armada would survive, those that did would grow into something of beauty and value. The lesson was worthwhile. There was a reason behind everything. You couldn't hope to understand what it was, but you were expected to carry out your role in the grand scheme of things, no matter how impossible the odds or how turbulent the journey. She realized that life was a struggle that often resulted in failure but that perhaps the only real failure was in not trying.

"Damn it," Bryce groaned, pushing himself to his elbows. "Where are we?"

Katie drew her knees up, rested her chin on them, and told Bryce exactly where they were and what had happened. By the time she finished, he was fully awake and listening with grim and red-eyed concentration.

When she ended by saying she was not leaving without her sheep, he appraised her with something like pity, then slowly crawled to his feet. Katie could see it was all he could do to reach his horse.

"I'm riding out," he announced in a tired voice. "I whipped Amos in front of his town and I know what that will do to him. He'll fester."

It took all Bryce's strength to drag himself into the saddle. Katie realized that he was in no condition to do anything but leave this valley.

"Good-bye," she said.

"Just like that, huh? Your sister told me you wrote all those letters because you loved me. Now you're saying goodbye as though I meant nothing to you."

"I made a mistake," she whispered.

"You're making a bigger one by staying here."

When she didn't answer, he tried to roll a smoke but did it badly, for his hands were severely swollen from the fighting.

"Here," Katie said. "Let me do that." She rolled one expertly.

"When did you learn that?"

"As a little girl. Rebecca and I used to make them for my father."

"I see." He lit the cigarette and inhaled. She watched his face relax and the twin plumes of smoke drift slowly from his nostrils.

"Katie, I don't like leaving you. If I hadn't left your sister, all our lives would be better."

"You had no choice." Katie thought she heard the faraway tinkle of a sheep bell. "I'm doing what I want. I'll be fine."

"No, you won't." His voice took on an edge. "They'll grind you down, even if it takes years; you'll marry among 'em. Probably Jude."

"No, I won't. I've got a plan."

"Let's hear it," he said.

Suddenly, Katie was a little embarrassed. It wasn't really a plan, just a vow to herself that she would be leaving. "Well," she said, "later this summer I'll be up in those higher mountains and I'll pick a day and drive our sheep into Wyoming Territory."

"That's a hell of a plan, Katie," he drawled cynically.

"Stop it! At least I'm going to try to save what is mine. I'm not just going to give everything to Amos Ludlow."

He was stung. She could see it in his eyes. "You can't do it alone," he told her.

"I won't be alone. I've a good sheep dog, and I know where I can find another to train."

Bryce's gaze shifted toward the east. "You'd have to cross those mountains yonder and reach the basin beyond before the snow falls. It may come early, Katie. You and those sheep could get trapped in the passes. You wouldn't have a chance up there."

"I'll make it."

"And if you don't?"

Katie had no answer to that, because there was none. If she failed to reach the lowlands before winter, all was lost "You'd better ride, Bryce. I've got to get back to my flock now. When we reach South Pass City, I'll leave word where you can get your sheep money."

"I don't expect ever to see a penny of it."

"Expect what you want. Next week is shearing time, and in a month I'll be up at the wagon camp."

"It would take you a good seven days to get over Bear River Divide and then drop down into Bridger's Basin. How fast do sheep travel?"

"Not fast."

"So I figured," Bryce said glumly. "You'd better make it ten days. A one-legged man could hoppity over 'em that fast if he didn't get caught in a blizzard."

Ten days! Katie had no idea how she could possibly keep her absence from the valley a secret for that long. Once they realized she was gone, the chase would be furious. So be it. Katie studied the rugged mountains she'd have to cross and tried not to show her doubts. Really, they weren't that much higher than she stood now. But they were wild and unknown to her. The responsibility of taking her sheep through them weighed on her like a millstone.

"You know what scares me the most?" she said absently. "It's not getting caught by the Mormons and being returned to Temple City. It's getting lost up there in that high timber and wandering around in those mountains, seeing my sheep grow thin and weak. And maybe watching the snow fall on them and knowing I was the reason they were all going to die. Bryce, when they're hurt, they look to you for help. They trust you and the dogs because they know they'll die on their own."

He frowned, took a final drag on his cigarette, and ground out its life on his saddle horn. "Come on, Katie," he urged. "I don't want to leave you here among these people. In five days you could be with your sister in South Pass City. I told her I'd help you. I mean to do it."

"Thanks. But no. Sometimes it's best to help yourself, and that's what I'm trying to do now."

He tipped his hat. "Where is that high country camp you'll be leaving from?"

Hope flashed into her mind. "Why are you asking?"

"Only so I can point out the way."

Katie averted her face so he couldn't see her disappointment. She indicated where she'd be staying.

"Good. You see that notch in the mountains just to the north? That's where you go through. You'll come to a river, but it will be shallow in the late summer. Beyond the river, there's a scar-faced mountain. Veer to the south of it and stay in the canyon. It will take you in the right direction."

"I'll remember that." Katie met his eyes. "Thank you."

He nodded, lifted his reins, then seemed to struggle with himself. "If you get caught and things go bad, ask Jude for help. I think he's man enough now to stand up to his father or anyone else in Temple City. Besides, he's sweet on you, Katie."

Her lips pinched together.

"Don't you make light of it," Bryce said. "You could do a whole lot worse."

"You'd better go now," she said stiffly.

"Okay, but I wish to hell you'd invested my money in horses or cattle. Either one and I'd have stayed and fought. But sheep? Jesus Christ, no! Ain't enough sheep in the world to die for, Katie."

He rode then. And not once did he so much as turn in the saddle to wave or look back at her.

Katie waited several minutes before she went to her own horse and started back to her flock. Never in her life had she felt so abandoned. Over and over she tortured herself with his last words. He wished she'd bought horses or cattle so that he might have had something worth fighting to save. What about her? Was she worth nothing? She had stayed for one reason, and that was to warn him and perhaps save his life.

How, Katie asked herself, could I ever have thought I was in love with such a man?

Jude appeared several days later. She caught him watching her from a distance as she tended the sheep, and, surprisingly, it was a comfort to know that she hadn't been completely forgotten by everyone in this valley. He waved to her but she didn't respond. After a time he climbed back on his horse and rode away. She could only wonder at Jude's thoughts and intentions. He'd said he was going to come courting, but she thought he'd first wait out the summer. By then she'd be gone.

A week before shearing, Katie had an unexpected visitor. Micah drove out from town with fresh supplies and, to her great happiness, a young female shepherd dog.

"Jude bought it from someone after he heard you wanted one," Micah explained, stepping down from the buckboard. "He said he hoped you like her."

The new dog was fawn-and-white-colored, with soft caramel eyes and a rich coat of curly hair. Her tail was bobbed, and her mouth was a natural smile. When she was panting, she appeared to be laughing in silence.

"She's beautiful!" Katie exclaimed, taking the dog in her arms and hugging it while it squirmed and tried to lap her face. "How old is she?"

"About six months. A freighter owned her; he said her mother was a good sheep dog. He'd gotten her in Idaho but just couldn't keep her near whenever she saw a flock of sheep. Said he guessed that meant shepherding was in her blood."

Katie set the new dog down, and instantly old Rebel was acting like a puppy as they began to frolic. She remembered Sabino's advice that two dogs were good, three a nuisance. "Tell Jude I'm very pleased and grateful."

Micah began toeing the earth the way he did when he was trying to dredge up his words. Finally, he said, "Katie, you going to marry Jude someday?"

"No." Katie was disappointed. "Is that why they sent you? To discover my true intentions?"

"Well, kind of," Micah said, refusing to look at her. "That, and I sort of do odd jobs for Mr. Ludlow anyway now. I've been assigned the job of hauling supplies to all the sheep camps."

"What happened to the leather shop? I thought you liked it."

Micah scowled. "It was all right," he said. "But I just got tired of always being ordered around as if I was a kid with no sense."

"Pa, did you quit?" Katie asked, knowing he had, and that this time he couldn't run from his failure.

"I was going to," Micah said bravely. "But I made the mistake of telling my wife I planned to open my own saddle shop. I was thinking of Ogden or even Salt Lake

City. Then she told a friend, and the next thing I knew I was out of a job. That's when I went off and seen the freighter who owned your new dog. I knew he'd have some cigars and whiskey. He's no Mormon, and that's a blessing."

Katie groaned. "Don't tell me you got drunk."

"We both did one night. And we got caught. They don't have much use for me here anymore. Got nowhere else to go, Katie." He jammed his hands deep into his pockets and stared at the ground like a beaten dog.

Katie knew a pang of remorse. Always before, no matter how badly he'd erred, Micah had been able to summon up a great storm of righteous indignation. Now even that was missing. The bluster, the facade of a man constantly being wronged by fate and nobly suffering great hardships, was no longer there. Now there was nothing but dull resignation. Micah reminded her of a spiritless animal, tractable and submissive to whatever was to be its fate. It made Katie ache inside. She resolved to help him if she could.

"Father, I'll be leaving this valley before long. Are you going to be all right?"

His eyes rested on some distant spot. It was a look she remembered—and one that had driven the family into tragedy and misfortune. Katie knew her father wanted to leave Temple City. She thought she might invite him to go with her, but she wanted no part of what might happen to him if they were caught. For such a man as Micah to be ostracized would be slow death.

He cleared his voice. "Katie dear, I know I got no call to expect anything from either of my girls, but I want to go with you."

She had to try to dissuade him, just in case everything went wrong. "I'm taking my sheep. It will be slow. We could easily be caught."

"I . . . I expect you'll need some help."

"I expect I will," she said.

Micah straightened. He looked right at her and came as near to smiling as he was capable. "When?" he whispered as though they might be overheard.

"Three days after I reach the sheep wagon. You can sneak out a week later and overtake me."

"Why can't I go when you do?"

"Because," she said, "the moment they discover you are missing, they'll send someone up to check on me. That's why you have to wait."

He could see the logic of that. "Maybe," he said, thinking aloud, "I can pretend to bring your supplies again and just keep going in the buckboard until I catch up with you."

At first Katie liked the idea, but then she shook her head. "No, that would make us thieves. We'll just take what is ours. That way, if we're caught, there's nothing they can legally do to us."

"Yes, but—"

"Father, they hang horse thieves! You'd have to steal a horse to pull the buckboard."

All his protest died. "I'd best start unloading your supplies, girl. They'll be expecting me back soon. They don't trust me worth a spit."

"They trust you enough to come out here alone to see me," she reminded him.

"Sure. But I bet there's someone watching." He looked about furtively. "I can feel their eyes."

Katie was about to say that was ridiculous until, far away, she caught a glint of sun on metal. He was right. Escaping this valley, even from the mountain pasture, was going to be almost impossible.

In many ways, her father was as helpless as the sheep. And just like them, his fate depended on her.

Dear God, she thought silently. What will happen if I fail?

Chapter Ten

*Rebecca had discovered that South Pass was not an awe-*inspiring cut in the rugged mountains. Like the thousands of previous emigrants who had rolled through its grassy gates expecting a spectacular cleft in the Rockies, she was a little disappointed to see that this famous opening in the continental divide was totally uninspiring. So much so that one did not really believe he had passed through it until he noticed that the rivers flowed from its crest in opposite directions, either east or west.

Dutch John had been almost apologetic about the gradual slopes leading up to the twenty-five-mile-wide pass that was covered by sagebrush and piñon pine. He'd explained that some thirty years earlier and guided by Kit Carson, even John C. Frémont hadn't recognized the summit. But this was the Oregon Trail, and in the years that followed, iron wheels had cut deep furrows through the pass. After the Indians, trappers, wagon trains of emigrants, and stagecoaches, the pass was finally going to get its long overdue rest; the Union Pacific railroad had decided to lay its shining steel fifty miles south.

They had ridden down the gentle eastern slopes along South Pass Road, overlooking Atlantic City, which was itself becoming another boom town since gold had been discovered nearby. This was hard land, Rebecca thought, and though it was summer and hot in the distant basins of Utah and Wyoming territories, here at nearly eight thousand feet the clean air had the snap of frosty mornings and pine forests. Rebecca noticed that up along the bases of the surrounding peaks and lurking under dense stands of aspen was last winter's snow. During the warm summers, enterprising Chinese from South Pass City would pack the snow under straw and peddle it to grateful miners who'd cool their whiskey down with it.

Dutch John stopped frequently along the way to chat with acquaintances and sell merchandise. The miners invariably rushed from their diggings with gold nuggets in their hands. They were rough sorts, clad in heavy trousers, woolen shirts, and serviceable boots. They reminded her of those she had seen panning gold along the Stanislaus and Feather rivers of California or trooping wearily into Virginia City after a hard shift in the mines, always dirty and tired, yet bright-eyed with gold fever.

Dutch John sat beside her on the wagon seat today, greeting just such a group of men. He introduced her as Mrs. Rebecca Woodson. At the word "Mrs." she noted the disappointment, then the curiosity. It was a question she had no intention of answering. Her past was just that—*her* past. Certainly there would come a time when someone from Fort Bridger would pass through, recognize her, and start tongues wagging, but she had decided to face that day when it came.

Almost as if reading her thoughts, Dutch John leaned over on the wagon seat and said, "You being a missus isn't going to protect you from whatever caused you to leave the captain, Mrs. Woodson."

"I know," Rebecca squared her shoulders. She had come to respect this little businessman, despite his persistent questioning. He had behaved like a gentleman, and she suspected he would help her get established when they arrived in South Pass City. She did not want to hurt his feelings, yet she felt that she had to say something in her own defense. "Dutch, right now my husband is on his way to Washington. He isn't coming back. What makes you so sure *I* left him?"

If she'd punched Dutch John in the nose his reaction could not have been more animated. Rebecca saw his eyes grow round with astonishment, then anger. "You mean he just up and left?"

"He has his reasons. I have mine. That's all I'm saying." Rebecca turned from him to gaze straight ahead.

"Why, Mrs. Woodson, I had no idea he was arunnin' out on you!"

It was not exactly true, yet in a way it was. Devlin hadn't given her any chance to explain the circumstances even to beg his forgiveness and understanding. That, more than anything, had hurt. Over and over Rebecca had relived those awful moments when he'd discovered her previous marriage. She'd wanted to tell him everything, but he'd banished her without giving her a chance to speak.

He'd been wrong to do that. She had loved him, and she'd proved her love every day since their marriage. Had the circumstances been reversed, she would certainly have given Devlin a chance.

"There it is," Dutch said, pointing ahead. "I can see we have another street full of new business just since I been gone. Hope none of 'em are competitors."

Rebecca leaned forward with interest. "I never expected it to be so large!"

"Growing every day. I reckon we have at least two thousand now; by next year we'll double in size. This here is opportunity. There is money to be made in this town."

Rebecca didn't doubt him at all. South Pass City fairly hummed with activity. Located in a canyon along a pretty creek, every square foot of land was in use. The main street was tiresomely familiar, with the rough-planed and mostly unpainted false fronts characteristic of western boom towns. There were hotels and plenty of saloons, as well as shops and businesses of every description.

Near the creek the marsh grass was a dark, almost blue-green shade that contrasted beautifully with the corroded brown and rust-colored canyon walls. Along both sides of the stream, miners' camps were in great profusion, many cut right out of dense stands of willow.

The walls of the canyon were not high, perhaps fifty feet, yet the site was such that the plains blizzards would race right overhead, leaving the people of South Pass City relatively protected from the icy blasts. Rebecca imagined that in spring the runoff might be a problem as Big

Hermit Creek swelled with melted snow, but most of the permanent structures were built on higher ground, and the miners could move their camps at a moment's notice.

"No wonder we couldn't see it until we reached this point," she said.

"Yep. First settlers lived here for quite some time and the Indians didn't even know. 'Course, now they do, and every once in a while some of 'em will sneak along the rim at daybreak and shoot arrows down onto the camps. Always a few miners dying in their sleep. Damned redskins get away before we can rouse up a chase. That's why some of the miners sleep under sheets of tin, though it's mighty uncomfortable."

"I should imagine."

As the wagons started down into the canyon, Rebecca decided she liked the appearance of South Pass City very much. It had a sheltered feeling, and being confined within the canyon gave a sense of closeness, as though everyone realized how vulnerable they were, so far from any Army post or the large cities to the east and west.

"When I left," Dutch John was saying, "there were four hotels, thirteen saloons, two lawyers, and a dentist—and all of 'em were doing quite well. Now, just what do *you* intend to do?"

"What I intend to do is ask you for a small loan," she said quietly. "I'll find lodging and set up a medical practice. I'll tell people that I am not a doctor but that I can remove arrowheads and deliver babies. I know how to clean out a wound and stitch it up neat, and I'm qualified to set broken bones and dispense medicines."

"You'll do all right. Pretty as you are, there'll be no lack of patients—most of 'em will just be plain lovesick."

Rebecca couldn't suppress a laugh. "Well, I hope that isn't a problem. I will need some money to get started. I'll pay you interest."

"And have Judge Carter get mad? No, thanks." Dutch John sighed and reached into his pocket. "You don't have any medical tools or medicine either. Want me to order some?"

"From where?"

159

"St. Louis. We can put your order on tomorrow's stage and have everything in less than a month." He frowned. "You can't practice medicine without any medicine."

"Will you order them on credit?"

"Sure. On one condition."

"What is that?" Rebecca asked, suddenly tense.

"That these loans are an advance against what you earn while working in my store until you get started."

"That's fair enough," she told him.

Dutch looked relieved. "You see, in a town like this, there are only two kinds of women—respectable and otherwise. All the respectable ones are married, or they wouldn't be here. The others work at places like Olive's Sugar Palace."

"Sugar Palace?"

Dutch chuckled. "Yep. I think you can guess what it is."

She knew. Houses of ill repute were as common as saloons in the West—and just as popular. In many of them the women became celebrities and were publically honored for their service to the community. Julia Bulette had been such a woman; she'd been loved and respected on the Comstock, and when a miner had robbed and strangled her, the whole town had mourned deeply.

"You'd better find a room with a decent family," Dutch commented. "It's certain our hotels aren't fit for a woman alone. These miners would get drunk some Saturday night and hack their way through the walls of your room. I'll drop you off in front of Mrs. Peterson's house. She's a good woman, and I think she could use the extra money from a boarder. Her husband got drunk and froze himself to death in a blizzard—and her expecting a baby this winter."

"Thank you," Rebecca said. "Does she have a place for my horse?"

"I'll take care of the mare along with my own stock."

"You're kind, Dutch. I'll work hard for you."

"I know that. You'll draw customers like bees to a honey tree, Rebecca. I have no idea why you and the captain separated, but I do know that until a real doctor like your husband comes along, we will all be grateful for your knowledge."

They rumbled down the central street of town, and Rebecca noticed how men halted to stare at her.

"See what you're going to be facing? Rebecca, you've been living a sheltered life at Fort Bridger."

She thought of how hard things had been since coming west, of cold, hungry days and nights, of burying her mother and hating her father, and of the loneliness she'd known since saying good-bye to Katie. And now of the heartbreak she was trying to hide.

"I haven't been sheltered."

But he didn't know her past, and so he said, "Sure, you have. On an Army post you had absolutely nothing to worry about except getting bored. You were a high-ranking officer's wife, so you had security and privilege. I'm not trying to say you didn't deserve them; all I'm saying is that here it's not going to be easy. This is a rough town, and I'm worried about you."

"I'll do okay. You worry about your business. I'll worry about mine."

Rebecca heard a woman singing in a slurred voice, accompanied by a badly tuned piano. A mule skinner popped his blacksnake over and over as his team strained in its traces to pull a heavily laden ore wagon around a corner. Everywhere she looked there was construction under way, and the sounds of hammering and sawing filled the air. She could smell green-cut pine oozing sap.

From the boardwalk, a handsome young miner whistled at her. A knot of men laughed, then saw her and began to whistle and yell for her to join them in a drink and some dancing.

"See you in ten minutes at Olive's Palace," one yelled, and he instantly was seconded by a chorus of men.

Dutch John brandished his whip at them. "Ignore that kind," he said angrily.

"I am." Rebecca's eyes searched into distance. South Pass City was losing its appeal.

"Don't let them upset you. As soon as they discover you aren't just another soiled dove coming to roost on a nest of their gold, you won't hear these kinds of insults."

Men were pouring out of the saloons to see what was causing such a stir, and a number of them fell in beside the wagon, grinning up at her and asking her name and making crude suggestions.

"Go on!" Dutch shouted at them. "This here is a respectable married woman. A doctor's wife. She don't deserve your foul talk." The men dropped back in silence.

Farther along, Rebecca heard a woman call and looked up to see a chubby, powdered face poking between red lace curtains. She wore a pile of blond curls on her head and enormous dangling earrings of bright red to match her lip rouge. Her eyebrows were inverted V's, giving her a permanent look of amazement. Yet when she opened her mouth, her voice was that of a young girl. "Howdy, Dutch honey, you bring me a new girl?"

Dutch looked pained. His mouth pinched with disgust. "Nope," he said. "This is a respectable woman, Big Olive."

"Respectable?" Big Olive leaned farther out the window, almost filling it. "Well, if she's respectable, what's she doing riding with you, Dutch John?" Shrill laughter floated down on them.

"She's going to practice medicine, damn it!"

Rebecca looked up at the madam, determined not to be intimidated. Big Olive had fish eyes, little black licorice drops sunk deep in flesh.

"Honey, you want to make some *real* money, don't forget Big Olive."

"Yah!" Dutch yelled as the wagon jumped forward and the team began to trot.

Rebecca heard Olive's laughter receding.

When they were almost through town, Dutch said, "I'm sorry for that. You see, Big Olive drinks too much of her own house whiskey. When she does that, she sure ain't no lady."

Rebecca said nothing. She wasn't a child, and she was going to have to make her own way in life now. Dutch pulled the team in before a neat log cabin. A white picket fence protected, of all things, a flower and vegetable garden. She saw tomatoes, squash, and carrots all neatly lined up and flourishing among marigolds, sweet peas, roses, and pansies. "My!" she whispered. "Who does this?"

"Mrs. Peterson. She could grow corn off the dust of a mule's back."

Rebecca climbed down. She gripped the fence, closed her eyes, and smelled the roses and the sweet peas. It was wonderful. "I can't imagine this clear up here." Given the almost eight-thousand-foot elevation, it seemed impossible that all these flowers and vegetables would flourish.

"Yep. The growing season ain't much, but she figures out just the right time to plant and harvest. Sells the flowers for weddings, but more often for funerals. Does pretty good at it too."

"They are lovely." Rebecca touched a rose with the tip of her finger. Like velvet. She had forgotten.

"You're going to like Mrs. Peterson," Dutch told her. "She is a fine woman. A little . . . oh, hello, Mrs. Peterson!"

Rebecca forgot the rose as the biggest woman she'd ever seen rounded the corner of the log house. In each huge hand she carried a wooden water bucket as effortlessly as if they were empty. The sleeves of her dress were rolled up to her elbows, revealing thick and muscle-corded forearms and big knobby wrists. Six feet tall with a miner's shoulders, she moved with stolid determination despite the fact that she was obviously pregnant.

"Hello!" she called with a smile. "I be vid you in a moment," she said, placing the buckets down and bending to her knees to fashion a miniature earthen dam.

Rebecca watched her carefully. Mrs. Peterson was in her thirties. The hair that had escaped from her sunbonnet was as yellow as straw, while her skin was nearly pink. She must be Scandinavian or German, Rebecca thought.

When the dam was completed, she carefully poured one of the buckets into her neat little canal system, and they all watched the water flood between the little dikes that divided the tomatoes and the roses. When the bucket was empty, the water stood an inch deep through a quarter of her garden. Already, though, it was seeping into the rich, dark soil.

The woman straightened, placing a hand against the small of her back, and Rebecca noticed a tight little movement indicating pain. Mrs. Peterson, once you got past her size, was actually quite handsome. Her features were attractive in a strong Nordic way, and her smile was wide and unaffected. Rebecca had a feeling that life hadn't been too easy for this woman.

"Dutch John, you bring me a boarder, yah?"

"Yah, Trudy, I think so. This is Mrs. Rebecca Woodson."

They shook hands over the fence, between the roses. Trudy Peterson's hand felt like rawhide. When her fingers closed, Rebecca's hand disappeared.

"I am happy to meet you, Mrs. Peterson. I think I'd like to live here."

"Trudy. You like flowers and good garden?"

"Yes. Very much."

"Good. Ve get along vell, den!"

Dutch John said good-bye and drove away with his wagons in tow.

"He is good man, Dutch John. I vould marry him, I vould," she said, watching him go. "Ve vould have some girls and dey not be so big as me. They vould be like you. Very pretty."

Not sure how to reply, Rebecca entered the yard and picked up the second bucket of water, though it took over every bit of her strength. "Where shall I pour this one?"

"Over der. By the roses."

Rebecca spread her feet wide apart, and, straddling the bucket, she began to walk frog-legged toward the indicated place with the bucket swinging between her legs, water sloshing her skirts, wetting her stockings and shoes. It was an awful job.

"You vill get stronger, Rebecca. Vait and see!"

Trudy was smiling again. Rebecca made it to the roses with the bucket only half full. She spilled a portion of it into each of the handmade reservoirs at the base of the rosebushes. When she was finished, she turned around to see Trudy beckoning her.

"Ve need much more vater. Come, I show you. Aftervard, I gif you a little secret on vatering roses."

Rebecca stifled a protest and hoisted her bucket. She wondered how soon Trudy might have to start tending a baby instead of her garden, and how long before the first night frost would come to rescue her from this bucket brigade.

"Coming," she called back. "Just give me a second!"

Jude stood beside his horse and watched the dust settle on the road back to Temple City. "Well, Katie, that's the end of it for another year. I'd say we got more wool than usual."

Katie said nothing. She was wondering why Jude had remained behind after the shearing crews. She felt nervous alone in his presence, though he'd been a perfect gentleman ever since his return. But the way he looked at her made Katie squirm. Oh, it wasn't with hunger or lust, the way Amos had for Rebecca. This was much different. Katie knew that Jude really loved her. Why couldn't he have fallen in love with a young Mormon girl? There were some far prettier than she who would jump at the chance to marry into Ludlow wealth.

"Katie?" he asked abruptly.

"Yes."

Jude frowned as if at last reaching some great decision. "I've decided you are going to need some help this year up at the sheep-wagon camp, and I—"

"No!" She hadn't meant to shout. She tried to regain her composure.

"Those are my father's sheep," Jude said doggedly. "We've a right to say how they'll be protected. That flock is too large for you to handle alone. I'm going to help out."

She *had* to stop this. "I'm not alone! There's Rebel and Taffy."

"Taffy doesn't know anything yet."

"Sure, she does! Why, all this past week during the shearing I've been training her."

"How?" he demanded. "How can you teach her anything without the sheep?"

"We had sheep. As soon as they were sheared, they were herded up where I made camp. Taffy is already showing me that she'll be perfect. Jude, please. I appreciate the offer but I'll be fine."

"Katie, even if that were true, don't you know that I want to help? I'd set up a camp away from yours. You can trust me. During the daytime we could be together. I never cared about sheep until now. You could teach me about them."

"It wouldn't be right."

"Why not? I said I'd stay in my own camp at night. In a month we'll be herding them down the mountain anyway."

Her mind was racing. There seemed to be nothing she could tell him that wouldn't make him angry and unreasonable or, even worse, suspicious.

"My mind is made up," Jude added.

Katie wanted to cry, even to scream, in hopelessness and anger. All at once her world seemed to be going to pieces. For weeks she had been dreaming of reaching the high sheep-wagon camp where at last she would be hidden from view among timbered forests and ringed mountain meadows. And now this!

She whirled away from him, trying to hide her tears as she stumbled toward the flock.

"Katie!" he yelled. "Katie, I swear I'll be a help to you and you've nothing to fear. I'm not like my father. I'd never marry you unless you wanted to. But . . . well, god damn it, how you ever going to want to if you don't get to know me!"

"I don't want to get to know you, Jude Ludlow!" she yelled back at him in anger and frustration.

He cursed then, a hard, bitter curse that normally would have burned her ears but now meant nothing.

As Rebel and Taffy trotted toward the flock, sensing it was time to cover ground, Katie began to saddle her old sheep horse. Everything was packed in the same buckboard that Micah had used. Let Jude tie his horse to the tailgate and drive the wagon! She would ride, and if this sudden complication meant staying another year or leaving her sheep, Katie thought she had no choice. When Micah arrived, somehow they would have to overpower Jude, tie him up, and stampede his horse, then run for Wyoming Territory.

If that were her only choice, she would save herself and her father, take her dogs, and abandon her sheep. The idea of it, though, the thought of losing all that she had worked so hard to gain, almost made her ill.

Katie took a deep breath and listened to the gentle whisper of the wind move through the pine needles. Gray squirrels overhead worked like diligent trapeze artists, leaping from branch to branch as they stored winter food while the jayhawks made raucous fun of their industry.

She loved these mountains, the brisk nights and glorious blue skies with pearly white clouds so close to the peaks that at times it seemed as though you could almost reach up and touch them. This was her second autumn at the sheep-wagon camp, yet its magic remained fresh. Was that old bear's den still unoccupied over on the east of Padre Peak? Did that spring still taste as wonderful as she'd remembered? And could the roof of that old trapper's cabin possibly have survived the weight of yet another winter snow without buckling?

Despite her resolve to treat Jude so coldly he might go away in anger, Katie's own excitement of discovery won out, and together they had explored these old finds of hers, even the stand of big aspen trees where Jim Bridger and other trappers had carved their names and the date of their encampment, 1850.

At the end of their first day in the mountains, Jude was obviously reluctant to return to his own small camp. And now, as he prolonged his stay, Katie knew that she must insist he leave the mountain at once, or it would soon come to the point where he would be camping on her wagon step.

"Jude, don't you see? You have to go or everyone at Temple City will think badly of me," she told him.

He was instantly defensive. "I don't care about idle gossips, and I didn't think you would either."

"Well, I do," Katie said. "I have to live among them this next winter, and I don't want to feel their scorn or have to defend my honor. There will be talk, and no amount of denial will silence what their minds put astir. It will be awful for me. It's not fair. And I'll blame you, Jude."

He glanced at her in brooding silence, then jammed his clenched fists deep into his coat pockets and raked pine needles back and forth with the point of his scuffed leather boot.

"I never thought it out like that. I didn't realize there'd be filthy talk among God-fearing women."

She felt hope stir deep inside and tried to smother her growing excitement. "They're good women, but they are only human."

"But why? My bedroll is a good quarter of a mile away. Katie, I want you to know that this has been one of the happiest days of my life, having you show me all of these things you found last year."

"Jude, I don't—"

"No, listen," he said in a firm but gentle voice. "I know how you feel about polygamy and what my father did to marry your sister, but I feel the same way. I'm not like Amos. You and I could be happy."

"I don't love you."

"But you could."

She shook her head as though confused. "Not if you stay up here. Not if you shame me in the eyes of everyone. If you stay here, even though you and I know it was only to help, those people down in Temple City will think differently." She continued, "It would be hard not to think of bad things."

"Yes, I can see that now," he agreed gravely. "I can even understand why you'd hold it strong against me. I love you, Katie."

He looked square into her eyes. "It doesn't matter that you don't feel the same way about me, because—"

"Jude, please stop!"

"I can't. You're the reason I came back to Temple City, even though I knew you were in love with Bryce. I had other women when I was gone."

"I don't want to hear about it."

"I had to tell you that. But each time I was with them I felt like I'd cheated on you. Then I'd get mad at myself, because you didn't give a damn about me. But that didn't help. Telling you now does, though."

Katie didn't know what to say. She'd had no idea that he'd suffered guilt or was capable of any real depth of devotion. He'd always seemed so brash and confident.

"I'm going now, and if I ride hard, I'll gallop into town before folks go to bed. It will lay to rest any talk."

"Thank you."

He tipped his hat. "Can I come up and visit now and then for the day?"

"Of course." Now that he was really leaving and doing it for her sake, she felt generous. "Come as often as you like, but just give me a week or so to settle in. Will you do that?"

"You bet."

Something in his expression warned her that he was going to try to kiss her. Katie stepped out of his reach. "Good-bye, Jude."

"Good-bye," he said. "Thanks for telling me straight out that I was wrong. It was honest. I appreciate that."

Katie said nothing as he left her, but she felt rotten about herself, because at daylight tomorrow she was leaving.

Jude waved from a distance, but she hardly noticed as big dark clouds piled heavenward.

Damn it, she thought, it looks like rain!

A bolt of lightning laid its finger of brightness across her canvas roof, giving it a soft yellow glow that was immediately followed by a crash of thunder. Katie sat up quickly. Her ears were sharply tuned now, listening for the familiar sounds that sheep make when they are about to run. She heard nothing, and after a moment she relaxed and lay back down on her soft, wool-stuffed mattress.

Sometime deep in the night she was awakened by Taffy's bark of warning and then Rebel's growl, almost on her doorstep.

She heard a low oath, and fear clamped its icy fingers on her heart. "Who is it? Jude! Jude, I've a gun, and I swear if you try to come inside I'll blow your head off!"

She fumbled for the gun, located it in the darkness, and drew back the hammer. "I hope you don't think I'm bluffing, Jude, 'cause I'm dead serious."

"I'm not Jude, and I know you aren't bluffing," came a tired but oh, so familiar voice.

"Bryce!"

Katie dropped the gun on her blanket and flew off her bed to yank the door open. There was Bryce, sopping wet and still astride his forlorn horse. He tipped his hat, and a sheet of water splashed across the steps of her wagon. She could barely see him, the moon was so shadowed by cloud.

"May I come inside?"

The weariness in his voice was obvious. "I'm sorry. Yes! I'll start a fire so you can get dry."

"Thanks," he said, easing out of the saddle. "Got any grain for my horse?"

"Side barrel on the left. Help yourself while I start the fire."

Katie lit the kerosene lantern over her bed and quickly started a fire from the dry woodbox under the stove. She kept glancing toward the door. Maybe now there was a way. He had come back!

He took off his hat and whipped the water from its crown, then stepped inside with squeaking boots. The firelight leaped up to touch his face, giving it color and magnifying his features. He was clean-shaven now, and his face was no longer thin and haggard. He looked tired but determined. He looked once again like the man she remembered in Echo Canyon.

He was studying her, too. And not like the last time, when she'd felt like a horse or cow being sized up. Katie blushed and pulled her night wrap close about herself; she backed up until she was against the bed.

"Why did you return?"

He took a deep breath. "Well, Katie, the fact is I've done lots of thinking these past few weeks, and I decided, sheep or not, a man ought to fight for what's his own."

She wanted to sing with happiness, yet she contained all outward sign of emotion. "So you're going to help me?"

"I am. If you can feed me. Haven't eaten much these last two days. I've been working for the stage line in Echo Canyon. I got used to regular meals again."

"There's some cold biscuits in that drawer. If you want, I could cook up some venison," she said.

"I'd like that."

Katie stepped forward. Steam was now lifting from his wet pants, and in the tight confines of the sheep wagon she was acutely aware of his maleness and how difficult it was going to be to move about in this small space with him in the way.

"I'd go outside," he offered, "but it's still raining a lick. Might be I'd catch my death of cold and then you'd have no help at all."

"We don't want that," she said, moving toward him and trying to squeeze by to get the biscuits.

He turned as she brushed past him and reached out and encircled her waist with his arm, pulling her up close.

"Bryce, stop it!"

"I can't," he said, slipping his fingers into her hair and then covering her lips with his own.

She struggled for a moment, then yielded to his embrace. She couldn't help herself, and her arms betrayed her as they moved up his back and pressed him near. Her heart was racing, and she wished this moment would never end.

His hand slipped up inside her wrap, and when it covered her breast, its cold hardness shocked and scared her. "Bryce, no!" she cried, rearing back and slapping him with all her might.

171

He stepped away, reached up, and worked the hinges of his jaw, He wasn't angry, but he wasn't pleased, either.

"You were liking it, Katie. Don't tell me you weren't," he said roughly.

It was true enough, but Katie didn't care. She'd been around animals enough to know what he wanted to do, and that was a lot more than just kissing.

"Admit you liked it," he demanded.

"All right, I liked it. But you had to spoil it. That wasn't fair."

"Well," he conceded, "maybe not, but it was just starting to get interesting. Besides, I must have been blind last time not to see how handsome a young woman you'd be. You've ripened plenty since that night I kissed you down in Amos Ludlow's cellar. And just now any man would have done what I did, especially if he knew how sweet you were on him."

Katie blushed deeply. She wished she could deny what he said, but he'd know she was lying and probably just laugh.

"You want another kiss?"

"No," she said, wanting to so bad she ached inside.

"Didn't Rebecca ever tell you anything about a man and woman together?"

"I think you'd better go now."

She could feel his eyes measuring her resolve, and they must have overestimated it, for he grabbed a sack of her biscuits, saying, "These will do until morning. I'll be sleeping under the wagon. Do you want to leave at first light?"

She nodded. "Bryce, was it just your investment you cared about here?"

"Nope. I got to thinking about how you and Rebecca saved my leg in Echo Canyon. That makes up for a lot. For most everything that's happened."

When he left her, Katie stood by the crack in the door and thought about him for a long, long time. She was excited, confused, not sure of his feelings, and a little afraid she wasn't going to be able to control her own. The rain had slackened. The blanket of clouds was breaking up, and here and there a star poked through. Maybe she'd awake to sunshine.

She brought the dogs inside, where they shed water all over the floor and collapsed happily into separate puddles, and then she slipped back under her blankets and listened to the rain until long after midnight.

With Bryce right underneath and the mountains to the east waiting to be crossed, she felt too excited to sleep.

"At last," she whispered, "it is finally happening. We are leaving. Oh, Rebecca, wherever you are, pray that we can all safely reach you and that I won't . . . won't let anything happen more than the kissing!"

Chapter Eleven

Dawn was inching over the eastern Wasatch Range toward the very mountains they would have to cross when Katie finished cleaning up the breakfast dishes.

Bryce emptied his coffee cup. "Katie, we are going to need your horse."

"It's not mine," she explained once more. "Nor is the saddle. I'm going to write Amos a note explaining that I have taken provisions but only in fair return for three of my ewes and their lambs."

"So you intend to walk. To carry all your supplies."

"Only if you refuse to pack them on your horse and walk too," she told him evenly. "We must have nothing of Amos Ludlow's, only what is our own, so that if he overtakes us—"

"If? Of course he will. The day your father is missing is the day they will know we are on the run."

"Micah is giving us a week's head start. It would take them another two days to catch us. I've been told that those highest peaks mark the Bear River Divide and once over them we are in Wyoming Territory."

"True enough. But those mountains are rugged, and it might take us two weeks to drive the flock through. And what about Amos Ludlow's sheep? They account for two-thirds of what we've got. If you won't take his horse, how do you account for taking his sheep?"

"I'm not."

"If you leave them there, the wolves and—"

"I know," she said. "We'll herd them only as far as the Utah Territory boundary. When we see Amos and his

174

men following, we'll cut ours off from the others and run."

"Run?" His expression reflected disbelief.

"We'll do the best we can." Even to her it sounded weak. "Amos is not the kind of man who would let his own sheep scatter into those mountains. He will have to stop and gather them, and, without sheep dogs, he will tie up a lot of men just returning them to the valley."

"Sounds as though you've got this all planned."

"I've had months to think about it."

Bryce was silent for a few moments. "It's a good plan," he finally admitted. "And with luck it could even work. It all depends on getting that week to ten days head start. There's only one little flaw."

"What's that?" Katie asked. She thought she'd considered everything.

"It's that Amos and his men will not let any territorial boundaries stop them. If they want our sheep bad enough, they'll hound us across Medicine Butte and all the way to Fort Bridger."

"I have the receipts from Amos that show we have a legal title to our sheep."

"That's good," Bryce said. He gripped his gun butt. "But I don't think it's nearly good enough. I'll be waiting outside for you."

Katie finished straightening things up. She could hear her sheep bleating, and she knew it was because they had become used to a morning routine that called for them to be moved to fresh pasture. Well, they were going to move, all right. And faster than they'd ever been herded before or likely would be again.

Amos and his riders weren't their only threat. Katie hadn't found the nerve to tell Bryce about Jude's resolve to marry her and how she'd tricked him into leaving. When he discovered she'd deceived him, he'd be hot on her trail.

Katie tried to push those worries aside as she stuffed a burlap grain sack with her belongings. She passed over the Colt revolver, because it was not hers. But then she decided she must have it, even though it would cost her a couple of ewes and their lambs in trade. Wolves, coyotes, and men all waited to take what was hers. She would not allow that to happen.

She was ready, yet found herself hesitating inside this wagon, which she'd grown to love. She took one final look around at the squat little cast-iron stove that she was so fond of. On cold fall nights it glowed a bright cherry red, and it had cheerfully provided her with heat and fire. And the cupboards for which she'd finally talked Amos into giving her paint last year. Now they were a bright yellow, and they gave the wagon's interior a light, sunny feeling to help drive away loneliness. Finally, Katie examined the dried flowers and leaves she'd collected last fall and pressed between the pages of a book before carefully pinning them to the canvas over her bed. There were even a half dozen or so butterfly wings, so brilliantly colored they rivaled even the most spectacular of prairie sunrises.

Katie lingered at the door, remembering the many nights she had lain awake, feeling a warm veil of protection from this sturdy little home on wheels, even as she planned to leave it to flee this valley. And now . . . now she was afraid. Afraid because Bryce and her father were risking their lives on her account. She bowed her head in prayer.

"Dear Lord," she whisered, "you know I'm nothing special, and only the day before yesterday when that big ewe with the black lamb tromped on my toes so hard she like to broke them, I took Your name in vain. Then last night when Bryce kissed me—well, You know what I thought of. I'm ashamed and have no right to ask You for anything so soon, but I have to. You see, Amos and his friends are probably going to catch up with us, and if they try to take our sheep, I know someone is going to die. Don't let that happen, Lord. I'm asking You for that, and in return I promise not to allow Bryce to handle me like that again. I know it was sinful, and I could feel the devil's own temptation. I'll be stronger next time. But we need Your help, Lord. Thank You. Amen."

* * *

Micah knew he'd have to stop by his house and say good-bye on the way out, but he didn't want to. He and the widow Evans—funny, he still thought of her that way—hadn't had much of a marriage. He'd never succeeded in meeting her expectations, financially or socially. He'd tried hard enough, even learned a trade and become so good at it that a growing number of customers had asked him to do their harnesswork. In another year he'd have been an expert saddlemaker. People said he was as good as they'd ever seen with leather.

That's what had set him to dreaming again, dreaming in the same way he had before giving up his life in Springfield and taking his family to the goldfields. And what was wrong with a man trying to better himself? His mistake had been to tell the missus that he wanted his own saddle and harness shop. My God, how she'd stormed! She'd wanted no part of leaving Temple City. Then she told his boss, and he was finished. Micah shook his head with a mixture of anger and disgust. No decent work anymore and no future, except running errands and doing odd jobs for those arrogant Ludlows. Thinking about that and living with a loud, mean-tempered woman had driven him to despair and forbidden whiskey.

"Micah."

He snapped out of his dark thoughts and sat up straight on the wagon seat.

"Yes, sir!"

Amos studied him closely. "I'm trusting you not to make some foolish mistake. You have three sheep camps to visit, and that will take less than two days. We'll be expecting you back day after tomorrow."

"Sure enough," he said, staring up the road.

Jude pitched the last salt block up onto the wagon and lifted the tailgate. "Tell Katie I'll be up to visit Sunday next. Don't forget, now."

Micah forced a smile that became easier as he remembered that by next Sunday he and Katie would be long gone. "I'll tell Katie. You can be sure I won't forget, Mr. Ludlow." He picked up the lines, cracked them sharply across the rumps of the team, and as he drove away began to sing the most beloved of all the Mormon handcart songs:

> Ye saints who dwell on Europe's shore
> prepare yourself for many more,
> To leave behind your native land
> for sure God's judgments are at hand.
>
> For you must cross the raging main
> before the promised land you gain,
> And with the faithful make a start
> to cross the plains with your handcart.
>
> For some must push and some must pull
> as we go marching up the hill,
> So merrily on our way we go
> until we reach the Valley-O!

It was crazy, singing out loud that way in this private farewell as he drove through Temple City, but Micah felt good, he felt more alive than he had in a long, long time. Almost as alive as that glorious day when he and Beth had loaded up Rebecca and Katie, along with everything else they could, on a Conestoga wagon and left Springfield. It seemed like a hundred years ago. Beth. Now, there was a good wife, a fine woman. Being married again had shown him how fortunate he'd once been. Now, of course, Beth lay deep in placer soil, and it did no good to think back. Only tomorrow counted, and he was on his way to it, starting right now.

Micah drove up to his house singing. He tied the horses to his rickety picket fence, noting with a smirk that he was going to get away without repairing and painting the damned thing. He kicked open the gate and strode up the footpath, singing the chorus once more at the top of his voice. When he stepped up and opened the door, his wife and her friends gaped at him.

Micah lifted his battered hat. "Afternoon, ladies!"

"Mr. Prescott," his wife said with indignation, "singing is for church, not the streets!"

Nothing could bother him now, not even this woman's sharp tongue. "It's a good Mormon song, by heaven!"

"Of course it is," one of the ladies said. "And you do have a very fine voice, Mr. Prescott. It's just that we have babies asleep in the other room and it would not be nice to wake them."

"Oh? That's a real shame. Because, you see, I have to go away to the sheep camps for a few days and need to go in there and pack a small bag."

Mrs. Prescott pursed her bloodless little lips into a hard line. She was steaming, and he didn't care.

"I wish," she said with exasperation, "you'd had the courtesy to do that before you left this morning."

Micah shrugged, passed on by, and entered their cramped little bedroom. It was dim inside, but he could see a pair of children asleep on their comforter. Comforter, humph! Small comfort or pleasure he'd ever had in this room. His packing took but a moment, yet so great was his desire now to leave that he accidentally knocked over his wife's favorite basin and water pitcher. They shattered on the polished wood floor. The children exploded into shrieks of fear, and the doorway filled with women.

"Mr. Prescott!" his wife screeched. "That was a gift from my mother!"

Micah studied the accusing faces, then he marched forward with his head up high. His wife held her ground until the very last moment and then stepped out of the doorway.

"Good-bye, Willa," he said.

"You'll have to buy me another. They aren't cheap, and since you were thrown out of the harness shop . . ."

The front door slammed shut behind him, and almost boyishly he skipped down the path. He was on his way.

His wife yelled something he didn't hear because he began singing again. "For some must push and some must pull . . . until we reach the Valley-O!"

Katie pushed over a rocky crest, only to see yet another rise lifting toward more forest. To her left, a high ridge, or what some referred to as a cuesta, met her view. On its extreme left end it fell away sharply, but on the right it sloped gently toward an alpine meadow. The meadow was small, and at its north end she could see a beaver's pond. Earlier she'd heard the sharp crack of his tail on the water. This warning signal would be relayed along untold miles of streams. Higher to the east she could see a marching line of snowcapped peaks. They marked Wyoming and, she hoped, sanctuary from her pursuers. Up here the air was so thin it gave nothing to the lungs, and the color of the sky was pale, almost translucent. Even the clouds that sailed overhead seemed wispy and diffused.

But if the sky paled at this altitude, the forests shouted in their most glorious moment of fall. Alder, aspen, and birch competed for the eyes' attention. They clogged the streambeds and the ravines, slashing the mountainsides with brilliant reds, yellows, and oranges. Katie never tired of rounding a corner of the trail to see a new breathtaking vista, lovelier than ribbons of rainbow. Never had she seen such beauty among trees, but never had she been in such high, wild country.

The sheep were not impressed. Comfortable in the lowland pastures and winter basins, they were out of their element in these unfamiliar mountains. They smelled danger at every turn, and the spoor of a grizzly or a cougar sent them running like frightened children. The sheep were tired and fearful, and it was difficult to keep them moving. Again and again a ewe would suddenly and for no apparent reason bolt for freedom. Her lamb would follow, bleating piteously, and then the entire flock would stop, mill about with indecision, and then attempt to follow this one self-appointed leader.

The instant this scenario began, Katie would unleash a shrill whistle and the dogs would whirl to see her point. Tired themselves, out of breath, and footsore from the rocks, they would go after the fleeing ewe. Taffy would cut off the ewe while Rebel punished her with nips that hurt but never broke the skin. Together they would hound her mercilessly all the way back to the flock.

Rarely would the same ewe make this mistake again. Her lamb would rejoin her, and together they'd share the indignity of her failure. But the lesson never sank in to the whole flock, and the act was repeated six or seven times each morning and afternoon.

The first time Bryce saw the dogs in action he was astonished at their speed and amused by their obvious enjoyment of the work. He'd been leading the flock, and Katie had seen him lift his arms and applaud silently. That had really pleased her.

"Give him time," she said aloud, "and he'll make a sheepman. And he'll see that there's more to raising woolies than meets the eye."

Katie was aware of the contempt horsemen and cattlemen had for sheepmen. The shepherd walked in dust and manure; the man on horseback rode above all that and felt superior. It was an illusion. The shepherd was likely to be the stronger, if only because he was walking instead of riding. Then, too, because he was alone he had to be more self-reliant. There was no one to help him if the sheep were attacked by a bear or he broke his leg in a fall. A cowboy might chance upon a shepherd napping for a few moments under a tree during midday. The cowboy would ride away in disgust. But that night, while the cowboy slept peacefully, the shepherd might be up five times, scaring off wolves or coyotes. Yes, given time, Bryce would come to understand.

They chose a small clearing ringed by dark pines in which to stop late that afternoon. The grass was good, the water cold and sweet. Katie was starting a cooking fire and Bryce was bringing in more firewood when suddenly a crashing in the forest sent them both leaping for cover. Bryce levered a shell into his Winchester as they crouched behind a log.

"Don't shoot! It's me!"

Bryce lowered his rifle. "God damn it! Your father wasn't supposed to leave Temple City for another three days!"

She closed her eyes, shaking her head. Micah hadn't

given them the head start he'd promised. The men of Temple City would catch them for sure.

"Damn him!" Bryce cursed, punching the rotting log with his fist. "I thought he understood!"

Katie took a deep breath. She wasn't going to panic, and yelling would only make things worse. "I'll handle this, Bryce. He's my father and he wants to get away as much as we do. What's done is done. We'll just have to make the best of it now. Don't get angry with him."

Bryce laid his rifle down, turned about, and stared off into the distance. "All right," he said grimly. "But I sure think you ought to at least tell him what he's done."

"Hello!" Micah called, kicking his horse into a trot and pulling on the lead rope of a pack animal. "Bryce Sherman? Well, good to see you! We're going to need your help. Wait till you see the supplies I brought."

Katie silenced Bryce with a glance and went to intercept her father. She could tell by his expression that he was in high spirits.

He half climbed, half fell, to the ground.

"Riding all this way bareback liked to kill me, but it was sure worth it to be here. Had to leave the buckboard yesterday, but I packed the best stuff along."

"You were supposed to give us a week, Father. We needed that time to reach Wyoming."

"I had to come when I had the chance, Katie. You know that. It'll be all right. Wait until you see the ham I brought and all the—"

"We need the time!" Katie said harshly.

He'd started toward the packhorse, but now he halted, and she could see his lean body stiffen. His face became red.

"Well, damn it, if I didn't think I did right! They weren't expecting me back for two and a half days. They'll lose another by going up to your sheep wagon. I thought it all out."

"So did I, and we need more time." She'd never spoken to him like this before, as if he were a naughty child. "Father, why didn't you listen for once in your life? Amos won't go to the sheep wagon. He'll follow your tracks, and in two hours he'll guess what you're up to. Do you think he's a fool? Do you?"

Micah stared at his feet. "No," he said quietly, his eyes losing their brightness and filling with doubt. He wrung his long, thin hands and said bleakly, "I didn't have any choice, Katie. They sent me out early, and I had to go or stay. There just was no choice. I . . . I couldn't stand it any longer."

Katie bit her lip. Damn it, but she couldn't find it in herself to condemn her father. Not like Rebecca. Yes, he was weak and selfish and foolish. Yes, he had ripped their family apart, torn it up by the roots, and dragged them across the western face of the continent to a land where her mother had suffered and died. But he'd never meant to hurt anyone. Amos was evil; Micah Prescott was just a failure.

"We're finished," Bryce said, walking up to stand beside her.

"Finished?" Micah cried. "Why, that Bear River Divide can't be more than fifteen or twenty miles ahead. We could be over it by tomorrow morning."

Katie shook her head. "Not with these sheep."

"I just don't know," Bryce said wearily, his eyes studying the distant range of mountains. "You and your father could be in South Pass City without these damn sheep in just three, maybe four, days."

"You mean you want to give it up?" Katie cried in outrage.

"I could work on the railroad for good money. It's already come into Wyoming."

"Then do it," she said between clenched teeth. "But if you walk away from this now, these sheep are all mine."

"Damn," he swore softly. "I'd give them to you right now if I knew they'd stay yours. But they wouldn't. That sonofabitch Amos would have them by tomorrow night, and the thought of it just kills me."

Katie relaxed. He wasn't going to give up after all.

"I hate Amos's guts," Bryce snarled. When he looked up at her his expression was deadly. "He took what should have been mine twice already; I won't let him do it again."

Vida and Rebecca. That's what he meant. "We'll fight them all the way to Wyoming if we have to," she told him.

"There'll be no quitting and no leaving this flock in those mountains. Father, are you agreed?"

Micah swallowed noisily. "We can't stand off Amos and his men if we're greatly outnumbered. Those damned sheep aren't worth our lives."

"Jesus!" Bryce screamed in anger. "You're the reason we're in this mess!"

"He didn't mean to bring it down on us," Katie said.

"But he did." Bryce stabbed a forefinger into Micah's chest hard enough to drive him back a step. "You let Amos have your oldest daughter without so much as a dog's whimper. You going to watch him marry off Katie, too? What kind of a man are you?"

Micah opened his mouth and closed it like a fish. His entire body started shaking, and then his fists knotted up at his sides. He leaned back, and with a cry of rage he punched Bryce squarely in the mouth.

Bryce staggered, touched his lips, and stared at his own blood with amazement. "Well, well," he murmured. "At least now I know there is a man inside you after all. Maybe even enough of one to stand up and fight for your own daughter."

Micah examined his bruised fist, then turned and walked away in silence.

"Father?"

Bryce caught her arm. "Let him be awhile. He needs to think this all out and understand that he's got to help us. He's probably always been a runner. It's hard for that kind to fight."

"He'll fight this time."

"I sure hope so, Katie. In the meantime, I think it's time we settled on a plan for tomorrow."

"I'm listening."

"We both know the only chance we have is in splitting the sheep up."

She didn't know that at all and began to shake her head.

"Katie, start thinking instead of feeling," he said roughly. "The only way either of us will keep our investment is if I take Amos's flock and use 'em as a decoy while you head for that divide I pointed out that leads to the Bridger Basin. I'll be leaving tomorrow at dawn."

He was right. All along she'd feared it would come to something like this, and now it was happening. She put her arms around him and hugged him with all her strength. "Take Rebel," she pleaded. "You can't move the flock without him. And when they get close, run! Run the very first moment you see them."

He stroked her hair. "I will. And I'll find you in Wyoming. Just keep pushing them toward South Pass City."

Bryce did not sleep well the first night out. He camped in a small grassy place, but a dense fog crept in around midnight and he had a difficult time trying to keep the flock from scattering. The fog remained through the early morning hours, and he had nothing better to do than smoke, try to keep warm, ponder the mess he'd bought for himself. Why had he come back? For the money? He'd checked around and quickly realized that Katie had been right all along—these damn sheep were worth a lot. Enough for him to buy a small ranch if he wanted, or just travel about the country for a while.

But it wasn't the money. He wanted a woman, and if he couldn't have Rebecca, her sister was the next best thing. She wasn't as pretty, but she had the same smile and the same fire, and if he ever got her bedded, he thought she'd probably even be able to make him forget she wasn't Rebecca.

He wished he could quit thinking and dreaming of Rebecca, but he couldn't. Katie might be his only chance. She could make him money and give him a woman's love. Maybe that would be enough. Nobody ever got all he wanted in this world, and he wasn't going to either.

Bryce pushed wearily to his feet. "Rebel, I'm damned near as stiff as you are this morning. Fog does that to the body's joints. Let's start walking it out and get these miserable woolies on the prod."

It was mid-afternoon when he saw a glint of sunlight on a distant mountain ridge. Bryce began to push the sheep faster. The chase was almost over. Rebel kept glancing back at him with a questioning look.

"I know you don't approve," Bryce explained, "but I don't want 'em to catch us before sundown, and that's when I plan to scatter these woolies all over this mountain. Knowing Amos Ludlow as I do, he'll go crazy trying to gather them out of the forest. It will give us a whole night's head start."

But the old dog didn't seem to understand. The dog was fretful when it came to the sheep. Bryce admired that. If all cowboys showed that kind of dedication, there'd never be an animal lost on a cattle drive or a roundup.

By sundown Bryce was staggering with weariness and the sheep were ready to drop.

"It is time," he said, gazing toward the growing body of approaching riders. "It is time."

He cocked his Winchester and entered the flock. Normally they'd have milled away from him; now they just stood with their heads down and waited to see what would happen next.

"I've got a little surprise for all of you," Bryce said. "All your stupid little lives you've wanted to scatter and run. Well, tonight is your big chance, eh, Rebel?"

The dog waited for his command.

Bryce lifted his rifle and fired at the setting sun.

"Ya!" he yelled, firing again and again as his rifle shots boomed off the hillsides and crashed through the trees. "Ya!"

The terrified sheep scattered across the grassy clearing in every direction.

"Look at 'em run! They're like a sackful of jackrabbits turned free! Reb . . . Rebel! Come back!"

But the sheep dog was gone. Streaking for the edge of the clearing, he slammed into a ewe and knocked her full circle, then snapped at others as he barked ferociously.

He raced along the perimeter of trees, driving the flock back into the open grass.

In the fading light, the old black and white dog was a darting shadow of color and movement. One second he was visible, the next he was not. For a long moment Bryce forgot everything in his admiration for the grit and dedication he was now seeing. Rebel was driving himself beyond the limits of his years, using every ounce of his muscle to do what he'd been born and bred to do. And it was a fine thing to see! A beautiful testimony of character and courage. The stiff old dog he'd seen only this morning was no more, and Bryce was awed.

"You sonofabitch," he whispered. "You're going to do it if I let you. Damn your heart, Rebel. Damn your big old heart anyway!" And he cursed himself, too, because he should have foreseen this and tied up the dog.

Distant gunfire rattled along the mountain ridge, and Bryce turned to see riders galloping to reach the far edge of the clearing.

He lifted his Winchester and yelled, "Rebel, come!"

The dog swerved and came to a halt. He lifted his head for a moment, but then he was off and running as a ewe and its lamb became entangled in the brush. Bryce watched him drive them back out and then race back to his work.

Bryce scrubbed at his eyes. "Damn it, old dog, we're dead out of time."

His rifle cracked a moment later and Rebel folded in mid-stride and went tumbling into sheep. He tried to rise, and Bryce sent a merciful bullet through his chest as the sheep ran in panic and Amos Ludlow's gunfire answered his own.

Bryce fired twice, and a horse and rider somersaulted in the fading light. Then he whirled and ran into the forest. Immediately he was in almost total darkness, slipping on pine needles, barely dodging fallen trees and branches. He could hear Amos's thundering voice and the pounding of hoofs across the clearing. Brush crashed and bullets blindly probed the forest. Bryce dropped on the undergrowth and went sprawling as a horse and rider charged by only a few yards to his left. He froze and waited until the gunfire faded. He knew they would find him in the morning and that Amos would overtake Katie unless he did something.

Bryce checked his weapons. He needed a horse and one hell of a lot of luck.

It was after midnight when Amos and his followers doused the fire and went to sleep. Overhead, cold gray clouds sailed in silvery silence across the moon; in the crowns of the tallest pines, a chilling north wind swept before an early winter storm. Bryce stared at the flock and the stiffening body of what had been one damned fine sheep dog.

A great horned owl launched itself from the bough of a pine and flew in silence to hunt. Bryce checked his weapons once again and began to move. A quarter of an hour later he closed his hand slowly over the muzzle of a picketed horse, then stroked its neck with more assurance than he felt. He untied it, then the others, without a sound except for the thumping of his heart.

He could barely see the animals, but by running his hand across the chest and foreleg muscles he thought he could tell the stoutest and fastest mount. When he found it, he looped its halter rope over its neck and joined it to the halter on the other side.

Wish I could find a saddle, he thought, casting about. He tugged, and the horse followed willingly enough. Groping forward, certain that he'd find a decent saddle, Bryce tripped over a sleeping man, who grunted in sharp pain.

Bryce kicked out and the man yelped. The horse reared back, and Bryce was lifted off his feet and dragged until he could jerk it about and swing up. Then, as a gun winked orange flame, he batted the horse across the rump with his rifle and saw the picket line scatter in fear at the sudden noise and commotion.

Curses and gunfire laced the night, and Bryce headed for the clearing. The Mormons had managed to round up quite a few of the sheep, but as Bryce thundered through the flock, they scattered again.

A man appeared, and Bryce flattened against his horse's mane and ran him down. Then he was across the clearing and plunging into the forest again.

"Whoa!" he hollered as dark formless shadows flew past.

But the horse was too strong and, free of any steel between its jaws, it plunged onward in spite of the man on its back. For one instant, Bryce saw the tree limb, and before he could duck, it caught him across the neck. A terrible pain blossomed inside of his head, and his mouth flew open as his body was torn from the horse. He dropped onto the forest floor, and his Winchester went sailing into the brush.

By all rights he should have broken his neck and died quickly. Instead he lay writhing on the pine needles, strangling for air that would not come. He cursed in anger, sure that he was going to die, die just as hard as a common horse thief kicking at the end of a noose.

He passed out, woke minutes later, gagged, and rolled, pulling at his swollen throat until a little air came. And then he just lay there, trying to breathe and wondering why he hadn't seen Jude Ludlow in that camp and if he'd already found Katie.

It was that question that burned away his pain and made him climb to his feet, hunt up the rifle, and set his sights on the cold blue snowcaps of the Bear River Divide. Quitting a thing while you still had the breath to see it through just didn't seem right to Bryce Sherman.

Chapter Twelve

Katie shaded her eyes and stared into the distance. The optimism that had grown since she and Bryce split the flock had faded. The Ludlows hadn't fallen for the ruse. They'd apparently also divided their pursuit, and now Katie knew that she and Micah would have to fight, because there was no time left for escape. A quarter of a mile back they'd climbed above the timberline, and there wasn't even a place to hide.

"There are only four riders," Micah said. "The rest must have gone after Bryce."

"Four or forty, does it matter?" she asked bitterly. "We've only one rifle and a pair of handguns. That won't stop them."

Micah cursed. "We're less than three miles to the divide. Two hours! We're so damned close!"

Katie whirled. In the high, cold air, the pass was magnified and appeared even closer than it was. Yet two miles was a fair estimate of the distance, and she guessed her flock could make it in an hour if pushed to the extreme. She frowned, then knew that she hadn't come this far to give up to the Ludlows.

"You'll have to push the flock on through alone, Father."

Understanding crept into his eyes, and he stiffened. "No, Katie!"

She had no intention of arguing and none whatsoever of allowing her sheep to be returned to Temple City.

Their rifle was lashed to Bryce's horse along with their meager stock of provisions. "Taffy will do most of what needs being done," she was saying as she pulled the rifle

190

free and checked that it was loaded. She'd never shot at a man before, but if they didn't turn back, she guessed she would. The thought of sending a bullet into a human being was something that she couldn't bring herself to think about. "Just keep them moving, Father. Don't let them stop and lie down, because I think it's beginning to snow."

He stared up at the sky. "Yeah," he said. "Yeah, it is, Katie."

"Good-bye, Father."

His eyes locked with hers, and his head slowly began to shake back and forth. "No," he grated. "By God, no!"

Micah tore the rifle from her hands. "*I* have to go," he said. "If I don't, I'll kill myself, I swear I will!"

He meant it. Katie knew that this time he wasn't making a show of false bravery. She mumbled something about how they'd probably turn back if he fired a warning shot, but it was a lie and they both knew it, so the words just died in the wind and she let them go.

"You'd better hurry, girl."

She nodded, reached up, and hugged his neck. "Damn it!" she choked. "Father, I don't want to lose you. Don't let them hurt you. Please, don't."

"You know I'm no hero, Katie. I'll just hold them off for a while and then give myself up." He pulled her arms away. "You go on now, before they catch us. Go on."

"Father . . ."

He half turned. "I'm still one of their congregation. I'll be fine."

Katie watched him walk away and couldn't help but feel proud. Striding purposefully down the mountain, Micah even looked different. He wasn't stooped over and shuffling now. His chin was up and his shoulders squared.

"I'll wait for you on the other side!" she called.

He glanced back and lifted the rifle in salute but did not break stride.

In the few days since Rebel had gone, Taffy had assumed total responsibility for the flock. She was young and inexperienced, but Katie was gratified to see how well she did on her own. Together they drove the protesting sheep over the stunted grass and lichen-covered rocks faster than they had ever been driven.

She topped a low ridge and glanced back; she could see Micah hunched down behind some granite boulders. He looked so small and vulnerable against the land she wanted to cry and to go back. Rebecca once had said he was a terrible shot.

The pass towered over them. Sixty feet across and twice that deep, it was a hatchet slice in stone. To the northeast, the sky was black and lightning splintered across the heavens. Far away, like the sound of distant artillery, thunder rumbled.

The snow she'd so feared was slanting hard with the wind, but thank heavens it was behind them. It almost seemed to be urging them to run faster.

But then she heard a new sound. When she realized it was rifle fire, she stopped and listened as Taffy pushed the sheep on alone.

The wind drove the gunfire at her, scattering it into snatches of sound. Katie looked back. "Run!" she yelled at herself. "Run!"

But she couldn't. Not with Micah back there alone. He was her father!

She heard Taffy's sharp barks as the flock entered the pass. How she had dreamed of watching her sheep move into free Wyoming! But always in her imagination it was a beautiful day, and she and Bryce . . .

The cry of a human in distress reached her ears, and she knew it was her father and that he had called her name. Katie sobbed and began to run back to find him. A bunch of sheep weren't worth her father's life! She ran straight into the rising snowstorm and let it numb her face and blind her with ice.

When she finally breasted the last ridge, she had to wipe the snow from her eyes to see the knot of men who were crowded around the form lying still before them. She knew before she even reached them that it was her father, and that he was dead.

"He's gone," Jude said, detaching himself from the oth-

GET FOUR BOOKS TOTALLY *FREE*—A VALUE BETWEEN $16 AND $20

PLEASE RUSH
MY FOUR FREE
BOOKS TO ME
RIGHT AWAY!

Leisure Western Book Club
P.O. Box 6613
Edison, NJ 08818-6613

AFFIX
STAMP
HERE

ers and coming toward her. "He wasn't supposed to die."

The men parted, and she knelt by her father's side. She brushed snowflakes from his face and hair and bit her lips to keep from shouting her pain. At least, she thought, he looks peaceful. He looks almost happy. His entire life had been a struggle, a disappointment. She wondered if maybe he'd tried to get himself killed.

"I tried to talk him into putting the rifle down," Jude said, cradling a bloody arm. "He just opened fire on me and the rest of us. He gave us no choice at all."

"He was always afraid of pain," she said. "I hope it didn't hurt him too much."

"He died instantly. I swear he did."

"It's better than him being hanged."

"We wouldn't have," Jude said in an injured tone. "We're not like Amos. I told them you wouldn't take any sheep that weren't your own."

"That's right," one of them said. He was a tall, sharp-featured man whose name Katie had forgotten. "We'd decided to help you get what was yours out of this valley. And that's the truth."

Jude cleared his throat. "And another thing that's the truth is that your pa, he wanted to die. He gave me no choice. I'm sorry."

"He did want to die, I think," she said, looking down onto his face. The deep worry lines she'd always remembered were gone now.

Jude squeezed her arm. "Bryce came back, didn't he? He's the one who took my father's sheep to the northeast."

There was no sense in lying. If Bryce was successful, he'd be on his way to meet her beyond the divide. And if he wasn't . . .

"I know it was him. If they catch him with Pa's sheep, he'll swing from a pine tree."

"They're not going to catch him!"

"I think they will. Just before we left town, Amos sent for an outsider. You may have seen him in Temple City once or twice. His name is Hubie St. Clair. His father was French, his mother Sioux. He's a tracker, a mountain man. Father hires him to . . . well, to take care of special problems."

When Katie said nothing, Jude continued. "Hubie is the finest tracker and hunter alive. He could outshoot Jim Bridger. Bryce shouldn't have come back. I gave him the only chance he'll get."

Jude's voice was urgent. "If you knew where he was heading, maybe I could save his life."

"I don't know where he intended to cross the divide," she said. "When we left, we were still below the timber-line. Trees were all around. We are to meet in Wyoming, but I'll not say where."

"Then you don't believe me."

"Do you blame me?"

"No," he said, pushing himself to his feet. "We'd better go back now. We'll bury your father right and proper."

Katie shook her head. "Bury him in the forest, not in your cemetery. He was always a private man and never one of you. Please, bury him quietly and alone."

"All right," he said. "None of us wants to get caught up here. Katie, are you sure you can go on?"

"I'm sure of only one thing, and that's that I have to try."

Jude wanted to protest, but he didn't.

Katie could see the struggle in him. "You were right. You're not like your father."

"Katie . . ."

"Good-bye."

She left them, not wanting to see them lift her father and drape him face and feet down across the back of a horse. Katie imagined they would just tell Amos she'd gotten away after being fired upon. It would save them all a great deal of trouble.

The pass was obliterated by the snowfall, and she put her head down and trudged grimly onward. If she lived to see Rebecca again, she'd tell her about the death of Micah, how he'd ended his life standing up for something he loved. It was very important for Rebecca to know that.

A sudden icy gust almost knocked her down, and Katie felt the cold seeping up from the bones in her feet through all the other bones. She had never before been so cold and so alone. It seemed that death stalked this mountain. She hoped to God Bryce was over the divide and out of Utah. Maybe this horrible Hubie St. Clair would not follow him into Wyoming. Maybe, but she doubted it. He would follow Bryce just as fiercely as this accursed blizzard would follow her. The odds were that neither of them would make it.

Bryce was gasping for air when he finally clawed his way up into the high branches of a big pine tree. It was rooted into a boulder-strewn hillock, thus affording him a commanding view in every direction. He could see a storm approaching and wondered if it carried snow and if Katie was locked in its grip. Bryce pushed the thought away. He could not help her now; he could only help himself by being vigilant.

Bryce inspected the land as a jeweler would inspect a diamond. He noted its colors, every facet of its shape, and how the trails and rivers crisscrossed. A full half hour later he was convinced that there was no pursuit. He twisted about and studied the divide, finally choosing a small gap that could be approached to within a mile via a gorge dotted with boulders. It would be slow, but possible only on foot, thus giving him an even chance. A gust of wind shook the tree branch on which he rested and a splatter of icy raindrops touched his cheeks. The rain would turn to snow after the sun went down. For him, that meant his tracks would be covered; for Katie and the sheep, it could spell disaster. Bryce shivered with the cold and vowed to be through the pass and on his way down by morning even if it meant hiking in a storm all night. He was a horseman, and every time he remembered how he'd chosen a horse as jugheaded as the one that had spilled him last night, his anger returned. He'd walk out, but it would be one hell of a long, miserable night.

He was just beginning to ease down from his branch when a glimpse of movement made him freeze. Bryce flattened against the rough bark of the pine and his lips formed a hard, bitter line.

It was they. Hubie St. Clair. Amos Ludlow.

They were less than two miles away, shadow figures in deep forest. Hubie was tracking him, leading his Appaloosa stallion, probably grinning with the fever of the hunt.

Bryce scrambled down from the tree, grabbed his Winchester, and started walking very fast. He needed to reach that gorge, and he hoped to find in it enough water to erase his tracks. Thank God he'd spotted them and knew they were on his trail. He also knew that Hubie's big Sharp's rifle had an effective range of at least six hundred yards, at least three times the range of his Winchester. Bryce had to stay outside that range-until past nightfall.

By the slant of filtering sunbeams, he guessed there was a good three hours left of daylight. That was not encouraging. Hubie and Amos could overtake him in half an hour if they spotted him.

He splashed into a stream, and a great cloud of mosquitoes and gnats lifted from the mossy earth. Bryce staggered upstream, beating frantically at the insects and trying to keep them out of his nose and eyes. One got into his ear, and he almost dropped his rifle in the water trying to dig it out. The stream was ice cold, and wet numbness seeped up into his body as he clawed his way on through the tangled trees and thickets. Twice he came upon beaver ponds, and, to avoid leaving footprints in the mud, he had to wade in hip-deep. With his arms stretched high overhead to keep his few provisions and his weapons dry, the mosquitoes layered his face with their bites. He wanted to go crazy with the pain and hate of them.

The canyon narrowed, and finally he knew he'd reached the gorge. The stream became swift and thunderous. The gorge was bathed in cold mist and moss. He climbed up onto the slippery rocks and studied what lay ahead. On either side of the water the walls of the gorge had broken away, leaving nothing but twisted trees buried in shale. Here and there a patch of brush had crawled out from under the rockslide and clung precariously to life, but both walls were essentially barren and scarred. They would be impassable. No, he thought, staring up at the rims nearly three hundred feet overhead, they wouldn't even have a good shot down into this canyon. He realized that he could settle in under the twisted trees until nightfall. They would have to come either up or downstream and climb over the scree of the rockslide. And that would be in his favor, not theirs.

In fact, the more he thought about Hubie and that monstrous old buffalo rifle he was so damned good with, the more Bryce thought he'd be a fool to go on and let them catch him higher up. And they would catch him. No government boundary would stop either Amos or Hubie from chasing him down or even allowing him to lead them to Katie.

Bryce dried the mist of the rain from his Winchester; it was just beginning to crystallize. Up on the divide, he knew it would be snowing. This gorge was not more than two miles long. He could see the top end of it where the last trees had made their stand on the mountaintop. Just beyond waited the divide and, probably, Hubie.

Bryce began to pick his way upward. Some of the boulders were larger than houses and a few even bigger than a fairsized hay barn. Just ahead he saw the massive remains of a pine tree that had been ripped off the wall and rolled down to the water. Its tangled roots were like tentacles reaching up toward a narrow slice of sky. He knew that he would find shelter under the tree from any overhead rifle fire.

He crawled down into the rocks and under the decaying trunk. The meat of the tree was infested with grubs and termites, and the bottom half of it was already eaten away. He chose a hiding place under the tangled roots; no man could crawl through such a barrier, especially a man as large as Hubie.

Bryce settled in to wait and tried to think if he had forgotten anything. After a while he decided he hadn't. It seemed his best—possibly his only—chance to beat Hubie.

Hubie had once spent a night at the Echo Canyon relay station, and Bryce remembered his ranting about the rush of new Oregon Trail immigrants. He'd hated them, but even more threatening to him was the rumor of the transcontinental railroad. Bryce had never forgotten Hubie's vow to wage all-out war on any rail crew or surveying party that tried to lay track over these Wasatch Mountains. His hatred for newcomers was vicious. He had boasted that there were some immigrants who had expected the Promised Land to be Oregon, but that he'd showed them a real quick shortcut.

Bryce had been only eighteen, and the other Pony Express rider staying there the same night was only sixteen. They'd both slept with their guns in hand and had expected to have their throats slit before daylight. He still recalled that Hubie stank of rancid bear grease and that his eyes were as black as obsidian. Bryce had been afraid of him eight years ago, and he was afraid of him still. If I have the chance, he thought, pressing his back to the rocks, I'll kill him first and worry about Amos later.

Time passed slowly but inexorably as the gorge filled with shadow. The sound of cascading water and his weariness made his eyelids heavy. Bryce set his rifle aside and dug in sand until he reached water. He cupped his mosquito-bitten hands and bathed his swollen face. Horseflies and mosquitoes were the two things he hated most, outside of Amos Ludlow.

It had stopped sleeting, but now it was starting again—only this time it was pure snow. Bryce knew he was growing stiff. He wondered if he might actually freeze to death if he didn't start a fire or begin to move about. One thing for sure, the temperature was falling.

Where were they? He pushed himself into a crouch. Maybe it was time to get this over with. When Hubie came, he'd just as soon see the man first. To have him drop down from the dark would be an awful thing.

"All right, let's see how it goes," he whispered.

Poking around in the rocks, he located a stick and removed his Stetson. Placing it on the stick, he raised it until it was exposed to a line of fire either up or downstream. Nothing happened. Bryce frowned, then moved the hat a few inches one way, then the other.

A rifle boomed. The hat disappeared. Bryce dropped the stick and grabbed his Winchester. He knew the sound of a buffalo rifle. And he knew Hubie was very, very close.

His bruised throat seemed to clamp down in fear, and he had trouble swallowing. Better to attack than to be attacked.

"Sherman, come out and die like a man!" Hubie called over the thundering water.

Like hell, he thought, tensing as he lifted the rifle to his shoulder. He peered up at the darkening sky. To the north, he saw a flash of lightning through a break in salmon-edged clouds. Along the rims there was a pencil line of sundown and the snow was spiraling in big lazy loops.

"Sherman!"

The voice was impatient but also uncertain. It occurred to Bryce that Hubie's refined sense of hearing had been neutralized by the water song, as had his advantage of greater rifle range. This was going to be close-quarter work, and Bryce decided his Colt .45 might be more useful than the Winchester. The gun felt comforting in his fist. Unexpectedly, he caught a whiff of bear grease. As he turned, the sky seemed to disappear. Hubie roared and dove for him with a raised knife. His Colt exploded lead and flame as fast as he could pull its trigger. The knife spun away to clatter on rocks, and Hubie's eyes widened as his big arms beat at the puckering holes blossoming across his chest. His roar became the scream of a wild animal as he fell. A root snapped but not before catching his body for an instant and twisting it half around.

Bryce tried to roll away yet only half succeeded. Hubie, still alive and thrashing, came down on him. His great bloody fingers clawed for Bryce's throat. Bryce jammed his forearm between them, levered Hubie away a fraction of an inch, and pulled his gun free. He shoved the revolver into Hubie's side and emptied the weapon just as Hubie's teeth sank into his cheek.

Hubie's mouth flew open, he reared back on his haunches, and then he shuddered and pitched forward, dead.

Bryce heard another sound, and he kicked Hubie's body aside and rolled. A bullet slammed down through the tree's roots, and Bryce clawed away dirt to pull himself deeper under them.

His gun was empty. He could hear Amos swear as bullet after bullet probed downward. One ricocheted off a boulder and nicked him. Bryce snatched two bullets from his cartridge belt, reloaded, and fired up through the tangled roots.

Amos cried out in pain. There was a crash of snapping wood, and Bryce realized Amos had lost his footing. The man was thrashing about in the roots, and his curses were terrible. Bryce aimed up through the falling dirt and shot again. A gun fell down into the hole. Bryce picked it up, and, barely able to stand, he gripped a root, pulled himself up, and stared at Amos Ludlow.

The man's complexion was waxy. His knee was shattered, and another bullet had driven up and into his hip. He had fallen backward and into the roots. He was too weak to break free and in shock; his head rolled from side to side. The snow drifted down to melt on his clothing.

Bryce felt a great wave of pity for him, but when Amos focused his eyes, there burned in them only hatred.

"Are . . . are you going to shoot me?" he rasped.

"No. I'm going to leave you to die or be found. Whichever. I don't care."

"Shoot me!"

Bryce hesitated. "If you were a horse or a dog, I'd do that," he said. "And if you were a good man, I'd help you. But you are Amos Ludlow, and so I'll do neither."

Amos swore weakly. "If I live, you'll regret this. I'll make you pay."

Bryce's mouth twisted cruelly. "If you live," he spat, "you'll be a pain-wracked cripple the rest of your days.

Every step you take will be living hell. No, sir, you are the one who is going to pay. You're long overdue."

It had begun to snow in Wyoming Territory, and Katie knew that she had to find shelter. She kept telling herself that this fall snowstorm was temporary, that tomorrow would be clear and warm enough to melt the snow, and that over in the Bridger Basin the sun would be shining and the grass still rich and nourishing.

Maybe Bryce was waiting just ahead and he had found a place out of the wind and snow where the flock could be sheltered. They would build a fire and dry out and be warm. How wonderful it would feel! Katie was so cold and exhausted she could barely place one foot before the other. She kept lifting her hand to shield her eyes from the falling snow, but her arm was too heavy, and through the falling whiteness she could not see anything beyond twenty yards. She was still above the timberline, though she could sense there were trees not far downhill. Just another mile or so. Katie knew that she could do it but that the sheep were finished. When she'd found them after leaving Jude and saying farewell to Micah, they'd been huddled in the pass. Together she and Taffy had struggled nearly an hour before the flock moved onward. To have remained up on the divide would have been sure death.

Now, out in this driving snowstorm without so much as a bush to hide behind, Katie saw her sheep beginning to buckle again and fall.

"No!" she shouted, running among them, lifting one only to see it drop when she tried to go help another. "Just a little farther!"

But though the young dog was trying her very best, not even her sharp teeth and Katie's yells could budge the flock again. They had been pushed as far as long as they could go, and they were finished.

Katie slipped on the snow and fell heavily. She groaned, pushed herself back up, and stumbled forward to a lamb that lay bleating weakly. Taffy was trying to worry it up, but the little creature was too exhausted. Its cries were piteous, its eyes pleading only to be left to die. Katie wanted to weep. This was all her fault! These poor, dumb animals had trusted her. They'd not asked or deserved to be driven into a snowstorm to perish.

"That's enough, Taffy," she said, kneeling beside the lamb and hugging it close. Its tired bleating made her heart ache, while beside them the young dog whimpered—confused, uncertain.

"We tried," Katie explained, gently stroking the lamb, feeling its heart beating next to her own. "We really, really tried, damn it, but we lost."

Tears froze on her cheeks, and Katie knew she had to go on ahead of the flock and hunt for shelter. Micah had died giving her a chance for a new life. And somewhere on this mountain, Bryce was trying to help her too. She couldn't give up on them, even though she felt like it.

"Come, Taffy," she said, easing the lamb down. "Maybe there is shelter close by. We have to try to find it. Some of these sheep can still be lifted and driven. We just have to show them the way."

The dog wagged its tail hopefully, and she followed it, trying to block out the sound of her flock.

Sometime just after dark she staggered into the trees and felt her legs buckle under her. She rose to her feet and went on but soon fell again, and this time she couldn't get up. She crawled until she was back out in the open, then rolled onto her back and gazed up at the starless sky. Powdery snowflakes spun down to melt on her face, and she watched the faint orange glow of moonshine fight to break through the clouds. She wasn't cold anymore, and she could feel a sense of peace quietly working into her mind. Katie thought it would be very nice indeed just to close her eyes and dream until even dreams sweetly slipped away.

Taffy whined softly, licked her face, and then sat up and barked sharply.

Her eyes opened but soon closed again. The dog licked her face once more, but her cheeks were numb. Katie dreamed of a long, shelf-sided canyon where the rocks were copper red and the grass rich and waving green.

Down inside the canyon the air seemed almost warm. Katie could feel that warmth, and she was happy to see that sheep dotted the valley's floor. She lay feeling the warm earth under her skin. She would have been completely content except for the barking of a dog. But the canyon was so lovely, and, besides, the sound of the dog was growing fainter and fainter. . . .

Rough hands were pulling at her, tearing apart the valley.

"Let me sleep!" she groaned, trying to push the hands away.

She heard a loud, solid smacking noise repeating itself over and over, and the valley of her dreams began to rock. Katie opened her eyes and realized her face was being slapped back and forth and that she could feel nothing. Above her loomed the impassive face of a squaw, and beyond her was an Indian chief. She was lying naked under a mound of buffalo robes.

The chief said something in his own language, and the squaw lowered her hand.

The chief bent down and pinched Katie's arm.

"Do you feel that?"

She nodded and tried to ask the questions that rose slowly into her mind like bubbles in a thick, boiling soup. But the bubbles burst and made her cough so hard that her eyes watered and her chest ached.

The chief spoke again in his own language, and the squaw left them alone. "She is going to prepare medicine," he explained. "I am Chief Washakie of the Shoshoni. Friend of Rebecca. You are her sister."

"My sheep," she groaned. "Did they all die?"

"We found them. Most alive. Some dead. My warriors carry to big cave and make fire. Next day sun shine and they grow stronger. We find grass."

"The next day. How—"

"Three days."

She stared around the teepee. On the earthen floor a fire crackled warmly in a blackened circle of rocks, and smoke curled lazily upward through a triangle of blue sky.

The squaw returned and forced Katie to drink a vile-tasting liquid that she almost threw up and that touched off another coughing fit.

"Taste bad, I know," Washakie said. "Tree roots and bark. Good medicine."

Katie nodded, hoping to God there was no more of the stuff to drink, though the squaw hurried away and she suspected it was to brew more. She felt hot and so tired.

"You've saved my life," she whispered. "I am grateful. You and your people are welcome to slaughter my sheep for food."

"We eat some. Not many. This snow is bringing elk to valley. Once we ate mostly buffalo. No more. Elk and deer now. Buffalo soon be no more."

"How do you know my sister?"

Washakie told her about his great friendship with Jim Bridger and Judge Carter at the fort.

Katie felt proud of her sister, but now there was another overriding concern, and that was for Bryce. "My friend was supposed to meet me here," she began.

When she was finished, Washakie said, "He came, and he is out with sheep and dog."

"He is?"

The chief nodded. "You want to see him now?"

"Yes. Yes, please!"

Washakie got up to leave, blew out his cheeks, then said gravely, "Him look like hell, Katie. Mosquitoes."

Katie didn't care. As fevered as she was, she wanted to laugh with happiness but knew if she did she'd start coughing again. Besides, as the chief left, in came the round-faced squaw with another bowl of steaming green liquid. Katie smiled at the woman, shook her head. "No, thank you."

The squaw bent down and pushed the bowl into her face, nudging it hard against her dry, cracked lips.

"No, thank you, I said it was—"

The squaw reached under her chin and started to pry her jaws open. Katie tried to protest but had no strength at all, and rather than suffer further humiliation she opened her mouth and drank the damned stuff. It was ghastly.

The squaw patted her on the head, rolled her big brown eyes around in a circle indicating lunacy, then struck her tongue out of the corner of her mouth and grabbed her throat as though gagging.

The effect was so comical Katie could not resist a smile. The woman stopped her antics, grinned without any lower front teeth, then picked up her bowl and marched out. She was going for more of the medicine. If I were dressed and well, Katie thought, I'd run for it.

"Bryce," Katie cried as the hot green liquid boiled back up her throat. "Help!"

Bryce crossed his legs and sat down beside her. His face was still puffy and scratched, but he was growing a full beard, and Katie thought it was going to look quite handsome. Mostly, though, she was just glad to see him again, to feel his presence beside her and to know that they had made it. He told her that the two hundred ewes and fifty-five lambs had survived. The Indians had butchered only three. Katie couldn't help but feel a sense of loss because of all the sheep that had perished—to have tried so hard and come so far only to die in an early snowstorm.

"We're lucky just to be alive." He told her about Hubie St. Clair and then about Amos. "There's something else I have to tell you, Katie. But let it wait until you're feeling better. I think you have pneumonia. You're still feverish."

She gripped his wrist as hard as she could, but there was no strength to her. "Tell me now."

He turned away to hide his face. Words seemed to choke in his throat as he explained about the final night when he'd been overtaken and had tried to scatter the flock and ended up having to shoot Rebel.

"Katie, I'm sorry. If there'd been any way . . . any way at all without shooting that dog of yours, I would have done it."

Katie squeezed her eyes shut, and with what strength

she had she pulled him down, wanting him to hold her as hot tears streaked down her cheeks. Oh, Rebel, she thought. Of course you wouldn't quit trying to save a flock. Oh, Rebel, I loved you!

"Go ahead and cry," Bryce said in a gentle voice. "I felt like it myself. I was almost afraid to tell you the truth."

She didn't trust herself to speak, so she just shook her head back and forth and held him close.

"Katie," he said. "I can feel the heat of you and the fever you carry. But it's going to be all right. The chief says we'll have to move you and the flock down into the valley where the Shoshoni winter. He says our sheep will be protected. But if we try to go on to South Pass City before spring, they could all die. The flock is in real bad condition. I don't know anything about sheep, but they don't even move away from a man they're so wrung out. I can count the ridges on their backbones. I say we have no choice but to stay with these people for the winter."

"All right. Yes, I agree."

Bryce took her hands in his own.

"Chief Washakie said we could have our own teepee. Just the two of us. I told him we weren't that way. He wanted to know if something was wrong with either of us. I said no."

He untied his neckerchief and carefully folded it, then dabbed away her tears. He smoothed back a stray lock of hair from her eyes and studied her face, then the curve of her neck. "Katie, we've both been through hell. Especially you. And I know you're a very sick young girl, but—"

"I'm a woman," she corrected. "I wish you'd remember that."

"I wish I had an excuse to. I'm wanting you real bad."

Her heart began to pound. "For right now, or for the winter, or what?"

"Damn it! What do you want me to say? That I love you?"

"Yes! That's exactly what I want. Do you?"

He ran his fingers nervously through his long hair.

"Maybe so, Katie. I told you about my childhood. My mother and father and how they died."

"I'll never forget that, but—"

"Every time in my life I ever really loved anyone, I lost them somehow. Loving for me comes hard because of that. Real hard. It might take a long time to love you."

"We have the time. All I have to be sure of is that it *can* happen. I've been in love with you for years. Ever since we met in Echo Canyon. But I'm not fooling myself anymore. I've seen what happened to Rebecca and—"

"She never gave a damn about me!"

Katie tensed, but he would say no more. It didn't matter. His sudden outburst told her that his wound still festered and might never completely heal. And yet she believed with all her heart that she alone might make him a whole man again, and that her love would prevail over anything that stood between them. If Rebecca could heal through her medicine, Katie thought, perhaps love could also prove a miraculous healer.

"Will you marry me? Chief Washakie said that if we keep house together we are man and wife. Shall I go, or stay?"

"Before I answer I have a question of my own. It isn't an easy one, but I have to ask. I want you to think it over carefully before you say anything."

"Whatever—"

"Let me finish. If we share a teepee, live as man and wife among the Shoshoni, will you legally marry me when we reach South Pass City?"

"Katie," he said after a moment. "You are the planningest woman I'll ever know. You never are satisfied with today but are always thinking about tomorrow. You want to build a sheep empire and you want me to promise you a preacher man. I'm beginning to wonder if you can ever be satisfied with what you have."

"Try me, Bryce. Give me love and respect and I'll make us both successful and happy."

Their eyes locked, and the amusement on his face slipped away. He saw she wasn't saying anything she didn't know full well was the absolute truth. "All right," he said. "I'll marry you before a preacher or justice of the peace in South Pass City when we get there next year if you'll agree to marry me right now according to the ways of these people."

Her heart raced; her mouth was dry. "You're what I want," she breathed. "And I can't change that."

She pulled back the buffalo robe, and he gazed at her soft, white nakedness. It was Katie who had the fever, but when Bryce tore off his clothes and climbed in beside her, she knew that the fever was his, too.

Chapter Thirteen

It was wintertime in South Pass City. Two blizzards had already swept the plains, and at night the temperature plunged toward zero. But underground the mining activity did not slacken its feverish pace, and the town was booming as men crowded the saloons and brothels. Let the blizzards roar! South Pass City was sitting on a mountain of gold, and they'd never reach its bottom. Whiskey flowed, Big Olive was getting rich, and no one cared a good goddamn about tomorrow. You worked, you fought, and a few of you got rich, but most just drank, and that wasn't altogether bad.

Trudy was awkward with child and even seemed to get tired, which bothered her tremendously. She kept busier than ever, doing washing, ironing, and mending, yet Rebecca could tell that her heart really wasn't in her work. Trudy loved her beautiful flowers and bountiful vegetable garden. Being inside made her fidgety, even a little short-tempered. Rebecca thought the new baby would change this, and besides, she was grateful she no longer had to struggle carrying buckets of water up from Big Hermit Creek. It hadn't gotten easier, and she suspected that her arms had been stretched two or three inches at least. Late in the evening, when she wasn't making emergency calls on her patients, Rebecca would help Trudy with canning fruit to sell. It was her main winter source of income besides the laundering. Bending over a steaming tub of water, she would proclaim, "Ve may freeze, but ve never starve!"

Rebecca would nod her head wearily. During the first two months in South Pass City she'd worked seventy hours a week for Dutch John to repay the loans he'd made to her for living expenses and medical inventory. Yet the arrangement had worked to her advantage as well as his. Dutch John's admiring customers had become her loyal patients.

There had been resistance, however. Her only competitor, a dentist, bitterly resented her practice—and her womanhood, which brought patients who sometimes just wanted to talk to Rebecca. Beeson told everyone who would listen that medicine and ladies did not mix. She might not have gotten so angry with him except that he was a terrible doctor. He'd never had a single day of training and clearly showed no indication of wanting to learn anything that would improve his sorely deficient medical skills. He was, however, very adroit in one narrow but important area of medicine, and that was pulling teeth. Everyone in town said that old Doc Beeson was a natural-born tooth-yanker. Rebecca scoffed at this after questioning several men. It seemed that Beeson insisted that a miner drink an entire bottle of whiskey before sitting in his dental chair. No wonder the miners thought he was painless! Rebecca had attempted to explain to him the advantages of using chloroform or nitrous oxide, but Beeson had laughed contemptuously and sworn that whiskey was better, easier to obtain, and a whole lot more fun to administer.

He'd make a great show of her attempt to get him to use chloroform, and he'd raised many a glass of whiskey in every saloon, shouting to all who'd listen that Rebecca was nothing but a quack. Even so, her medical practice had grown steadily. For the first time in her life she was financially independent.

Every night she counted her money and entered a running total in a little black account book. She'd taken it upon herself to raise her board to the limit of what Trudy would accept without a fuss. Also, she intended to deliver Trudy's baby. Rebecca had delivered a number of them with Devlin at Fort Bridger and more here in this mining town. Still, in an effort to increase her knowledge of childbirthing and medicine in general, she'd subscribed to one of Devlin's old journals, *The Physician's Friend*. The monthly magazine was obviously written with an eastern physician in mind, one who attended to a sedate and well-financed clientele. There was an abundance of articles on gout, in which Rebecca had scant interest. Also, because medical terminology was evolving so fast in the East, there were a frustrating number of articles that made no sense to her at all. Still, many were helpful, and she was encouraged by her slow but steady progress in gaining knowledge. It was most exciting to read about the many new fields of research. One day she hoped to see Devlin's name in print. He was never far from her thoughts, especially when she was setting a fracture or stitching up a wound. At such times she would remember the procedures they had used together when they were a team and in love. There was so much to learn, and at times she felt hopelessly incompetent.

"Dis husband of yours," Trudy asked one night as they huddled before the fire. "Is he ever coming back?"

Rebecca shook her head in a way that left no room for argument. "No. He is in Washington. D.C., probably teaching medicine or doing research." At least she hoped he was, rather than drinking himself to death.

"Vat's dis research?" Trudy asked.

"It's trying to discover new ways to do things better."

"Dey do dis research on showing me how to grow roses and vegetables bigger?"

Rebecca smiled. Most universities had started out as landgrant colleges, founded primarily to promote agricultural interests. "Yes, I think so. In fact, I'm sure of it."

"Den I like to do research too someday," Trudy decided. "I tink I show dem a ting or two maybe. Yah?"

"Yah," Rebecca teased. "I tink so too."

Trudy laughed gaily, the way she did whenever Rebecca slipped into her idiom. "You tease dis time."

"Yes, I tease," Rebecca admitted, thinking how fortunate she was to live with this woman. Trudy was a delight. Rebecca knew her life had been a struggle. Trudy's deceased husband had been a hard-living, hard-drinking man whose uncontrollable rages had terrified his wife. From bits and pieces of information, Rebecca had constructed a very unflattering picture of Olaf Peterson, and though Trudy would never admit it, most folks thought she was better off a widow.

But Trudy carried few if any emotional scars and openly admitted she would remarry as soon as she found a good, willing man. Trudy was a catch. She was big but not coarse or vulgar, and she had no illusions about becoming wealthy and having fine possessions. She just wanted a husband and a father for her child—someone kind, not ugly, and of temperate habits and an even disposition. She candidly told Rebecca she favored Dutch John, but there were others, big men mostly, who called out in greeting to her and came up to her gate to buy her canned vegetables.

With the advent of winter, fire became a real danger in a town made of rough-hewn boards and pitch-green posts. Men drank heavily to warm their insides and sat by cherry-red potbellied stoves to toast their outsides. Whiskey and fire were a bad combination, and in early December two miners were seriously burned when their rusty barrel stove collapsed, showering their shack with glowing embers. Too drunk to run for water, they struggled out of their coats and beat at the flames, making the fire roar ever more greedily. The miners had nearly died before abandoning their efforts. This kind of tragedy occurred over and over.

Cases of frostbite and pneumonia were just as frequent, and Rebecca was kept busy from morning till night. Now, as she examined a thin, ascetic-looking man in his late twenties, she was strongly reminded of that awful day when Devlin had lost his fingers. This man had frostbite and faced a similar fate.

"Well," he said nervously. "I know I had no business chopping wood all day without gloves, but I've been out of work since coming here and I needed the money."

Rebecca took a deep breath. How did you tell someone that they needed to have their fingers amputated? "Mr. . . ."

He smiled. "Ames. Bob Ames."

"Well, Mr. Ames, I'm afraid this is very serious. You don't have any feeling in these fingers, do you?"

He swallowed. "No, but—"

"What that means, I'm afraid, is that your . . ." She was struggling now, searching for some way to say this thing so that it would be easier on him. She couldn't find one. "Mr. Ames, I'm sorry, but I'll have to amputate."

He gasped. Jerked his hand away from her. "Absolutely not!" he swore. "I'm a bookkeeper."

"It's gangrene that will invade your hands, Mr. Ames," she told him gently. "Gangrene doesn't care about occupations or anything. I'm sorry."

"Sorry!" he cried, grabbing his hat and almost running toward the door. "Don't give me that! You're not sorry at all. And it's goddamn clear to me that you have absolutely no sympathy for your patients!"

Rebecca turned white with anger. "The last thing I want is to amputate your fingers. But I'm trying to save your *life*!"

He sagged against the doorway. Never had Rebecca seen such a hopeless and desperate look on the face of a man. "It can't be that bad! Yes, my fingers are swollen and discolored, but they'll heal! Can't we just give them a little time? Maybe you're wrong. Everyone is wrong one time or another. It's nothing to be ashamed of, Mrs. Woodson."

"I'm not wrong. I wish I were, but I'm not."

"How do you know for sure?" he cried. "Maybe there's something else you could do. An ointment. Can't you give me some kind or slave or medicine?"

"Mr. Ames," she said with compassion. "What has happened is that the tissue has died. It was frozen, and if you don't—"

He clamped his terrible hands over his ears and bawled, "You're wrong!" Then he fled the room, leaving her standing and wondering what she should have said and did not. If those fingers weren't removed, Bob Ames was a walking dead men. She was almost certain of it.

She waited for days for his return, and by the end of the week she was almost searching for him, asking strangers if they had seen the young bookkeeper. No one had. Finally, when she couldn't think because of the worry, she realized that he must have gone to Dr. Beeson.

Doc Beeson's office was a small, shabby room over a leather shop just to the west of the main street. Rebecca knew she would be extremely unwelcome, and the idea of going into her enemy's den was not in the least appealing, yet she felt there was no choice. Squaring her shoulders, she marched up the rickety stairway and entered. The office was empty, though she thought she could hear voices in the back room. Rebecca noted the big steel barber chair with its ankle and wrist straps, which Beeson no doubt used to restrain his patients during especially difficult dental surgery. The back wall was floor to ceiling with dusty bottles of every size and description. Rebecca moved forward to scan the labels of hundreds of brands of lotions, syrups, and medicinal powders. There was a scarred desk, a door covered with a dirty gray Army blanket, several dated calendars depicting healthy easterners who touted various medicines, and a box of dirty surgical instruments. The room reeked of cigar smoke, whiskey, and several other odors she did not even want to consider. On one wall was a picture of a nude. Rebecca smiled wryly to see that its anatomical parts were labeled inaccurately. On another wall was a crudely drawn sign: ONLY GOD WORKS ON FAITH. I DEMAND GOLD OR CASH.

"Are you quite through spying?" Beeson asked coldly.

Rebecca looked up at his voice. Her eyes jumped to the pale, sickly-looking man beside him. It was Bob Ames. "I'm not spying. I'm here to see my patient. How are you, Mr. Ames?"

"*Your* patient! By God, that's ripe!" Beeson sneered contemptuously. "Good heavens! You poor misguided woman. Are you so desperate for business that you chase those who have forsaken your practice, your ridiculous idea of medicine?"

She scarcely even heard him. Rebecca was staring at Bob Ames and feeling a rising sense of alarm. The man looked very ill. His eyes were sunken into his prominent forehead. A waxy sheen of perspiration covered his drawn features. His eyes were dull, and his lips cracked and crusted, indicating a raging fever.

"Mr. Ames, how have you been?"

He opened his mouth to speak, but Beeson cut him short. "You have no right to question this man. He is my patient now. Leave at once!"

When she stood resolute he rushed forward, grabbed her arm, and propelled her roughly toward the door. "Let go of me!" she cried.

Ames seemed to awaken as if from a dream. He walked out on the landing and escorted her down the stairway. Rebecca wanted to help him, but he seemed almost in a trance.

Beeson followed them down the stairs and out into the street, raving at the top of his lungs. "He's my patient!"

When he tried to grab Bob Ames, Rebecca slapped him. He staggered, cursed, and advanced with blood in his eye.

"I'd think twice about your next move," a man said as he stepped in between them.

"Damn right he'd better," another added as a crowd began to form.

Barely under control, Beeson shrieked that she was stealing a very ill man from his care. A man too incapacited in his mental facilities to resist. "I'm on my way to curing this man!"

"He's killing him," Rebecca told the onlookers. "For proof, we have only to remove those bandages from his hands."

"Don't you dare. There could be contaminants in the air."

"That's ridiculous," she argued. "His office upstairs is a pigpen."

"Best take off the bandages," one of the miners said. "Wyoming air never killed a man. Only bullets and bad medicine."

"Very well," Beeson said. "I'll show you."

He grabbed the frostbitten hands and quickly unwrapped first one, then the other. Rebecca stared in silent wonder. The fingers were also waxy, but gone was the swelling and the evil black color of a gangrene infection or any sign of frostbite.

"Are you satisfied?" he hissed.

Rebecca dumbly nodded. She could scarcely believe her eyes ! She'd been so certain of her diagnosis.

"So there we have it, folks! Maybe some of you are now ready to believe me when I say that a woman has no goddamn business posing as a qualified practitioner such as I am. This . . . this imposter of a doctor swore that Bob Ames's fingers had to be sliced off at the nubs. Sliced off! You men are miners. How would you feel about losing your own fingers to fatten this woman's bank account?"

Rebecca looked up and was not surprised to see doubt and accusation in the hard, unforgiving expressions of the onlookers. She didn't blame them for that even a little. "I'm sorry," she mumbled. "I made a mistake."

"A mistake!" Beeson roared as he began to howl with derision. "The only mistake you made was in telling these good folks that you knew something about medicine. Go back to Fort Bridger or whatever place you came from. We don't need or want you here in South Pass City!"

Rebecca left them. She was crushed, and all afternoon she wandered about in the nearby hills trying to imagine how she could have made such an unforgivable error in judgment. It was after dark when she finally returned home and told Trudy what had happened. "I was just plain wrong. I thought his fingers were every bit as dead and gone as Devlin's had been. Beeson is right about one thing: I am no doctor, and I've proved it again. I'm uneducated, just a pretender, and they can be dangerous."

"Den stop pretending," Trudy told her gently. "Go to school and become a real doctor, but den come back to us here."

That night Rebecca searched through her copies of *The Physician's Friend*. There were a number of medical schools back east, but she rejected many of them whose advertisements read like the labels and potions she'd seen in Beeson's office. One of the more colorful was the

Occidental School of Medicine, which claimed to teach the science of hydrotherapy, a method by which everything from constipation to warts and tumors could be painlessly soaked from the body with special extracts and oriental herbs and spices.

It was nearly two in the morning before Rebecca sent a letter to a school in Philadelphia whose advertisements were modest yet convincing, and that was affiliated with a local land-grant college.

> Dear Sir:
>   Today I realized how very badly I need a formal medical education. I have had some informal training, but there is much of which I am ignorant.
>   I would like to know how much your school costs and how long it would take to complete training. Besides the ability to diagnose frostbite, I would like to learn how to properly extract arrowheads and bullets, and to treat several frontier diseases endemic to railroad and mining boom towns.
>   I beg your assistance and your time in this matter, which is of the greatest concern to me.
>   Respectfully,
>   Rebecca Prescott

When Rebecca finally went to bed that night she still had a great deal on her mind. Once Devlin himself had suggested that she become a real doctor, yet she'd sensed he was not genuinely pleased by the idea. And he'd also told her that she had the hands of a surgeon—only knowledge and technique were lacking. She'd never forgotten how proud that had made her feel.

If I had the money, Rebecca thought, *I'd go to that medical school and become a doctor. And then I'd return to Wyoming and help these people.*

The next day, as she was on her way to see a patient who'd hurt his back righting an ore cart, Rebecca was caught by a man who was out of breath and in a great deal of agitation.

"Mrs. Woodson!" he shouted. "You've got to come quick!"

"What's wrong?"

"It's that bookkeeper fella, Bob Ames. He shot himself!"

Rebecca was racing after the man in an instant. When they reached Ames's hotel room on the second floor of a dirty flophouse she saw a large knot of men crowded around the door.

"Move aside! Mrs. Woodson is here!"

The crowd parted and Rebecca entered to see Beeson bent over his patient. Bob Ames appeared near death. His breathing was shallow and labored, his eyes already starting to glaze, though he still seemed to recognize her. He was trying to tell her something. There was a desperate urgency in his voice, and Rebecca leaned very close to hear better.

"Beeson," he gasped. "Beeson!"

"I'm here, young man. Don't worry. I'll attend to you."

"You . . . you and your goddamn leeches have killed me!"

The doctor reared back as though he'd been slapped. "You must be delirious!" he cried. "You have killed yourself."

Ames tried to lift his hands, and there was little doubt in anyone's mind that he wanted to grab the throat of the doctor. But the effort was a dying one. With a wrenching convulsion, he shuddered and lay still.

Rebecca was speechless for a moment. Never had she seen such pure hatred in a dying man's eyes. Then she said, "Why is this man wearing gloves?"

"His . . . his hands were still tender. It was a precautionary measure against infection."

Rebecca didn't believe that even a little. She yanked the gloves off before the doctor could stop her, and there was a gasp of horror from the onlookers. Bob Ames's hands were swollen and purplish with gangrene. Gangrene and the suction marks of leeches. Now she understood why his hands had appeared so pale yesterday on the street. Leeches had sucked away the subcutaneous blood and swelling.

Behind her, a man gagged and whirled for the door. Rebecca quickly covered Bob Ames's wrists and hands.

"He did have gangrene after all. It was spreading throughout his entire body. He realized he was dying and simply did not want to suffer any more agony."

"That's not true!" Beeson shouted. "My treatment was working. He died of a self-inflicted gunshot wound, not gangrene, and that's what the coroner's report will read. He wouldn't apply the leeches. I told him it wasn't pleasant, but—"

"Quack!" a miner yelled, yanking the doctor around and smashing him to the floor. "Goddamn bloodsucking murderer! You did kill him!"

Beeson's eyes widened in fear. "I did my best. I meant him to get well. Surely you men, my patients and friends, must believe that!"

"He ought to be strung up," someone in the room growled.

"No!" Rebecca said harshly. "He was doing his best. Let him go away from here if that's what he wants."

Beeson drew himself up. "If it's you they want, then by God it's you they shall have. I'll close my practice as of now," he promised, grabbing his bag and leaving the room with as much dignity as he could muster.

When he was gone, the tension and the bad feelings eased enough for one rugged miner to say, "Now that he's leaving us, Mrs. Woodson, I reckon you'll be the one who'll be pulling our fangs."

"Fangs?"

He opened his mouth and pointed to an incisor. "This one," he garbled. "Hurts like the dickens."

Rebecca felt a sense of dread. She'd never extracted teeth, though she'd watched Devlin do it. The practice of frontier dentistry required strength and determination. There was little finesse involved on the part of the practitioner, and a great deal of pain for the patient.

"Every Saturday afternoon," the miner was explaining, "Doc Beeson expected us to get drunk after the mines closed and come over so he could yank fangs all at once. It was a real party. Yes, ma'am, it was!"

"I'm quite sure it was. What was a normal attendance?"

The man shrugged. "Depends on how many fights

there was that week. Generally five or six of us. Sometimes more. We each had to pay five dollars. Doc, he'd buy some more whiskey if we ran out, so it wouldn't hurt so bad. He'd drink some too. Once he told me that he made more money pullin' teeth than anything else. You going to charge a whole five dollars too?"

Rebecca didn't want any part of yanking out teeth. But someone had to do it, and being the only doctor in town meant the job was hers. "If Dr. Beeson received five dollars," she said heavily, "then I shall charge exactly the same. Furthermore, I'll expect anyone who wants his tooth pulled to be at the Bull Dog Saloon Saturday at five P.M."

"Drunk, I hope," another man said. "I can't hardly stand it when you put them big hoof nippers in my mouth and start to jumpin' up and down. Drunk was bad enough. Sober, I'd go crazy."

"Then I suggest you stay out of barroom fights," she advised testily. "But if you must have a tooth pulled, then you have my permission to choose between the new and painless chloroform I recommend, or your whiskey."

"Reckon we'll all stick with the whiskey, ma'am."

As it turned out, Rebecca was unable to pull teeth that next Saturday, because she was busy delivering Trudy's infant son. "He's beautiful," Rebecca said with pride, holding him up for Trudy to see. "The biggest infant I've ever delivered. This one is going to be well over six feet."

Trudy reached for the child, her eyes shining with joy. "I was so afraid it vould be a girl," she confessed.

"Would that have been so tragic?"

"Yah," Trudy said quietly. "Girl be big cow like me."

Rebecca stared at the woman and felt her throat swelling up so that she could hardly swallow. "You're no cow," she said thickly, squeezing Trudy's hand. "You're one of the finest women I've ever met, and I predict you'll be married before your son is a year old."

Trudy beamed, then squeezed her son so tightly he squirmed. "You tink so really?"

"Yes, I do. And if Dutch John is half as smart a man as I'm sure he is, your son will be John Jr."

Trudy closed her eyes with a look of contentment. She began to rock her baby gently, saying, "Ve see, Rebecca, ve just vait and see. . . . I vish your husband could come back to you."

Rebecca turned away quickly. "I don't think that could ever happen, Trudy. He has gone far, far away. He'd never return."

"Are you sure?"

"Yes. But never mind that. For the present, we both have a new man in the house."

Devlin Woodson II sat beside the broad Potomac River and watched a flotilla of gray-bottomed clouds scud across a cold, pale sky. Out on the river he heard the sounds of fishermen and sailors calling out to one another as boats sailed by in busy confusion. The seagulls were fighting a stiff wind, diving and squawking around the fishing boats.

He disliked seagulls. Clean and sculptured for graceful flight, they gave the impression of being noble birds, while in fact they were profane and ill-tempered, with thoroughly disgusting habits. Seagulls were deceptive, just like sleek and pretty women.

He was in sight of his father's mansion, which glared down on him from the bluff above. Perhaps his father was even now spying on him again, using a mariner's glass to see that he didn't become too drunk to navigate his way up the bluff along the footpath he'd played upon so often as a small boy.

Devlin raised his pocket flask and toasted a close-passing boat. "To truth and honesty in love!" he bellowed.

One of the sailors happened to be watching him, and he waved and smiled. Unable to hear the toast because of the wind, he nevertheless returned the gesture. The sailor was the picture of health—tall and dark-skinned, happy and vital; he was probably returning to his wife and children after a long day of fishing. Rather than cheering Devlin, the sight of the sailor depressed him. He drank on in silence.

"I'm killing myself," he muttered as he stared at his mutilated left hand. He then added, "But not nearly fast enough."

If I had the courage, he thought, I'd use a gun. Slow destruction is not very gallant, but for that matter neither is suicide. He'd seen it on two occasions he'd rather have forgotten.

That was his trouble—he forgot almost nothing, not even the most minute detail of how Rebecca had felt, and laughed, and smelled, and . . . He drank deeply. And how she'd deceived and dishonored him in marriage and in a sacred trust they'd shared as husband and wife and in medicine as partners.

He knew that he could consider the marriage void both legally and morally. God knows that was what he wanted to do, what his father pleaded for almost daily. But that would be too easy, and he'd never taken the easy way out of anything.

Whiskey wasn't the easy way. He might have chosen to forget Rebecca in the arms of other women; they were his for the asking. But whiskey was a western opiate, and the West was still alive in him. Day and night, in a cozy fog of inebriation, he dreamed of great blue skies, the pageantry of a cavalry outfit on parade, and the sad dignity of the old Indian chiefs staring into a future they could never hope to understand.

Earlier that fall, in this very spot, he'd watched the sky darken with thousands of Canadian geese, and he'd wept unashamedly until the noisy birds' last cries had faded into the southern horizon. He relived how he and Rebecca had once held each other tightly and watched the great flocks wing southward out of the freezing north, down toward Mexico.

The crunch of a boot made Devlin stiffen. He took a deep breath, then raised his flask again, but as it touched his lips his father's hand lashed it away, sending it spinning in a silver arc into the murky Potomac.

"Damn you, son! When is this going to end?"

He was sorry he hadn't drunk faster; the flask was still half full, and whiskey was expensive.

"I insist this nonsense cease now. You've been home long enough, and you can't hide in a bottle any longer. People are asking about you. They want to know why you haven't come in to the university to visit and to work in the laboratories."

"Tell them the truth."

The old doctor's voice shook with indignation. "I'll be damned if I'll allow you to destroy everything the Woodson family name stands for in this town!"

"We have no family," Devlin responded. "So we have nothing to lose."

His father's cheeks puffed out in rage, and he planted his feet in the sand. "How dare you say that! After everything you've been given! You're a spineless ingrate!"

Devlin belched. "I may be an ingrate, but there is a First Sergeant McConnell at Fort Bridger who will tell you I'm not spineless."

"Then why can't you face up to life? Is being a drunken sot noble?"

"Not noble, merely vital to my sanity."

"Keep drinking and you'll have no sanity." His father's voice softened. "Devlin, I know you loved her very much. But that is over, and you have to forge ahead with life. Do something to make yourself and all the family proud."

He thought to remind his father again that there was no family—at least not that he cared about. Yet there seemed little point in it, so he mumbled, "Yes, sir."

Dr. Woodson knelt and squeezed his son's shoulder with manly encouragement. "Tonight is that special dinner I told you about. The one at the university where some of the older professors will be honored by our former students and colleagues. Will you be good enough to attend?"

Devlin wanted to say no, but as he stared at the gray flesh of his father, it struck him that this man was really quite old and not in a particularly good state of health.

"All right," he said. "I'll come."

"That's wonderful!" the old doctor said, his voice rich

with emotion. "It would mean a great deal to me. You might even enjoy yourself. Everyone still remembers your impressive record as a student. Why, just last week Dr. Sinclair was telling me that he never had a more outstanding—"

"I'll be there," Devlin interrupted. "Just tell me where and when."

"Ebel Hall. Seven . . . no, eight o'clock."

"I can find my way. I'll meet you there."

His father's expression clouded with worry. "You won't come . . ."

"Drunk?" Devlin chuckled. "I'll arrive sober."

"Fine! Wait until I tell everyone you're back!" he said, pounding him on the back with enthusiasm.

Devlin watched his father labor up the footpath and then turned his attention back toward the river. The party, he knew, would begin at seven o'clock and there would be a bartender to pour drinks. The dinner and speeches always got under way at eight, and things would go downhill for the remainder of the evening. These faculty gatherings were stuffy affairs at best. University professors and surgeons had a tendency to be bigoted, highly opinionated men, and if the whiskey were left in their midst longer than one hour, things would degenerate into a roaring confrontation as egos were unleashed.

Still, it had been a long, long time since he'd swum in these waters, and it would be interesting to do so once more. From seven to eight, everyone, including him, would be drinking like fish.

On a whim, Devlin elected to wear his United States Army uniform. There was nothing to prevent it, since he had not formally resigned his commission, nor had it been formally taken away. Besides, Rebecca had always loved the dark blue broadcloth coat with the gold buttons and silk sash with its bullion fringes. Most officers wore buff-colored sashes, but since he belonged to the medical corps, his was a dashing emerald green. He had an urge to wear his sword and belt yet knew that this would be going a bit too far. He would have to be content with the dress gold epaulettes with his rank of captain denoted by two gold bars and the wreath of a medical officer.

Once he had the uniform on, Devlin stood before the mirror smiling and nodding with approval. Now he took the best part of the outfit—his Jeff Davis hat—and placed it carefully on his head at a jaunty angle. The hat was magnificent even by eastern fashion standards. Wide-brimmed, one side looped up, the other down, the effect was to give the wearer a certain roguish élan not to be duplicated by any civilian hat. The hat cord itself was of gold and black silk tipped with acorns, and there was a beautiful velvet insignia embroidered in the front.

Devlin stood a little taller now that he was fully outfit-ted in his dress uniform. He hadn't seen an Army officer since leaving Fort Bridger, and the once familiar uniform that had been commonplace in the West now appeared gallant to the extreme in the East. On his way out of his room he grabbed another flask of whiskey and tucked it under his sash. At the door he bowed toward the mirror and gave himself a smart salute. If Rebecca had been so taken with the uniform, so might any other attractive ladies in attendance. But going downstairs to the livery, he took out his flask and drank some more, because, so-ber, he just couldn't stand the thought of another woman.

By the time his father's liveryman and driver had de-posited him before the venerated stone walls of Ebel Hall, Devlin was back in high spirits. It was only a little after seven o'clock, and he made his entrance with a well-planned flourish that stopped conversation. His uniform raised the eyebrows of the elite among the medical fra-ternity, and Devlin played on that fact. "Relax, ladies and gentlemen! The United States Army is *not* here in force tonight, and no guns or cannon or drums and bugles will violate this venerated hall."

Surprise was replaced by amusement now. He contin-ued. "So if someone will tell me where the devil I am tonight, and find me a horse or even a cooperative mule,

GARY McCARTHY

I will gallop away to glory on some distant battlefield to leave this kind audience wondering how many whiskies it has already consumed!"

The laughter was immediate and enthusiastic. Devlin flushed with pride and strode in among these men with the thought that he really might belong among them after all. Rather a good entrance, he thought, aware of the sensation he was causing. Rather good indeed!

There was some delay with the food, and the whiskey hour stretched on toward nine o'clock. By the time the assembly began to move toward their seats at the tables, Devlin was unsure that he was capable of locomotion. All about him, physicians seemed to be in various degrees of a similar state, and the discussions were both passionate and more than a trifle disjointed. Devlin had grown quiet, for the simple reason that he doubted he could speak very intelligently on any aspect of medicine, politics, or even the American West. His tongue was fuzzy. Also, he was concerned to discover that there seemed to be an entirely new vocabulary here as doctors argued on specialties of which he knew very little.

"I say there, Woodson," a young man his own age called as he shouldered his way toward the bar. "It is good to see you again. You look marvelous."

The beaming face swam before him, and Devlin squinted, trying to improve his focus. "Who are you?" he asked, finally giving up on it.

The smile dissolved. "Alexander Crowell. Don't you remember me? You and I did a six-month internship together. We shared the same room."

"Oh, yes," he said, vaguely recalling the man. "Sorry. Bartender, this calls for another round."

Crowell glanced nervously toward the head table. "Perhaps we just ought to go and sit down. Your father is waiting at the head table. There's a place for you to his left. It's a proud night for him."

"Did he send you after me?"

The man shifted uncomfortably. "Well," he stammered, "he did suggest that you might be hungry."

Devlin laughed out loud. He lurched about and picked

226

up two waiting glasses of whiskey. "Here you go, old sport," he said, concentrating fiercely in order not to drop them. "Let's drink this one to internships!"

Crowell nodded unhappily. He kept glancing back toward the head table. Most of the crowd was seated.

"Come now," Devlin snapped. He didn't appreciate someone approaching him, exuberantly claiming friendship but all the time working at another purpose. "One drink and you can lead me up to his table like a leashed puppy dog."

Crowell reached out to accept his glass. His right hand brushed Devlin's left, and he was visibly jolted at the sight of the ugly stubs of amputated fingers. The glass of whiskey fell between them and smashed wetly across the floor and their shoes.

Crowell swallowed in embarrassment. "I'm sorry. I didn't realize . . ."

Devlin threw his drink down his gullet with a vengeance. The room had fallen silent, and he dimly sensed that all eyes, and especially his father's, were once again directed to him. Only this time he had no well-rehearsed entrance.

He banged his glass down on the bar, and it sounded like a shot. "One more, bartender!"

"Really, Woodson," Crowell said in a hushed voice. "I think we ought to sit down."

Devlin ignored him and concentrated on getting his left hand to wrap itself around the sweaty little glass. With just a thumb and forefinger, it was like manipulating a pair of kitchen tongs. Satisfied the glass was finally in his control, he reeled about and said in a loud voice, "Gentlemen, I regret that I must be leaving this splendid gathering. But . . , but first I offer one more toast—to my father, old Devlin Woodson the very first!"

Beside him, Crowell groaned, then had the presence of mind to pour his own drink for the toast.

That made Devlin chuckle. "Thanks, old sport. Looks as though we might have to do this one alone. To you, Father!"

As they drank, the crowd also felt compelled to sullenly

GARY McCARTHY

raise their glasses, even though most of them were filled with plain water. Through the sea of faces, Devlin saw his father standing beside an empty place at the head table, his face pale and downcast. Devlin carefully placed his empty glass down on the polished bar, then staggered toward the doorway, desperately needing to get some fresh air before he passed out cold.

He never made it.

Chapter Fourteen

Katie grew strong and healthy on buffalo meat and Shoshoni medicine. At night she held the man both she and the Indian people considered to be her husband, and they made love between piles of buffalo robes or simply lay in their teepee and watched the fire dance on the leather walls. During the days they walked hand in hand, learning more and more about each other and also about themselves. Katie taught Bryce about raising sheep, too. There were cold, raw days when they huddled out of the wind and feared for their flock, but the snow was never heavy. There were also deliciously crisp days, when icicles hung on the trees like garlands of diamonds and the frost shimmered like a sea of silver. Like the Indians, they wore buffalo robes to keep out the cold, and, as often as possible, they spent the long winter days inside a teepee, laughing and watching the elaborate antics of the warriors as they told their stories.

This winter, buffalo had given the tribe food, though Katie would gladly have provided them with sheep. The children were well fed and happy, and she and Bryce spent many hours watching them play a game in which they would race across the snow toward the river and then begin to slide. The object was to see who could come the closest to the water without getting wet. It was a game that worried Katie; she much preferred the sledding. The children would tie buffalo ribs to wooden sticks and construct crude but effective sleds on which they raced from morning to night. The sound of laughing children had a new and growing meaning for her.

It was a mild winter and an early spring. One crisp

March morning as she and Bryce lay in the buffalo robes, Katie told him she was pregnant.

"You are?" he cried, instantly wide awake.

"I think so," she said, looking deep into his eyes, afraid of seeing disappointment because they'd hoped to have more time alone together and even to have a start in ranching.

"Katie, Katie." He chuckled reprovingly, yet with a smile. "You said we were going to wait. You told me life was to be planned. I said no, that it was a crap shoot. Remember?"

She squeezed him with her body and laughed softly. "Maybe there are a few things you can teach me after all."

"I'm afraid raising a kid isn't one of them."

"We'll do all right," she said, trying to hide her own concern.

He kissed her eyelids, her nose, and her lips. "I know. I'll just be glad when we get to where we're going and stake out a hunk of Wyoming and put down roots. This Bridger Basin suits me. Why don't we find a piece of it and ask Chief Washakie if we can stay?"

"Because I have to see Rebecca in South Pass City, and I think Washakie plans to live in the Wind River country. I want to see it, Bryce. I just have a feeling it's where we should begin."

He frowned, lay back, and cradled her head in his arm. "Katie, I don't much want to see Rebecca. There's a bad feeling in me about her."

"She's my sister, and she's waiting. I have to tell her about us."

"Well, I don't want any part of her," he groused. "And as for this Wind River country, I just don't understand why we have to trail sheep clear over there this summer when we ought to be building a cabin and pens starting here and now."

"There are many reasons," she argued forcefully.

"I'm listening."

"In the first place," she said, "Chief Washakie and his people call it the Black Valley or the Warm Valley, because the winters are extremely mild for Wyoming and the snows are never deep. That's what we need, Bryce."

"The winter has been mild here."

"Yes, but we've been lucky. The chief admits that there have been years when the snow was five and six feet deep. That won't happen in the Wind River. And for another thing, this country is wild, unsettled, and unsafe. It's a corridor for war parties of the Crow, Arapaho, Cheyenne, and Ute—a disputed hunting range. As long as we are with the Shoshoni, we're safe. If they go to Wind River and we remain, there will come a day when we'd be scalped."

The contention washed right out of Bryce. "I see. You feel that if we stay near enough to the Shoshoni, we'll be protected from raiding Indians."

"Yes. Chief Washakie and the elders of this tribe believe they owe a debt to Rebecca for helping Eagle Wing. And even more important, you saved that young hunter and gained their loyalty and respect."

"And what about you? Washakie favors you over me. I can tell that."

Katie laughed. "The chief just likes me. I think of him almost as a father. After all, he saved my life, and there's an old saying that when a person does that, he feels responsible for your welfare forever."

Bryce looked skeptical.

"It does make sense," Katie added. "But the important thing is that we'll be safer, and if we can find the valley we're looking for, we'd be much closer to the gold strikes at South Pass City and Atlantic City. They need fresh meat, and they'll buy all our wool until we're large enough to start shipping it east on the railroad."

"Railroad? Why, they haven't even crossed Wyoming with it yet. And here you are already planning to ship mutton and wool to the East Coast."

"And Salt Lake City, Denver, and wherever else we can get the best prices," she said, smug with confidence.

Bryce chuckled. "My dear, I have to hand it to you. For outright determination, you win the prize."

She pulled him down close to her. "I've got you as a

husband and partner, don't I? How can we fail?"

He nuzzled her with the rich beard that she had come to like, which was almost the color and texture of the buffalo robe.

"We can't fail," he agreed with a smile as his lips covered her own.

Less than a week before it was time to break camp, they had an unexpected visitor. Judge William Carter, of Fort Bridger, paid a visit to the Shoshoni camp to see his old friend Chief Washakie.

"I bring good news," he told them after he was settled in. "A bill has been introduced in Congress to give Wyoming territorial status this summer. That means we'll finally be able to elect our own officials. And the federal government has decided it must enact treaties with the Plains Indians."

Chief Washakie nodded. If there was any excitement in him over the announcement, Katie could not see it.

"This time the treaties really will last," Judge Carter predicted solemnly. "The Army built Fort Phil Kearney up in the Big Horn Basin to protect the Bozeman Trail two years ago. Your old enemy, the war leader of the Ogala Sioux, Red Cloud, put a Circle of Death around the fort. To date, about a hundred and fifty soldiers have died and the Sioux are slaughtering the advance Union Pacific Railroad crews all the way from Cheyenne east. Congress is up in arms and determined to settle things peaceably."

"The Shoshoni people have always been the white man's friend, the Sioux their enemy. Do arrows speak louder than the peace pipe?"

Judge Carter sighed. "My old friend, I know it sometimes appears so, but this is no longer true. Red Cloud and the Sioux leaders have agreed to leave the transcontinental railroad in peace if the Army will give them land in the northeast part of the new territory."

"And what of us?"

"It hasn't been totally decided yet, but if you and your friends come to Fort Bridger, I promise you I'll do all I can to help you obtain a reservation. You have proven your friendship many times, and Congress is grateful. You've earned it. On my honor, this summer the Wind River shall be yours."

Now she saw the emotion. Washakie didn't smile, and he didn't say a word. But his eyes sparkled with joy, and he sat a little straighter, a little taller. He gripped the judge's hand in his own, and the picture of these two great men was one she would treasure and remember always. Katie felt Bryce reach out and squeeze her hand, and she knew he was as deeply moved as she.

The peace pipe traveled the circle many, many times that day. In the evening, Judge Carter came to see Katie. In very few words he told her about Rebecca's influence on the soldiers and their wives at Fort Bridger and the deep sadness they'd all felt when she'd run away and Devlin had abandoned his promise to remain their doctor.

"They were a beautiful couple, and I loved them like a father. I never saw two people so much in love."

Bryce stood up quickly, and Katie tried to see his face, but he excused himself and hurried outside. She wanted to listen to the judge, but the realization that Bryce would never forget her sister made it hard to concentrate on his words. Perhaps, she thought sadly, it burns even stronger in him than I'd thought.

"I want you to tell Rebecca," the judge was saying, "that we at Fort Bridger will always be her friends. She is welcome to come back to my house as a member of the Carter family."

Katie forced herself to pay attention. "I will," she promised.

"Thank you. Tell her also that . . ." He hesitated, and her attention focused.

"Tell Rebecca I know about her past. About the Mormons. Tell her that no one else does except my wife, and that it is a secret we shall always keep. *But* if she ever decides she wants to wipe the stain of that marriage from the record, I have friends in Utah who would gladly help her. Free."

"Why? Why free?"

"Like many of us, they abhor the idea of polygamy. If your sister was forced into that marriage, my friends would welcome the opportunity to expose polygamy for the despicable practice it is."

He frowned. "There is one more thing, however. I did legally marry Rebecca to Captain Devlin Woodson. If she chooses to fight the Mormon marriage, there is no way she can avoid publicity, which might ruin Devlin's career, even in the East. I have received one letter from him, and it appears he may be on the way to recovery. It is too early to say. He loved your sister very, very deeply. If the affair were ever uncovered by the eastern press, they would crucify the poor man. I don't think he could stand the humiliation. His father is adamant that Rebecca's name never be mentioned, not even between them."

"Tell me," Katie said, "about the good things you remember about my sister. Rebecca has had so little happiness. Not like me. I would be forever grateful if you could tell me if she ever laughed."

For the first time the judge really smiled. "Laugh? Well, of course she did! Often, in fact. Your sister has a beautiful laugh, and I remember the first time I heard it, she was . . ."

The stories Judge Carter had given her of Rebecca were worth remembering during that long, hot summer as she and Bryce grazed their small flock southeast along the base of the Wind River Mountains. They spent a month lambing in the beautiful meadows bordering Little Sandy Creek. Katie was eager to see Rebecca and then to journey on to Wind River, yet Bryce seemed almost reluctant. He delayed their start in the mornings and insisted they camp early in the afternoon. Katie did not object, because their sheep were still underfed from the winter and the new lambs were not as big or strong as they needed to be in order to climb the South Pass.

Also, five months into her pregnancy, she tired easily. She was beginning to wonder if she would ever regain the stamina that had once carried her to California and halfway back. She felt clumsy, and as her midriff broadened there were times when she stared at herself in the reflection of a still pond and wondered if Bryce might abandon her because she was so ungainly. Though it was hard to admit, she was jealous of Rebecca's beauty. She'd always felt that way—a little colorless and unattractive—next to her sister. Bryce had assured her it wasn't true. And Jude had thought she was prettier. Still, by the time she reached South Pass City she would be as big as a horse and just about as appealing. Bryce would see them both and . . . Dear God, she fretted. How could any man fail to compare?

So they dawdled the summer away as if there were no yesterdays and no tomorrows. It was wonderful. They watched the delicate pronghorn antelope roam the hills by the thousands. It broke Katie's heart to have to shoot them for meat. The antelope ranged in bands of up to twenty, and their speed could match the shadow of an eagle. Sometimes she and Bryce came upon prairie dog towns that covered acres of range. They skirted these towns because of the obvious danger they posed for hooved animals, yet Katie found the prairie dogs fascinating to watch. The sentinels would stand frozen like statues, ever alert for attack from coyotes, the terrible badger who would dig right down after them, or the dreaded hawks.

The prairie sage grouse provided a welcome change in their diet. These birds traveled in large groups, scratching busily for food. Katie couldn't help but be amused by their antics during mating season, when the males would stand almost on their toes, raise their wings and tails, then inflate their chests like bullfrogs. The hens, clucking and pecking in blissful indifference, seemed both to enrage and arouse the males to greater exertions. Their feathers would porcupine outward, making them look like fat little pincushions. For a grand finale the males would begin a ridiculous croaking song. Strutting, croaking, dragging their chests in the dust and fighting, they were a real comedy act that Bryce and Katie loved dearly.

One night, however, they woke to a terrible roar, the

sound of stampeding sheep, and Taffy's frenzied barking. It was a grizzly.

"Stay here!" Bryce shouted, grabbing his Winchester and racing into the darkness. Katie pulled on her sturdy boots and waited anxiously.

It seemed like hours, yet only minutes passed before the rifle shots began. Unable to stand the thought of Bryce facing the huge and vicious beast alone, Katie clutched her Colt .45 and ran after him.

She found Bryce in the moonlight, kneeling, cradling Taffy in his arms. Katie glanced around and saw two broken and dying sheep as she knelt beside the whimpering sheep dog.

"It's not too bad," he gritted. "Torn shoulder. She's lucky to be alive. One good swipe with those claws and she would be gone."

Katie brushed tears away and stroked Taffy's muzzle. The dog licked her hand and thumped its tail. "It's going to be all right, Taffy. You're just going to get to rest awhile. Good dog!"

They carried her back to camp and stitched up the shoulder as best they could. Katie was upset about the wound and the loss of her sheep yet grateful that the grizzly had decided to run rather than attack either Bryce or the dog.

"It takes a little luck to bring down a charging grizzly with a carbine," Bryce said. "And this one looked about nine feet tall. When he took off, I just let him run."

"Will he be back?"

"Sure he will, but we'll be gone. We'd best cover some miles today."

"I'll make a travois for Taffy. She'll have to be tied down or she won't stay."

"Do you think that's necessary?"

"Yes. If need be, I'll pull it myself."

She didn't pull it, of course, but she would have if Bryce had made it an issue. Instead they tied the dog on their makeshift packsaddle, and she seemed content to ride. It made the work of herding far more difficult, but they got by until Taffy's shoulder healed enough to allow her to herd. Still, it tore at Katie's heart to see the valiant little dog limping along.

"Don't worry," Bryce said. "It's what she was bred to do, and she's far happier herding sheep than sitting atop a packhorse."

Katie nodded, but she couldn't help thinking of her beloved Rebel, who also wouldn't quit the flock.

They began to climb the shoulders of the continental divide in August. Almost an entire year had passed since their escape from Temple City. The Wind River Mountains reminded her of the Bear River Divide, where Micah had given his life to save her from recapture. It was a memory Katie knew she'd always carry, and one she longed to share with Rebecca.

Rebecca. The closer they came to a reunion, the more Katie found herself thinking about her sister and recounting the stories that Judge Carter had told her. What kind of a man had this Captain Devlin Woodson been that he could drive away someone he loved so much? Hadn't Rebecca explained to her captain the terrible circumstances regarding her first marriage in Temple City? Perhaps not. Sometimes Rebecca's strength and pride seemed to be almost her worst enemy. Katie sighed. What was her sister doing now? Had the loss of her Army captain driven her into despair and bitterness?

These were the questions Katie asked herself again and again as they toiled up and through South Pass and began the last few miles of their journey. She was almost certain that Bryce loved her more than Rebecca. More than once he'd stated that he preferred never to see Rebecca again. This saddened Katie, but she would not allow the past to cloud the future. Her plan now was to visit Rebecca and then go on to Wind River with her sheep and her husband to start their ranch and have her baby. First, though, they would need shelter for the winter. There would be no time to build a cabin before the first snow. They would need a sturdy sheep wagon, one in good enough condition to withstand the icy blasts of a Wyoming winter.

Katie knew such a wagon would be expensive, but it

was essential. They would have to sell many ewes to fully provision themselves.

On the day they crested the hill overlooking distant South Pass City, Katie's heart was pounding with anticipation. "Oh, Bryce, look at it! There are stores and everything. There's even a church steeple! That means there must be a preacher who will marry us."

"We *are* married," he said gruffly. "Married as good as anyone can be. I'd feel kind of stupid going up to a preacher with you almost ready to have our baby and asking him to marry us."

Katie swung around, the wonder of the distant city dying in her eyes. "Stupid?" She could not believe her ears. "Why? You said you loved me, and the Shoshoni people married us. If you're ashamed, then I feel very sorry for you, Bryce Sherman. But you promised, and by God this child I carry will have a legal father!"

He wouldn't meet her eyes, but the muscles of his jaw were rigid, and he spit out, "We'll marry, then. I'll not break my promise."

Katie fought back tears. He didn't want to marry her. She felt sick and old inside. Trying to pull herself together, she stood a little straighter and spoke very evenly. "Bryce, let's not fight again. We've been through too much together, and I just know that once we get to Wind River country and start to build and grow that things will be good between us."

She reached out and took his hand and brought it to her cheek. "Bryce, I really want a legal marriage for this child. You won't be sorry. I'll be a good wife and stand by you all the rest of my days if you treat me with love and respect. I promise that with all my heart and soul."

"You've got to make a choice between your sister and me," he grated.

"I have. You're my husband, and you come first in my life—before Rebecca and even before this child I'm carrying. But you have to place me first in your heart, too. I just can't love a man who doesn't truly love me in return. I could try, but in the end I know it would cause me to become bitter."

When he said nothing, Katie released his rough hand and said, "I'd better get along so I have time to find Rebecca before it gets dark. I have no idea even where to begin looking."

"Most likely the whorehouses, Katie."

She was stunned for a moment as she stared at this man who could say such a terrible thing about Rebecca. Then, with a growl, she raised her hand and slapped him with all the anger and strength she possessed. His head rocked back and his eyes radiated what she could only call hatred. Katie stepped away from him. "Don't you *ever* say anything like that again about my sister!" she said in a low, trembling voice. "Not ever."

His bruised lips twisted into a smile that was anything but pleasant. "You've made your choice, Katie. Now go find her."

She'd left him in a fog of pain and hopelessness. They seemed like strangers now, and she wondered if they would ever be able to ignore the wounds that were ripping them apart. Oh, how she wished she and Bryce could be back in the Shoshoni teepee, under the buffalo robes, laughing, lying warm in each other's arms and making love—sweet, gentle, and ever so passionate love. But last winter now seemed a thousand years ago, and there was no bringing back what was lost.

Katie let the sun dry her tears as she marched through the sagebrush toward the freight road leading down into South Pass City. She told herself she must smile and try to appear to Rebecca to be happy. Rebecca had trials enough without having this one to share.

"Hey there, missus, you need a lift into town?" a grizzled old freighter bellowed down from the heights of his ore wagon.

Climbing up to accept his offer was the last thing on earth she was prepared to do in her condition. "No, thank you. I'm looking for my sister. Her name is Rebecca."

He hauled in on the lines and ten weary mules came to a grateful stop. The freighter squinted. He had a white beard and was chewing a cigar. "What's her name?"

"Rebecca," she answered, not certain what last name her sister might be using, though she suspected it was Woodson. "She is practicing medicine here."

His face lit up. "Why sure! You must mean Mrs. Woodson. Why, most folks swear by her, though I figure a lot just play sick to watch her. Once or twice I done it too. Now that," he said almost reverently, "is one beautiful woman."

Katie looked down at her swollen stomach. "Yes, I know," she said quietly. "Can you tell me where she is living?"

He was more than happy to give her directions. "Only thing is," the freighter said, "I've heard your sister has gone to bed with the ague."

"Are you certain!"

"Yep." He cleared his throat and his voice was sympathetic. "Guess you didn't know, huh?"

Katie shook her head sadly. The ague wasn't fatal, but she could well remember all the miners who'd contracted it in the goldfields of California; they'd suffered badly with recurring chills and fever.

"You sure you don't need a lift?" the man said. "You don't look too healthy yourself."

"No, thank you," she replied, beginning to walk down into that valley. Rebecca's illness had shaken her to the core. First Bryce, now this. Dear Lord, she thought disconsolately. Please, no more bad surprises today. I just can't handle any more now.

By the time she reached the house that had been described to her, Katie was back in control of her emotions and more determined than ever to put on a smiling face to cheer Rebecca. The flowers in front of the cottage lifted her spirits. She passed through the front gate and stooped several times to smell and admire them. Someday, she thought, knocking on the door, I will have a flower garden.

The door opened, and one of the tallest women Katie had ever seen looked down at her. "Mrs. Peterson?"

"Yah. Who are you?"

"Katie," she said hesitantly. "Katie Sherman."

The woman's blue eyes dilated, and she cried. "Oh, my Gott! You are Rebecca's little sister!"

"Not so little," she answered looking down at herself.

The woman reached out with a squeal of happiness, crushed her in her arms, then yanked her into the house. "You are a Gottsent! Go in to see her. I vait out here."

Katie followed her glance, and as she moved forward, she was hardly aware of the rugs, the blue curtains, or the cheap handmade furniture she passed. All she noticed was that the little cabin was spotlessly clean. At Rebecca's door, she hesitated a moment before taking the glass knob in her hand and slowly turning it, to see Rebecca sound asleep. The room was yellow. The curtains, a soft white muslin, were pulled, and yet the sun was in such a position that the light had a glowing quality about it and bathed Rebecca's face, giving it a soft, golden radiance that was almost unreal. It seemed to Katie that she must be staring at a fairy-tale princess.

No wonder Bryce couldn't forget her. Katie tiptoed forward to stand beside the bed. Rebecca looked almost serene in repose, as though she had never loved and lost, never known heartache and sorrow. And yet Katie could see the faint signs of Rebecca's trials, how her cheeks were sunken and her eyes ringed with dark circles. Katie was surprised at how slight Rebecca now seemed. She remembered her older sister as being a little taller and considerably stronger-looking, but this young woman seemed almost fragile. Her face was pale, and her skin had what Katie could only describe as a pearllike quality. So perfect was her complexion that Katie could almost see the dark shadows of her veins.

She chewed her lip. And this was the woman who had carried their family through the mountains and the awful deserts on pure strength of will until that fateful day when she'd first met Bryce. Katie felt a catch in her throat. Afraid she might begin to cry, she reached down and whispered, "Rebecca. Rebecca."

The long eyelashes Katie had always envied fluttered, then opened. For a heartbeat and a lifetime, Rebecca just stared. Suddenly her eyes seemed to take on focus; they grew round with joy, and then a surprisingly loud shout of happiness burst from her lips. "Katie!"

They held each other for a moment, and Katie heard herself say, "I'm going to have Bryce's baby."

Rebecca's arms tightened around her, but she didn't say a word. Katie felt her excitement go flat. "Rebecca? Aren't you happy for me?" she asked, sitting up.

"Well . . . well of course I am." Rebecca smiled, but it clearly took some effort. "It's just that, waking up and seeing you, and then hearing you say you're pregnant . . ."

Katie relaxed. "I guess it probably is a little too much all at once. But I was so happy, I just blurted out the first thing that came to my mind."

"And who could blame you?" Rebecca said, squeezing Katie's hand.

"You are happy for Bryce and me, aren't you?" She needed Rebecca's blessing badly.

"Very happy. It's just that I kind of felt responsible for you, and now you're pregnant and I haven't even gotten used to thinking of you as a woman."

Katie understood that completely. There had been times, plenty of times, when she'd looked to Rebecca for strength and support. It had been Rebecca who'd gotten them out of California and then off the Comstock Lode. Rebecca had been the head of their family from the moment their mother died.

"You were more to me than a sister," Katie told her quietly. "You took mother's place in so many ways, and yet I never thought of you that way. I was . . . Oh, hell," she said self-consciously. "Never mind."

"Come on," Rebecca urged. "It's not fair to start something, then quit and leave a person wondering."

"Okay. I was always kind of jealous of you. Of how pretty you are and the way men and boys gawked at you all the time and just looked past me like I was some old stick or something."

"You're pretty now," Rebecca said. "Very pretty. I just wish you'd waited a few years so you could have seen all the attention you'd get from men."

"I don't care about that," Katie said staunchly. "I've got the man I'll always love."

"Are you married?"

Katie's chin flew up. "We will be soon. Bryce promised."

"Then I'm glad for you. Very glad."

She didn't sound so glad, but Katie did not allow herself to dwell on it. "I'm afraid I have some bad news that shouldn't wait."

Rebecca stiffened.

"It's our father. He was killed helping me escape from Amos Ludlow and his men."

Rebecca's eyes shut tightly. "Did they hang him?"

"No, he was shot," she added quickly. "I was there, and he died instantly. I'm sure there was no pain. You know how afraid he always was of being hurt."

"I remember."

"Rebecca," she said firmly, because she wanted to make certain her sister understood her next words perfectly. "Micah died bravely. I almost wish you could have seen his face. He found peace with himself. After all those years of struggle, you could tell he was finally happy."

Rebecca opened her eyes. There were no tears, but they were bright and shiny with pride. "I'm glad he died helping you, Katie. I always thought he'd live to be a hundred and he'd get smaller and smaller until you couldn't think of him as a man anymore."

Katie was appalled. "He'd changed for the better. You were wrong about him in some ways."

"I guess I was at that," Rebecca said. "Someday I'd like you to tell me exactly how he died and how he acted. But not now. I didn't hate him, you know."

"You sure acted like you did."

"I know, but I didn't. I was always more . . . more disgusted with him than anything. He could charm the rattles off a snake, and yet, with all that, he did nothing but whine and spin his dreams that only mother believed."

"He loved our mother."

Rebecca's eyes flashed. "He married that awful widow in Temple City."

"And never forgave himself. In his heart, I know he still loved our mother."

They were silent for a long while, each remembering him very differently. Katie wished her sister had seen him in that mountain blizzard and how he'd gone back to save her and the flock.

"Katie?"

"Yes."

"Let's not let this spoil our happiness. Micah wouldn't have wanted it to do that. When are you expecting?"

"In December."

"A Christmas baby! Now Trudy and I will have two babies to knit for. Wait until I tell her. She'll be more excited than the two of us put together."

Katie laughed and then told Rebecca all about the Wind River country that had been described to her by Chief Washakie. How it was called the Warm Valley and how the water was sweet as sugar, the sage and grass ideal for the sheep ranch she and Bryce intended to build.

"The name is familiar," Rebecca said. "Wind River. Is it far?"

"Not at all. That's what's so wonderful. We'll be close together again. Not more than twenty or thirty miles. That's if you plan to stay here. You will, won't you?"

Her voice was so earnestly hopeful that Rebecca had to smile. "Until a real doctor arrives, I'm all these people have."

"And even if one did, do you mean you'd just leave?"

"I might have to. When people are deathly sick, they want the best they can get."

"Come December, real doctor or not, you're the one I'll need."

"Thank you." Rebecca brightened. "Actually, I am about the nearest thing you can get to being a physician. If I were a man, I could get through medical school far quicker than most because of my background. But it doesn't matter. Not really. I'm quite happy the way things are. I've managed to save a little money. I love being self-supporting and totally independent of men."

It seemed to Katie that her sister was forcing a note of cheeriness that didn't quite ring true. She thought of the Army captain but knew this was not the time to mention him. "If a real doctor did arrive, what would you do then?"

Rebecca shrugged. "What I'd really like to do is to enroll in a reputable medical school and become a qualified physician."

"Perhaps you should anyway." It sounded like a wonderful idea.

"What? Leave again just when you've returned and I'm about to become an aunt? Not a chance. Actually, I did inquire to a school in Philadelphia. They turned me down flat."

"Why?"

"They said that the practice of medicine was better suited to a gentleman, not a lady."

Katie was incensed. "That's stupid and totally unfair! They accept women as nurses. There were hundreds of them in the Civil War. There's no reason why you couldn't be a fine doctor."

Rebecca gestured toward a stack of opened letters. "Yes there is. Right there on my commode are about ten reasons. Most explain they're fully enrolled, but others admit they are simply opposed to a woman who is trying to improve her station. Why, one even advised me to get married and have a great many children if I lacked the proper direction in my life!"

"I never realized people felt that way about us."

"Oh, they do all right," Rebecca said hotly. "The day will come when women will have the right to vote, to be on juries, to hold office, and, yes, to become doctors and lawyers and engineers."

"And you'll be one of the first."

"Will I? I'm afraid that by the time it happens, I'll be an old spinster. I don't understand it at all. The same men in Northern politics who led this country to war in order to free the Negroes and give them the right to vote are still willing to deny that right to their mothers, their wives, sisters, and daughters. Men! I give up on them."

"Don't give up. Fight them, Rebecca. You've always been a fighter, and you still are."

"Would you like to help me?"

Katie shook her head. "How can I? I've a husband I love, and he wouldn't appreciate that. Besides, what I intend to do doesn't require any change in the law or in men's attitudes. You go after gaining us the vote, Rebecca. I have my own ideas about equality between the sexes."

"You've changed, haven't you? Some women I've seen become more timid and afraid with pregnancy. You've become more sure of yourself. What you intend to do sounds very exciting and courageous, and I give you all my blessings. If I can make just one request."

"Name it."

Rebecca propped herself up on her pillow. "When you become a rich and influential sheep rancher, I want you to create a medical scholarship for women. There's no big hurry. Twenty years from now will be fine."

"It's a deal." Katie laughed. "But you must promise to teach there."

They shook hands very formally then, and soon Katie was asking about Rebecca's illness.

"I'm feeling better every day," she insisted. "This ague is very unpleasant, rather like a bad cough or chest cold that you have to let run its course."

Katie knew it was far worse than either of those, but chose not to say so. "Is there any cure?"

"Not as yet." Rebecca smiled almost wistfully. "Perhaps Devlin is working on one. He always did say that there ought to be some kind of cure."

Devlin. Rebecca's husband. "Judge Carter asked me to tell you he is doing better now in Washington, D.C."

"Good. I'm so relieved to hear that."

"You really loved him, didn't you?" Anyone could plainly see that she did.

"Very much. I guess I still do, though he hurt me deeply. We needed each other, and I think we always will.

It's because of him that I'm much more qualified than most men to practice medicine."

She reached out and patted Katie's swollen abdomen. "My specialty is delivering babies. This one is going to be very, very special to all of us."

Katie's face must have reflected the sudden anguish that filled her heart, because Rebecca sat up quickly. "What's the matter?"

"I'm afraid Bryce and I have decided we have to go on to Wind River. I can only stay here with you a day or two."

"But the baby! Katie, you and I are both narrow in the hips, like Mother used to be. She almost died giving birth to us. You'll need my help."

Katie steeled herself. "Bryce can help me. We'll be fine."

Rebecca grabbed her by the arm. Hard. "Listen to me and listen well. I know what I'm talking about, Katie. You must have an experienced doctor or midwife in case of trouble. For your sake and the baby's. We are talking about something that could cause your death."

"What are the chances?"

Rebecca was astonished by the question. "Chances! If it is only one chance in one hundred and we can eliminate it, isn't it worth your remaining here?" When Katie didn't respond, she continued. "The chances of a complication are high in your case. I'm saying that because of our bone structure and mother's history. It's even more serious because your husband is a large man and this is your first delivery. Please, I don't understand what is going on in your mind, but you *must* stay here."

"It's . . . it's Bryce," she confided in a hushed voice. "He has strange feelings for you, Rebecca. He's not the same man he used to be even a few months ago. I don't understand him at all now, but he is insisting that you have nothing to do with this child."

Rebecca was silent for a long time. Finally, she said, "Bryce is strong-willed, and I understand why you don't want to go against him, especially if it involves me. But he's not worth the chance of losing your life, or your baby's. It's your decision, and I'll say no more of it, but leaving behind all medical help borders on the irresponsible. If something went wrong you'd never forgive yourself."

Katie found herself nodding her head. "You're right," she whispered. "But I just don't want to lose him."

"When you love someone, they also have to love you enough to be concerned about your happiness. Loving them harder and harder won't make them do that. It's something they have to feel inside for themselves. I don't understand it. Lord knows I failed with Devlin. He left me, and I guess he had every right to, but . . ."

"He shouldn't have," Katie declared. "And you don't think he should have either."

"I guess that's true enough," Rebecca admitted. "If it had been the other way around, I would have at least listened to him and then, because I loved him, I'd have been forgiving. But he wasn't. To have begged would have just caused him to scorn me."

"I wouldn't beg either," Katie decided. "But I've a baby to think about now, and that makes it harder."

"No matter what," Rebecca said, "I'm going to be here to help you. I want that baby to be delivered in a house, safe and warm and where you can get the best care I can give. The very best."

"All right," she pledged. Katie was remembering how dreadfully some of her ewes in Temple City had suffered during birth and how a few of them had even hemorrhaged and died. "You've my word on it, Rebecca. When the time comes, I'll return."

"Good! Just hearing you say that is going to allow me to rest and sleep better."

It was easy to see the peace of mind her promise gave Rebecca. Katie wished she shared it, but deep inside she was riddled with uncertainty. Bryce seemed so unstable, and she didn't understand him at all these days. And even if he did marry her for the sake of the baby, what then? Would he be gone one morning when she awoke? The thought of being abandoned in an untamed country with a newborn child filled her with cold dread.

Katie pulled her attention back to what Rebecca was saying about Trudy's summer garden. It was happy talk, and she smiled, even laughed with this sister she'd missed so dearly. But the thought of Bryce deserting her now lay crouched in the deepest caverns of her mind like a black, poisonous spider.

Chapter Fifteen

Katie stayed with Rebecca for two days. She didn't want to leave while her sister was still bedridden.

"You have to go," Rebecca said. "I'll be up and working in a few days. Besides, Bryce is expecting you, and I'll not come between you. Ever."

"All right," Katie said reluctantly. "But first, tell me what you know about this ague. What causes it? Why can't they find a cure?"

Rebecca explained that she had read many differing opinions on this frontier disease. She'd caught it in the spring when snowmelt caused the canyon floor to become mushy and mosquitoes filled the air. Ague was a common name; others referred to it as malaria, or just "chills and fever." Whatever it was, most doctors seemed to feel that it was caused by miasms in the air, little creatures too small to be seen that entered the body either through contaminated food or simply through the air as you breathed. Rebecca had suffered two bouts, and they'd each been composed of three distinct and unpleasant stages. At first she experienced an overpowering feeling of lassitude, her pulse raced, her feet and hands became cold, and she felt weak. This stage ended with the chill spreading throughout her body, giving her the cold shakes. It lasted for ten or fifteen minutes and was awful.

The chill was soon replaced by stage two, a blinding headache and then waves of intense heat. In the final stage, the high fever broke and Rebecca wanted to die. She had perspired so freely she'd been certain a poison was being flushed through her very pores. With dehydration came exhaustion so absolute it was an effort even to drink tea or water, though she'd known it was essential for her recovery.

"We're certain it's not contagious," Rebecca explained in conclusion. "But whatever you want to call it, it leaves me so weary I can't find the strength to get out of bed for days."

Katie shook her head sadly. "It's a terrible affliction. I remember sick miners in California. They wanted to die, and their whiskey seemed to make it worse. Rebecca, I'm sorry. I almost feel guilty, being so healthy. I get tired carrying this baby, but I'm very healthy."

"Good!" Rebecca said, squeezing her hand. "And by this time next week you'll see me as spry as ever. I've got patients to care for! Teeth needing to be pulled!"

Katie laughed. "You can't be kept down for long. Even when things were at their very worst, you saw them through."

"And so did you." Rebecca paused. These next words would not come easy, but, for Katie's sake, she had to say them. "So now you must go to Bryce. Tell him hello for me, and that what is in the past is in the past. I never wanted anything to happen between us, Katie. Neither of us has anything to hide. We were never more than friends."

"I know."

"And so does he. Make him understand."

"I'll try. But we can't stay in South Pass City."

"Why not?"

"It's too high. Deep snows would bury my flock or starve them."

"Of course. I should have realized that," Rebecca said. "It's funny, I haven't thought of sheep in so long. It's almost as though I'd pushed them and Temple City out of my mind—as if they never existed. And now you appear and tell me that you're going to establish a great sheep ranch. That's exciting."

"Rest," Katie said. "I'll be back to say good-bye as soon as I can, but then we must hurry on to Wind River. We'll buy a sheep wagon and save the cabin building for next spring."

"You mean to winter in it?"

Katie could hardly have missed the disbelief and now disapproval she saw in Rebecca's face. "It will be fine. There is no choice. We certainly can't leave the flock, and what little time we have left before winter must be spent cutting firewood and building holding pens."

Rebecca didn't say any more. She let Katie go, but worry kept her from sleeping. A canvas-topped sheep wagon was no place to nurse and care for an infant during a long winter. Perhaps Wind River did have a milder climate, but it was still in Wyoming, and that meant hard freezes, strong icy blasts from the north, and snow until you thought you'd never see the earth again.

And what about Bryce? Why would he refuse to let his wife remain in South Pass City? Rebecca felt heartsick to think that he hated her enough to risk Katie's life. After all, Rebecca thought, it was I who suffered in Amos Ludlow's bed. She shuddered to remember his coarse roughness and animal rutting with her at night. Until Devlin, she had never thought she could let another man make love to her. How she missed him still!

Rebecca reached into a small bag hanging on her bedpost and removed a daguerrotype. It had been taken at Fort Bridger just before their separation. Devlin was dressed handsomely in his Army officer's uniform. She'd loved it, though he'd felt the gold braid and buttons were pretentious. In the picture, they were posed before their cabin, next to a little plot of flowers. Rebecca studied it for several minutes, feeling a rush of loneliness and a deep sense of loss. She slipped the daguerrotype back into the bag. "Do you ever think of me, Dr. Woodson? Or has your father gotten you back into the world for which you were always intended? Are you happier without me than I am without you? I hope so, my dear. I sincerely hope so."

Devlin's footsteps were unsteady and the hour late as he trudged along the dimly lit streets of Washington, D.C.

He wasn't drunk but neither was he sober after visiting half the saloons on Second Street. It was a pleasant evening. The stars were out, and winter was finally at an end. And, he thought, I am still alive, in body and mind if not in spirit.

Heavy drinking had not made things any easier between him and his father. After his abominable behavior at Ebel Hall, the senior Woodson had refused even to look at him, much less speak his name.

Devlin stayed away from his father's home as much as possible. Almost every afternoon he passed by the university on his way downtown to have a few drinks. Sometimes he stopped across from its ivy-covered stone walls and tried to imagine himself as a member of the university staff; he never quite succeeded. It was a good life, a fine life, but it simply was not *his* life. And yet, what other choices existed? Surgery, which had always been his forte, was now impossible. In respect to teaching, he was quite as out of date as a dinosaur, and the same could be said for his aptitude in a laboratory, where complex new experiments were rapidly expanding the arena of medical science.

But Devlin understood that he badly needed a harbor, a safe port from the storms that constantly raged inside and threatened to destroy the last threads that bound him to some degree of rationality. And that was why, every afternoon and every night on his way to and from the downtown saloons, he felt the pull of academia. Felt it growing stronger as his need increased with the passage of time.

Tonight the magnetism was even greater than usual, and it finally drew him onto the campus itself to wander among well-loved and remembered footpaths, around dignified old stone lecture halls, then the two-storied medical hospital, which had once been the center of his life, and eventually to the musty old amphitheater, where he'd spent so many hours listening to lectures and watching the best surgeons in America at work.

Tonight the door was open and lamplight poured out onto the walk ahead. Devlin heard voices and was drawn forward by curiosity. At once he saw three young men who looked barely out of their teens huddled together in more or less a state of exhaustion. Devlin knew instantly that they were studying for an examination. When they saw him, they grew silent.

He might have left at that moment but was arrested by the almost forgotten sleep-starved eyes and the pale, haggard face of a medical student. My God, he thought, did I once look that drawn and harried, that exhausted?

Devlin slid his left hand into his coat pocket and said, "You men are studying a little late tonight, aren't you? It must be eleven-thirty."

A young man with thick glasses and magnified black eyes answered, "It's almost midnight, actually. Who are you?"

The tone of voice wasn't challenging, and yet Devlin hesitated, caught up with indecision.

"Are you all right?" another asked, studying him keenly.

"He looks drunk," said the third.

"I am not," Devlin protested with indignation. "I've had a drink, but I am definitely not drunk. And furthermore, if that is how you form your own diagnosis—by snap judgment—I pity your future patients."

The boy colored. He was fair-haired, with freckles and red-rimmed blue eyes. He looked more like a future dairy farmer than a medical student, and he was miffed. "Sir, it was not a snap diagnosis! Your hair is disheveled, your tie is crooked, and your entire appearance is a bit . . . unsteady. If I were closer, I could confirm my judgment by smelling the alcohol on your breath."

Devlin swallowed his anger. "Your powers of observation are not entirely deficient. However, I am still not drunk, so your diagnosis, however well reasoned, is incorrect. You should think in terms of diagnosis by elimination."

"Elimination?" they echoed.

"Yes. Aren't they teaching it here anymore?" A survey of their blank expressions told him they were not. "That is a pity and a serious mistake."

"Not if you know the correct symptoms," one challenged.

Devlin grinned combatively. He was warming to his topic. "But what if the symptoms are identical for two different disorders? You then have no idea which to treat unless you first do a thorough case history, then make a list of all the diseases which the aggregation of symptoms could possibly suggest, then compare the two and eliminate the obvious."

"You were wrong, Peter. He isn't drunk."

"Of course I'm not," Devlin said. "But allow me to finish. Now, you shall have eliminated all but a few possibilities, and this would be the proper time for what?"

They stared blankly at him until the one named Peter ventured, "To consult your medical encyclopedia?"

"No! This is the precise time to do a complete medical examination, to listen to the heart, the lungs, and the digestive tract. To palpate organs for distension and to eliminate all but the proper disorder."

"Sometimes," the pimply one with weak eyes said, "you might not have time for all that."

"Phooey! Unless the patient is in shock or hemorrhaging, you *must* take the time. As my old professor once said, 'A snap diagnosis is just a rapid method of arriving at a faulty conclusion.'"

"Who *are* you?"

He knew that they'd immediately identify him as the Army captain who'd made a drunken fool of himself at Ebel Hall; such a juicy scandal involving the son of a professor emeritus was bound to sweep the campus and be told, retold, and elaborated upon. Still, there was no help for that except to turn and run.

"My name is Devlin Woodson the Second."

Their eyes widened. They were no longer jaded and exhausted. "You're the famous Army officer from Wyoming!" Peter cried.

"Infamous. I'm afraid my reputation is well deserved."

They stood. The blond one said, "Is it true that as a second-year student you once proved to Professor Omar

Bidwell that his physics equation on the laws of optics was incomplete?"

Devlin shifted his feet self-consciously. "Physics," he explained quietly, "was long one of my favorite subjects. Only a few weeks before that, my father was honored by the visit of a very prominent German physicist, Muhlenberg. I was fortunate to have had an entire evening to discuss the theories of optics and biophysics."

Peter's mouth dropped open. Closing it, he blurted, "Sir, I would not, I mean, I'm certain you wouldn't want to . . ."

Devlin grew impatient with his stammering. "Want to what?"

"Well, the reason we are here is because of a physics examination."

"That's right, sir," another chimed in, grinning broadly.

"And," Peter continued, "it so happens that we are bogged down in a bit of a muddle right now on a few points. We're in a fix, sir."

The other two nodded emphatically. They all bore such expressions of anxiety that Devlin had to struggle not to smile. He knew the panic. "What exactly are you in confusion about?"

"To begin with, the connection between the laws of optics and the human eye."

Now he did smile. It happened to be one of the areas he felt particularly well versed in. He might be outdated in the new specialties, but the laws of physics, once mathematically proven, remained immutable.

Devlin removed his coat. His flask tumbled to the hard floor. He stooped and glanced up at the students and saw nothing but respect and hope. He rolled up his sleeves, tossed the coat across a seat, and strode toward the blackboard beside the lectern. He listened to the trio scrambling to take seats nearer to him as he selected a piece of chalk and took a moment to gather his thoughts before writing in bold letters: The Theory of the Nature of Light.

"To begin with, Isaac Newton was one of the most brilliant men in history. It was his studies and experiments concerning prisms and lenses during the late sixteen hundreds that laid the very foundation of this science, and . . ."

Devlin pushed a new book on materia medica under his pillow at the sound of a knock on his door. "Come in."

The elder Woodson entered the room and studied his son carefully. "Are you sober tonight?"

"Reasonably, yes."

The professor characteristically came straight to the point. "What is this I've been hearing about your 'midnight lecture series' in the university amphitheater? Have the drunks in all those saloons along Second Street already sent you packing?"

The corners of his father's mouth were edging toward a smile, and Devlin relaxed. He had more than two hours to prepare for tonight's lecture. "The other drunks aren't very interested in medicine."

"I should guess not! But our medical students are. I'm told your audience is approaching a full house."

Devlin said nothing. Four weeks of intensive lecturing had created more attention than he'd ever have imagined.

"You know, son, university professors are not going to be grateful. You are infringing on their well-defined areas of expertise."

"I can't help that. Some of the professors are miserable instructors."

His father scowled and began to pace the floor. "In my opinion you should be specializing in research, not teaching. Research is where the acclaim and honors are to be found. No one recognizes a brilliant teacher."

"Only the students," Devlin clipped, "and their future patients."

The older man stopped pacing. He looked uncomfortable with himself. "Yes, just so. All right, son," he said. "Are you happy in this teaching business?"

"Very."

His father's lips formed a thin line of resolution. He slammed one hand into the palm of the other. "That settles it! I'd hoped you would change your mind in favor of research. I had a laboratory all ready for you. But since what is not to be is not to be, you shall teach."

"I already am."

"You will teach at a respectable hour, then. Starting Monday, you will begin as a full-time lecturer on the university staff."

"After what I did? You can still do that?"

"Certainly. Do you think one night of embarrassment could totally erase all the years I've given to this institution? Or that anyone has forgotten that you are still my son, and a very gifted one at that? The damned bleary-eyes students who are defecting to your midnight lectures certainly have not."

Devlin swallowed. "What will I teach? You give me no time to prepare!"

"You'll teach physics of the human body, of course. Who knows more around here than you? And oh, yes, you will also fill in teaching materia medica for Professor Brindon Wheeler twice a week. His health is poor, and he told me he would be very grateful."

"Father!" Devlin was dumbstruck by this sudden responsibility.

"I suggest you get back to your reading. Materia medica is a tough subject."

Devlin gaped. "You've searched my room!"

He was halfway out the door. "Damn right I did. It's my house. Besides, when I started finding medical books tucked under your mattress instead of whiskey bottles, I knew my son had finally returned," he said, his voice starting to break.

Devlin shook his head and then winked as his father disappeared. "Good night," he said, "you sly old bastard, you."

Katie left Rebecca resting quietly and began the long walk back to camp. Worry about her older sister made her forget her own fatigue for a while, but when a passing

freight wagon slowed down beside her, Katie swallowed
her pride and accepted a ride. "You ought not to be walking alone," the young driver said. "You a decently expec-
tin' woman."

He was probably her age, yet her condition made her
feel older. "I judge myself safe with you, sir. In a suit or
in working clothes, a woman can recognize a gentleman."

This compliment pleased him immensely, and for the
remainder of the ride up the canyon road, he confided
that there was great wealth to be made by investing in
nearby Atlantic City.

"It'll be bigger than South Pass ever thought of, and
claims are still cheap. If you had fifteen or twenty dollars,
I could sell you property that could yield thousands."

Katie smiled. "No, thank you," she said, pointing to her
band of sheep grazing in the sage-covered hills beyond.
"Those woollies of mine will also yield thousands. Only
difference is, they're a sure bet, if you husband them
properly."

"Sheep!" he spat, glancing sideways at her with disgust. "Are you a sheepwoman?"

Katie lifted her chin. She didn't understand this contempt, but here it was again.

"Yes, I am a sheepwoman."

"Pee yew!" he said in a nasty voice. "I can't stand the
smell or the sight of 'em!"

Anger flashed in her. "Stop this wagon. I'll be walking
now."

"You sure as the devil will. Sheep stink up and ruin the
range. I got no use for them or the people who raise 'em.
I thought you were smarter."

"And I thought you were a gentleman!" Katie climbed
down and walked away without a backward glance, trying to appear as dignified as a woman six months pregnant could, tromping through the sagebrush.

Katie reached camp at sunset. Bryce was hunkered
down on his heels nursing a fire, and their sheep were
bedded down for the night. Taffy ran barking to greet

her, but Bryce hardly even raised his head to nod. He was angry. Katie's spirits plummeted. She knew he was hurt, and now the prospect of informing him that she must return to South Pass City to have their child was going to make him furious.

He poked the fire and cleared his throat. "I've already eaten. There's more if you want. Beans, some pork, and gravy."

"No, thanks." She searched for words. "Bryce, I don't want this to come between us."

"It won't," he said abruptly "Just say we're leaving as soon as we can find a sheep wagon and buy our winter supplies."

"All right."

He glanced up in surprise; he'd been expecting an argument. His body relaxed, and he almost grinned. "Well, good! I think we can be on our way day after tomorrow."

"We'll have to sell a dozen or so ewes in order to earn enough money to go on to Wind River. I don't like to do it, after all they've been through."

Bryce did chuckle now. "Katie, if we're going to be big operators, we'll be sending thousands to slaughter every fall."

"I know. But these are special, Bryce! They're our foundation stock, and I've had them a long, long time. Hardly a day passed that I didn't tell them about my dream canyon in Wyoming. To sell them to a butcher now just seems unfair."

He laughed. "There you go again with that 'fair and unfair' stuff of yours. You've got to think of these critters as money, Katie. It's a few of them now, or us later." He stuffed his hands into his coat pockets, retrieved the makings, and began to roll a smoke.

"How much do you figure we'll have to pay for a sheep wagon?" he asked.

"A hundred dollars ought to be plenty. We'll get good prices for our sheep here, and a hundred dollars is tops if a wagon is in first-class condition."

"I could do some fixing on it. I'm handy enough. All I need are tools, and I plan to buy them in Atlantic City."

"You'd do better in South Pass," she told him. "More stores. Besides, Rebecca told me she has a friend named Dutch John who owns the dry-goods and mercantile in town. He'll treat us fairly."

"No! I told you I wasn't going down there to buy."

"Then I will," Katie said sharply. "Bryce, you're acting foolish, and we can't afford it right now. Just because Rebecca is living there is no reason why you can't go into town on business."

"It sure as hell is! I don't want to see her."

"You won't. She's ill. She has the ague."

He was visibly jolted. In the fading light, Katie still was able to see the shock and concern on his face. "How'd she get it? Is it the same as the malaria?"

"Yes. But she's going to be all right. She said to tell you the past is past. I know she wishes us well."

He recovered. "That's nice of her, but it doesn't change things."

"Yes, it does. It means tomorrow we drive sheep into town and we buy our supplies at Dutch John's. I'm going to see Rebecca once more before I go."

Bryce forgot the cigarette he'd rolled. His voice took on a sharp edge. "Reckon I'll go down there right now and have a drink. It's been a long time."

"Go ahead," Katie said. "While you're wasting good money on bad liquor, ask around for a wagon to buy."

He strapped on his sidegun and strode out of camp without even saying good-bye. Katie watched him go, feeling worry build. Something was eating at him, and she was afraid that all of her fears were justified; it hadn't been her imagination when she'd seen the color drain from his face over Rebecca. He still cared. Katie sank down on her bedroll and softly rubbed her distended abdomen. It soothed her and made her feel better. The baby gave her hope and reassurance. It loved and needed only her.

Taffy crawled over and licked her cheek, and Katie scratched the sheep dog, saying, "I think I'd better wait to tell him Rebecca is going to deliver my baby. He's got enough on his mind now. December will be better."

The sheep wagon they found was in good working condition. They bought a stout horse to pull it and enough supplies to last them the winter. Dutch John gave them a discount on everything in addition to helping arrange for the sale of enough ewes to pay for it all.

"Have you heard the news about the treaty at Fort Bridger?" Dutch John asked.

"No. What happened?"

"Well, I just learned it a couple days ago, and I guess that's why Rebecca didn't mention it to you, but the treaty is official. Washakie is getting his Wind River Reservation."

"Good!" Katie said fervently. "I hope they got everything they wanted and more."

Dutch John explained to her that the Shoshoni had gotten over two and a half million acres along the Wind River, and their reservation was to have buildings, a school, an allowance of three hundred and twenty acres of land for cultivation for each head of a family, and an annual clothing allowance.

"I'd sure like to get the contract for that clothing allowance," Dutch John said. "Though I suspect Judge Carter wants it too. Each man and boy over fourteen gets a suit of good woolen clothes, which means a hat, heavy coat, pants, flannel shirt, and a pair of thick woolen socks. The women and girls over twelve get a flannel skirt or the yardage they'll need to make one, twelve yards of calico and another twelve of cotton, and a pair of long woolen hose. The kids get pretty much the same."

"But they wear leather," Katie objected.

"Oh, they probably always will during special dances and ceremonies. But the chief realizes the buffalo are gone. He was smart, Katie. Smart enough to demand that the federal government build a fort to protect him and his people from their enemy, the Sioux."

"And they agreed?"

"Yes. No one trusts Red Cloud to keep the peace. Next year they'll build the fort, and that's when Washakie has agreed to relocate his woman and children permanently."

"Then I won't have any protection until then?"

"I'm afraid not," Dutch said. "I'd say you ought to wait until next summer to go into that country. I know several cattlemen who are going to hold off settling it until then."

Katie's chin lifted. "Then that's all the more reason why. I must go now and stake my claim near the reservation lands.

Chapter Sixteen

It was hard leaving South Pass City, as hard a leaving as Katie had ever felt, but there was a sense of urgency in their departure. It was September, and in this high country the nights were already getting cold. Within a month these mountains could be dusted with snow, and ice would be crusting along the river. They had to go, and now.

Katie remembered Rebecca's parting words. "Don't wait too long. Be here by the first of December, Katie. You'll need time to rest and gather your strength."

"I will," she'd promised. But now, as she tried to maneuver their sheep wagon through the pines and rocks and down the steep shoulders of these Wind River Mountains, she could only hope that she'd have the chance to return early. Maybe they would have to travel thirty or forty miles in order to find her valley. Katie knew she'd recognize it the moment it came into view, and she prayed it would be close.

The first night out they camped at the base of a cliff where a spring-fed meadow clung like an emerald to the mountainside. The meadow was only an acre, but the grass was rich and the water as sweet as any she'd ever tasted. Bryce hunted frogs, and though Katie couldn't bear to see them being killed, she did love the rich meat of their legs cooked in flour and oil.

That night the baby inside her kicked ferociously. Katie gazed out her tiny window at the brilliant shower of stars and wondered what the future would bring. Because there was so little feed up at this altitude in September, she and Bryce had pushed the flock steadily. She guessed they'd come ten miles from Atlantic City, and she knew that Wind River was just below.

They were up before daybreak and moving at first light. The weather was perfect, and they were following what seemed to be an old frontier trail, possibly one that the earliest fur trappers had used to reach the headwaters of the Wind River, where they'd held their famous rendezvous not long after the turn of the century.

Katie was following her sheep while Bryce walked beside the wagon, helping to guide it over rocks and deadfall, when she suddenly looked up and realized they were on a crest.

"There it is!" she cried, standing erect in the wagon box. "Oh, Bryce, I see Wind River!"

He jumped up beside her, and they gazed out into the soft distance at the great valley beyond. It was miles and miles across, and she could see that it was surrounded by a necklace of mountains, tall and proud and stretching forever. The Wind River was not sparkling green, the way she had imagined it would be; instead, it was blue-gray, and she could see silver links of the rolling river shimmering and looping along the broad valley floor. The mountains formed a V in the northwest, but at a point so distant Katie couldn't see them meet.

She took a deep breath and closed her eyes just to listen and to smell. She wanted to sense and feel this place that would become her home forever. Chief Washakie had said this was one of the last great hunting grounds for his people and, from his boyhood, he remembered thousands of buffalo and antelope ranging together in this warm earthcup. Yes, it was a paradise, but one drenched in the memory of Indian warfare, of coups and scalps taken. She held no mystic powers, yet Katie could feel the sense of history, conflict, and never-ending struggle here, and she wanted to be a part of it.

"Let's go on!" she urged. "We can reach it before late afternoon. Look! The sheep! They sense it too."

The sheep had begun to flow down the mountainside with more energy than she'd thought possible. Katie imagined it was because they too smelled the grass, or perhaps they even felt a warm breeze lifting from the valley.

It took all her strength and skill to drive the wagon down the steep rocky path to the valley floor. Sometimes, when she could not exert enough pressure on the screeching wooden brakes, Bryce would leap up beside her and together they'd ride the bucking, sliding sheep wagon down the rocky slope, hanging on for their very lives.

They hit one particularly vicious slide and the wagon nearly capsized before it came down on all four wheels again. When Katie caught her breath and looked up, they were topping a low ridge.

"Bryce," she whispered in awe, "it's just the way I'd dreamed!"

Katie's eyes filled with wonder and thankfulness as she gazed at the canyon that lay shining like polished copper before them. A river tumbled happily down from the mountains; the water had probably been carving away rock and dirt for centuries to form this deep and spectacular valley. Katie noted the richness of the tall grass, how it waved softly in the breeze and followed the river around a distant bend on its way down to the great Wind River country beyond. She smiled and whispered a silent prayer of gratitude, because there was no sign of habitation, and she knew it would be theirs if they could but hold it. Katie loved the copper red of the canyon walls against the green grass and powder-blue sky. She took a deep breath and felt almost heady with the promise of their future in this place.

"It will be our home," she told him. "Right at the doorstep of the Shoshoni reservation. This is the place where we will raise our family and build our future."

He placed his big, work-roughened hands on her shoulders and nodded. "I believe you now. It's just like you said it would be, only prettier. And we'll do it, if Red Cloud doesn't find us before next year. It's worth the chance."

Of course it was! Somehow, someway, they would survive and prevail against every force that might rise

WIND RIVER

against them. And when they were too old, the child she carried and the ones to come would do the same. They would breed fighters and visionaries, men and women worthy of this country; she would see that it was so.

Bryce figured it was less than twenty-five miles from their sheep ranch to South Pass City. Granted, on a cold November day like this it seemed a lot longer, but he'd managed to make it in less than four hours, and he'd go back even faster, because it was all downhill.

He tied up his horse a block from Mrs. Peterson's house and leaned against a building to wait for Rebecca. He just couldn't shake the thought of her. The memory of Rebecca was like a raging thirst he could not quench. She was in his mind and even in his soul. Sometimes it seemed he'd go crazy trying to drive her from his thoughts, and even when he did, she always crept back into them the moment he lowered his guard.

That's why he'd come here this day, not that it was the reason he'd given Katie. Oh, hell no! He'd carefully fabricated some errands and even practiced what he'd say to her, trying to anticipate every objection. But Katie had offered none, just a simple request.

"Bryce, you made a promise. I want our child to be respectable and legal. You find a preacher. It doesn't matter what he'll charge to come out here. Tell him we'll pay."

"He might not want to come at any price."

"Then change his mind!"

Bryce hadn't met her gaze. He'd just nodded and walked away.

Well, that was how it was now between them, and he knew it was his own damn fault. All he had to do was quit thinking of Rebecca and get the preacher.

Sure. And now here he was, hunched down in the cold shadows of a frame building, just waiting to see her again. Yes, but he was going to tell her she couldn't deliver Katie's baby. That's what he'd do, and then he'd get on his horse and go to that church he'd seen and find a preacher who'd marry them and who'd know of a good midwife for Katie. After that he'd have done what was right and needed doing, and he could look Katie straight in the eye and not feel so mean and low.

He smoked one cigarette after another and waited until she came out of the Peterson house. He saw her pass through the gate and walk briskly toward town. His eyes drank deeply of her, and the cigarette burned the flesh of his fingers. He stepped from the shadows and angled across the street.

"Rebecca." It was a whisper, softer than the pounding of his heart. He managed to raise his voice and shout, "Rebecca!"

She spun around, and he froze in his tracks. It seemed to Bryce that everything stopped as their eyes locked. He expected her to run or maybe just cut him cruelly. She did neither.

"Hello, Bryce." Her smile was fleeting but genuine, yet her voice expressed concern. "What are you doing here? Did you bring Katie?" she asked, glancing past him.

"No, I came alone."

"She's out there all by herself?" Concern became outrage.

"I'll be back by this evening. She's all right."

"What do you want?"

"I don't want you fooling with Katie or our baby," he said, surprised at the anger in his voice.

She blinked, took a deep breath, and waited a moment before speaking. Very slowly, she said, "Bryce, you're not being reasonable. We are talking about what I believe will be a difficult childbirth. I'm . . . I'm no doctor—you know that—but I'm better than anyone in this part of the country. If something went wrong, do you want it on your conscience that you prevented me from at least trying?"

He shook his head stiffly. The only reason he'd objected was that he'd wanted her to beg. And now she wasn't even going to give him that much.

"Bryce," she said, "I don't pretend to understand—"

"Yes, you do. I think you know how I'm all twisted up inside for you."

"Don't say that! It isn't true."

"I wish to God it wasn't," he said bitterly.

"I've got to go see a patient." She didn't want to hear another word of this.

He grabbed her arm.

"If you turn your back on me, I swear I'll tell Katie all about you."

"She already knows. You've no hold on me." She began walking very fast.

He caught up with her. "Do these good folks know you're married to two different men?" he asked viciously.

Rebecca stopped to lean against the wall in defeat. "You plan to tell them, don't you?"

"Why should I do something like that?"

"Because you hate me." He didn't need to answer. His eyes said this was so.

Late that night Bryce returned to the sheep camp and hoisted his bottle toward a cold winter moon. "To the Prescott women. The one I loved and the one I married."

Katie lay in her bed awake. He was drunk and he was alone. There was to be no preacher. And right down in the pit of her ripening womb there was an awful feeling there never would be and that her child would be illegitimate. She squeezed her eyes shut very tightly, wishing it didn't matter. It wouldn't to Chief Washakie and his people, but somehow it did to her.

The wagon rocked under his weight. She tensed.

"You ain't asleep," he muttered as he fumbled with his matches.

The wagon's interior blossomed with light, and Katie rolled over on her side, drawing a sleeve across her eyes. He staggered, cursed, then began to undress. When he crawled into bed and began to pull up her nightdress, Katie tried to fight him, but she was afraid of hurting the baby and so she gave in to his rough demands. She felt sick, used, and revolted. And afraid. Very afraid.

When he'd finally gone to sleep, she lay biting her lips and trying not to sob aloud. Dear God, she thought, what has gone wrong? Why has it become this way when just last winter it was so beautiful?

And though she tried to ignore the answer that echoed over and over again from deep within, she knew that she could not: The difference was Rebecca.

On Thanksgiving Day, Katie had Bryce dig a charcoal pit, and they roasted a sage hen and had it with canned peaches and sugar cookies. They both tried to make the day festive, and yet a veil of suspicion and anger hung between them. Katie hadn't told him about her decision to go to South Pass City to have her baby, and he hadn't offered to take her.

The nights grew steadily colder until an icy northern storm dusted the valley with several inches of snow. Katie sat down that evening and reckoned it was the seventh day of December and she'd pushed her luck far enough. She waited until after dinner when he was relaxed and then said, "I want Rebecca to help me have this baby."

He'd been stretched out on their bunk with his eyes closed, just listening to the wind ripple the canvas. Now he sat up and glared at her.

"You know we decided to do this together. We'll have the baby here, Katie."

"I can't take the chance with our baby. If something went wrong, it could die and we'd be helpless to save it."

"And maybe Rebecca couldn't either. She isn't a doctor. Everything will be fine," he snapped.

Katie turned away. There was no sense in discussing it any more. She'd come to recognize that tone of voice. His mind was set, and trying to reason was just wasting words. Let him think he'd won tonight. Tomorrow, if the weather was fair, she'd go anyway. With or without him. By horse or up that snow-crusted mountain on foot.

But the next day the wind strengthened, and by late afternoon it was cold and a bad day for travel. She decided to wait another day.

That night she slept poorly. Twice she felt the baby shift inside her. The movement brought sharp pains and, though she wasn't certain, what seemed like weak contractions. Katie was alarmed. She'd decided to go to

South Pass City even if it meant defying Bryce, but now she realized that nothing could be worse than to get caught on the trail during labor.

By morning she was fretful and mentally exhausted. She made them both breakfast, but it took all her energy, and she had no appetite. Bryce eyed her with concern, but he left to tend their flock alone.

Katie wasted no time in packing. She would take the absolute minimum and hope that Rebecca could provide whatever else was required. Besides, Katie thought, what do I know about babies? Nothing, that's what. She wished she were having a lamb! It would make things so much simpler.

At eight-thirty the baby twisted violently, and Katie gasped with pain and bent over double. She gritted her teeth and it passed, then she crawled to the bunk and lay down to rest. She felt terrible and a little afraid. She shut her eyes and tried not to worry. She thought of all the nice things she could, and tried to imagine how her ranch house would look someday. It would be big, of course, at least a half dozen rooms, with great big ones for the kitchen and dining room. She'd like a piano, too, and if she had a daughter, she would hire a piano teacher. Their daughter might tend sheep, but she'd grow up with some refinement. Boy or girl, they'd find a tutor, a very educated, scholarly sort who'd teach the child to read the classics, including Shakespeare. If it were a boy, he would inherit Bryce's size and rugged good looks, but Katie also wanted him to possess the ability to deal with U.S. senators and railroad presidents. A man who felt comfortable not only on saddle leather but also in the leather chair of an executive boardroom.

The images drove away her fears one by one until she fell into gentle dreaming.

"Katie?"

She heard the voice. It woke her from a deep sleep.

"Katie, are you in there?"

Her eyes fluttered open, and her spirits soared. "Rebecca! Rebecca, you came for me!"

271

She flew off the bunk and threw open the door to hug her sister and to see Dutch John.

"Come inside, where it's warm!"

They needed no additional urging.

"This is very nice," Dutch John said, glancing around as he entered.

"It is nice," Rebecca said. "But it's no place for a baby. Not all winter, it isn't."

"Katie!" This time the voice that called her was flat with anger and belonged to her husband.

Katie felt her heart begin to pound. "Here comes Bryce. Wait here. I'd better go out and talk to him alone. He still doesn't want me to go."

Katie hurried outside, wondering how she could make him understand.

"Send them packing!" he yelled. "Or I'll do it for you."

She shook her head. "Bryce, listen. I'll return as soon as I can. No later than a month, I promise. You must be reasonable!"

He pushed her aside so roughly she fell, and he marched toward the sheep wagon with both fists clenched.

"Get out of there, both of you!"

Dutch John was no coward, but neither was he a match for someone as big and strong as Bryce. He shot Rebecca a helpless look, raised his hands innocently, and moved outside. Rebecca stood her ground.

Bryce charged inside. "You too, Rebecca. Git!"

"Not without Katie," she vowed passionately. "This is no place to have a baby. I can help."

"Sure you can. By getting the hell out of our lives!"

Rebecca didn't know what to do or say. They stood in the small wagon, facing each other like enemies. This bearded, hating man bore no resemblance to the young man she'd met in Echo Canyon.

"What is it, Bryce?" she probed. "Is it because I married Amos to save your life, or because I fell in love with another man?"

He closed the door behind him, grabbed her wrist, and

twisted it until she had to bite her lip to keep from crying out in pain.

"Let go of me!"

He smiled wolfishly as she squirmed, and then suddenly he was crushing her in his arms, touching her in places she did not want to be touched.

"Get away from me!" she murmured, trying to tear her mouth from his.

He mashed her lips even harder, then he shoved her sprawling across the bunk. "If Katie wasn't outside, I'd take you like I should have in Temple City but didn't because of your innocence. An innocence that was soon to be lost to other men."

"I'm leaving," she hated him. "And if you ever try—"

"You want Katie to go with you? Then you'll do as I say when I choose to visit. South Pass City isn't far away. You're going to become my mistress."

"How dare you even think that?"

He grinned. It was savage and frightening. "Oh, I 'dare,' all right. I dare plenty."

"You've become a twisted creature, Bryce. I can't believe you're the same man I once respected."

"I've changed, all right. Before, I was a lovesick fool, but no more. It's clear to me now. All you have in this world is Katie. You'll either do as I say or I'll destroy what you have left. I can ruin your precious little medical practice just by informing people that you are legally a bigamist."

He laughed when he saw her resolve crack. "How long do you think the decent citizens of South Pass City would allow you to practice medicine knowing that little fact?"

Rebecca stood up. "I don't know," she admitted in a trembling voice. "But I suspect I'm going to be finding out."

The door flew open and Katie stared at them. "What's going on in here?"

"Nothing," Bryce said coldly. "We just had a little catching up to do. Isn't that right, Rebecca?"

She managed to nod but failed to summon the nerve to look at her sister.

"Katie," Bryce said expansively, "your sister has just convinced me that you should go along to South Pass City."

Katie's eyes darted from one to the other of them. Somehow she managed to smile at him and say, "Thank you."

They left within the hour. Neither Rebecca nor Dutch John wanted to wait a moment longer than was necessary, not even for some badly needed coffee. Rebecca heard Katie offering Bryce some last-minute instructions about caring for the flock. She told him they'd send for him as soon as their baby was born.

Rebecca sat beside Dutch John in the buggy and neither of them spoke a word. There just wasn't anything good to say. Rebecca's throat ached, and one of her breasts ached too, where Bryce had clamped his hand over it and squeezed. Even Amos Ludlow hadn't hurt her in such a cruel manner.

Bryce would probably manage to do as he threatened and destroy what remained of trust between her and Katie. And then he'd wreck her medical practice and she'd be driven away in shame. After Temple City and Fort Bridger, all that had kept her alive was the thought that someday she might help Katie and perhaps even manage to become a real doctor. But now Bryce had the power to shatter both those possibilities if she didn't submit to his carnal desires. She was trapped.

Somehow she managed to push these thoughts aside. Let tomorrow bring what it would; right now Katie was beside her and very close to having her baby. Perhaps the child would bring Bryce to his senses again, drive away whatever dark evil ate at his brain and fouled his mind.

The barking of a dog made them all turn around.

"It's my dog, Taffy," Katie said. "Go back," she said to Taffy. "Take care of the flock until I return. Go on, now!"

The dog hesitated. When Katie remained stern, its tail drooped and, crestfallen, Taffy turned away to race back to her sheep.

Rebecca heard a catch in Katie's throat and realized she was trying to keep from crying. She reached out for her hand to offer comfort, but Katie stiffened.

My God, Rebecca thought, Bryce won't even need to say anything—she's already beginning to distrust me.

The wind had started gusting, and it was a miserable ride as they jounced over rocks and brush. It was all Dutch John could do to keep them on the steep mountain trail. Going down to Wind River had been rough but beautiful; going back was a jarring torment.

A sharp intake of breath caught Rebecca's attention, and she turned to see Katie jerk upright in her seat, her body rigid, color draining from her face.

"Dear Lord," Rebecca groaned, more to herself than Dutch John. "Katie is in labor."

Dutch swore. "We're still a good eight miles from town."

"Katie, is this the first?"

"I think so. I had a few last night, but they didn't keep up."

"Dutch, we must all stay calm," Rebecca said, wondering who she was fooling. Yet she reminded herself that she was in charge now. Katie was depending on her, and there was no room for panic. She might not be a real doctor, but she was a professional, and she'd have to behave like one if they were to see this through.

"Relax, Katie, this is just beginning. You'll probably be in labor for hours. Have you broken water yet?"

"No."

"Good." She turned to Dutch and said calmly, "As fast as possible."

"This ain't a team of goddamn mountain goats, Doctor. But we'll do what we can!"

The buggy whip whistled through the air and they shot forward, bouncing violently up the winding mountain trail.

"Dutch, please slow down a little," Rebecca ordered, "or this awful jarring might hurt her insides."

He pulled the excited team into a brisk trot. Rebecca squeezed her sister's hand comfortingly. "You are going

GARY McCARTHY

to be fine. You'll be safe and warm and in fresh linen within two hours."

"Hour and a half," Dutch John swore, grim-faced.

"Thank Heavens! Katie, before the contractions come closer together, you must try to relax and conserve your strength."

"I'll try," Katie said nervously. "But this isn't exactly the way I'd expected it to go."

"It rarely is. Especially the first time. Now, listen. You'll probably want to hold your breath during a contraction and go rigid. You mustn't. You must breathe as normally as possible. Try to breathe deeply and evenly, and don't fight the pain, but relax and let it work as it must."

"Why does it hurt so much?" Katie panted, hanging on to the seat for her very life.

"It's the muscles inside you. They are stretching, and that's painful. Normally, your uterus is not much larger than a fist, but now it is as big as your baby. You know that from being around sheep. After the first delivery, it's easier, the muscles have already become loosened. This first birth is the most difficult."

Katie laid her head against Rebecca's shoulder. "I'm afraid," she whispered. "Afraid of what's going to happen if I do something wrong and hurt my baby."

"You won't," Rebecca was firm. "You will do it beautifully. When Bryce comes to South Pass City, he will see what a fine child the pair of you have produced."

"I hope so," Katie said, "because, to be very honest, I'm starting to become a little afraid of him, too."

"Nonsense!" Rebecca pulled her own coat around her sister. There was no sense in admitting to poor Katie that she also was frightened of Bryce.

"What did he say to you?"

Rebecca stared directly ahead. "He . . . he said that he wished we could be friends again."

"Oh, Rebecca! Did he?" Katie almost laughed with happiness.

"Yes."

"He still loves you." Katie sighed. "I don't know what to do about it, but he does."

276

"We can talk about that another time. Now, just relax and breathe easily. That's a girl."

She looked to Dutch John just as another contraction caused Katie to gasp. Her eyes pleaded with his. She mouthed but a single word.

Hurry!

By the time the buggy slurred around the corner to Mrs. Peterson's house the contractions were less than five minutes apart. Katie had broken water and was in such extreme discomfort that Rebecca marveled she had not started screaming. When the contractions came now, they were so intense that Katie's legs would shoot out stiffly and she would lift completely off the wagon seat.

Dutch carried her inside as Rebecca yelled at Trudy to put on a kettle of water to heat. One look at Katie and even Trudy knew this was no time to ask questions. Fortunately, a bed was ready, and Rebecca helped her undress and then climb into a loose nightgown.

"There," she said, finally able to run her hands over Katie's protruding stomach to try to determine the exact positioning of the baby.

"Ahhh!" Katie sobbed as another contraction twisted her mouth and brought her knees up.

"Relax. Breathe deeply. Think of what a beautiful baby you're about to deliver."

"I'm trying," Katie panted. "And there's nothing in this world I'd like to see more."

Rebecca palpated the abdomen as gently as she could. She closed her eyes to allow maximum concentration. Here, she thought, this is where the head should be. But it wasn't! She began to rub the stomach firmly in a circular motion. She had to determine the baby's position; the child might be breech and would be born feet first. Rebecca knew that her sister's small pelvis meant a difficult delivery. The abnormal presentation would make it immeasurably harder, and there was the additional danger to the baby of strangulation by the umbilical cord.

"Is it . . . is it all right?" Katie asked, begging to be reassured.

"Yes, its going to be fine."

Where was the head? If not down in the normal position and not up in the breech position, then where! She fought down a mounting sense of alarm.

"Roll over on your side, Katie," she said, feeling beads of perspiration popping out across her forehead and a trickle of sweat running down her spine.

"I felt it move!"

"How?"

"I don't know," Katie breathed. "It just moved!"

Rebecca placed her palms flat against Katie, one at the small of the back and the other on her stomach. Then, pressing them together in a slow, rhythmic churning motion, she again closed her eyes and concentrated with all her powers on the mass of life between them. At first she still felt nothing and then, finally, she did recognize the familiar curve of the baby's head. It was low now. Lower than she'd dared hope. Rebecca said a silent prayer, and yet the more she felt of the baby, the more she realized something still was wrong.

Suddenly she knew. Katie's baby was locked in the transverse position. Devlin once had told her this was the most dangerous complication imaginable. Somehow the baby had to be turned up or down. Anything but crosswise.

"Rebecca, your . . . your face! What is it?"

She calmly explained it to Katie, leaving out how dangerous the situation had suddenly become. "You must get out of bed, Katie. I know you don't think you have the strength, but you must find it."

Katie nodded weakly, placed her feet on the cold wooden floor, and shivered.

"Vat are you doing?" Trudy cried, almost dropping the kettle of steaming water.

"Trudy, help me get her up."

"You vill kill her!"

Rebecca's eyes flashed. "Do as I say!"

The big woman looked stunned by her fury, but Re-

becca didn't care. "Now, Katie, turn around and place
your hands on the bedpost. When you feel a contraction
coming, you must not push; I am going to try to move
the baby into the proper position."

Katie was breathing hard just from the effort of rising
and standing. She nodded limply. Rebecca bent forward,
once again placing her hands on Katie's spine and abdomen. She took a deep breath and located the curve of
the baby's head once more.

As she was about to begin manipulating the baby, Katie had another contraction. Rebecca felt it coming and
said urgently, "Katie, don't push. *Don't* push!"

At that very same instant, Rebecca applied pressure,
her hands sinking into Katie's swollen flesh as she tried
to force the baby's head downward.

"Oooh! Ahhh!" Katie bawled as she slumped in Trudy's
arms and started to faint.

"Get her back in bed now."

Trudy lifted Katie and set her down on the bed. "Vat
is wrong vith you, Rebecca?"

She ignored Trudy and ran her hands quickly across
the abdomen. A flood of grateful tears washed down her
face. "Oh, Katie, you did it! The baby is finally in position."

Rebecca pressed her ear to her sister's belly and listened for the fetal heartbeat; she could barely hear it over
Katie's heavy breathing.

"It's going to be all right," she said with a smile.

"Here it comes again!"

This contraction was even more powerful. They were
coming fast now. Katie was fully dilated, and Rebecca
knew it was only a matter of minutes until the delivery.

Katie's eyes fluttered open. "Oh, Rebecca, I hope it's
worth this. You'll never know how terribly it hurts."

She tried to smile and felt like telling her little sister
that she would have loved to have suffered this pain and
birthed Devlin's child. But she wouldn't. Not ever.

Katie's lips formed a hard white line as she clenched
her teeth, and her thighs trembled as another contraction passed.

"Rebecca, it's coming! I feel the baby coming!"

"Push now, Katie. Push hard!"

The exhaustion and pain seemed to vanish, and Katie pushed harder than ever. The end of this ordeal seemed so very close.

Rebecca's heart was pounding with excitement. What was about to occur was nothing short of a miracle, made all the more wondrous because this was her sister's child.

"Katie, push now! That's it. Keep . . . I see it! Its head is crowning. Push. Don't stop!"

As she reached down, the head with its hair plastered down under a film of mucus appeared and, bit by bit, the forehead, then the eyes and now the nose and . . . suddenly she was staring at the perfect face of a little human being.

"Oh, Katie, you've a son!" Rebecca said excitedly as she guided out its wet, slippery body, as yet attached to the pulsating cord.

Moments later the baby was in Katie's arms, clean and crying lustily. His color was pink, and there was no doubt as to his intention to make his presence known.

Rebecca was drained of all strength, so weary she thought it surely must have been she who had given birth. She managed to help change the linen and clean the new mother. Now, ready to collapse with exhaustion, she gazed with admiration at the child, whose hair was as coppery as the rock in Katie's beautiful Wind River Valley. His eyes were green and fixed intently on her.

"Come here," Katie whispered, reaching out to take her hand. "I owe you my life, and so does he."

"My pleasure. You know that."

Katie's eyes still glistened with tears. "I won't ever forget these past few hours. You were born to be a doctor. I swear you'll have my help in becoming one."

"Rest," she advised, pulling gently away. "This is no time to talk of the future. Enjoy now. I envy you more than you'll ever know."

She left Katie, hardly aware that Trudy had taken her arm and was leading her to her own bed, pulling back the blankets, helping her undress, covering her up.

"You haf great gift. I vill never again doubt dat." Trudy bent over and kissed her cheek. "Ve luf you, Rebecca."

She smiled, and then she fell into a deep and dreamless sleep.

After the buggy left, Bryce felt an overwhelming sense of bitterness mixed with guilt. Uncorking a bottle of whiskey he'd saved to get drunk on when the baby arrived, he decided he was definitely a bastard and, since he hadn't gotten a preacher, his son or daughter was going to be a bastard, too.

He couldn't help it. Rebecca had poisoned his mind and fired his blood. She would, of course, come around to his terms. Give her time. He'd loved her since the moment he met her, and it wasn't just gratitude for saving his leg. He'd loved her, and she'd never given him the time of day—except to save his life by marrying Amos. Why had she done that? To save her precious sister, that's why. All along, she had plotted to have him end up with Katie, and now he was stuck with her—her and a lot of smelly sheep. Well, he'd fix that soon enough. He really had the goods on Rebecca now, and he'd use everything he had to get his way with her.

"Hello inside!"

Bryce snapped out of his reverie. Who the devil could be outside? He checked his gun and stepped to the door. Cracking it open, he lifted his gun and said, "Who's there?"

"Passin' stranger. Name is Guy Wilson. Seen your smoke, then your sheep." He was young and boyish and smiling. "And now I smell your coffee brewing. Sure could use a cup. It's been a long, cold day."

"Come on inside," Bryce said, kicking the door open and flourishing his bottle. "I've got something here that'll warm you better than hot coffee."

The young man's eyes widened with pleasure. "Well," he said, "I sure could use a shot. It's still a ways to South Pass City, isn't it?"

"Four hours at least. Come on in." Bryce liked the man

instantly, and he was grateful for a drinking partner. Luck was with him this day.

The man stepped inside and rubbed his hands together briskly, warming them beside the stove. "Boy, this here is a real nice wagon you got. See you have some pretty good-looking sheep, too."

"Yeah." Who the hell really noticed the difference? He damn sure couldn't. A sheep was still just a stinking sheep.

"Where they from?"

Bryce ignored the question. He poured the man a cup of whiskey and raised his bottle in salute. "To cowboys turned sheepmen, God forgive 'em," he said acidly.

He drank, then wiped his lips as the man set down his tin cup.

"Ready for . . . ? Why, I seen hummingbirds thirstier than that, stranger!"

"I'm sorry." The young man smiled with an apologetic shrug. "Guess I forgot to say that where I come from, we don't believe in drink."

Bryce stiffened. A warning sounded, and he reached for his six-gun, but an explosion filled the room and he felt himself being thrown backwards. His body slammed against the edge of the bunk, and went numb. So numb that even his hands wouldn't obey his command.

Through the gunsmoke and the mushrooming terror rising in his throat, he saw the man step closer.

"Who are you?" he gagged, tasting blood.

"Wilson. Guy Wilson, like I said. Amos sent me. I've been watching Mrs. Ludlow for weeks, hoping she'd lead me to you. " 'Bout gave up. Sure glad I waited just a shade longer."

The gun lifted. Bryce found himself staring at it and seeing eternity down that long black barrel.

"I'll tell Amos you said you were real sorry. Sorry you made him into a hateful old cripple who had to send someone to do his own job."

Bryce tried to speak. His lips formed words, but the words sounded far away and garbled even to him.

"Not . . . sorry."

The man chuckled in soft disapproval. "You're lying to me, old horse. You're sorry, all right. I can plainly see it in your glazin' eyes."

Another explosion filled the sheep wagon, and with it Bryce felt as if the lid of the world had slammed down tight.

Forever.

The young man backed up to the stove, opened its door, and studied the licking flames. After a moment, he turned, found a long-handled water ladle and used it to scoop burning coals onto the floor. The embers popped noisily on the wood. He kicked them with the toe of his boot, and some lit on the bedding. They began to smoke, and then a long, dancing flame shot up the wall.

The stranger opened the door, and the fresh, cold air caused the fire to unleash a whooshing sound and almost explode with hunger. The man from Utah left the door open. He unsheathed his rifle, and with long, purposeful strides he walked toward the sheep. Behind him, Taffy whined fitfully and kept turning back as the canvas of the sheep wagon ignited into an inferno.

The man's orders were to slaughter the sheep, but that would take hours. He was cold and hungry. Seeming to reach a decision, he levered a shell into his rifle and methodically began to drop one ewe after another. The flock went crazy, scattering like leaves before the wind. The man grinned, because this was more sporting and he was an expert marksman. He shot them on the run until they vanished in the dusk and the great copper canyon beyond.

The growl of a dog made him twist around, and he saw a brown and white blur launch itself at him. His smile disappeared and he howled with surprise and pain as the sheep dog's fangs pierced skin and sank deep into the calf muscle of his leg. He swung his rifle around and fired. The muzzle blast seared the dog but the bullet went wild. The dog yipped once, then took off running through the tall grass.

Cursing, he shot at it again but missed.

Wilson hobbled to his horse, pausing several times to inspect his injured leg. It was going to be stiff and sore but nothing to worry about.

He rode toward South Pass City, hearing the dog's frantic barking in the distance. Maybe the coyotes would kill the bitch. He sure did hope so. It would serve her right.

Chapter Seventeen

Katie was asleep with her baby, and Rebecca sat with Trudy and her own young son before the crackling fire. Outside the wind moaned softly, and through the window the cold night sky glittered with stars. It was a good night to sit in front of the fire, watch the flames dance, and hear the logs pop and sputter.

Rebecca rocked softly and let the flames hypnotize and lull her into preparation for sleep. Nearby, their little Christmas tree stood garlanded with its snowy strings of popcorn, bright ribbons, and bits of colored paper. Rebecca had fashioned a star for its crown the way her mother once had done for all those Christmases in Springfield. This year, she thought, they would really have a Christmas. She would forget Bryce's threats until after Katie left, and face them when she must. Until then she intended to try to be thankful that the three of them were safe and warm and very happy in each other's company. Most of all, they were thankful for the two babies, both of whom were bright-faced and healthy. Trudy's son, John, would be a giant. Though Rebecca had no scale, she guessed he'd weighed close to fifteen pounds at birth. His wrists and ankles were outlandishly thick for someone his age, and his sparkling blue eyes gave one the impression that he was going to be a real hellion; that is, they did until he laughed. John was always cooing and smiling. It was clear from the very beginning that if he was going to be a giant, he would be a gentle one.

Katie's son, Christopher, was quite the opposite. His hair was a dark copper color, his eyes a deep green that was almost brown. He was long and thin and a fretful and demanding child. His cries were shrill and urgent, his lips set with determination. Rebecca hoped that he was not going to be difficult all his life. Katie was going to have a hard enough time with Bryce and the building of a sheep ranch without the additional burden of a truculent son. She wondered if the events of a baby's birth could somehow stamp its personality. Certainly little Christopher had experienced a great deal of trauma during his entrance into the world. Maybe he'd even sensed it deep in Katie's womb and had cried out silently in the warm security of her, struggling not to be born.

Rebecca blinked at the flames. She *was* tired. It was bedtime. She was just about to rise when there was a loud pounding on the door.

Trudy's head snapped up. She'd been dozing.

"I'll get it," Rebecca said, going toward the door. "Who is it?"

"Dutch John! Open up!"

She swung the door open and he hurried inside. Anyone could see that this was no social call. Dutch hurried over to the fire and pivoted to say, "Is Katie asleep in the other room?"

"Yes," Rebecca answered.

Dutch shook his head. "I don't know how the hell you're going to tell her this, but her husband is dead."

Rebecca sat down hard. "Are you sure?" she whispered in a hushed voice.

He nodded.

"How did it happen?" she asked, looking toward Katie's room.

"He"—Dutch struggled—"he burned up in their wagon. But it was no accident."

Rebecca jerked her head around. "You mean he was murdered?"

"Yes. There are at least a dozen sheep out there with bullets through 'em. There's no question of it. Bryce Sherman was murdered and left to burn to ashes. The man I sent found Katie's flock bunched up tight at the end of the valley. It seems even her dog was shot at but apparently just took the muzzle blast." Dutch shook his head with admiration. "According to my man, that little dog of hers was just about to take on a pack of coyotes."

Rebecca expelled a deep breath. Bryce's death had come as a shock—one that would greatly affect her life. Perhaps it would mean she could at last be free from the hold of any man. But then she realized how hard this would be on Katie. Certainly it would hurt her deeply— yet she too had feared Bryce. At least, Rebecca thought, she still has the flock—and the baby.

Trudy knelt beside her. "She vill stay here until she vants to leave."

"Yes. Yes, I know. But . . . well, I also know Katie, and when she sets her mind to a thing, she won't give up. How many sheep has she left?"

Dutch shrugged. "As far as I can tell, all but the ones that were slaughtered."

"Are they being tended now?"

"I'm afraid not. My man doesn't know how to trail them, and he couldn't get within forty feet of the dog. Said she looked ready to attack anything that came close to those woollies."

"So they're still at the mercy of the coyotes," Rebecca said. "And they'll be back."

Dutch nodded almost with embarrassment. "The fella I sent killed two of them and chased off the others. But you're right, they'll come back soon enough. We'll have to go after the sheep and drive them all up here to be watched."

Abruptly, the door to Katie's room swung open. She was holding Christopher, her face marred by suddenly interrupted sleep and the tragic news she'd obviously overheard.

"Katie!" Rebecca threw her arms around her sister. "I'm so sorry."

"Who did it?" Katie said numbly.

"We don't know," Dutch said. "There's no sign of anyone still there, and it wasn't Red Cloud or any of that bunch. Just one shod horse and rider."

"I've got to save my flock," she said, more to herself than to anyone else.

Rebecca took Katie's face between her hands. "You can't," she said gently. "You're not strong enough to go out in the cold, and Christopher needs you here."

Katie's lips began to tremble; her eyes brimmed with tears. "They'll kill my sheep and poor Taffy too, Rebecca! And Bryce, he . . . he has to be buried or they'll . . ."

Rebecca squeezed her sister. "We'll go tonight. Right now."

Dutch said, "There wasn't nothing left but a pile of ashes and blackened metal, mostly parts of the stove. Nothing will bother your husband 'cause . . ." His voice trailed off as he realized how bad this sounded. He added lamely, "We'll bring your flock up here to safety, Katie. Don't worry."

"Dutch," she protested. "If you bring those sheep up here, and if we have a bad winter, they'll die at this altitude. Just lie down in a blizzard and die!"

Dutch shrugged helplessly. "Then we'd best pray for a warm, dry winter, 'cause those woollies of yours ain't going to make it in Wind River alone. And no man in this town would go down there with 'em to stay until next spring. Not with the chance of Red Cloud showing up."

It took another half hour to make Katie go back to bed—and then only because there was no choice. She was too weak to travel, and Christopher needed her milk. Rebecca closed the door to her room. "Dutch, do you know anything about sheep?"

"No, but—"

"Then tonight you'll learn plenty," she predicted, taking Trudy's big sheepskin-lined leather coat off a hallway peg.

"Maybe I can scare up some help."

"That won't be necessary, even if you could. Pulling miners out of the saloons wouldn't help. If the dog is still alive, you and I can do it alone."

"Then let's get started." Dutch came over and pecked Trudy on the cheek. "We'll be fine. Christmas is less than two weeks away. I've a big surprise for you."

Trudy smiled hugely and almost managed to look coquettish. "You be careful. Both of you."

They hurried out, and the bone-chilling wind struck Rebecca so hard it made her lungs ache. It was going to be a very bad night, but they had to go now before those coyotes returned. Coyotes would slaughter for sport as well as for food. She remembered that little dog of Katie's, and the thought of her being torn apart by coyotes was unbearable.

What remained of her sister's dream hung in the balance this night. Rebecca meant to see that it wasn't destroyed, as her own had been so often these past few years.

The little dun Indian pony that Eagle Feather had given her was more than eager to run as she and Dutch John galloped into the night. The wind cut through her jacket as if it were a mere paper wrapping, and the cold night air left Rebecca's face numb.

For two miles they raced, and finally Dutch could stand the chill no more and began to pull his horse into a walk. When he spoke, his breath came in long blasts of steam. "The road is getting bad. We can't see well enough to gallop any farther."

It wasn't exactly true. The intense cold gave the moon a frosted look and the stars a special intensity. Their light bathed the mountaintops, flooding the snowy peaks and giving them a bluish appearance that, had it not been so numbingly cold, Rebecca would have thought strangely magical.

They had stopped by Dutch John's store, and he'd given her a woolen scarf and the heaviest gloves he had in stock. Even so, her fingers were like icicles as she pushed the sheepskin collar up around her face and breathed down into the woolen coat lining. Her breath finally began to warm her cheeks. After a few minutes Dutch John swallowed his pride and imitated her. For most of the night they rode on with little clouds of steam floating out from around their collars.

Rebecca spent her time weighing in her mind how she could best help Katie now that she was alone. Katie wasn't about to give up her dream of ranching in this great Wind River country, but clearly she could not do it all alone. Rebecca decided she would help her get established in the spring. Then, by fall, Katie might have enough lambs and wool to hire a shepherd for next winter. Rebecca hoped so. She wanted to help Katie, but she was not the kind of woman who would be happy living in wilderness isolation. Rebecca needed to be needed, and if not by her husband, then at least by the sick and injured in South Pass City.

Katie was going to need a new sheep wagon, and Rebecca thought she knew where she could find it. During one of her medical calls, she'd observed a pair of miners living in just such a wagon north of South Pass City. It would probably cost her dearly, but she knew it would be a symbol to Katie that her dream would endure. Rebecca knew the miners; they would sell to her, and perhaps she'd give the wagon to Katie for Christmas if she could get it cleaned up and in proper order. Just the thought of what it would mean to Katie made her feel warmer.

It didn't matter that this purchase would use up all her savings and dash her hopes of going to medical school. Rebecca no longer thought that was much of a probability anyway, while, deep inside, she believed that, given half a chance, Katie could become a successful rancher. All she needed was to lay claim to her land and hang on until Chief Washakie and his people assumed ownership of the valley and the United States government built its fort.

They stumbled into the canyon as dawn was topping the Antelope Hills against the eastern horizon. This was the second time she had been to this place, yet with the sunrise bathing the reddish hills, she now realized what a magnificent valley it was and how protective it would be for livestock. Yes, she thought, Katie and I must come back early, before someone else settles here first.

"There it is," Dutch John said. "That's what's left of their camp. Look! See the dead sheep."

Rebecca saw them, and she could smell death on the cold wind. There wasn't much left of the wagon. The fire must have been extraordinarily hot, because even the heavy iron wheel rims were twisted into tortured shapes. It was all just rubble—white ashes, the lump of Katie's precious cookstove, the stovepipe now blotched gray and white and snapped like a toothpick.

The sun burst over the canyon wall, and they halted to observe the scene. "Christ!" Dutch swore. "Do you have any idea who did this or why?"

"No," she answered. But even as she spoke, she thought of Amos Ludlow and the people of Temple City. It was possible, yet she'd heard Katie say that Amos was probably dead or crippled at least. Those people would have left some sign and probably would have tried to drive the sheep back through Echo Canyon and into Utah. This was a random killing, the kind of brutal, senseless murder that occurred in the West every day. Rebecca suspected that someone had stopped, probably shared a bottle, and then had shot and robbed Bryce.

To her surprise, she discovered that tears were freezing on her cheeks. Staring at that pile of ashes and knowing that they'd been his funeral pyre brought into sharp focus what he once had been, and what he'd become. The Bryce she now remembered wore two faces. One youthful, strong, and ardent; the other twisted, aged, and centered by a pair of eyes that were filled with self-loathing.

Saddle leather squeaked in protest as Dutch dismounted. "I'll poke around and bury what's left. You go on and see if you can find the sheep dog and flock. Hope they're not dead too."

Rebecca saw him grab the blistered stovepipe, tear it loose, and use it to begin poking through the ashes. She scrubbed at her eyes, then rode past before he found the bones of Bryce Sherman.

They located the sheep and managed to drive them up near South Pass City the very same day. Coyotes had slaughtered five of them, but Taffy and the earlier gunfire had kept them from entering the herd and killing for sport.

Rebecca paid sixty dollars for the sheep wagon, and

Dutch John persuaded a capable old hermit to oversee the sheep until spring. If the winter was halfway accommodating, Katie's flock would survive, though there were now less than two hundred. But that was a start, and even though they were a little thin, Rebecca thought it obvious that they were far superior in conformation and general health than most of the sheep she'd once tended for Amos Ludlow.

The last days before Christmas were frantic. The mines shut down early, and many of the big operations gave their employees small bonuses, which were promptly exchanged for whiskey. Rebecca found herself patching up more broken faces and knuckles and pulling more teeth than at any time since her arrival. But she was glad for the business, because she was happily spending money to fix the rickety old sheep wagon.

"It's going to be beautiful!" she confided excitedly to Trudy one night when they were alone. "I've cleaned and scrubbed it out with soap and lye until you could do surgery on the floor."

"Yeck, vat a ting to say!"

"Never mind that. Yesterday I hired a man to paint the inside of it yellow and then the outside green and red."

"Vat?"

Rebecca laughed. "It will look perfect. Just the color for a Christmas present. Green body, red wheels. I can hardly wait to see it myself."

"Did the blacksmith fix it to vork?"

"He did, and he charged me only ten dollars to weld up the springs, repair the stove, and tighten the wheel rims. He says it'll go up or down anything we've the nerve to drive it on."

Trudy's eyes clouded. "I vish you vould not go to dat place. You belong here. Ve need you."

"I know. Maybe I can figure out something. But that's months from now. And guess what?"

"Vat?"

"I talked Mrs. Galina into patching up the canvas top. She said the material was good, but it was just riddled with bullet holes and knife slashes. I knew that, of course. Those two old miners admitted to getting drunk and shooting and trying to stab flies and mosquitoes."

"Damn fools," Trudy said in disgust. "Viskey turn men into animals."

"Yes, but you should see that canvas now. Mrs. Galina patched it all up tight. I'm afraid she couldn't find enough canvas, so she used any cloth that looked heavy enough. It's a very interesting pattern. I didn't realize how many holes there were."

Trudy rolled her eyes upward. "Goot Gott," she sighed.

"No, no! It looks wonderful. Grab little John and come along. I'll show you."

So they hurried over to the livery. When Trudy saw the canvas top all splashed with colors and waterproofed with hot wax and boot grease, she wailed, "It looks awful!"

"No, it doesn't," a man said.

They turned around to see a group of spectators.

"Half the town has been in here to admire it, Mrs. Woodson. We all heard about what you're doing for your sister, and tomorrow we're going to help make sure this big honey gets down the street safe and easy."

"That's kind of you, but it really won't be necessary. Dutch John has a team of horses—"

"Horses? Why, we don't need no horses! It'll be an honor to push this big honey along tomorrow morning."

Rebecca's eyes narrowed suspiciously. "Just you remember that I won't be amused if anyone gets drunk and so much as scratches the new paint. No more bullet holes in the top, either. I mean it!"

The grins disappeared and were replaced by looks of stern responsibility. "No, ma'am!"

"Good."

That night, Christmas Eve, they all shared a fine dinner and went to bed early. Rebecca was worried, but, true to their words, the next morning almost every able-bodied man in South Pass City advanced on the livery. Laughing and shouting, they jostled good-naturedly for their places along the wagon. Because of the rush and the cold weather, the green and red paint was still tacky, and most of them left big handprints, but nobody seemed to care as they wheeled the sheep wagon onto the main street and began to sing Christmas carols.

Inside Mrs. Peterson's snug cabin, Katie looked up from nursing her son. "Oh, listen!" she said. "Someone is caroling. Rebecca, we haven't heard that since we left Springfield!"

The song grew louder. Rebecca glanced at Trudy, who looked ready to burst with expectancy.

"Katie, you vant to come here and vatch dem?"

"No, thank you. I'll just listen. My, I've never heard Christmas carols sung quite so . . . so exuberantly."

Rebecca went to peek outside. Neither had she. The singing could best be described as controlled shouting. They were off key, some a half stanza ahead of others, but all having an absolutely wonderful time as they pushed and pulled the big, gaudy, and gleaming sheep wagon through town.

"Sounds like they're right outside," Katie said, buttoning her blouse as Christopher finished nursing.

"Come and see!" Trudy insisted.

Katie lifted Christopher and headed for the window, but Rebecca caught her arm and steered her to the door. Katie's quizzical expression transformed into one of stunned bewilderment and then absolute joy as she stood in the doorway and gaped at the jubilant crowd.

"Oh, my goodness!" she gasped with delight. "You . . . you found me a wagon!"

She threw her arms around Rebecca and began to jump up and down with poor Christopher crushed, forgotten, between them. The miners sang on lustily, many raising bottles in salute and others gesturing toward the big letters they'd painted across the canvas sides: WIND RIVER OR BUST!

The next few minutes were almost indescribable as the miners surged up to the door and grabbed the women and their babies. Laughing, shouting, roaring with the fun of it and at how many it took to carry Trudy, they deposited them in the wagon. Then, for nearly an hour, they muscled it up and down the street, singing at the top of their lungs while, inside, Katie lay on the bunk, grinning up at her brilliant little patchwork sky.

Remember this Christmas Day, Rebecca thought, for there will never be a better one, or even one anything like it. Never mind what is lost, or what could have been but is not.

This feeling was heightened later that evening when they exchanged small presents and Dutch John shyly asked dear, wonderful Trudy to be his wife. That night there were four of them before the fireplace, and Dutch provided a rare and delicious champagne. They sang and they laughed and, together, they shared their dreams for the new year and whatever was to come.

In late January they had a heavy snowstorm, and nothing could keep Katie indoors while her sheep struggled to survive. She left Christopher with Trudy, and Rebecca followed her out into the storm. For four long, agonizing hours they alternately beat and carried stranded ewes and yearling wethers into the cover of rocks and trees. Two days later they had a chinook and the snow was gone. Big Hermit Creek roared with melted snowpack, and several of the newer cabins built downstream were swept away. Up on the plains, grass poked through a half-inch layer of unfrozen ground, and small white and yellow flowers bloomed overnight. The flock ate greedily, and before the thermometer plunged again a week later, the sheep were round and healthy again.

"God is watching out for me after all," Katie said. "But He doesn't like anyone to push His luck. I'm going on to Wind River as soon as I can pack my wagon."

"Katie . . ." One look at her sister was enough to kill the protest Rebecca had started to make. "All right, then I'm going with you."

"No," Katie said. "Rebecca, you belong here. I'll do fine."

"You can't take care of your baby and several hundred sheep all alone," Rebecca said. "Please don't argue. You know I'm every but bit as stubborn as you are."

Katie didn't argue, because she knew she wasn't equal

to the needs of Christopher, her flock, and whatever emergencies might occur. And if she fell ill or was hurt . . . well, she just couldn't risk the baby's life that way.

"I swear, Rebecca, you are needed. But once Washakie comes and the fort is built, I'll expect you to return here and to your medical practice. One of us has to be making some money."

"I agree. That's why I plan to spend a day and night here each week. It will pay for all our food and provisions until those woollies of yours start paying off. It's less than four hours from here to your ranch, so I can be reached in an emergency, too."

"Then you've got it all figured out."

"Not really," Rebecca said. "I'll be honest with you. I almost wish you had other plans. Going out there by ourselves worries me."

"We won't be alone for very long. The Shoshoni are our friends. They'll protect us. And there will be an Army post."

"I've seen my fill of them, Katie."

"We'll have neighbors, too. Cattlemen, I'm afraid, but I hope they'll be good people. Without setting foot on Shoshoni land, Wind River can support a ranching community and dozens of families. You've seen the size of it. There's no better country around for building a future. By this time next year Wind River will be crawling with people. You may even want to move your practice."

Rebecca had to laugh at that. "I think you're exaggerating a bit. It's too far from the proposed transcontinental railroad."

"A hard day's ride is all." Katie grew serious. "Mark my words, someday that country will be worth far more than these mining towns, and the people who settle it will put down roots and stay. Railroad or not, Wind River will put its stamp on the history of Wyoming—and we'll have a part in it. It has everything that Temple City had, and it's a hundred times bigger."

Rebecca shook her head. "I'll never forget that time and what happened to us all. Not ever." She paused. "Katie?" she asked suddenly.

"Yes?"

"Do you think much about Bryce?" She hadn't meant to pry, but the question popped out.

"Sometimes I do," she answered in a quiet voice. "But not so often. Sometimes I even feel guilty for not grieving any more than I do. Bryce had changed, Rebecca. There at the end he was like a stranger. Maybe the baby would have helped. I don't know."

"It's impossible to say," Rebecca added. She too felt guilty for the relief she'd felt at his death.

"You know who I think killed him?"

Rebecca looked up quickly.

"I think it was someone who plans to settle that valley and wants it for themselves."

"I hadn't thought of that. It could be true."

"Who else would do such a murderous thing?"

Rebecca shook her head, but she saw no point in raising old ghosts. She never wanted to think about Temple City and its Mormons again.

Christmas in the Ludlow household was more somber than usual. It was snowing lightly on Christmas Day, and Jude defiantly had skipped church. Despite the weather, he'd saddled up his horse and ridden out to the log cabin where Katie had once lived. He was wrapped in melancholy. There was a pretty girl in Temple City hoping to become his first wife, yet Jude found himself thinking of Katie and wondering if she'd reached the Bridger Basin safely and located Rebecca. In a way, Jude hoped Katie hadn't found her sister. He'd never really known Rebecca, but that woman sure had been the ruin of Amos. Bryce, too, until he'd realized what a two-timing bitch she really was. Bryce had loved her, and she'd gone off and married somebody else.

Yes, he thought, dismounting to shake the snow off himself and jar open the cabin door, Rebecca had been a real sinful woman. Jude believed in God and the devil, and he was sure Rebecca Ludlow was the devil's own creation. He'd heard it preached that where the flesh was too beautiful, there stood the devil's work.

Jude wasn't sure of that, but he guessed it might be true. During all those months he'd been riding with Bryce, he'd had his fill of bad women, but there were times he wanted them still. He guessed that if the devil didn't get you right away, he kept working at your mind until you finally weakened and gave in to desire. The thing of it was, though, he didn't want to marry into his church and live like a saint, but neither did he want to be an outright sinner. What he wanted was a compromise, and Katie, or a girl just like her, seemed to be the answer. She was a fine person, but there was a look in her eyes that jolted him to the core. He'd liked everything about her, especially her sense of humor, her spunk, and her boundless determination.

"Freeze or die!"

Jude stood motionless. He wasn't even wearing a pistol!

A young man stepped out of the shadows. He was slender and boyishly handsome.

"Who are you?" the stranger asked softly, holding a gun pointed at his stomach.

Jude cleared his throat nervously. "My father owns this land and this cabin. Who are you?"

The gun inched downward. "Name's Guy Wilson. Your father told me I could stay here. I was hoping he might have sent you to pay me."

"For what?" Jude had never seen this man before.

Guy Wilson smiled. "If he hasn't told you, then I sure ain't. But you go back to town and let him know that I don't much like waiting out here while he fiddles around playing the big shot."

Jude's eyes narrowed. "Why don't you and me ride into town and settle this? I'll take you to his office.

"It can wait. Today is Christmas, ain't it?"

"That's right."

"Then what are you doing clear out here by yourself? You and your pa have a falling out?" The man smiled, and Jude knew he was being goaded.

"My father and I get along all right."

"Sure you do," Wilson said. He sounded sincere. "It

must be hard living in a wheelchair all the time. He told me all about it."

"I've never seen you before."

"And you won't again, once I leave."

"Then what's he paying you for?"

"I think you'd better climb back on your horse and ride. Don't come back unless you bring your pa's money. Tell him I want it tomorrow. Now, git!"

Jude stiffened. Being the eldest son, this cabin was as good as his own, and if he'd been armed . . .

"Don't," the stranger said quietly. "Don't even think about coming back with anything but money. Your pa, he's rich, and so will you be, too, if you let things that don't concern you pass on by."

Jude stared hard at the man. He felt like a schoolboy being dismissed for the day. It wasn't pleasant, but he made himself swallow it. Next time perhaps he'd be packing his gun. "See you tomorrow."

"I'll count on it, friend."

Jude left in a hurry. He had no idea who the man was or what services he'd performed for Amos, but he was going to find out.

It was after supper by the time he'd grained his horse and headed for the house. The snow had stopped falling and the storm had passed, moving south. Somehow, though, the air was colder, and the snow crunched and squeaked under the soles of his leather boots. The footing was treacherous.

At the door, he stomped the snow from his boots, stepped inside and removed them, then pulled on a dry pair. His mother saw him arrive, and he could tell she was both angry and relieved—angry because he'd not gone to church, relieved that he'd returned. She started to come across the huge kitchen, but he shook his head and quickly moved toward the library, where he knew Amos would be working on his accounts.

The room was big and filled with overstuffed chairs and heavy desks covered with ledgers and kerosene lamps. Against the far wall a massive rock fireplace barely contained a roaring inferno. The heat shut down on Jude like a stove's lid, and he began to perspire.

"Sir, I have to speak to you."

Amos glanced up from his desk with irritation. Jude noticed he did not even set down his quill. Christmas or not, he had work to do, and he did not appreciate interruptions. His hair was disheveled—thin now and a sick yellowish white that made him look jaundiced. Studying him, Jude realized how terribly the man had aged in the past year since Bryce Sherman's bullets had left him bleeding and crippled up in that desolate, freezing river canyon. They'd found Hubie St. Clair with a wild expression on his face—an expression more of disbelief than of fear or pain. And it had taken four strong men to lift Amos off the tree roots and haul him out of that canyon. He'd been as close to death as any man could get and still pull through. Now, seeing him before the fire, shrunken and shriveled, trapped in the rolling prison of his wheelchair, Jude thought it would have been kinder if he'd simply died.

"Is something wrong?" Amos demanded imperiously. "What are you staring at?"

"Nothing, sir. And no, I don't *think* anything is wrong."

Amos's lips formed a hard and unforgiving line. "You weren't at services today. I won't tolerate that. You're a man now. You've got to set an example and show this town you've changed your ways."

Jude's nostrils pinched in a little and his lips flattened against his teeth. "You're never going to let me forget I went away, are you?"

"No, I won't. Nor will I ever forget that you allowed that girl to escape while Sherman was making me a cripple and killing one of us."

"Hubie St. Clair wasn't one of us. He never belonged to anything."

"He took the vows!" Amos shouted. "And God will judge him as one of us. You know He will."

Jude mopped his forehead with his sleeve. He could feel the sweat flooding down his spine, and he wanted out of this room, out of this house, out of this town and the whole damned territory! But it wasn't that easy. Here, he was the son of a wealthy man, and since Amos had been crippled, he'd largely taken over the day-to-day management of the lumber mill and sheep operations. He'd surprised everyone, including himself, by exhibiting an initiative and dedication that had raised the Ludlow family profits by more than twenty percent. Jude asked plenty from those he paid yet was quick to praise, and he had finally shamed his father into paying decent wages. He liked what he was doing; the thought of giving it all up and riding away as a nobody left him with an empty feeling.

Amos finished with his ledger and snapped it shut. "What do you want now?"

"Money for Guy Wilson," Jude replied, studying his father intently.

Amos blinked, then his eyes shuttered. Suddenly he slammed one big hand down on a wheel of the chair, swung around, and propelled himself across the room.

"Damn you!" he said in a white fury as he spun the tumblers on his huge iron safe. "Damn you, anyway! None of this concerns you."

"Who is he?"

Amos ignored the question. He opened the safe and grabbed a fat envelope, hissing, "Here is what I owe the man. Tell him he's to be out of this valley by tomorrow evening without fail!"

"Then you're not going to tell me who he is?" Jude asked, taking the envelope and knowing his father would not.

"You're dismissed!"

Jude glared right back into those fierce, bird-of-prey eyes. "I'm about done up with you."

Amos snickered: "No, you're not. You will stay until I die, because you want what's mine. You've a rebellious nature, Jude. Your mother had it once, and at times I think she still does. A little rebel in a man or woman is fine. It adds spice and gives character. But not too much. Not near as much as you still have."

"I may surprise you," he said without conviction.

"And you'd come back again, begging for a place among us and for my forgiveness."

"Never!"

Amos seemed to look right through him. "I have other sons more obedient to me and our church. You have nothing outside of this valley, and I understand you like being the boss. Now," he said icily, "I said you were dismissed."

Jude spun on his bootheel and stomped out of the room.

"Jude!" his mother called.

"What is it?" he asked tightly.

"I want you to be . . . to be patient with your father. He is in pain," Anna said.

"So am I," Jude told her. "I can't take this place much longer."

"You must. Outside, it's a sinful world. You know that now."

When he remained silent, her voice became urgent. "Your father is a *good* man. A fair man, though one with all the human faults we each possess. He is *honorable*, Jude. Whenever you quarrel with him, remember that he is an honorable man and forgive the rest."

"I'll try," Jude finally said. "Goodnight."

Her lips brushed his forehead. They felt as dry as dead leaves and very cold. She glanced around to make sure no one could hear them. "My son, I live for the summer when I can be with my sheep and, God forgive me, for the day when you will become the head of this house."

His expression softened. "God hasn't anything to forgive you for, Mother. You're paying your dues right here in Temple City. Everyone in this house is, including me."

He rode out early the next morning with a gun strapped on his hip, though he'd no intention of using it except in self-defense. Whoever Guy Wilson was, he was not a lumberman or a sheepman. No, he looked more like a gunman or, yes, a gambling-house shill or perhaps a professional bounty hunter. To Jude, the man had all the signs of a man who hired out to solve problems—permanently.

Jude kept his own gun hand buried warmly inside his coat, just in case. He hummed a tune as he rode along, and though he was a little afraid of Guy Wilson, he felt very much alive this morning. The hills were blanketed with glistening snow that would be melted by midday, but now it was absolutely dazzling.

"Hello the cabin," he yelled, turning up the road.

Guy Wilson pushed open the door. A Winchester rifle was cradled in the crook of one arm.

"You bring the money?"

Jude rode in close enough that he could have tossed Wilson the envelope, but instead he nodded and then stepped down from his saddle. Wilson glanced at the six-gun he wore, but his eyes reflected no concern. "I'd like my money *now*, please," he said.

With his left hand, Jude reached into his coat pocket and brought out the envelope. He extended it to Wilson.

The man relaxed and took the envelope. "How much?"

Jude didn't answer. He was staring at the rifle. Its stock had been cracked and repaired with a small brass plate and screws.

When Jude didn't respond, Wilson took a menacing step forward. "You took some of it for yourself, didn't you?"

"No," Jude said, taking his eyes off the Winchester.

"The hell with it. Git out of here."

Jude had no intention of leaving. "That rifle of yours. I once knew the man who owned it. I recognize that brass plate on the stock."

Wilson had been thumbing the money, trying to watch Jude and yet make sure he hadn't been shortchanged. Now the money was forgotten.

"Rifles change hands. I bought this one in a gun shop in Cheyenne."

Jude said, "Oh." He stepped forward, as if to look closer, and, as Wilson reached out to push him back, Jude slapped him across the eyes.

The man swore and dug for his pistol, but Jude had

anticipated the move and his own gun was out and cutting an arc that terminated across the bridge of Wilson's nose. The nose popped and the gunman roared with pain even as Jude drove a fist from boot-top level straight up and under Wilson's rib cage.

Jude disarmed him and took back the money. He placed the barrel of his own six-gun over the broken and bleeding nose and said, "Who are you and why is my father paying you and, most of all, how'd you come by Bryce Sherman's rifle?"

"He's the man who crippled your father."

"I know."

"Well, he didn't get away with it. There's no more shame on your household now. I killed the bastard."

"How?" Jude asked in a trembling voice.

"Shot him over in Wyoming. Don't worry, I left no traces."

"And the girl? What—"

Something in Jude's voice or eyes told Wilson that he was making a second mistake and this one could, and probably would, be fatal. With a strangled sound, he made a desperate grab for Jude's pistol and it exploded point-blank in his face. He was thrown back through the doorway of the cabin, and Jude stared at him, letting the gun fall to bang on the floor. Wilson didn't even twitch, and it didn't take a doctor for Jude to realize he'd just killed his first man. He spun around and walked out into the yard, where he promptly emptied his stomach.

Jude finished the burying and smoothed the grave, then sprinkled it with dead leaves and clean cold snow. He tried to think of something to say over Wilson but no words came. The man had killed Bryce Sherman for money paid by Amos Ludlow. That meant Jude could either ride out and not look back or he could return to Temple City and stand before the elders. If he accused Amos of hiring a killer, half the town wouldn't believe him and those who did would say Amos was within his rights after what Sherman had done to his legs.

All that would come of it would be shame and sorrow

for Anna, his mother. Jude couldn't do that, so he would ride—what he'd been wanting to do but hadn't the courage.

If Katie had married Bryce, she was now a widow and the money he carried was rightfully hers. That gave Jude an honest reason to hunt for her, but it also meant he had nothing left of his own. He might sell Guy Wilson's outfit, but that was risky. Someone might recognize Wilson's gear, just as he'd recognized Bryce's Winchester. No, he'd take a shovel and bury Wilson's stuff, then turn the man's horse loose once he put some miles between himself and this valley.

Jude quickly packed everything and closed up the log cabin. There wasn't anything about it to remind him of Katie now, and as he swung into his saddle and rode away, he did not glance back. To the east lay Wyoming, and now he was as eager as Katie had been to leave Utah. His father would assume he'd ridden away with another fighter, just as he'd once ridden away with Bryce. He'd be totally disinherited this time. His mother, bless her soul, would grieve deeply over his absence, but, come spring and her flocks up from the Salt Lake Basin, she would smile and even laugh again.

He cut south and east, because the snow would be too deep over the Bear River Divide country, where Katie had fled. Better to go down to Echo Canyon and then head east along the route of the advancing Union Pacific Railroad. Bryce had always said there'd be plenty of jobs open along that line, and that's where the towns would flourish. Jude thought maybe he could find work and Katie, both, along the railroad tracks.

At a final crest of hill, he reined up his horses and twisted around in his saddle to gaze back at distant Temple City. "Good-bye, Mother," he murmured, sure that he could pick out the Ludlow home, which was the biggest in town. "They'd never forgive me, and I couldn't forgive him for what he did to Bryce. And you were wrong about Amos, anyway. He is *not* an honorable man."

Jude yanked his Stetson down to his eyebrows and tried to shield out the blinding reflection of sun on snow.

It was melting fast, and his tracks would be gone before sundown's freeze. By then he planned to breathe the cold, free air of Wyoming.

He was wrong. A blizzard caught him in Echo Canyon, and he took refuge with hundreds of cold but determined Union Pacific track layers. He learned that the main vanguard of the railroad was trapped up in Wasatch, Utah, just a few miles east. These men were trying to build a roadbed up to them, but there was a seven-hundred-foot climb in less than four miles.

"Only way it can be done is to build a couple of big old trestles and a damned tunnel over seven hundred feet long through the shoulder of a ridge."

"No way easier than that?" Jude asked.

"If there was, we'd be doing it," the Union Pacific employee said. "It's frozen sandstone, and she's harder than granite. Dynamite won't even tickle it, so we're using nitroglycerine."

"Never heard of it."

"You will if you go to work for us. Want a job?"

"Doing what?"

"Blasting in the tunnels we're working on."

"Nope," Jude said flatly. "I prefer to work aboveground."

"Not in this weather, you don't. This is when being a driller is good work. Pays good, too. Three-fifty a day. Double time on Sunday."

Jude carried an envelope stuffed with money, but it wasn't his, and he preferred not to touch it. "I do need the money but not bad enough to work in a tunnel."

"Then go on up to Wasatch and help them poor bastards dig their way out," the man said irritably.

"Reckon I will," Jude called. "Soon as this damned blizzard stops."

It didn't stop for seven days, and Jude had to use some of Katie's money just to pay his hotel and livery bill. It was that or starve. He'd repay Katie with his first paycheck.

Now, less than fifteen hard-fought miles later, he was

in sight of Wasatch, and it was a view he'd never forget. This was the very backbone of the Wasatch Mountains, seven thousand feet above sea level. The Union Pacific's Irish army was buried under thirty feet of snow, but instead of guns, they wielded picks and shovels. Jude stared at this high mountain railroad town of four thousand brawling track graders, layers, and trainmen and marveled at their snow-covered saloons and their network of ice tunnels, their railroad cars and roaring bonfires. It was a miracle that anyone could survive in this place, where the temperature hung suspended at a bone-chilling twelve degrees above zero for weeks.

He had arrived just in time to witness a desperate effort by the railroaders to break out of their icy prison. Strapped for supplies and with its track buried under tons of snow, the Union Pacific had mounted a huge slicing snowplow to the front of a lead engine, then hooked four more locomotives behind, and was now attempting to break through and run for help.

Jude saw more than a thousand men with shovels, furiously slinging snow in a pathetic attempt to help free five linked engines, which were poised to charge snowdrifts taller than their stacks. The signal was given. His eyes widened as the mammoth iron driving wheels spun on the icy tracks and the rails grew hot with sparks and smoke. The locomotives jolted forward like a line of prehistoric beasts. They had two miles of clear track to gather speed, and they filled the great gulley of snow with thick, choking smoke. The track workers threw down their tools and scrambled for safety. The locomotives were running on a downgrade. In the lead, the huge slicing snowplow gleamed, and Jude could see the engineer bracing himself for the impact. Jude drew a sharp, cold breath, held it, and tensed as the snowplow ripped into the mountain of snow, sending a great shower of it into the sky. He gaped as the lead engine thrashed and knifed its way forward until it vanished completely in the white explosion and the one behind shuddered to a frozen standstill with its wheels spinning and sparks ripping a hundred feet along the track.

Suddenly, the throttles were silenced. The great wheels stopped their shrieking revolutions and the smoke and fire were almost gone. Now down came the Irish, whooping and cursing. Jumping and sliding into the snowcut, they began to work furiously to clear away the snow and free the two lead engines once more. Eighty feet from where the snowplow had first entered the drifts, Jude saw something appear from the whiteness and laughed when he realized it was the buried engine's stack, melting itself free. The Irish swarmed to dig around it. A quarter of an hour passed as the crews dug out the locomotives, and then boilers were heated to maximum steam pressure. Now the driving wheels reversed themselves and spun. The engines bucked and yanked and fought to pull the snowplow back out of the snowpack.

Out came the lead engine, then the plow. In went the Irish to dig back the sides of the new trench. The locomotives retreated, wheezing black smoke. To Jude, they looked resentful, and when they'd backed into town for another charge they seemed to crouch like sullen, ill-used beasts. Across their boilers, snow sizzled, steamed, and ran like sweat, only to freeze along their flanks.

Jude nudged his horse forward over the snow. For reasons he didn't completely understand, this struggle of the Union Pacific seemed more dramatic than anything he'd ever seen. The mighty locomotives, the swarming track crews, all fired his spirit. He wanted to locate Katie, but first he just had to be a part of this epic battle to link the country by rail.

And from the looks of it, the Union Pacific needed all the help it could get.

Chapter Eighteen

Katie watched Rebecca ride out of sight and immediately felt the loneliness. This was the second time she'd been called to South Pass City for an emergency. Katie hoped she would return soon, but she was glad her sister could visit the town. The isolated canyon didn't suit Rebecca.

When she was in town, Rebecca stayed with Trudy and Dutch John, who had married in mid-January. Unwilling to give up her garden and roses, Trudy had persuaded Dutch to vacate the crowded little apartment he'd kept over his shop. Katie hadn't been back to town, but, according to Rebecca, there were changes in Trudy's house. Dutch had added a new bedroom for little John, which, along with a big new parlor, now made it a very respectable-size home. The walls were freshly papered, and there was a huge new piano. It was widely reported by their neighbors that whenever the baby began to cry too loudly in the middle of the night, Dutch and Trudy would pound on the piano and sing lullabies. The fact that they could neither sing nor play seemed not to matter, because after a couple of hours the baby would always fall asleep. Trouble was, the neighbors would not.

Katie spent the remainder of the morning washing clothes and cleaning up the sheep wagon. She still tired easily but could feel her strength returning week by week. When Rebecca came back, she would be exhausted from the long ride and the rigors of her medical practice, and she'd need to rest for several days. Katie hung out the clean bed linen on a rope that stretched from her wagon to a nearby cottonwood. She wasn't at all sure it would dry. There were dark clouds on the northern horizon, and that meant the possibility of a storm. It was cold, and after making sure her flock was settled in close by on the bedground, Katie took down her washing, though it was still half wet. Inside the sheep wagon, she hung it on ropes and lit her little stove. The wagon grew warm almost immediately, and she fixed herself a hot broth for dinner and went to bed early. When she touched the canvas, it was icy cold. Katie cradled her son very close and knew that she would have to replenish the fire at least three times before dawn to keep warm. She hoped there wasn't going to be a storm, and yet she was sure there would be. It didn't take a lot of sense to realize that when the temperature was plunging toward zero and the wind was freshening, you were in for bad weather.

That night she slept fitfully and dreamed of Bryce. Around three A.M. she was awakened when the sheep wagon began to rock violently. The wind had risen to a low but steady howling. Katie braced herself in fear and gripped the bed frame. Someone once had told her that they'd never heard of a sheep wagon being blown over; the rounded canvas top would bend and buckle and yield just enough to kick the wind over its top. No, they'd said, a log cabin, square and solid, was likelier to be blown over than a sheep wagon. Katie hoped that was true. The wind was so strong she could hear the wagon's springs squeezing as it rocked back and forth.

Christopher woke up and began to fret. She nursed him and hummed a lullaby until he slept again, and then she arose and fed the fire. Her windows were plastered with snow, and she now felt a rising sense of uneasiness. Over the next few hours the wind increased to a steady roar, and Katie finally gave up trying to sleep. She dressed sometime after dawn and shoved open her door, to see everything covered with snow. When she looked up, there was no sun, only a dark gray sky with snow pushed before a hard wind. In this canyon, the wind beat against the rock walls and seemed to come from every direction, or no direction at all.

"Taffy," she called. Her words were snatched from her

lips and went nowhere. Cold air flooded into the warm wagon, and snow rushed through the open door as if seeking the warmth, only to disappear at its touch.

"Taffy!" She leaned into the wind, feeling it bite deep into her exposed cheeks. Katie heard nothing but the wind in reply, and though visibility was poor, she knew her sheep were gone and that they'd drifted down toward the Wind River basin. She could only hope they'd not end up in some draw. This was a possibility every shepherd had nightmares about, because woollies would pile up. They'd pick a low spot where the wind wasn't so fierce and just stand until they were buried and suffocated.

Katie considered her options and found them uniformly bleak. Christopher was too young to leave or to take out in a snowstorm. Yet, if she could just overtake the flock before it drifted down into the basin, she knew that between them, she and Taffy could turn the sheep around, force them back into the wind and up near her sheep wagon, where she could protect them from harm.

She decided to wait. Maybe Taffy would manage to turn the flock herself. An hour passed, then another. Katie was sick with worry now. Twice she opened the door a crack to see if the storm was dying, and each time the cold hit her in the face like an open fist. She reached down and pitched in the last of the firewood. Rebecca might have piled some extra under the wagon, but perhaps not, since she'd intended to return by this evening.

Katie took stock of things. There was enough food to last a week, so there was no danger of starving. Outside there was a whole stand of cottonwood trees and a good sharp ax that she was strong enough to wield. It would be hard, bitterly cold work, but she had cut logs before in these conditions and could again. Wyoming blizzards might last hours—or days. Her life and Christopher's depended on the wood, and she had better cut it now while she could still reach it.

Katie pulled on her coat and mittens. "I'll be right back," she told her baby, trying to sound soothing and yet hearing her voice come out almost reedy with anxiety. Christopher looked at her with wide-eyed attention, his little fist thrust in his mouth and the covers bundled up around his face. If the fire went out, he would feel the cold very quickly.

Outside the wind battered her from every angle. It seemed to be toying with her as she plunged through two feet of snow toward the trees. She found their ax buried in a stump, and it took all her strength to pull its blade free. Eyes narrowed, nose watering, she shuffled up to a fallen tree and measured her swing. The ax felt very heavy, and its handle was slick with ice. Katie eyed a thick branch and swung the ax, cutting neatly through wood. Yes, she thought with grim satisfaction, I can handle an ax when I have to. A half hour later she couldn't raise the ax above her waist, and she was missing badly. Her lashes were frozen, and her entire body was numb. Rebecca had often told her of the dangers of frostbite, and she suspected she was in danger of becoming its victim if she didn't get warm.

She leaned on the stump, trying to catch her breath, pulling the icy wind down into her chest and willing herself to move. It took all of her determination to bend down and scoop up an armful of wood and carry it to the sheep wagon. Katie reeled about like a drunk, lowered her head, and went back for more. She made three trips before she sagged down at her doorstep and reached up to unlatch the door. Christopher's screams roused the last of her will into action. She began to throw her precious firewood up into the open door of the wagon until it was all inside. Then she dragged herself up the steps and fell inside, pulling the door closed behind her. For long seconds she lay on the snow-crusted wood, and then she raised herself up and filled the stove. It hissed and steamed yet burned anew, and the wagon began to heat up again. Katie crawled over the fresh wood and reached her bed. She bowed her head, bit each mitten and yanked it free, then fumbled out of her coat. She was shivering so badly that she didn't even try to speak. She just crawled in beside her baby and pulled the blankets over them. After a while Christopher fell silent, and she unbuttoned her blouse. She expected him to shriek at the coldness of her skin, but he seemed grateful and too hungry to protest. Katie listened to the fire pop and sizzle and to her baby suckling. They were good sounds, sounds much nicer than the howling of the wind. She closed her eyes and drifted off to sleep.

She guessed she'd slept an hour, maybe two, and it was now early afternoon and the wind had died a little. Katie knew she could wait no longer if there was any chance of saving her flock. Christopher was well fed and asleep. Perhaps, with luck, she could go out and return before he awakened. She had to try.

Once again she dressed, and this time she took her Winchester carbine down from its rifle pegs. It was a new purchase—one Rebecca had insisted on for each of them, even though it had been on credit from Dutch John. Katie was glad enough to have it as she opened the door and hurried away. Every fifty paces she turned to gather her bearings. It wasn't snowing nearly so hard now. The visibility was much improved, and unless the storm suddenly intensified, she was in no danger of becoming lost.

But it was very cold. The sun was nothing more than a pale milk stain on a gray table of sky, and she inwardly chided it for being so weak.

She had hiked down-canyon perhaps three miles and was very near its mouth. Just beyond lay the Wind River basin itself, and she strained to see the flock yet could not. Her heart sank in despair. She was too late. They'd reached the valley and scattered.

Katie hung her head in dejection and tried to decide whether to risk going a little farther or heading back. She turned as if she might see the sheep wagon and sense if Christopher was all right.

That's when she saw the timber wolves on her trail.

There were three. Gaunt, slavering beasts with hunger-pinched eyes and heads too massive for their rib-ridged bodies. One growled menacingly and came closer than the others. Its coat was black and silver, and it was somehow chillingly beautiful. It had a blazed face, silver with a masklike appearance around the eyes. The other two were grayish, long of fang, and with scarred muzzles and torn ears. Though their coats were thick, Katie could still see the outlines of their bones.

She raised the Winchester, though they were still some distance away. The wolves shrank back under some snow-covered pines where she couldn't see anything but their faces. Katie saw a scree of boulders just up ahead and knew that beyond them she would have an unobstructed view of the valley. She glanced back at the wolves and decided to press on. Wolves would not attack a human being unless they sensed their quarry was defenseless, and these three certainly had been shot at before.

It seemed to take forever to reach the field of boulders, and Katie was acutely aware that the wolves were following her. She was afraid, wishing she'd gone back. The day was growing short, and the strength was draining from her body. Every labored step was taking her farther from the sheep wagon and her baby. Even worse, the wind had strengthened, and the storm seemed to be gathering its fury for the approaching darkness.

I must stay calm, she kept telling herself as she pushed onward. And if I do not see them at once, I will kill the wolves and go back.

At the rocks, she halted, her breath a fire in her chest. She sagged to her knees with weariness, and that's when the wolves closed in on her. Katie sensed rather than heard them. She swung around and threw the Winchester to her shoulder. The mittens! She couldn't get her mitten inside the trigger guard!

The wolves peeled away from their line of attack at the sight of the upraised rifle, and by the time Katie was able to tear her mittens free, they were into the rocks. She was so frightened that the rifle was jumping in her hands, and she knew she had to settle herself and kill the wolves the very next chance. Kill them while they watched her. Perhaps if one died, the others would eat it and leave her to go free.

Katie lowered the rifle. Her pulse was racing, and her

hands were already going numb. She pulled on her left mitten and used it to balance the rifle while she plunged the bare right hand back into her pocket. When she turned to scan the valley, she still didn't see her flock, but she did see a huge party of Indians.

Katie's eyes widened, and she dropped into a crouch. My God, she thought, what next? She raised up and studied the horsemen. They weren't Shoshoni. Katie guessed there were nearly two hundred, and they were heavily armed. Though the distance was almost a mile, she could distinctly catch snatches of their talk on the wind. She stared so hard her eyes ached, and it was only when she realized that they were going to ride by her canyon that the sick dread that had coiled up inside her stomach began to unwind.

Who was it? Red Cloud? It had to be. Where were they going, and would they return this way, perhaps to discover her? These questions beat at her until she wanted to scream. And if they saw her sheep, what then? Surely they'd come searching for a shepherd.

Katie leaned her head back against a rock and closed her eyes in momentary defeat. It seemed everything—the weather, the wolves, the Indians—was against her now. She didn't even want to think about how close she'd just come to firing a shot that would have been a certain death sentence.

A dog barked somewhere, and Katie's head snapped up. It was Taffy! She'd recognized her voice anywhere. The Indians did not hear the dog, and now they were riding past her valley. Katie glanced wildly across the canyon, and now she saw her flock, across the stream and against the far wall, down in a low place near a lightning-splintered stump. The three wolves had forgotten her and were silently running toward the flock.

"Taffy!" she cried, breaking from the rocks and pounding through the snow.

Katie reached the stream but fell heavily crossing the ice. On the far bank she labored up a slight rise and saw the black wolf closing toward Taffy—Taffy, who had the heart of a lion but stood no real chance against a wild, hunger-starved timber wolf.

She shouted, knowing the sound would not carry. When the black wolf did not hesitate, Katie began to run again. The Indians were out of sight, but were they beyond the distance of hearing gunfire? She couldn't risk it. Not with Christopher's own life at stake.

Taffy and the black wolf rolled in the snow, twisting and snarling. They were just a blur of pale brown and silver black, and their sounds were terrible. Katie saw the other two wolves sweep by and attack a ewe. The sheep, half-buried in drifts, floundered in terror but were unable to run.

"Taffy!" She was almost on them now.

The black wolf surged to its feet, and its long, glistening fangs and dark lips were covered with blood. Beneath it, Taffy tried to rise, but the flashing fangs drove her down into the snow and sought the jugular vein.

With a cry, Katie gripped her rifle by the barrel with both hands and brought the stock crashing down on the huge wolf's beautiful mask-face. The wolf grunted. Its jaws were clamped on Taffy's throat, and it was trying to tear flesh and tissue, to rip into the lifeblood of its victim.

Katie swore, then bought her rifle up and chopped it down again with all her strength. The skull was crushed, and the wolf gurgled and began to flop as Katie kicked it away and pulled Taffy free. When she stumbled about and saw the other two gray wolves slashing at one of her ewes, Katie forgot the Indians. She raised the Winchester and shot both wolves. The first died with a bullet through its head; the second took off running on three legs. Katie used two more bullets to finish it off near the frozen stream. A final bullet went to the dying ewe.

She crumpled in the snow and wrapped both arms around Taffy, who licked her gratefully. The dog's skin was severely torn and bloody, but there seemed to be no serious damage.

The sheep were still bleating in terror as Katie gripped her dog and waited, expecting to hear a bloodcurdling Indian scream. But none came. They had not heard her.

Katie raised her head and kissed Taffy on the nose. "We almost lost it all this time, dear girl. The Lord must be watching."

She glanced over at the black wolf. Its jaws were filled with Taffy's hair, and there was nothing beautiful about the animal now. Katie fished into her coat and yanked out a very good pocketknife that she'd bought a long time ago from Sabino Echavarria for castrating lambs. Now, gritting her teeth, she sliced off the black wolf's tail.

Taffy whined nervously. "It's all right, girl. The Basque shepherd told me to hang this on the bushes around camp to keep wolves and coyotes away."

Taffy's own tail thumped on the snow. She sniffed at the trophy and growled.

"Come on," Katie said with a tight smile of triumph. "Let's get this flock back up to their bedground before dark and this storm gets any worse."

The dog rose to its feet, and together they started to work. It wasn't easy, and it took them until long after dark to finish. Katie was past feeling and past exhaustion when she finally threw open the wagon door and toppled half frozen into the dark, cold interior. Poor Christopher was crying hoarsely, and the fire was nearly dead. She pulled Taffy inside and lit her kerosene lamp, then threw a pile of wood into the stove—wood she'd cut only that morning, a lifetime ago.

In a few minutes she had the fire licking with a fresh hunger, and she was peeling out of her clothes and burrowing under her blankets.

"You poor, poor baby," she said quietly. "Someday, this might make a fine story for your children or grandchildren. They'll shake their heads, maybe judge me wrong for leaving you. I'm sorry, Christopher, but I had to. For both of us."

When the baby finally quieted, Katie found herself so tired there was absolutely no hope of sleep. In her little cast-iron cookstove the cottonwood snapped and pinged as sparks shot against metal. The wagon grew luxuriously warm, and little reflections of firelight escaped to dance on the shivering canvas overhead. Katie sank deep in her bed and found herself shaking still, though now more from the aftershock of how near she'd come to dying and how her baby might also have died of exposure, since Rebecca had been unable to return as planned. That realization frightened her more than the thought of her own death. Katie swore at herself for taking such an awful chance. Twice that night she dressed and went back out in the storm to check on her flock. They weren't going anywhere. Had they wanted to, she doubted she'd have had the strength to hold them.

It wasn't until an hour before dawn that Katie finally managed to forgive herself and taste the mercy of sleep. An hour later, Taffy awoke, studied her mistress, then pushed outside to guard the flock. She moved very stiffly toward the sheep. When she turned her neck, it was obvious she was in pain. Yet, as she padded a snowy circle around the woollies, it was also clear that the dog was in command, ready to fight to the death if need be.

The storm lasted three more days, then broke under a turquoise sky. By noon the creek was running full, and the pines, heavily burdened with snow, were raining water in sheets. Not far from the wagon, Katie sat on a rock, holding Christopher while her sheep grazed on the higher slopes of the valley, up where the sage and brush provided a nutritious winter browse. Katie was at peace. She leaned far back and let the sun soak pain from her muscles. Her eyes were closed, and she felt a deep sense of relief and growing optimism. The snow would not last another day in this weather. Far out in the Wind River it had already disappeared except for a few stubborn patches.

From a nearby tree hung the black wolf's tail, and she was resolved not to tell Rebecca but to let her find it instead. Then, as though nothing really had happened, she'd let her sister drag the story out, bit by bit. Katie smiled with anticipation. Yes, it was a prideful thing, but she was proud of herself and Taffy. Katie realized that luck had played no small part in her success and that if she hadn't forgotten to remove her mittens before trying to shoot . . . well, she was just thankful she had.

"Katie!"

Her head snapped up. Taffy began to bark, and Katie smiled to see Rebecca galloping up her canyon, a rifle cradled across the saddle. She reined her horse in, and almost the first thing she saw was the wolf's tail.

"Katie, what happened?"

She shrugged indifferently, but it wasn't easy pretending she wasn't proud. "Not much. Just a little excitement during the storm. Climb down and I'll tell you all about it."

Rebecca wasted no time in accepting the offer, and there was a real look of concern in her eyes.

"Actually," Katie said, fighting not to blurt everything out in a big rush, "it's quite a story."

Ten minutes later Katie was finished with the telling. Rebecca said, "That's it. I'm not leaving you alone again."

Katie laughed and glanced up at the sky. "Winter is over. Look out there and you'll see flowers pushing up through the ground. Rebecca, I can feel the change. No more blizzards or hungry wolves. The worst is over."

Chapter Nineteen

His name was Yancy Dover, and he had been twenty-seven years old when the South fell and Texas submitted herself to the indignities of the carpetbagger government and the Reconstructionists. He was a Texas Ranger until the Northerners disbanded them, leaving the citizens at the mercy of the Indians, Mexican banditos, and the hated Comanche. During those blighted Reconstruction years, life along the Texas frontier was bloody and frightening. Without the Rangers, there was no law except that of the gun. As hundreds died and small ranchers and settlers fled to the cities for protection, Yancy Dover saw an opportunity, and he grabbed it in his big, rough hands. Moving westward, he'd taken the best of the vacated lands and forged for himself a cattle empire down near the Pecos River. It was hard, dry country and squarely in the path of Indian and Mexican raiders, yet Dover was as dangerous a man as any and hunted those who raided him and killed them with such savage vengeance that he was soon left in peace. Dover quickly prospered. Within three years, he had married, had an infant son, and claimed enough land to make him wealthy.

He cut a mighty figure. Standing six-foot-four and weighing two hundred and twenty pounds, he possessed massive sloping shoulders, a granite jaw, fierce black eyes and bushy brows, a fist-flattened nose, hair as wild and profuse as the Texas mesquite, and a voice rougher than the horses he rode. Yancy loved a fight, and that usually meant taking on a saloon crowd all by himself—a feat that sent his wife into near hysterics and made his three-year-old son cry to see his battered face.

Yancy was in the process of mellowing when he trailed a herd of longhorns to the San Antonio market, but while he was gone, the Comanche, drunk on tequila, struck his ranch. They came at sunset when the sky was red, and not even the small army of marksmen Yancy had left to defend his family could withstand their attack. It was over very quickly, and the Comanche raced a cold moon north with more stolen horses, guns, and whiskey than they could possibly have hoped for. Normally, they'd have taken hostages, but not Yancy's wife and little boy. Instead, they took their scalps and those of the ranch defenders and left in their wake only ashes and the smell of death.

Yancy Dover went berserk. He forgot his ranch and cattle and spent more than a year hunting Comanche. No one knew how many he killed, only that it was never enough and that it did not stop until his health was almost broken—until his great strength and spirit were exhausted and he was consuming a quart jar of whiskey between sundown and sunup.

In the fall of 1869, while drunk and idly considering suicide around a lonely campfire, he was visited by a drifter from Wyoming. He couldn't remember the man's name, only his face and most especially the way he'd talked about southwestern Wyoming. "High and dry," he'd said, with great tough plateaus, good nourishing grass, and the sweet scent of pine drifting off the Wind River Mountains. Soon there'd be a railroad, and cattlemen wouldn't have to drive their herds very far to cash in on both the California and the midwestern livestock markets.

Yancy and the drifter got drunk, and Yancy bragged about Texas a little, too, so that, come morning, hairy-tongued and acid-eyed, they'd ridden off in opposite directions, each thinking the other was a fool for leaving his native country. Yancy went back to San Antonio and closed out his bank account. During the next month he rehired most of his scattered crew and scoured the brush for what cattle he could find. They tallied forty-seven hundred, and a quarter of them were the wild ones, the "cimarrones" of the brush. They were all thin, mean, and wily—but as tough as West Texas. Yancy thought of these cattle as survivors, much like himself, and once they learned trail manners, he was proud of them. North they rode, up the Chisum Trail. They saw the Red River and then crossed the Washita, Canadian, and swung to the northwest along the Cimarron. Cattle buyers flocked to his camp at Dodge City, but Yancy ran them away. When his herds passed that railhead, the townspeople called him a goddamn fool.

And maybe he was. Yancy kept hoping the Comanche would attack his small herd, for he was still in a killing frame of mind. But it was not to be his fate to die in battle. They rolled north out of Comanche territory, through Kiowa Kansas and then into the lands of the Arapaho and the Cheyenne. It was as if he and his outfit led charmed lives, and it stayed that way clear to the Wind River. His first impression was only mildly favorable. It was cattle country, but he'd seen, even trailed over, better. Yet he liked the land, and it grew on him almost from the first day. It had a hardness about it that he appreciated; what grass there was was tough but nourishing. He liked the rolling hills and the badland buttes covered with short grasses, sagebrush, and greasewood. And best of all, the memories of Texas were now only an ache, and he could live with that.

Someone told Yancy Dover this was an Indian reservation, but that meant nothing to him, for land belonged only to those strong enough to take it. Three days after they arrived, they were resting their stock when a man named Bill Teacher pushed four hundred head of eastern-looking cattle down into the valley with every intention of grabbing some range. Yancy had other ideas, for he was in no mood to accommodate would-be neighbors.

"Hold up!" he ordered, galloping out to stop the advance.

Bill Teacher was a reasonable man; there was room for others. He sized up the approaching riders and knew at once they were Texans. He didn't like Texans; his son had died a Union soldier.

"Where are you going?" Yancy demanded.

"Up a ways. There's a canyon with red rocks I fancy," Teacher said.

"Big canyon?"

"Big enough. Nice stream. Good grass."

"Then I'll be wanting it," Yancy decided. "Turn your herd around."

Bill Teacher *was* a reasonable man, but neither was he a weakling or a coward. "I guess there's enough for all of us, mister."

Yancy grinned wickedly. "Maybe for *you* there is, but I'm from Texas, and this whole valley seems almost crowded. Ride out."

Teacher knew a moment of sharp disappointment and even a little bit of fear. He had, he knew, but two choices. He could go and be labeled a coward, thus spending the rest of his days in shame, or he could fight like a man. He chose the latter.

They buried him with respect that afternoon, and someone even said a prayer. Yancy got drunk for the first time in months, and so did both crews. That night he talked the Wyoming cowboys into hiring on to help him with those funny-looking eastern cattle they called shorthorns.

"They'll cross well with those longhorns of yours, sir," a brave Wyoming cowboy ventured after long deliberation.

"They look like pigs," Yancy said, squinting meanly around his bottle of whiskey. "Little splotchy-colored pigs."

The cowboy stared down at his feet and wished he'd kept quiet.

"Where's the canyon?" Yancy asked.

"What canyon?"

"The one you was agoin' to settle in."

The cowboy spluttered, "About twenty miles up this valley. Stream comes out of it. Red rocks and you can't miss it."

Yancy rolled a cigarette. "You'll show me tomorrow."

"Yes, sir. First thing tomorrow." He excused himself then and moved away into the darkness.

Rebecca saw them first. Six cowboys riding up from the basin beyond, and they weren't looking any way but toward her and the flock. Rebecca lifted the rifle, then levered a shell into the chamber. They saw her, and she guessed it wasn't a very friendly greeting, but there seemed nothing friendly about these hard-eyed strangers. All but one were dressed quite strangely for Wyoming cowboys. Their hats were too wide-brimmed, and they wore big jangling spurs and smooth chaps instead of the wooly type characteristic of this part of the country.

Rebecca took hope. Perhaps they were just passing strangers and only wanted information.

They reined in their horses, and she found that the big hawk-faced man in the center just naturally commanded her attention.

"Can I help you?" she asked, cradling the Winchester.

The big man stared until Rebecca felt her cheeks warming. "I said—"

"I heard you. Now what I want to know is, what are you doing here with them sheep?"

The tone of his voice left no doubt that he wasn't pleased. Rebecca somehow had the feeling that he viewed *her* as the intruder. "We've taken this canyon."

"We? Where is your man? I want to talk to your man," he said, eyes skimming the rims of the canyon.

"He isn't here now. You'd better leave."

Yancy spurred his horse forward. Rebecca had to jump to avoid being knocked over. "This is *our* land!" she cried.

A rifle shot boomed and Yancy threw himself from the saddle.

"Freeze!" Katie snapped.

For maybe the first time in his life, Yancy took an order; the rifle was cocked and pointed right at the center of his broad chest.

"You're trespassing," Katie said. "You and the rest

aren't welcome in this canyon, Now, catch your horse and git!"

He relaxed and climbed to his feet, just going higher and higher. Rebecca thought he was the biggest man she'd ever seen, and his demeanor gave him a hungry, almost predatory appearance.

"Ladies," he said. "My name is Yancy Dover and I'm from Texas, where they know I could kill you both if I willed it so, but I'd never shoot a woman."

"Then leave," Rebecca said.

"I want to ride up to the head of this canyon."

"No."

"I like the looks of this canyon," he said in a voice loud enough to echo off the red walls. "I'd pay you a fair price."

"It's not for sale at any price," Katie said defiantly.

Yancy frowned, thumbed his hat back, and chewed on her words. "You're a pretty woman. Both of you are, but you're not long on sense." He remounted, and his eyes dismissed them as he studied the rocks and the grass and the stream. He rolled a cigarette by feel and scratched a light off his saddle horn. "You women best hope I find another canyon as good, right close, or you'll have to leave and take those damned stinking sheep."

"In a box," Katie hissed. "That's the only way we'll go."

Yancy inhaled deeply. "I'm a reasonable man, ladies, but don't try and take advantage of my own generosity and good nature. I don't cheat folks, but I step aside for no one."

He tipped his hat then, and he rode away.

Rebecca and Katie were tight-lipped with worry, and that night neither of them slept. For two more days they carried their rifles cocked and at the ready. They were nervous and irritable and afraid. By the end of the week they were just too tired to worry about Yancy Dover anymore. He would have to take his place in line with the wolves, the grizzly whose tracks they'd found, the weather, and the Indians.

"Maybe he'll stumble into Red Cloud," Katie said hopefully.

Rebecca shrugged. "Then I don't know which one to feel sorrier for."

"Yeah, it would make a hell of a fight."

"Maybe they'd kill each other off and then we'd have neither to fret about."

"You know," Katie said with a dry smile, "you stick around out here long enough, we're going to think so alike it will be spooky."

Rebecca merely nodded. No sense in telling Katie all over again that she had no intention of remaining longer than necessary. But that might be years—and if Yancy Dover didn't find himself a good canyon, it could even be what was left of a short lifetime.

The spring crop of lambs arrived late, perhaps because the ewes had been in poor flesh and needed a few extra weeks to prepare for birthing. Rebecca learned how fast and exciting lambing could be. Katie showed her all the tricks that the Basques had taught her only two summers earlier. Rebecca was able to go one step further and saved a ewe and her lamb by using some of her knowledge of midwifery.

"I'm sure Mr. Echavarria wouldn't approve of my methods," she commented later, "and that his knowledge of sheep far exceeds my own. *But* he's a man, and when you come right down to it, I think a woman's instincts are superior to any man's in this kind of thing."

"I won't argue with you on that," Katie said, remembering how Rebecca's skill had saved Christopher's life and her own. "It's just too bad that the presidents of those eastern medical schools won't believe you."

"Funny, I was thinking the same thing."

The summer grew hot in August, and they pushed the sheep up into the mountains, though Katie was loath to abandon her sheep wagon and canyon for more than a night. One day, Captain Taylor assigned to survey the grounds for the Wind River Army post appeared and told them that Washakie's tribe had been attacked by Red Cloud. "The Shoshoni lost thirty warriors and many, many horses."

"Was it the Indians I saw during the blizzard?" Katie asked.

"Yes, and what's ironic is that the Shoshoni were armed with cap-and-ball pistols and rifles and Red Cloud's Sioux had only bows and arrows. The blizzard made the Shoshoni guns useless and gave the Sioux a victory. Now Washakie swears he won't come here until the Army can guarantee the safety of his people. That may take another year or two."

"Have you met a cattleman named Yancy Dover?" Rebecca asked.

The captain's expression left no doubt he had. "That man is dangerous. He's moved in to settle along the Popo Agie River. We keep having to crowd his herd back out of the basin. There's been a time or two when I've had the impression he'd be willing to attack the fort and do battle with the U.S. Army."

"How far is his valley?"

"Less than five miles from you, just over that ridge."

Rebecca felt a chill.

"He has a message for you. He said he'll be wanting this canyon when his herds get larger. I told him the United States government would not stand for his threats, and, should he take action against you or any other settlers, we'll deal swiftly and with force."

"He won't listen to you," Katie said.

"He'll have to, or he'll go to a cemetery or a federal prison."

When the captain and his small detachment of cavalry had ridden away, Rebecca said, "Mr. Dover would never try to oppose the Army. I think we can both sleep easier now."

Katie glanced toward the ridge beyond which the Texan had settled. "Five miles is stepping all over each other to a man like Dover. Army or not, he'll return, and he'll want this canyon."

"And our answer will be the same," Rebecca said tersely. "Let's stop worrying about the man and worry instead about these damned sheep of yours."

*   *   *

By late summer, they could not avoid shearing any longer. To delay would mean the flock would go into winter insufficiently protected with wool. Dutch John had to order shears from Omaha, and by the time they finally arrived, the wool was longer, greasier, and dirtier than it should have been. They knew they were in for an awful time.

Rebecca dubiously tested the new shears, which were like grass clippers. "Do you really know how to do it?"

"Sort of," Katie answered. "When the Basques were shearing in Temple City, I was responsible for watching the flock and trying to keep those that had been sheared from those that had not. It wasn't easy."

"Well, this isn't going to be easy either."

"Not if we keep talking, it won't. Let's have a go at it. We need the wool money."

Rebecca sauntered into the flock, trying to look casual. The sheep eyed her suspiciously. Spying a ewe whose coat looked a little cleaner than some of the others, she tackled it and the animal began to bleat and thrash about.

"Katie, hurry up!" she shouted.

Katie laid Christopher on a blanket and rushed to her aid, just as the ewe's lamb began to butt Rebecca and bleat piteously for its mother.

"Well, don't just stand there!" Rebecca gritted, with her fingers dug into the wool and both legs wrapped around the ewe in a body lock. "Start cutting!"

Katie knelt beside the ewe. When it saw the clippers, the poor thing almost went crazy. It apparently remembered shears, how they could slice, even amputate the flesh.

"Help!" Rebecca groaned as the ewe got a leg into her stomach.

Katie smothered the floundering ewe and tried to push the lamb aside. "Here we go," she said, jamming the shears into the thick, greasy coat, only to discover they wouldn't open. She yanked them out again.

"Didn't you learn *anything* about shearing?"

"No, but I'm fixing to now!" she said, snipping madly.

Wool began to fly, and after several moments Katie grunted, "This isn't so bad."

"Isn't it supposed to come off in a fleece?"

"Don't be damned picky. I'll take it any way I can."

"Yes, but snipping it off like that will take forever."

"We've got nothing better to do," Katie replied.

Rebecca's hands were filthy with grease, her dress was hiked up around her thighs, and the wool was already making her legs itch. It was hot, and she was perspiring, and the sweat made her eyes sting. "Nothing better to do!" she howled. "Well, I'll be damned if I'll spend all summer in this position!" She had slipped underneath the animal, and it was tramping all over her with its sharp little hooves.

"We'll get faster," Katie said, avoiding her eyes and working the shears furiously. "I remember Sabino Echavarria telling me that a good shearer can do a hundred a day."

"Well, I wish to God he was here now," Rebecca gasped, trying to shut out the constant bleating, which threatened to drive her mad.

"We've got to walk before we run. It's going to be a long time before we can afford to hire a sheep-shearing crew."

She was about to answer that, but just then Katie accidentally cut into the ewe's tail. For the next ten seconds, Rebecca held on for dear life as the ewe squealed and battled insanely.

"Be careful, damn it!"

Katie pressed on with grim determination. Flies buzzed, ants crawled over them, Rebecca's legs kept itching, and the ewe and her lamb kept bleating. Rebecca had never been more miserable in her life. When Katie finally finished and they released the bloody ewe with its hacked, uneven coat, Rebecca thought she was going to cry.

"Now, now," Katie said, returning with her baby. "It wasn't *that* bad."

"Yes, it was, and we've got almost two hundred to go!"

"We'll definitely have to get faster," Katie said. She

reached out and balled up the dirty, greasy wool. "I wonder how much this fleece will bring?"

Rebecca bit back her reply. To her, it certainly wasn't worth the hell of this past hour. She'd yank teeth first any day.

"Come on," Katie urged. "I'll hold the next one and you can shear. I've already got a couple of big thumb blisters."

It took them twelve days to shear the flock, and it was a miserable job, in spite of the fact that they became much more proficient toward the end of the ordeal. Rebecca swore that never again would she shear sheep, no matter how badly they needed the money.

Besides, the return wasn't all that good. Due to their inexperience, they'd rendered part of the wool useless, and they were lucky to get eighteen dollars for the entire crop. But the money was the first they'd earned from the sheep, and it made Katie very proud. To her, it was a landmark, a symbol of what was to come, and a long-awaited beginning.

"I wish Mother were alive to see us, Rebecca. She'd be proud of her two daughters and how we're going to make it on our own."

They were sitting on a rock, watching the sun tumble down to meet the skyline in an incredibly beautiful explosion of gold and silver along the rimrock edges of their canyon. It was a warm evening, and Rebecca could smell the grass and the flowers, hear birds nestling down for the night. Katie was right. Being financially independent was a fine thing, and it brought on a deep welling of satisfaction that could not be denied. Their mother had always been dependent on Micah, and he'd invariably failed her. Yet Rebecca could now objectively compare this kind of satisfaction to the ones she had felt when she and Devlin worked together. She'd never tell her sister this, but the other was better, even more deeply fulfilling.

Perhaps in time Katie would come to see this. Until then she seemed quite determined to go on alone if need be, seeing her flock multiply until she could hire shepherds and until Christopher was old enough to help. Katie talked about that quite often. It worried Rebecca that Katie seemed so driven to establish a foundation for her son and his offspring. Rebecca wished her sister would live more for the day, take a little more care of herself.

Devlin had taught her that lesson. In some ways he'd been a moody and difficult man, but in others he'd been a joy to live with. For one thing, he was one of the few people she'd ever met who were perfectly content to be exactly what they were. Now that she looked back on those days at Fort Bridger, she realized they were the best days of her life. And sometimes, like now, with the sun so indescribably beautiful, she wished, really wished, she could be there to stand again beside Black's Fork.

Katie squeezed her hand. "You've slipped away from me again. Where is it you go?"

"A secret time. A secret place. Even sisters can have secrets from each other, you know."

"Fort Bridger. Captain Devlin Woodson. I'm sorry, Rebecca, but that is not a secret to me."

The sunset was dying, the flame turning the color of smoke. Rebecca pushed herself to her feet. It was time to get busy just as Michael, a young Irish friend Jude had met working on the railroad, came up to speak to her. Smiling broadly, his eyes were alight at the discovery of so many books; he could read, though not as well as some. Jude accepted a cigar from the judge and sank deep into his chair, brandy balanced on one knee. "Will you sell them to me, then?" he asked, trying to appear relaxed, even a little indifferent.

The judge studied him carefully. "Are you certain, young man, that you really want to buy a thousand head of ewes and go up to Wind River?"

"I am."

"And what if the young woman rejects your . . . proposal?"

Jude frowned. He didn't even want to consider the possibility, and yet he must. "If that should happen, then Mike and I will raise them ourselves. I've explained everything to you and hope it meets with your approval. Obviously, there is a risk that Katie will not be pleased to see either me or the sheep."

"Obviously," Carter agreed. He seemed to change the direction of his thoughts, as if he wanted a little more time before making a final decision. "Do you know that my sheep are the finest crossbred flock in the entire West?"

"No, sir, I did not," Jude said truthfully.

"Well, they are. How much do you actually know about sheep, young man?"

Jude shrugged apologetically. "Not much, I'm afraid."

"And you, Michael Killeen?"

"I'd rather catch fish, sir."

"Hmmm," the judge mused aloud.

"But we both really want to learn," Jude said desperately.

"If you are going to raise woollies, you'd better learn all you can about them. A fundamental knowledge of breeding will determine your success or failure, your profits or losses. Besides," he said, winking at Michael Killeen, "fishing is more pleasurable, but there's not much money in it in Wyoming."

"No, sir," Michael said with his slow, warm smile.

The judge steepled his fingers. "I have several volumes on sheep here in this very library, but if you are going to pioneer in Wind River country, you'll never have time to read one. Let me give you a brief history lesson."

"Please do," Jude said.

"First, Columbus brought over sheep on his second voyage to America, landing them on the island of Hispaniola in 1493. Later, when Cortez conquered Mexico, he relied on sheep to feed his invading army. When Coronado and the Spanish explorers trailed their sheep into Texas, New Mexico, and Arizona, the Spanish missionaries were busy introducing them to the California Indians. Sheep have always thrived in America, but back in those days they were a much different kind of animal from the ones you are familiar with."

"How so?"

"Well, they were half-wild little beasts, more like goats

than today's sheep. They were called 'churros' or even 'Mexican bare-bellies," because of heavy wool growth along their backs. A hundred years ago the Spanish dons owned millions of them and hired thousands of 'pastores' as shepherds. These people were treated like serfs, paid almost nothing, and not even provided with rifles to protect their flocks. They were expected to fight off wolves, cougars, and grizzlies with swords or rocks. As you might also guess, they bred very big and ferocious dogs."

Jude chuckled. "I imagine they did."

"Yes. These fighting dogs were considered more valuable than the churros and the churros more valuable than the pastores. But let's stick with the churros. They were incredibly hardy little animals and perfectly capable of thriving in the furnace heat of a desert, or the terrible cold of a Wyoming winter."

"They sound perfect for this country," Jude said.

"They are, except that they are ugly animals and their meat is as tough and stringy as a jackrabbit. Furthermore, they produce only small amounts of coarse, inferior wool."

"Exit the churro," Jude said dryly.

Judge Carter shook his head. "Not at all. They are still to be found, mostly among the Indians in our Southwest. But they are being replaced by fine European stock, especially the Spanish merino, a breed largely unsurpassed for its rich quality and amazing quantity of wool. So superior is the merino that Spain did not even allow them to be exported until the beginning of this century. Eastern breeders, as well as the French and English, paid fortunes for merino rams. Over the years, they have been crossed with the churro and the French Rambouillet, also a superior dual-purpose animal."

" 'Dual purpose' meaning wool and meat?"

"Yes, the sheep I will sell you retain more of the merino blood than any others you will find. This is important for you to understand, because your wool will be of a higher quality than anyone else's and you should demand a higher price beginning with your first wool crop this fall."

"And what of meat production?"

The judge smiled apologetically. "I have concentrated on the quality and quantity of the wool. To do that, I've had to lose a bit on the meat. In time, I expect to increase meat production. You see, I keep detailed weight records of both wool and meat on all my flocks and carry on a strict breeding program. If you simply turn all your rams loose into a flock of ewes, you cannot hope to understand the effects of a breeding program, nor ever improve the blood and the performance."

Jude grew pensive. A range sheep operation was just that—a range operation. There was no way of telling which ram bred which ewe.

"I know what you are thinking," Judge Carter said. "It wouldn't be easy. Yet it is something I'll insist upon if you buy my sheep. I'll sell you purebred merino rams and you must agree to keep breeding records. From time to time I'll visit to inspect those records. I am interested in how my sheep will produce in varying climates and ranges."

"Sir," Jude protested. "I'm afraid I can't promise that. It would require pens and, during the breeding season, a separation of the ewes into bands."

"Exactly. And it is for that reason and because I very much care for Rebecca, and Katie, too, that I'm willing to defray those costs for you."

"You mean pay them?"

"Yes. *If* you agree that these sheep are to be used as foundation stock for Rebecca and Katie."

"And where do my own interests fit in? If, say, those women want nothing to do with Michael or me, then we'd be broke." Jude glanced at Michael and saw his own concerns reflected in the boy's keen eyes. Only now were they both beginning to understand how Judge Carter's mind operated.

"Those women need help," the judge said simply. "Without it, they cannot possibly repulse the cattlemen who will come to slaughter their flocks and drive them to ruin. You look like a pair who *can* help them. Am I wrong?"

"No, sir." Jude glanced over at Michael. Michael had

no doubts. Jude cleared his throat and winked at the boy before addressing Carter. "There is one thing, however, that I must make very clear. We mean to *own* sheep, not just work as hired hands."

"Then you know exactly what is required. Should you be successful, I'll be more than happy to perform the marriage ceremony."

"Thank you." Jude's worries were now at rest. They both understood the matter perfectly. All that remained was to woo and win Katie.

"By the way, I hope you realize that Rebecca is legally married."

Jude was shocked. Apparently, they did not yet understand each other fully. "I know that. It's Katie I'm interested in," he said stiffly.

"Excellent!" Judge Carter said, relaxing. He now raised his glass of brandy in a flourishing toast. "To your success—in business *and* in love."

Jude drank deeply.

Katie saw them first. Her mouth fell open and she stared in amazement at the sea of woollies pushing into the lower end of her beloved canyon. So great was the shock that it took her quite some time to recover and grab her Winchester. She'd been expecting an invasion of cattlemen; it had never occurred to her she might also have to ward off other sheep operators.

Rebecca was back at the wagon, tending to the cooking and the baby. There was no time to go for help, so Katie hiked up her long skirts and raced forward to intercept the flock and turn them around. She was running downhill, skirts and hair flying, when a rock turned under her heel. Her ankle twisted, and, with a cry of pain, she fell heavily. For a moment, at least, everything went out of focus, and she groaned, trying to clear her head.

"Don't move!" the voice yelled as a horse slid to a halt nearby. Katie heard crunching boots and managed to raise her head and see Jude Ludlow. For just an instant, she had a wild fear that he'd come to take her sheep back to Utah.

GARY McCARTHY

Something of that fear must have been evident because as he knelt beside her and brushed dirt from her hair he said, "I'm a friend. Remember?"

She *did* remember. It had been Jude who'd tried to save her father and had allowed her and her sheep to pass over the Bear River Divide in that blizzard. Katie quit struggling, but then the pain in her ankle made her wince. "I sprained it," she said. "It really hurts."

He reached under her arms and knees and lifted her.

"What are you doing? And those sheep! You can't bring them in here!"

He ignored her protest. "We'll have to set you down on the bank of that pretty stream. Cold mountain water will make that ankle feel better and hold down the swelling."

The water did feel good, and it was pointless to deny it, though she was furious at Jude and blamed him for the injury. Even worse, *his* sheep were now spreading out and grazing hungrily on *her* grass.

"Damn it, Jude! What are you doing here?"

"I came to find you," he said, kicking away his own boots and peeling off his socks, then setting his feet beside hers in the icy stream. "Feels good, doesn't it?"

"Not for long, it won't. I want you—" She saw a boy approach.

"Katie, this is Michael Killeen. He's my partner and friend. I've told him a great deal about you."

"It's an honor," the boy said gravely, removing his formless wool cap and wringing it in his hands. "Honest to Christ, it is."

Katie forgot what she was going to say. The Irish boy was staring at her with such intensity that she was a little unnerved. "Well, thank you," she sputtered.

"Oh, it's I who should be thanking *you*," Michael said fervently.

"Why?"

The boy looked to Jude for help and found it. "Perhaps you'd better go watch the dogs," Jude suggested.

Katie saw Taffy playing with a beautiful pair of sheep dogs. The boy hurried away. "What's going on here?"

Jude wriggled his toes in the stream. "You remember I said I loved you?"

"Yes."

"Well, I still do. I heard about Bryce. I left Utah to find you. Thought you might need me now."

"But I don't! And if you came all the way here to find me, you're crazy."

"No, just in love."

Katie sighed. She had no wish to hurt this young man's feelings, but . . . "Jude, I don't love you. This canyon belongs to Rebecca and me. We haven't many sheep left, but we've enough for a start."

"It's a magnificent canyon," he said, gazing at it with admiration. "And you've plenty of sheep now. Most of these I've brought are yours. But first, there's something I have to confess. It's a bad thing, but I can't keep it a secret."

Katie grew still. Jude looked more than distraught, and she could not imagine why.

He removed his Stetson, nervously ran his fingers through his hair. "Katie, I had no part in this or even any knowledge of it until last winter."

"What are you trying to say?" she demanded in exasperation.

"Just this. The reason most of those woollies are yours is that I took the money for them off Bryce's killer, and . . . and he was paid for by my father."

Katie stopped breathing for a moment, then let the words sink into her mind and eddy about inside her until she really understood what Jude was saying. "Did you kill my husband's murderer?" she whispered.

"I did." His mouth formed a hard, unforgiving line. "And I'm glad."

"And your father?" She wanted Amos Ludlow dead.

"No. It would have destroyed my mother. I just rode away."

Katie rested her forehead on her knees and closed her eyes. For nearly half an hour they sat quietly beside the stream. Finally she raised her head and looked at the man from Temple City.

"How much did your father pay?"

"A thousand dollars. I used it to buy part of those sheep from Judge Carter."

"And the rest?"

"Money that Michael and I earned working for the Union Pacific. Katie," Jude rushed. "The judge says we all ought to go into partnership."

"No."

"Katie, listen to me," he argued.

Her eyes sparked defiantly. "Why should I? This is my canyon, and I'll not give it up."

"I don't want this land!" he shouted. "I want you!"

"But I never want to be ordered about like a wife. I've lived in your house, remember?"

Katie pushed herself up and tried to put some weight on her ankle. "I'm beholden to you for ending the life of my husband's killer."

"Bryce was my friend."

"And I thank you for the sheep," she said brusquely.

"Judge Carter practically gave them to us!"

"But after you've separated what is mine from what belongs to the boy and you . . ."

"Katie!" He scooped her up in his arms. She slapped him, but he would not let her down, so she slapped him again and split his lip open.

"Damn you, Jude, just leave me be!" Tears sprang to her eyes.

"I can't," he said raggedly. "I already tried, and it didn't work. If you don't want me as a husband or a partner, then I'll find someplace close by and be your neighbor. You can't stop me from that."

Katie's face was only inches from his own. Never had she seen such unspeakable sadness in a man's eyes. With her sleeve, she dabbed at the trickle of blood she'd caused. He wasn't going to put her down, and he wasn't going to go away. "I can't walk, and you can't stand here holding me forever," she ventured.

"Then I guess you've no choice but to invite me to your camp to stay."

Katie wrapped her arms around his neck and said, "I

don't love you, Jude. I don't even understand you."

He grinned broadly. "Don't feel bad. I don't understand myself; either. I think I'm a fool."

Katie chuckled at that. "Only a fool would come here to be my partner. Let's have some tea, and you can tell me about Judge Carter. Rebecca—"

"She's up there now?"

"Yes." Katie felt him stiffen. "Why?" she asked cautiously.

"No reason," he answered as he marched up the canyon.

Over his shoulder, Katie could watch the sheep, all the dogs at play, and the young Irish boy who now waved. She beckoned him to follow, and he did.

"You have a baby."

It was a statement. "Yes, a son named Christopher."

"Now *that* is a nice name. Christopher Ludlow. Goes well together, doesn't it?" His tone was half in humor, but half serious, too.

Katie refused to answer. She studied Jude out of the corner of her eye. This man had freely given up for her what amounted to a great inheritance and a high position in Temple City. Given it up and avenged Bryce's death. That was, all considered, quite a testimony to his character and his devotion.

And he was handsome. Not ruggedly so, as Bryce had been. His jaw wasn't as strong, nor were his shoulders. Yet he carried her easily, and there was an intelligence about him and a hard determination that had been the best parts of Amos Ludlow.

Katie allowed herself to rest her head against his shoulder and relaxed. She would talk to Rebecca about this. Maybe they could use a couple of partners. She liked Jude and needed his help. But no more. Katie did not love him nor think she ever would. That was a fact of her life, and it was something he must understand if he were to remain.

The last thing in the world she needed or wanted was another husband to blur her shining vision of a sheep-raising empire.

Chapter Twenty

Rebecca had welcomed Jude, because he was needed. The welcome had not been returned to her. Though Jude was civil, even polite, it was obvious that he did not like her and that he blamed her for Bryce's death and Amos's crippling injuries. Rebecca could not bring herself to confront Jude about his suspicious and, instead, hoped time would heal and bring forgiveness.

In spite of Jude's hostility, the days were full and happy ones. Their large flock of sheep demanded constant attention, and there were always a hundred things to do. As the summer swept past and Katie still indicated no willingness to accept Jude as a partner, Rebecca became concerned.

"You can't expect the man to stay here if he's not given some encouragement, Katie. And you do need a partner."

Katie frowned. "I don't understand you. You're the one who's always talking about how a woman has to do things for herself because the law says she has no rights."

"You need his help. You can't do it alone, and I don't want to stay here another year."

"But what if he turns out like his father?" Katie asked, almost in a tone of desperation.

"He won't. Jude left everything to come and find you. Besides, Judge Carter is a very intelligent man and a sharp judge of character. He'd never have sent Jude unless he believed in him and Michael."

This appeared to relieve Katie. "He does seem to want to build for the future."

"Jude is smart and working hard. Michael Killeen is too."

WIND RIVER

Katie placed her hands on her lean hips and gazed at the flock. Jude saw her and waved. A slow smile formed on Katie's lips, and she waved back. "Oh, hell," she mused aloud. "Perhaps I've been too hard on him and you're right. I can't do this alone, and I do need help. Besides, those are mighty good-looking sheep. Jude told me all about their history. About sheep breeding and why he's set on keeping production records. And it all made sense. I was amazed at how much he knew."

"He's no fool," Rebecca said.

"That's true enough. He's done some fancy figuring on what we need to make this operation the biggest and best in the territory."

"He'd make a fine partner."

Katie looked almost convinced now. Still, her brow was furrowed. "What do I do about Michael? I can't see splitting into a three-way partnership."

"You wouldn't have to. Give Michael an incentive—a part of the lamb crop each year until he's a man and ready to go off on his own."

Katie nodded. "You like the boy better than Jude. I can tell, and I've wondered about it from the moment they came."

Now Rebecca understood that the ill feelings between her and Jude had been apparent to her sister and that Katie was troubled. She chose her words of explanation with care. "That could change, will change, someday. Right now he blames me for some things in the past about Bryce and his father. Then, too, it's hard for him to understand what I did. To Jude, it probably seems immoral."

"Immoral!"

"Katie, it's not his fault. I'm a bigamist. I left his father."

"He knows why. Jude left Amos for a lot of the same reasons you did—the man is a tyrant, a beast. I'll never forget what he did to you."

"He's paying for it now," Rebecca said.

"Not enough, as far as I'm concerned."

"Is that why you've treated Jude so coldly?"

GARY McCARTHY

Katie frowned. "Maybe."

"It's not his fault."

"I know. He really is a wonderful man. I wish you two could be friends."

"We will. In time."

But time was running out, and Rebecca knew she would be leaving before the winter snows fell. As the first leaves began to fly like beads of copper and gold from a fiery morning sun, they began a small cabin down near the stream by the cottonwood trees. Its dimensions were modest, even by local standards. Just eight by ten and a dirt floor. Even so, it was a difficult job, cutting the trees and notching their ends, then hoisting them into place. It took all their skill and determination, but it was done, and done well.

Their sense of accomplishment was heightened when they learned that Dutch John had gotten a top price for the wool that they'd gathered after weeks of hot, back-breaking labor. It had been Dutch who'd urged them to hold their wool until the crisp fall weather, and his advice had paid off handsomely. With eight hundred dollars of wool money, they thought they were rich.

By November the ice was thick enough for them to walk across their stream, and Rebecca wanted to return to South Pass City. The canyon's walls now seemed to press in on her, and the glorious fall colors were no more. She chose to leave on the day that Dutch John and Trudy finally arrived with the new cast-iron stove for Jude and Michael. Rebecca waited until late that afternoon when they were about to depart before she said, "Katie, I didn't tell you this, but that rider who stopped by last week from South Pass City said a good friend of mine, Esther Morris, is running a dangerously high fever. I must return to my medical practice. I'm needed."

"You're needed here!"

"No. I'm not. You'll be fine."

Rebecca turned to Michael. During the last few months, as Jude and Katie had spent more and more time together, she and the boy had grown close. "You make sure those two don't get careless around here."

342

"No, ma'am," he said, his voice filled with disappointment. "Wish you could stay."

"So do I in many ways." She gazed at the canyon, trying to lock it into her mind, because she knew the days would come during her life when she would want to return even when it might be impossible. "But I will be back. And soon. That's a promise. Good-bye, Jude."

"Good-bye," he said curtly.

Rebecca tried to cover up her disappointment. Give him time, she thought. Just time.

Katie reached out and they embraced. "Take care of yourself," Rebecca whispered. "If you get sick, or just need to talk, I'll be close."

Katie nodded. She understood. Rebecca would always come back.

Rebecca studied the thermometer and visibly relaxed. Esther Morris's temperature had fallen almost to normal. Her color was good, and her pugnacious jawline was set to argue if Rebecca instructed her to remain in bed even one more day.

"Well," the stout, middle-aged woman said. "Are you going to tell me I'm fit to leave this bed or not?"

"You really should rest a few days. You were a very sick woman."

Esther whipped off her blankets. "No time for that now. Not with our territorial elections coming up."

She stood in her shapeless woolen nightgown, a thick-bodied woman with gray in her hair and a tough, honest face, one incapable of hiding her feelings on any subject. "Are you going to help us get an official elected who'll vote for woman suffrage?"

Rebecca placed the thermometer in her bag. Esther was waiting for an answer, but Rebecca wasn't quite ready. "I haven't decided yet," she said.

Esther sat back down. "We need your help. You're a highly respected woman in this town and our most successful. If you don't help us buttonhole support, people will say you are opposed to our aims."

"I'm not opposed to you at all, Esther. I'm just not interested in politics. Surely you can understand that."

"Sit down," Esther ordered. "I can see you need some instruction."

"I've patients who need some care."

"They'll wait a few minutes. Rebecca, the women of this new territory have a chance that will never come again—a chance to help elect men to our legislature who'll give us some rights. The rights to vote and hold public office; the very same ones the United States of America gave to her freed slaves after the Civil War. Now, is that so much to ask?"

It wasn't. Of course it wasn't, and Rebecca knew that Esther was pushing for Wyoming to be the first state to give women these rights. It seemed unbelievable that they might be won here in this raw and not really civilized country, which was just now being granted territorial status.

"Esther," she said gently, because she realized how very important this cause was to her friend. "I just don't think it can be done here. Women in the East have been fighting for years to vote and hold office. Even Susan B. Anthony, Elizabeth Cady Stanton, and Lucy Stone haven't been able to win our vote. Why do you think we can do it in this little boom town on a mountaintop?"

"Do you know that when a woman marries, all her property automatically becomes her husband's?" Esther demanded.

Rebecca shook her head. She'd known that was the case among many Mormon wives, but had not believed it to be so among Gentiles.

"It's true! A husband's debts can be paid from his wife's income even against her wishes. Many a poor woman has seen her inheritance of wages gambled or drunk away while she stood helpless in the eyes of the law."

Esther took a sip of water from her bedside table. This was her favorite subject, and she was quick to warm to it. "Rebecca, you once told me you wanted to be a registered doctor trained and educated in a university. Why don't you save your money and go east to a school?"

"You know the answer to that. No women are allowed."

"See!" Esther cried triumphantly, bouncing to her feet again. "Now how can you say you aren't interested in politics? Unless you become interested, things like that are never going to change."

"How is my helping you talk to a few candidates going to change the mind of someone back east who decides on medical school applications?"

"Maybe it won't this year, or next. But if we win the vote, then other territories and states will follow. And if you have the vote"—she raised one stubby forefinger dramatically—"if you have the vote, you have the power to influence the decisions of our leaders *and* all of our public officials. University staff are supposed to be public officials."

She took a deep breath and studied Rebecca intently. "Winning our rights isn't going to get you admitted to a university; you are wise enough to know that. But it's a start. We have to try—you and me and all the others who are being denied our God-given rights."

The truth of Esther's words was undeniable. Rebecca didn't give a fiddle for politics, but she could see how they affected her life. "What exactly do you want me to do? Just come to this party of yours on the eve of election day?"

Victory assured, Esther smiled broadly. "Just wear a new dress and charm the hell out of them."

"Esther! I'm disappointed in you. First you talk of equality based on fairness and equal pay, then you tell me to charm the candidates."

"Well, *I* sure can't. I'm too old, and my husband will be there."

Rebecca's brows knitted in disapproval. "I'm also a married woman, or have you forgotten?" she demanded, turning away in hurt and anger.

"I'm sorry," Esther said. "It was unfair of me to say that. But no one in South Pass City can figure out why a man would leave someone like you alone here. And if you weren't married . . ."

"But I am," she said, pivoting around. "And I'm not going to fawn over a couple of politicians for anyone."

"Then just be nice to them. I know they both admire you, that you've doctored their friends or families. Simply be charming and say you support our cause. Is that so darned much to ask for all of womanhood?"

It wasn't, not at all. "Very well, I'll do my best."

Now that the pledge was given, Esther beamed. "Come on Rebecca. Show me how you're going to smile at all those candidates and melt their hearts and their resistance."

This woman was exasperating! Rebecca drew her lips back and gave Esther an idiotic grimace that threw the older woman into a fit of hysterical laughter. "Perfect," she squealed. "Just perfect!"

Rebecca shook her head, closed her bag, and left her friend howling in the bedroom. But by the time she reached the street, she was also struggling not to break out in laughter. She had to maintain her composure at all costs. There were dozens of familiar people on this street, and it would be unseemly for a doctor to complete a house call in the throes of uncontrollable laughter.

Still, it wasn't easy.

South Pass City was still growing. Its population was nudging four thousand, and its main street was half a mile long. Its school system was touted to be one of the best in the territory. Big Olive had long since sold her Sugar Palace, and the establishment was making a fortune for its new owner, a woman called Naughty Nellie. There were five hotels now, thirteen meat markets, four law firms, a dress shop, a weekly newspaper, a shooting gallery that was failing, and a beer garden that featured German music and turned away crowds. The fire company also served as the municipal band and was totally inept at both functions but looked splendid marching up and down the streets in new gold uniforms.

"Now," Esther Morris said as they halted outside the dress shop, "before we go inside, I want you to make up your mind that you're going to buy something pretty. Tonight is important."

"I know," Rebecca said. "But I can't see spending a lot of money on a dress I'll probably never wear again."

"Horsefeathers!" Esther snorted. "You'll wear it to lots of parties. This is just the beginning. I've invited the candidates, and I want you in a pretty new dress, standing out like a rose in a weed patch."

Rebecca smiled with tolerance. "Esther, a dress won't matter."

"Maybe, maybe not. I'm leaving nothing to chance."

They pushed inside. The owner, Beth Fisher, was waiting on a customer, and so Rebecca just stood admiring the beautiful dresses, parasols, bonnets, and bags that were on display, while Beth made a sale with practiced professionalism. The total came to over twenty dollars! Rebecca grew nervous. She hoped Esther didn't expect *her* to spend that much. That was a day's work of yanking teeth, and no dress was *that* pretty.

Beth Fisher was a slender woman with dark hair, a rather longish face, and wide-spaced, lovely eyes. No one would say she was pretty, but she did have an air of refinement. When she spoke of the latest eastern fashions, women believed her, and the few who had gone east to visit found they had not been misinformed.

"Oh, Mrs. Woodson, do come over here!" Beth called when she was free. "You don't know how many times I've watched you march past my shop and wished I could pull you inside for a fitting."

Rebecca suddenly felt self-conscious in her drab dress amid all this fluff and finery. There were dresses and bonnets in every color of the rainbow stacked to the ceiling, so pretty that it almost took a woman's breath away. "I've never had the time or money for anything like this. I have no idea of what to buy."

"Trust me," Beth said. "I know why you need the dress, and I want you to look stunning tonight." She began to circle Rebecca, eyeing her like a storefront mannequin. "Mmmm. Yes. Exactly."

"Exactly what?"

"Please. Don't move." Beth's left eye closed; her right eye narrowed in measurement. "It's perfect!" she cried. "Even the sleeves will fit."

"But—"

"Don't you worry, Mrs. Woodson. When you see this dress, the price will not be an issue."

She hurried into the back room and a moment later appeared with a dress so lovely that Rebecca drew a sharp breath in admiration.

Beth held it up and said, "This was *made* for you."

She couldn't argue the point. The dress was a pale pink, a shade Rebecca had seen only in the glow of sunset, and it was sprinkled with perfectly exquisite tiny red rosebuds. The sweeping overskirt would accentuate Rebecca's graceful figure. She especially loved the dainty scarlet bows so perfectly stitched into the rather low neckline, a neckline that made Rebecca wonder if she dared wear such a gown.

Esther was effusive. "You'll kill 'em, Rebecca! They'll be pouring my punch all over their shirtfronts staring at you."

"That is *not* the desired effect." Her doubt showed on her face.

"Maybe not, but compared to the dresses I saw Big Olive wear and squeeze her girls into, that one ought to pass muster in Sunday school."

Rebecca wasn't convinced. She loved the dress, but she would not be comfortable with that much of her bosom revealed. "I'm just not sure."

Beth said, "Rebecca, on you the dress will be wonderful. Furthermore, it's entirely respectable, and that neckline is only alluring. There will be other women at Esther's party with far more revealing dresses."

"I don't care. I'm . . . well, I just can't."

"All right, then I will make a small change that will put your modesty at ease. Just one moment, please."

She vanished into the back room.

Esther was unhappy. "You should have at least tried it on first."

"I didn't need to."

"Here," Beth called, hurrying forward. "I think you'll appreciate my ability to improvise."

Rebecca clapped her hands together with pleasure. Right at the base of the neckline Beth had placed a white lace flower. It seemed to her a touch of genius and made the dress perfect. "I'll try it!"

"You're stealing it for only twenty-eight dollars. No extra charge for the alteration."

Rebecca tried the dress on and paraded before Beth and Esther.

"It's perfect," Beth said. "May I ask if you have any appropriate jewelry?"

Jewelry? She hadn't even thought of it and shook her head. "And I can't afford any now."

"Then I'll lend you some. I've just the right pieces to go with this."

Again she vanished. Rebecca heard her rummaging about in the stockroom, and when Beth reappeared she was holding a huge jewelry box.

"None of this is expensive, so don't worry, but it is of some quality."

She continued to survey her stock while Esther and Rebecca patiently waited. "Here they are!"

"They" were a lovely pearl necklace set off by a delicate coral medallion, matching earrings, and a mother-of-pearl bracelet. Rebecca's eyes shone, and she felt a tightness in her throat as she accepted the pieces. "I'd have given anything in this world if my mother could have worn these and a dress like this one for just one night. She never had a store-bought dress; the only jewelry she ever owned was a thin wedding band of German silver."

Esther nodded. "We have so much that our mothers never had. The telegraph, the safety pin, Mason jars for canning, sewing machines, store-bought teeth! Now they're even coming out with a machine that types words in ink. Our mothers never even imagined these things. But there's one thing that hasn't changed. Women still cannot vote or hold office. In that way, we're not a stitch better off than they were—that's why tonight is so important."

"Esther, you've a one-track mind," Rebecca said.

She winked. "And just like a big old noisy train, I'm just going to keep coming."

Rebecca wished this overbearing newspaper reporter would finish his interview. His name was Samuel Pickney, and he was a short, unattractive man with deep-set, watery eyes, a doughy complexion, and a red, bulbous nose lined with blue veins. His breath was a nauseous combination of cigar and whiskey.

"So," he said, "you claim Mrs. Esther Morris is the one responsible for bringing the issue of woman suffrage here to Cheyenne for a vote. And yet yours is the name on everyone's lips. It is you, Mrs. Woodson, who are being regaled and pursued for interviews. How do you account for that?"

The tone of his voice was slightly accusatory, and if he hadn't been representing a large newspaper, Rebecca would have terminated the conversation. This, she thought, is the price one paid for championing a cause—the subjugation of one's own wishes to the attainment of the idea.

"Mrs. Woodson, I asked—"

"I heard you," she replied. "And it was a good question, but a difficult one. Perhaps you should ask your colleagues instead."

In his fat, nail-bitten hand, the pencil hung stationary over a smudged pad. "Let's try another one. Do you believe you have the support you need to win?"

"Yes. Colonel Bright is a strong supporter of woman suffrage, as evidenced by his introduction of Senate Bill Number Seventy, which I'm sure you've studied."

The Pencil wrote: Senate Bill No. 70. Read.

Rebecca suppressed a smile. "Colonel Bright endorses our position. Now that the Fifteenth Amendment gives Negroes the right to vote, it is only fair that we be given the same right. Our secretary of state, Edward Lee, has urged this legislature to distinguish itself by being the first to give women the vote."

"Yes, I know that, but you do have your detractors

among the new officials. Mr. Sheeks has attempted to kill the measure. He's even urged that the word 'women' be struck and replaced by 'all colored women and squaws.'" The reporter chuckled obscenely. He was obviously very amused.

Rebecca controlled her temper. She would not be goaded into name-calling. "Mr. Ben Sheeks considers himself a wit, and he laughs loudest and longest at his own jokes. That ought to tell you something. Besides, Governor Campbell supports the bill fully and has promised to sign it tonight if it clears the legislature."

"Ah! That is the question. And what will you and Mrs. Morris do if Bill Number Seventy dies in committee?"

"See that it is reintroduced."

"For what purpose? The waste—"

Rebecca stood up. "Mr. Pickney, I'm afraid I'm developing a headache. It has been a long day. If you will excuse me?"

He bounced to his feet so suddenly the notepad fell to the carpet. "Come now! This is history. In just a few hours we'll know if you can pull this off. If so, your name and face will be on the front page of every newspaper in the country."

Rebecca felt a chill. "No, that's not fair. It is Esther Morris who deserves the credit."

"She isn't here!" Pickney said with exasperation. "Besides, you're the pretty one. I've seen Mrs. Morris. She won't sell copy."

"Sell copy! Damn you and your copy!"

"Now we *are* getting some copy. I'll use that quote."

"You wouldn't dare."

"Oh, yes, I would. Passion sells, Mrs. Woodson, and I was about to decide you were passionless." He bent down and retrieved the pad, scribbling furiously and talking even faster. "Now, tomorrow morning, if you pull this off—"

"Quit using that term. 'We are not 'pulling off' anything except justice." She was losing control.

"Sure," he growled. "*If* you win, my editor wants an exclusive story for which I'm authorized to pay you one hundred dollars. Of course, you will have to pose for our artist and photographer, and I'll insist on knowing more of your background than you've been willing to give up to now."

"I am a skilled medical practitioner. The rest of my background is immaterial."

He studied her with his deep-set little eyes, his nostrils dilated as if sniffing for secrets. "It is *you*, Mrs. Woodson, who chose to be a spokesman for this. You must have known that victory would make you a celebrity, a household name along with other prominent suffragists."

Her voice was shaking, but she couldn't control it. "Listen, it was not I who brought the candidates together in South Pass City, nor did I introduce Bill Number Seventy, nor will I be the one who signs it into law. *Those* are the celebrities. My interest is medicine, not the sales of your newspaper."

"I believe you. I actually do. But don't be so naive. If the bill passes, you're a story, and no one cares whether you enjoy it or not. You'll be public domain."

She had a sick feeling that he was right, and even to herself her protest now seemed feeble. "I'll refuse to grant interviews, Mr. Pickney. No one can force me to speak out. I'll become reclusive."

"If you take that position, I'll crucify you in print. I'll not leave you alone for a moment. I'll hound you in the present and dig into your past until I have your story—and what is missing, I'll fabricate. Sensationalize. I am *very* creative, but you won't like my versions of your life."

The man made Rebecca shudder. Up to now, the journalists who'd pursued her had been pushy but courteous, annoying but not threatening. Some of the younger ones had seemed pathetically grateful for anything she'd tell them. Not so this vile Samuel Pickney. Not so at all.

He scratched his potbelly and consulted his pocket watch. "Two more hours. I hate waiting."

"Mr. Pickney, you can wait or not. I don't care. I'm going up to my room. I will not consent to an interview or pose for you again. Good night."

"Wait a minute, damn it!" he swore. "You can't walk

out on me now!" He was pursuing her across the lobby. Strangers gaped, and newspaper reporters moved quickly. Rebecca lowered her head and plowed through them all, wanting only to escape. How she suddenly longed for Wind River!

"Who are you, *Mrs*. Woodson? Who are you really?" Pickney bellowed. "Where is your husband? No one has asked, but I will. Where is your past, and what are you hiding?"

"Leave me alone!" she cried, reaching the stairs.

A hotel employee grabbed Samuel Pickney's arm.

"Let go of me!" the reporter demanded.

The hotel man was big, heavily muscled and scarred. Pickney made no attempt to get past him. He seemed content to hound Rebecca with his shrill voice.

"Mrs. Woodson, you haven't seen the last of me. I swear you'd better talk to me in the morning!"

"Go away!" she shouted, hurrying across the top landing. When she reached the sanctuary of her room, she pushed inside and threw the bolt lock. My God! she thought, trying to slow her heart. What can I do? For a long time she stood with her back pressed tightly against the door as wave after wave of despair washed over her. If the bill passed, her life would be destroyed as surely as Devlin's. She would be exposed for what she was, and all who had trusted her, befriended her, and had faith in her would be smeared in the shame of her past.

The answer, she realized, was evident. These people didn't need her, but her patients did. She would slip away, and she would do it tonight.

Chapter Twenty-one

Rebecca sat behind her office desk. The last of her patients had gone for the morning, and now she faced the city editor, Mr. Paul Lyman. There was an expression on his round, bearded face that told her the news was not good.

"All right," she said. "I'm sitting down, and you might as well tell me the worst of it straightaway."

Lyman was a short man. He was also dynamic, a man who never could sit still and to whom pursuing a good, honest story was the most important goal he could imagine. South Pass City's paper was lively and far more accurate than its contemporaries; the city was fortunate to have such an editor.

He steepled his pudgy fingers and looked uncomfortable. "I'm afraid you can expect some company—a lot of it and soon. I have a copy here of a Philadelphia newspaper. I think you'd better remain seated while you read."

Rebecca warily took the paper. She'd been expecting this, and a quick glance at the byline told her that Samuel Pickney had not forgotten her. The dateline read Cheyenne, which meant that he'd telegraphed the entire story to Philadelphia and chosen to remain in Wyoming; it seemed reasonable to assume the worst—that he and his ilk were on their way to South Pass City.

The bold headlines were strung clear across the front page:

WYOMING GIVES ITS WOMEN THE VOTE
MYSTERY WOMAN VANISHES

Cheyenne, December 12, 1869. History was made at the

stroke of midnight, when Governor William Campbell signed into law the very first legislation ever to give American women the right to vote and hold office. This ends for the present what had been a hotly contested issue and one sure to arouse the passions of fiery debate throughout our land.

Upon awakening to the discovery of this new law, many of Cheyenne's staunchest critics of the measure did gather in public to raise glasses of beer and toast, "To the lovely ladies, once our superiors, now our equals!"

Reflecting this cynicism, a great many here are treating this new piece of legislation as a poor joke intended to succeed only in attracting both publicity and women.

To this reporter, the irony is that the infant Territory of Wyoming, so wild and such a bastion of rugged individualism, should be the first to grant equality to its women. Perhaps this is because to survive in this harsh environment many Wyoming ladies must think, act, and even dress like men.

Now the question that remains is, will they *vote* like their men or even dare to vote at all?

Rebecca's eyes sparked with anger. "This man is a bigot!" she cried. "I don't know why they allow him to write such opinionated copy as this. And on the front page! Of course the Wyoming women will vote."

"Read on," Lyman urged. "If that upset you, what follows is going to send you through the roof."

Almost as interesting as that question is the strange and sudden overnight disappearance of Mrs. Rebecca Woodson, whom I shall call the Doctor of Mystery. It is around Mrs. Woodson that much of the publicity has centered in recent days. This woman has a flourishing medical practice in South Pass City, yet she has absolutely no credentials. She is strikingly beautiful, charming, and seemingly intelligent, yet remains an utter enigma even to her closest friends.

Where did she go, and where is she from? These questions are beginning to be raised from all quarters. Yesterday, this reporter's attempts to provide the public with answers regarding her credentials as a doctor

or as a spokeswoman for woman suffrage were rudely
ignored by Mrs. Woodson.

"I told him I wasn't the spokeswoman for anything! I
made it clear that it was Esther Morris who'd been behind it from the start."

"Apparently," Lyman said, "he did not choose to believe you."

The paper began to quiver in Rebecca's hands.

> It could be argued that Mrs. Woodson or whoever
> she is has returned to her medical practice in South
> Pass City and that her past should be of no concern to
> the issue of woman suffrage. And yet, when one takes
> up the gauntlet of a public cause, does not the public
> have the right to know the reason for such action on
> order to determine its fundamental legitimacy?
>
> This reporter believes so. And now that she has won
> her victory, the public is waiting for answers from Wy-
> oming's Doctor of Mystery, a sketch of whom will be
> appearing soon in an upcoming issue of this paper.

Lyman handed her a page saying, "Here's the drawing.
I cut it out of the *Cheyenne Leader* for you to see. It's
already being reprinted all over this territory and will
probably be out in the big eastern papers by next week."

Rebecca's hand involuntarily lifted to her mouth when
she saw the sketch. It was like staring at a photograph.

"It's an amazing likeness, isn't it?" the editor said.
"Quite a piece of art."

"But how? I gave no one a sitting. It would be impossible to get this level of detail without my knowledge."

"Were you photographed unexpectedly in Cheyenne?"

"Yes, but—"

"That's it, then. The sketch was made by an artist using
a photograph. A top artist."

Rebecca groaned. "And I suppose this can easily be
copied by all the other papers." The very last thing she
wanted was her picture splashed all over the country.
Devlin would be shamed.

"Most assuredly so," Lyman answered. "We even have

a man in my small office who anxiously awaits your permission to copy this."

"For what purpose? I was not the story!" Rebecca shouted. "History has just been made, and yet you and the others insist on doing this type of reporting."

Lyman forced himself to take a chair. He crossed his stubby legs, then tried to hide his own exasperation. "We are businessmen first, my dear Mrs. Woodson. You must understand that. If you failed to take in enough cash, your medical practice would cease to exist."

"I could practice medicine from a porch."

"Well, I can't print a newspaper from one. It takes money. Those books on medicine you get, the journals, your instruments and medicines, they all cost money. We have to sell newspapers, just as you must collect fees. Mr. Pickney clearly recognizes this as a fact of life, and he also recognizes what none of the others did, namely that you lend an element of mystery to this story that greatly sharpens readership appeal. Now, please, will you give me permission to tell the full story and for my artist to recopy this sketch?"

"No!" she stormed. "I will most definitely not. I thought we were friends. I have trusted you."

"With good reason!" he bellowed, leaping out of the chair. "All right, then, I *won't* tell your side of the story. Let all the other newspapers in the West do it."

Rebecca felt washed out with relief.

"But may I give you some sound advice?"

"You may," she said wearily.

"You're going to have to tell someone before your past is discovered and then distorted and sensationalized beyond all truth. I swear I would publish it accurately. No one else will give you that much Think about it. Please."

Rebecca stood up and moved trancelike to the window. Out in the streets it was cold, and the surrounding mountains were mantled with snow. In three days it would be Christmas, and though she'd promised Trudy and Dutch John she would share it with them and remain in South Pass City to attend to her patients, Rebecca needed Katie and the Wind River more than anything in this world. Katie and her baby, Christopher, were her real family. That's where she belonged at Christmas, not here, facing reporters like Samuel Pickney.

"Rebecca? May I have your story so that I can do us both an honest service?"

"It is not just myself that I shield," she told him quietly. "I risk hurting someone else. How can I justify that?"

"I don't know. I expect you are referring to your husband, the one all of us have been wondering about since the day you arrived. Is that who you are trying to protect?"

"Yes."

The newspaperman expelled a deep breath. "I can't answer that. All I can say is that you will not be able to hide your past. Everyone knows you came from Fort Bridger. If you refuse to speak, that's where the questioning will begin."

"Damn it!" she raged, turning on him in anger. "This is not fair."

"The issue has nothing to do with fairness."

"What . . . what if I run?"

"To where? Your sister in Wind River? When the weather clears, they will come and find you. They are being sent from the East and West coasts. Do you really believe that thirty miles of icy, rutted road will stop them after coming this far? It is common knowledge that your sister has a sheep ranch nearby. They'll find out where it is. They are very good at asking questions."

She glanced up at the clock on her wall. It was only eleven A.M. "Have you met the new doctor yet?"

He frowned, clearly disappointed by this sudden change of topic. "Why, haven't you met Dr. Henderson?"

"No."

"He's a fine man. Has a wife and two children. I know he's anxious to meet you. I've been told he delivered Mrs. Kinney's baby and did an excellent job. Though I'm sure not," he added quickly, "as good a one as you'd have done."

Rebecca smiled at this obvious diplomacy. "It's nice of you to say that, but I doubt very much that it's true."

"Well, anyway, the fellow seems experienced and quite agreeable. I'm sure you'll have a good deal in common."

"I'm sure," Rebecca said, wondering why she was almost dreading the meeting instead of looking forward to having a colleague with whom to consult. Was she afraid that he would be more knowledgeable or skilled than she?

"Rebecca, I have to go," he said. "I'm sorry your own paper will not be permitted to give a true story of your past."

He was almost at the door when she stopped him with her words. "Paul, I'll come by your office in a little while and give you my decision. No promises. I just need to think. To be sure."

"Thank you!" He slapped his hands together, and his feet did a small, involuntary shuffle as if he were already off and running with the story. "You wouldn't regret it. I promise you."

When he'd left, Rebecca put on her heavy coat and went for a walk. Snow was blowing off the rim of the canyon and swirling down on the buildings. There were few people outside, for there was a wind that numbed the cheeks almost instantly. The saloons were packed. She could hear piano music and laughter.

Rebecca had a destination firmly in mind, and yet when she came abreast of Dr. Martin Henderson's new office, she wavered in her purpose to speak with him. Across the street she could see figures inside, and she told herself that he was too busy now, that she could meet him some other day. She also tried not to feel a small sense of betrayal; the people in there had probably been her patients before Henderson's arrival. It was going to be hard for two doctors to make a living this winter. In the spring, when the weather improved, the population would triple as miners poured in and production shot up, but spring was a long time away.

Rebecca pulled up her collar and walked on until she reached the livery stable. Inside, she halted and breathed in the smell of horses and hay, of leather and manure. It was a heady combination, but one that always lifted her spirits, for it usually meant taking her mare for a run, and that was her favorite escape.

"Well, Mrs. Woodson! What brings you here on a day like this?"

It was the livery owner, a wizened, bald-headed man, yet one possessing the most agreeable disposition imaginable. "Too cold to go riding today, Mrs. Woodson."

Rebecca said nothing in reply. She entered the stall, and the mare nickered in the dimness and then came to nuzzle her with anticipation.

"You're tired of being cooped up in here, aren't you, dear lady?" She slipped a piece of sugar candy into her palm. The mare chomped down on it. "Frank, please grain her and tighten her shoes before you saddle her."

"Sure you want to ride out on a day like this?" he yelled as she hurried past, now filled with decision.

"Yes!" Rebecca called from the barn door. "And please hurry!" She rushed out into the daylight. Overhead, the blue sky stretched on forever. The weather was as fine as you could expect at this time of year. She'd pay a quick visit to Dr. Henderson and ask him to attend any of her patients who might need assistance during her absence. Then she was going to give Paul Lyman his interview and she'd tell him everything—her forced marriage to Amos Ludlow and then the terrible mistake she'd made in falling in love with Devlin. She didn't expect that many readers would condone her shocking behavior. It was really unfair. A man could beat his wife or neighbor senseless, get drunk in public, raise hell and destroy public property, visit the Sugar Palace, or do any number of things, yet a woman was expected to be virtuous in all matters or she was labeled loose and immoral. It wasn't right, and maybe with the vote, women would start to be treated fairly.

All that mattered now, however, was to make sure her story was told with honesty and that it was perfectly clear that she alone was at fault regarding her bigamous state. Then she would let the cards fall where they may. Rebecca was sick to death of running and hiding, of keeping her past a secret even from Trudy and Esther Morris, knowing her secrecy wounded their feelings.

She paused outside Dr. Henderson's office, suddenly a little afraid. Here was a real doctor, an upright married man who, after tomorrow, might well find his business doubling as Rebecca's own shocked patients switched alliances during her holiday visit to Wind River. But would they desert her so easily? She paused, remembering all the babies she'd delivered, some of whom would surely have died without her skill, and the gunshot wounds, broken bones, and raging fevers she'd attended to. Rebecca's chin lifted. She might not have the university diploma, but by heaven she had earned the right to practice in this hell-raising boom town. And diploma or not, no man could deliver babies the way she could!

Rebecca strode inside to meet her colleague. She would stay but a few minutes, and then she'd tell the South Pass City editor story while an artist had a chance to correct any imperfect lines in the sketch he'd be making.

She would stay through the noon hour. And then she'd leave for Wind River. Very probably the reporters would come after her, but perhaps by then she'd have had a chance to decide on her future—and she desperately needed time.

Katie would help her find the right answers. Katie, whose strength would meld with her own until, as in days long past, they would both become stronger, more sure of themselves. And when the reporters found her, she would be ready. Yes, with Devlin gone, Katie and Wind River were her sanctuary.

Rebecca reined in her weary horse at the crest of the ridge for a short breather. It was nearing sundown, and the temperature was probably in the twenties. The air snapped with crispness, and the snow-covered road snaking down to Wind River was unmarked by the passage of man.

Just below was Katie's beloved red rock canyon, and it had never seemed more beautiful to Rebecca than now. The canyon walls were dusted with snow, and the snow, and piñon and juniper that jutted out into the sky clung to their foundations with knotted roots, sinewy and twisted like tortured, arthritic fingers. She noted the wispy plume of chimney smoke and, very faintly, heard the soft, reassuring bleat of sheep, which now seemed almost musical. Rebecca's eyes lifted to the great valley, which was dark compared to the white mountain ranges that encircled and protected it from the high plains blizzards.

"Wind River," she said. "You look so peaceful and safe." It is little wonder, she thought, that this is the favored ground of the Shoshoni, the place where Chief Washakie chose to settle his people forever.

As her eyes swept over the landscape and drank in the vast grandeur of it all, Rebecca desperately wished she were the kind of person who could find a lasting peace in such a place as this. She patted the mare with affection. "Come on, let's get down off this mountain and get to that sheep wagon before we freeze in the dark."

The little mare did not need any urging. Head up, tail switching with anticipation, she moved forward with such excitement that Rebecca wondered if she remembered former days in Wind River. Perhaps her Indian pony had been born and raised here, spent long winters grazing near Shoshoni teepees, first tasted snow and felt her heart race as someone vaulted to her back and taught her how to hunt the buffalo that had until recently covered this valley. She wished the dun could speak; the animal would tell her some fascinating stories.

The road was icy, but the mare was surefooted. She came to the canyon's floor at dusk, just when the sheep wagon's patchwork canvas was beginning to glow with the light of Katie's potbellied stove. Rebecca gave the dun her head and let her race across the brown grass for the final mile. When the dogs began to bark and the door of the sheep wagon flew open, to reveal Katie holding Christopher, Rebecca let out a whoop of joy. Her voice rippled along the snowy canyon sides. This was as close to a homecoming as she was ever likely to know.

*   *   *

Rebecca let her troubles slip away in the ensuing days. The weather grew unseasonably warm; all traces of snow melted from the canyon sides, and thousands of small rivulets gleamed like strands of silver. The earth, saturated with runoff, became mushy; creating a danger for their sheep, which were not intelligent enough to stay out of boggy places. They would sink to their bellies, then bawl for help.

They all spent countless exasperating hours pulling sheep out of the mud and sometimes becoming so mired and muddied themselves that it became almost comical if they didn't let themselves take it too seriously. Most days, however, were uneventful. In the morning, she and Katie would have breakfast, then pack a good batch of biscuits for their noonday meal. Jude had made a sort of papoose cradle for the baby, and she and Katie would take turns wearing it as they herded the flock down into Wind River for the day's grazing. There they'd play with Christopher and just visit for hours.

Sheep raising was Katie's whole world, and though the subject became tedious sometimes, Rebecca was glad that she was so excited and optimistic about her future in this place.

"The biggest danger is overgrazing," Katie said. "It could ruin the land in just a few years. When my flocks build up into the thousands, I'll need to use this valley more and more. Chief Washakie will let me lease grazing rights down at this end; I've nothing to worry about there. Yancy Dover may have a problem, though. He's not exactly a friend of the Indians."

"You're sure he's not a threat to you anymore?"

"Not at all. We sat down one time right out here and I let him play with Christopher for a few minutes. We talked then, talked for hours, and when he left he promised that there'd be no trouble from him or his cowboys, most of whom hate sheep."

"That surprises me," Rebecca said.

"Me too, but that's what he said, and we shook hands on it. I even told him I hoped that someday there'd be a town right over yonder and that I wanted it to be a good town."

"What did he say to that?"

"Said there wasn't no such of a thing. All towns were bad." Katie chuckled with the remembering. "Of course, I told him that wasn't at all true. Probably the only towns he knows are the cattle trail towns and the boom towns. I explained that the kind of town I have in mind would be made up of families. There'd be a school and churches. You should have seen the look on his face!"

"What did it look like?"

"Like he'd swallowed castor oil. He jumped up and stomped over to his horse, saying that if that happened less than a hundred miles from his ranch he'd up and sell out. I told him I'd like to make the first offer."

Rebecca shook her head. "You said that?"

"Yep. And he laughed until he almost pitched out of the saddle. I tell you, he isn't anything like we thought he was. Oh, he's tough, all right, but fair, too. His cowboys think he's like God."

"That's because he acts like Him," Rebecca said shortly. She was relieved that Katie and Yancy Dover were going to live next to each other in peace, but that didn't change the way she'd felt about him from the beginning. Still, it wasn't her place to say anything more.

They began to talk of the breeding program that Jude and Judge Carter had worked up for the flocks.

"That's why they're working so hard to finish up those pens," Katie said. "The judge gave us the money to build everything."

"I think Michael looks awfully thin and tired," Rebecca said. "Is he working too hard?"

"I'm sure he is," Katie said. "Why don't you and he take this flock out tomorrow. There's a hundred things I need to do back at camp."

"All right, I will. Michael and I have always gotten along well together. I wish I could say the same for Jude."

"He'll warm to you," Katie promised. "He'd better, if he and I are going to get along. But it's Michael who worries me more. He seems so moody, and sometimes he doesn't say anything for days. I can't tell if he's mad at me or what. Jude doesn't know what the matter is either."

"Michael has had a hard life. Leaving his country, having his mother and father die—it couldn't have been easy. We, of all people, ought to see that."

"I do, only I'm not sure what to say or do to make him happier. Sometimes he just goes off for an entire afternoon, and then you'll see him up against the skyline right at sunset, just standing all bent over with his hands sunk deep in his pockets."

"Have you told him he's going to be paid when the time comes for him to strike out on his own?"

"Sure! But that doesn't seem to matter to him one way or the other."

Rebecca frowned. "I'll see if I can find out what the trouble is."

She didn't get the chance to talk with Michael until noon, when it was time to eat. They were sitting on a rock gazing out at the valley when Rebecca offered, "I envy you, Michael. You and Katie and Jude. This valley is so peaceful, I wonder why I don't just stay. I haven't felt this relaxed in months."

He thought for several minutes and then replied, "After six months here you'd go crazy."

The statement caught her off guard, and it was a moment before she recovered enough to say, "Do you feel as though you're going crazy?"

"At times. In fact, most of the time. Not since you've been here, though. You're different from Jude and Katie. You and I are a lot alike."

"How so?"

"You've a wandering spirit, the very same as mine." Michael spoke with more calm assurance than a fifteen-year-old boy deserved. "We both crave adventure, new places and faces."

"I'm not so sure about that," Rebecca told him, thinking about all the reporters who had hounded her in Cheyenne and would probably again in South Pass City.

"Oh, I guess I can tell that you're weary of the world

and all of that for now, but you'll soon be ready to go back, for all this talk of peacefulness."

"Michael, the entire West is full of men just wandering about in search of one thing or another. Most of them end up broke, alone, and in shallow, unmarked graves. Jude discovered that during his travels, and you would too."

He stared out at the land. "I've come too damn far to bury myself here."

"Listen to me. Here you can have a stake. In a few years you'll be a man and have a flock of sheep all your own."

He laughed at that, and it wasn't a pleasant sound. "I'd rather have adventure and excitement than money or sheep."

Rebecca was at a loss for what to say to that. "Have you told Katie and Jude how you feel?"

"Not yet. I'll know when it's time and how I can do it without hurting their feelings."

"Are you homesick?"

"For Ireland?" He looked at her strangely.

"Yes."

"Sometimes," he conceded. "I miss the green of it. This valley is pretty enough, but it's all gray and blue. The people in Ireland would call this a desert."

"It's no desert," Rebecca said. "You haven't seen desert until you cross parts of Nevada."

"Jude told me the same thing. I intend to see a desert or two someday. I'd like to see a lot of things before I finally settle down, if I ever do at all."

"You will."

"Maybe. But it's like my father once said. The Irish are a wild and restless breed of men not given to settling down easy or making money."

"Phooey," Rebecca said. "I think all you're doing is giving me a lot of blarney. And at your age, too!"

This time when he laughed there was a ring to it that made her feel good. He finally drew a small briar pipe from his jacket and filled it from a sack of tobacco.

"Michael, you're too young to smoke!"

"Humph," he grunted around the stem of the pipe. "We Irish are born old."

He had the size and face of a boy, yet as she studied him closely and watched him light the pipe, she saw that he was much older around the eyes. Michael Killeen was not going to be short and stocky, like most of his countrymen, but taller and more broad-shouldered. Rebecca knew it was pointless to try to make him change his mind about leaving. Michael looked right back at her with his old, sad eyes, and it was she who almost felt the younger.

"When are you going back?" he asked.

"I'm not sure. Soon after Christmas, I think."

"You don't sound very happy about it."

"I'm not." Rebecca forced a smile. "Actually, I'm dreading it."

"Why?" He must have seen the sudden alarm on her face, because he quickly said, "Never mind. I'm sorry. I didn't mean to pry. It's just that I haven't had a chance to talk about anything but sheep for a long time."

They sat quietly together while Rebecca sorted out her thoughts. She really liked this young Irishman, and it seemed important that it be *she* and not someone else who told him about her past.

"Michael . . ." She groped for words.

"You don't need to tell me anything," he said.

"I want to. We're the closest of friends, aren't we?"

"Damn right," he swore. "Always will be, too."

"Then you should know why I'm dreading to return." She took a deep breath and said it all at once, knowing that was the only way she'd get the telling done. "I'm a bigamist. A woman who married one man while still married to another."

He didn't look away, but his face paled. "Why?" he asked gently.

"I was forced to marry a Mormon, and then I ran away from him and fell in love with an Army doctor at Fort Bridger. Now it seems the entire country wants to know all about it. There are sure to be newspaper men waiting for me in South Pass City."

"To hell with them! Go somewhere else."

She couldn't help but smile at this. If only it were that simple. "They'd find me someday, or, even if they didn't, I'd always be afraid of them. No, since I came here I've had a chance to think and talk to Katie and make a decision—I'm going to Salt Lake City. I'll ask for an annulment because I was forced into the marriage. If they won't give me one, I'll push for a divorce."

"Will they listen to you?"

"I don't know. It's probably never been done before. But my circumstances are so unusual they might make an exception. I married someone who has always taken the law to mean whatever he wished. Besides, I think Judge Carter may know of someone in Utah who will help me."

"We will all help you," Michael vowed.

Rebecca took his rough hand in her own and squeezed it tightly as they watched the sheep graze along the Wind River. It was very, very good to have friends.

It was the middle of January when she hugged Katie for the last time and whispered, "I'm afraid. I can't help it, but I am."

"There's no need to be. Amos Ludlow can never force you to return to Temple City."

"I know, but I'm not sure I can face all the questions and the smirks and the whispering. You have no idea how people imagine a Mormon household, a Mormon bedroom. It would make you sick, Katie. I can see what some of them are thinking by the look in their eyes."

"Ignore them. Rebecca, you are doing the right thing this time." Katie swallowed noisily, and her voice was shaking with emotion and a sense of conviction. "Think of it this way. For the rest of your life no more running or hiding from your past."

"That's all I do think about now."

She kissed Christopher and then embraced Michael, who whispered, "I'll be there."

Even Jude now seemed concerned for her. "You will face a hard man. My father will never allow you to go freely."

"I understand that," she said, climbing hurriedly onto the dun before she lost her will to go.

She heard their shouted farewells as she let her pony race toward the high mountains. The wind numbed her cheeks but not the fear inside. In all her life, Rebecca had never felt so overwhelmed by futility and dread.

She was going back to Utah.

Chapter Twenty-two

Devlin's mind was not on his lecture. Twice he found himself writing equations that had no bearing on the subject at hand, and yet his students did not correct him. They knew the reason for his distraction.

Because of the overnight sensation caused by the national publicity regarding Rebecca Woodson, Devlin's stature had soared to an all-time high among his medical students. In less than twenty-four hours they'd collected no less than eighteen eastern newspapers and compared the articles on his bigamous wife with a more penetrating eye than they'd ever used in the university laboratory. They'd unanimously agreed that Rebecca ought to ethically and legally be Mrs. Devlin Woodson II and that she was one of the most beautiful, courageous women in the world. Why, then, they wondered, was her brilliant professor husband in Washington, D.C., instead of racing to her defense in Salt Lake City?

Devlin stared at the blackboard, his expression vague, his eyes scarcely focused. "That will be all for today," he finally said, rousing himself to the present.

They remained seated, watching him.

He shuffled back to the podium, collected his lecture notes, and was turning to the door when he realized the amphitheater was silent. There was an air of expectancy.

Devlin slowly turned back to them. "What is the matter? Did I . . . Are there any specific questions?"

"Sir!" One of his brightest students rose to his feet, holding a newspaper.

"Yes?" he asked, suddenly wary.

"Is . . ." The young man nervously cleared his throat.

"Is this an accurate drawing of your wife, sir?"

Devlin blinked. Opened his mouth. Clamped it shut. And finally got himself under control. "Your question is impertinent!"

"Yes, sir. I apologize."

Devlin's heartbeat quickened. He had not seen a picture. "Let me see the thing," he said impatiently.

He stared at the sketch, and his sharp intake of breath was clearly audible. Even he had forgotten her beauty. It took him a long time to tear his eyes from the page, but he finally did so, and now he skimmed over the accompanying article. She was on her way to Salt Lake City and was going to ask for an annulment or a divorce from her Mormon husband. Again the reasons for her circumstances were given, and this newspaper was just as sympathetic as the others. Rebecca had captured the public's fancy, and all eyes were turning to Utah, though few newspapers gave her any chance of succeeding in the courtroom, even if everything she'd said was the absolute truth.

She *was* telling the truth. He saw that now, and finally understood the terrible error in trust he'd made that nightmarish afternoon at Fort Bridger. What a fool he was! He'd nearly destroyed himself and had certainly thrown away any chance for happiness he'd ever had. God help him, he'd deserted—no, banished—the woman he loved.

"This sketch really doesn't do her justice," he mumbled to no one in particular. "Nor did I."

Devlin handed the paper back to the student and then went to the podium. His shoulders lifted, and he shook off the daze that had been with him since he'd been visited by the first newspaper reporter, less than a week before. He cleared his voice and looked up at the sea of young faces, the men who would someday go beyond his knowledge. "If you are all wondering why I'm standing here instead of racing for Utah, you have asked yourself the same question that I'm asking myself."

He gripped the podium tightly. The muscles in his forearms knotted, and he said, "And the answer is not to be found in mathematics or in the theories I've given you. It's to be found in the human heart. Once, I was a very good frontier surgeon, until my wife had to amputate the fingers of this hand. She excised the gangrenous tissue, but I should have begged her to excise my stupid, excessive pride."

Devlin raised his head. "We can learn. You are proof of that, and I think I've learned my lesson as well. So this is good-bye. On Monday, this class will be taught by someone at least as capable as I am. I don't know if I will see you again, certainly not for a long time. Teaching you has been a singular pleasure. But Utah is a long way, even on the transcontinental railroad. The question your eyes shouted at me a moment ago has been answered. I only pray it is not too late."

He swung about and moved toward the door as the medical students rose to their feet and the amphitheater filled with applause. It was an ovation he appreciated yet thought was ill-deserved. His father would be insane with anger upon hearing of his decision to leave once more for the West.

It couldn't be helped. Rebecca needed him now to shield her from the world. The only verdict that counted was her forgiveness and love.

Rebecca climbed down from the Union Pacific coach in Ogden, Utah. It was a rough, windy day and very cold outside. The mob of reporters she'd been warned to expect was waiting at the far end of the railroad siding.

A tall, distinguished man with a long, angular face and silver-gray hair jumped out of a buggy, hurried across the platform, and said, "Come quickly, Mrs. Ludlow, before those reporters recognize you!"

"Are you Mr. Thomas Henry?" she asked, giving him her valise and rushing after him.

He glanced back. "Well, certainly. Do I look like an abductor? Didn't Judge Carter give you any description? Never mind. Let's hold the introductions until we make our escape."

Rebecca took a seat in the buggy and they trotted away

just as a cry of dismay arose, indicating that she had been discovered. Mr. Henry's whip snapped like a Fourth of July firecracker and the buggy careened through a row of back streets before they were on their way south toward Salt Lake City.

"Excuse my abruptness," Henry finally said, reining in the horse. "But as you can see, there wasn't any time for explanations. In another minute, you'd have been mobbed. As it was, I had to give them the wrong coach number in order to spirit you away."

"I was wondering about that." Rebecca studied the man. "I know that Judge Carter wrote at my request, and I'm grateful for your help. I really can't afford to pay you very much."

Henry removed his derby and placed it on the black leather seat between them. His hair was long and thick, and he was still a virile-looking man, though well into his sixties. "Never mind that. Money is not the issue in this case. It is justice, Mrs. Ludlow."

"Mrs. Woodson," she corrected.

He studied her with concern. "You misunderstand that, in Utah, you are legally Amos Ludlow's wife. That marriage nullifies the second ceremony, despite the fact that it was performed by a man as eminent as Judge Carter."

Rebecca bit her lip with anxiety. "What are our chances of changing that?"

"Almost zero," he answered, looking straight ahead.

She was still a long time, and her eyes burned with disappointment and the cold wind. "And for a divorce?"

Thomas Henry twisted about to ensure that there was no pursuit. He slowed the horse to a walk. "You know that Mormons, like Catholics, do not believe in divorce."

"But the circumstances! Surely Judge Carter told you—"

"Of course he did." Henry leaned forward a little. "Mrs. Woodson, I have arranged for a preliminary hearing tomorrow, during which I will argue that a federal judge decide this case rather than a territorial one, who would clearly be influenced by the Mormon Church. To win, we must have this trial conducted before a United States district judge."

"And if you are unsuccessful in doing so, then we quit?"

"No. I never quit, and Judge Carter said neither would you. However, our only real chance of winning is to create such embarrassment concerning the entire issue of polygamy that the Mormons will decide that somehow the marriage was indeed invalid, because you were forced into it in order to save a man's life. Also, you must understand that Amos Ludlow has never been one of Brigham Young's favorites."

"I'm aware of that."

Henry leaned back. "That is why you must say nothing more about your life in Temple City to the newspaper reporters here. If the past is to be revealed at all, it must be done in a courtroom. We shall call witnesses and—"

"What witnesses?"

"Anyone who can substantiate your claims. The most obvious being Mr. Bryce Sherman."

"That's impossible. Bryce is dead."

The lawyer glanced at her in surprise and dismay. Clearly, Judge Carter had not written to him explaining everything. But to his credit, Thomas Henry recovered quickly. "That *is* a severe blow to our cause, but not a deathblow. Who else is available? Perhaps if your second husband would testify?"

"That is entirely out of the question. Such an appearance would seriously damage my husband's medical career back east, and I wish him no more pain than I've already caused."

Henry's brows knitted with disapproval. "Commendable, but he could at least testify to your fidelity during your brief marriage at Fort Bridger. The judge also informed me that there are a number of officers' wives who would testify as to the good works you performed at that Army post. One of the ladies is the wife of the commanding officer."

Rebecca smiled, remembering Linda Barrett and the others. They hadn't forsaken her in the midst of all this scandal. "I'd prefer to keep them out of this too."

"Mrs. Woodson!" he protested in anger. "When I was asked to accept your case, I was led to believe we had many character witnesses, and now you are refusing me the right to call them. You leave me with little hope of a defense."

"I was *forced* into that marriage, Mr. Henry. I never even joined their church."

"I'm aware of that. But your marriage is written into their records." He was silent for a moment, intent on the road and his thoughts. "Mrs. Woodson, are you familiar with the Mountain Meadows Massacre?"

"Yes," she whispered. "Bryce told me of it. One doesn't forget such a thing."

"Did he also tell you that Amos Ludlow was one of the leaders?"

"He did. But what bearing does that tragedy have on any of this now?"

"A great deal. The Mormon leadership simply will not support him if the public pressure becomes too severe. I doubt he's ever been forgiven."

"Then we have a chance."

"Yes, even if we lose the preliminary hearing and are given a territorial judge, there is still hope. The ghosts of Mountain Meadows may yet haunt Amos Ludlow. But remember, our strongest hand is not a plea for justice but rather the antipolygamy sentiment that exists in our United States Congress and in the hearts of the American public. To all but the Mormons, polygamy isn't a holy doctrine—it is an excuse for lust."

Rebecca swallowed. Amos Ludlow certainly had been a lusting man.

"Mrs. Woodson, before we reach Salt Lake City, I have to ask you a very personal question, one the court also will ask. Was your marriage to Amos Ludlow consummated?"

She squirmed with shame.

"Against your will?"

"He made my very flesh crawl!"

"Then that is what you must tell the judge, and you

must tell him more," the lawyer said. "I'm sorry. I know it won't be easy."

"Easy?" She looked right through him. "Sir, I would rather die."

He opened his mouth, then closed it, then finally seemed to find words to express his thoughts. "Mrs. Woodson, none of this will be easy for you, and as I've already pointed out, we could easily fail. But I must know right now if you have the will to fight for your independence, your God-given freedom. Because if you do not ... if you do not, then let's save ourselves the ordeal that faces us and go our separate ways in peace."

She thought about it hard. Weighed in her own mind whether or not the price was worth the chance for success. It was. "No, Mr. Henry, I've come too far to quit now."

"Good! Judge Carter wrote that you were courageous. He also said your beauty was your curse."

"What did he mean?"

"Only that it caused Amos to want you enough to take you against your will, and that it's also the reason this case will attract the attention of the most sensationalist newspapers in America, even the world. Your circumstances and your beauty will be used to incite the basest instincts of their readers. Their articles will be phrased in order to excite, even to titillate. It will sell newspapers by the tens of thousands."

He paused reflectively. Clearly, he had his own fears and misgivings. "Knowing all that, can you still go through with it?"

Rebecca said, "I've already said yes. I must, because I have no choice. I won't quit in the middle of the trial, Mr. Henry, if that's what you're thinking."

"It's worth the sacrifice," he said. "You have the unique opportunity to help abolish polygamy, but also to push this territory into giving its women the right to vote, just as was done in Wyoming."

"I find that difficult to believe," she said honestly.

"But it's true. The Mormons are eager to prove to the United States Congress that their women are not slaves

or poor, ignorant creatures deprived of all their free-
doms."

"May I ask you a question?"

"Certainly."

Rebecca had no wish to offend or to pry, but she had
to know. "Why are you doing this if not for the money?"

"I told you, for justice."

"There's more to it than that," Rebecca said. "I know
there is."

"All right. If I should win, I'll become famous, long remembered by historians. For the here and now, my practice would flourish, my legal fees soar. Isn't that more
than enough reason?"

"If the odds were in favor of our winning, then yes."

"You are not only beautiful; you are a very perceptive
young woman," he said finally. "Very well, before this
mess is finished, you'd find out anyway. So I shall relieve
you of the unnecessary suspense. I once was a Mormon."

"You?" She found this startling. People quit their
churches, but rarely attack them afterward except from
guilt, and this man did not seem that sort at all.

"Yes," he said. "I was a good one until about twenty
years ago. My mother was then in her fifties and devoted
to my father, who was a civil engineer. He helped plan
the great irrigation projects that made this desert bloom
into what it is now. He grew prosperous, and by and by
my father was visited by the leaders of his church and
strongly urged to do his part and accept his responsibil-
ities. What they were asking was that he marry a number
of lonely, deserving widows."

Rebecca *knew* the ending to this but did not try to stop
him. Thomas Henry lit a pipe. Its tobacco had a rich
aroma.

"My father was a good man, but he weakened and took
three more wives, all of them meddlesome, grasping ladies. It killed the heart of my mother; despair drove her
to slow madness. I have never forgiven my father, though
in his final days he begged for mercy. Both of them are
dead now, but polygamy"—he shook his fist—"polygamy
still exists, still destroys and ruins the lives of the inno-

cent of heart. I mean to do all in my power to destroy that institution, if not the Mormon Church itself!"

He drew a ragged breath. "I apologize for my lack of control, Mrs. Woodson."

"Please don't apologize. I understand."

"I thought you might," he said. "And now you will understand why I've waited for this, for someone like you, for a long, long time."

Salt Lake City was a testimony to both the vision of Joseph Smith and the dedication of his successor, Brigham Young. It was a sea of greens and winter grays, of fields and farms brought to life by the Mormon people when no others even dreamed it possible. The valley was enormous, yet it seemed to Rebecca to be overshadowed by the towering mountains and the Great Salt Lake itself.

Less than twenty-two years before, Brigham Young had told his starving, beleaguered followers that this was their City of Zion. Once a wasteland, it had been transformed into a model city, one for all the world to see. Nowhere else in the raw West did one find a metropolis so clean, and with broad avenues, verdant lawns, and spacious gardens. Rebecca could not help but be impressed by the wide, tree-lined streets, all of which ran precisely north and south, east and west, and were numbered so that even a stranger knew his position in relation to Temple Square at all times.

"Impressive, isn't it?" Thomas Henry said.

"Very. But it's . . . it's a little too perfect. I guess that sounds ridiculous, but so much order seems somehow . . . disconcerting."

"I don't understand that, but you are not the first to make such a statement. Anyway, don't let all this intimidate you, Rebecca. Mostly, it just reflects planning and hard work. Over there is Temple Block, which was set aside for the Assembly Hall, the Tabernacle, and the Temple."

"Is that where we'll go to court?" She studied it with interest.

"Very close by. Come now, relax and smile. You are

passing Brigham Young's famous Lion House."

Rebecca stared in fascination at the huge, three-storied home of colonial design. The house was constructed of native sun-baked adobe, and its proportions were enormous, with twenty gabled rooms upstairs. Almost a dozen smoking chimneys poked from the roof. The entire house and grounds were surrounded by an impressive wall, which prevented a good view, yet she noted the great stone lion that reclined majestically over the front entrance and gave the house its name.

Henry reined in the horse for a moment for her benefit. As you can well imagine, I haven't been invited into Mr. Young's house, though the description of its interior is common knowledge. On the first floor there's an enormous dining room more than forty feet long where fifty people can eat at one sitting. There is also a buttery, a pantry, a weaving room, the coachman's quarters, and a schoolroom. I'm told it also has a flagstone storage cellar with enough provisions to last the household one year."

Henry continued the recital. "On the main floor is the parlor, used for meetings, prayers, and entertainment, and bedrooms for children. I'm told the central parlor rivals those in the great European houses for its splendid furniture."

"And upstairs? What is upstairs?" she asked, quite sure she could guess.

"Twenty bedrooms for his wives. They are quite small. Brigham's enemies swear the entire place is riddled with secret passages and underground rooms. I'm sure this is quite untrue. Mr. Young has his faults, but they do not include being secretive."

"Neither was Amos Ludlow," she said, turning away in disgust. "What would happen to all those wives if we were to help eliminate polygamy?"

"That's a good question. In truth, I don't know. I rather think most of them would live out their lives unchanged. A few of the younger ones would rejoice. How about the other wives of Amos Ludlow?"

Rebecca thought of them. "Most would feel as if given back the very breath of life," she said.

Thomas Henry glanced sideways at her. "I'm glad," he replied. "Very glad, for that is my mission."

A short time later they were trying to get through a crowd of journalists at her hotel. In the crush of bodies and jostling, she was separated from Thomas Henry and barraged by insistent questioners.

"Are you suing the Mormon Church itself?"

"No."

"Then you're challenging the validity of plural marriage."

"Yes."

"May I quote you?"

"Where is Mr. Henry?" she called, and then she saw him, under as fierce an interrogation as she was.

"Have you heard anything from the Church of Latter Day Saints itself?"

"No."

"Then are you aware of the rumors that they are considering allowing their women to vote?"

"I have only just arrived. I hope—pray that those rumors are true."

"Do you realize, Mrs. Ludlow, that your trial may be having some influence on this decision?"

"I think not. And besides, I *have* my vote."

"Excellent! That will sell newspapers."

"End of questions," Henry said brusquely, grabbing her arm. "Any more discussion could prejudice our case, gentlemen."

"Mr. Henry, aren't you afraid of being harmed?"

This one he did not try to avoid. "Not at all. This is a God-fearing, law-abiding town, safe for everyone, even those who would rally against the practice of plural marriage. My safety could not be more assured."

"Will Brigham Young be called to testify?"

"Don't be absurd, man! Of course not. Come, Rebecca."

Cameras, already loaded and posted beside the stairs, blocked the passage, and Rebecca tripped and almost fell in her haste to pass. Hurrying upstairs above the shouting and the clamor, she and Thomas Henry found her room. Before he left her, he smiled grimly and said,

"Sleep well, Mrs. Woodson. We will need all our wits about us in the days to come."

They lost their plea for a federal judge. No one needed to tell Rebecca that winning now was going to be almost impossible in a court presided over by a Mormon. The national press was incensed, and even some Mormon journalists privately expressed anger. Public attention had focused on Rebecca until she was not able even to venture out of her room.

And then, on February 10, 1870, Utah gave its female citizens the right to vote. The impact in the United States Congress and on the American public was profound and instantaneous. Never mind that the move was calculated to avert pending congressional action making polygamy illegal or that the Mormons, alarmed by increasing numbers of Gentiles pouring into their territory, had now doubled the voting power of the resident Mormons with a single stoke.

Rebecca was ecstatic. She devoured the newspaper accounts of the Utah victory sent to her by woman suffragists all over America.

Her fame increased, became heightened by her seclusion, and, when the day finally came when she was scheduled to begin proceedings against Amos Ludlow, she had to be escorted from her hotel by a detachment of law officers. On her way to the courthouse, the streets were jammed with spectators trying to catch a glimpse of her. Some shouted encouragement, and there were a few oaths.

A description of her entrance into the courtroom appeared later in an eastern newspaper.

> Mrs. Rebecca Ludlow's arrival was a swirl of human confusion, but like the proverbial eye of the hurricane, she appeared calm and composed. Her great beauty contrasted with the ugliness of what promises to be a vicious and wholly unfair trial. Mrs. Ludlow appeared very pale, most likely because of her self-imposed confinement. Yet in her eyes could be seen the look of a

woman deeply committed; one who hungers for her freedom.

The packed courtroom sparked with electricity. Rebecca sat in the front row behind a railing. She could feel the tension growing by the moment as the crowd awaited the arrival of Amos Ludlow.

"Damn him!" Thomas Henry swore. "He's making us all wait just so his entrance will create a big stir. I've heard that he was paralyzed from the waist down by Bryce Sherman. Is that true?"

"I don't think so." Rebecca kept her eyes riveted straight ahead. Four days of testimony by church authorities as to the validity of her marriage according to the Book of Mormon, the Doctrine and Convents, and the Pearl of Great Price had left her confused and drained.

She had listened without really understanding any of it or why these endless theological arguments had anything to do with this court. What it all seemed to boil down to was that these people believed that Joseph Smith had truly been visited by God and Jesus Christ, who'd commissioned him as a prophet and given him the authority to decree that polygamy was a holy practice as commanded by the Lord God.

"Here he comes," Henry said, twisting around in his seat as the courtroom doors swung open.

Rebecca sat frozen in dread. She heard the uneven whisper as the wheels of Amos's chair revolved up the aisle toward the witness stand. Then she felt him passing her, smelled the scent of him, and tasted all the awful memories of what he was, what he'd done to her not so very long ago.

She made herself look up as he passed, but his back was still to her and he was bent over, sitting deep in his steel and wood contraption and propelling himself forward with grim determination. He reached the place beside the witness stand and he seemed to straighten, grow larger than he had been moments before. Rebecca stared with a mixture of fear and fascination. She noted his great rack of shoulders, even now starting to twist as he began to turn the chair and face her. His back was immense, and it seemed to her humped with muscle even now, and she saw the bulge of his arms and remembered how those arms had once pinned her beneath him in a rutting embrace. She looked away, suddenly faint.

"Rebecca," Thomas Henry said urgently. "Are you all right?"

Her heart was laboring so hard it seemed to squeeze in on her lungs until she felt a shortness of breath and had to tell herself that she must not faint, must sit upright and face this man, or he would beat and ridicule her in all the hours of this trial.

His voice exploded through the courtroom. "Look at your husband, Rebecca, you whore!"

The room itself seemed to draw in its collective breath and hold it until Thomas Henry shouted, "Your Honor, I object to this vicious attack. This is a court of law, not an inquisition!"

The judge, a small but scholarly-appearing man in his early fifties, peered down through his thick glasses and said, "Objection sustained. Mr. Ludlow, you have been called to the stand to testify to the validity of your marriage, and *not* to make slanderous statements about this woman."

Amos said nothing, but his lips wore a twisted smile.

"Now then," the judge continued. "This woman seeks a divorce on the grounds that she was forced into matrimony."

He glanced down at his table and thumbed through a sheaf of papers. "I have with me the written statement which reads in part: 'I was forced to marry Amos Ludlow under the threat that Bryce Sherman, now deceased, would be shot to death upon his return to Temple City if I refused.'"

The judge cocked his head. "Mr. Ludlow, if this can be proven, then I will have to rule that your marriage is invalid. Also, as you must be fully aware, this woman must have been a member of our church before she could enter into a plural marriage."

"She was one of us," Amos vowed solemnly.

"That is a lie!" Rebecca found herself on her feet. "Your Honor, I *never* joined your church."

Amos tore an envelope from the inside of his coat pocket. In his haste, it went sailing to land on the polished wood floor. He slammed his palms down on the big wheels and drove the chair forward so violently that the front of it lifted completely off the ground. One of the court assistants jumped to retrieve the envelope, but Amos beat him to it and deftly snapped the envelope up. Spinning the chair around, he said, "Read this, Your Honor."

His agility and quickness surprised everyone but Rebecca. He wasn't a young man, but there had always been an animal strength and vitality about him that was frightening.

The judge opened the letter and studied it for a moment before adjusting his glasses and turning his attention to Rebecca. "Mrs. Ludlow, these are certificates of marriage and baptism confirming that not only were you legally married, but that you were a member of the Church of Christ of Latter Day Saints."

Rebecca was shaking her head back and forth. Her mind rebelled at this sudden treachery and refused to accept what Amos was doing to her. "I swear I've never been baptized in your church. You *must* believe me."

"How can I when these documents say otherwise? They even bear your signature."

"The marriage certificate, yes. But not the other. I . . . I would not have done it for anything. It would have been an affront to God. No, sir. I swear the baptismal certificate is a forgery."

The courtroom became very still. The judge peered down at her for a long moment and then sighed loud enough to be heard around the room. "Mrs. Ludlow, I'm afraid the document in question appears authentic in every respect, including your signature. However, I am not fully qualified to judge if a forgery has been done here. So, for the time being, I will withhold this baptismal certificate from consideration."

"Thank you."

Amos was smiling.

"Mr. Henry, you may cross-examine Mr. Ludlow."

"Your Honor," he said, coming to his feet and striding forward with a confidence that Rebecca could not begin to understand. In fact, so far he'd almost seemed over-confident despite the preponderance of testimony in Amos's behalf. And today, she thought, is the day of summation.

"Your Honor," he repeated. "It is not my intention to deny that the marriage ceremony took place. Mr. Ludlow and his attorney, Mr. Butler, have witnesses to attest to the fact." He gestured toward the audience, and Rebecca followed his gaze to see, over by the far wall, Anna Ludlow and several of the other wives. They looked miserable, all of them.

"Then what, exactly, is your intention?"

"To prove the marriage was completely against Miss Prescott's will and totally invalid."

The judge raised his eyebrows. "Begin your questioning, then."

"Yes, Your Honor." He turned to study Amos, who sat tightfisted and who was no longer smiling. "Mr. Ludlow, did you or did you not force Miss Rebecca Prescott into marrying you so that she might save the life of Bryce Sherman?"

"I did not," Amos snapped. "The man was a renegade, a horse thief who would have been shot or hanged under any circumstances. That's the law. Everyone knows that."

"Everyone?" Thomas Henry swung around to face her. "Did you know that Bryce Sherman would be brought to justice under any circumstances?"

"He swore that all charges would be dropped. He ran an ad in the paper and showed it to me. I believed him."

The opposing attorney yelled. "Objection! Mrs. Ludlow is not under oath, and her statements are not to be considered."

"Objection sustained."

The attorney sat down with a pleased look on his face.

He was young, handsome, and quite sure of himself. He almost swaggered before the audience.

Thomas Henry continued his questioning, and now his manner was very brisk. "How many wives do you have, Mr. Ludlow?"

"Five, including her. They're all here to swear that the marriage took place in my house."

"That won't be necessary. How many children do you have?"

Amos scowled. "What's that got to do with all this?"

"You have fifteen, Mr. Ludlow. And isn't it true that the oldest, the one named Jude, also went away with Bryce Sherman and, in fact, helped him escape?"

"No! That boy didn't help him do anything."

"Your son urged Bryce Sherman to take him out to see the city lights, Mr. Ludlow. He knew the kind of man you are—vicious, without conscience, and—"

"Objection!"

"Objection sustained. Mr. Henry, the character of Amos Ludlow is not on trial here."

"Well, it damn sure ought to be!"

"One more outburst such as that and you will be dismissed from this courtroom! the judge cried. "I will not stand for such behavior."

Thomas Henry's jaw muscles corded, but he did not lose control. "Mr. Ludlow, is it essential that Miss Prescott was baptized into your church for the marriage to be valid?"

Amos blinked. Whatever he'd first been about to say was now forgotten, and his eyes narrowed as he stared at the attorney. "I showed the court that baptismal certificate."

"I'm aware of that. What I want to be sure of is this: For the marriage to have been legal, was it absolutely essential that she be a member of your church?"

Amos licked his lips, glanced nervously over at his attorney, then said. "That's right, but—"

"Then how in God's good name," Thomas Henry roared, "can this marriage be legal when you, a leader in the Mountain Meadows Massacre, were formally excommunicated!"

Rebecca gasped as the full impact of what had just been said slammed home. Now she realized why her attorney had thought they had a case! A surge of hope filled her breast as the courtroom erupted with the excited voices of the spectators. Pounding feet could be heard in the hallway, and she knew that the reporters were racing toward the telegraph office. The judge was banging his gavel again and again and shouting for order as the court assistants tried to silence the audience.

Amos seemed to shrivel in his wheelchair. His bluster and arrogance were gone now as his attorney bent toward him and whispered rapidly into his ear.

"Get a doctor!" someone yelled. "This woman is ill!"

Rebecca started to rise, but Thomas Henry stopped her from going over. The woman was immediately attended to and in just a few moments was on her feet and being led sobbing from the courtroom. Oh, my God, Rebecca thought as she recognized one of Amos's younger wives. If this is all true, those women are living in sin and have borne illegitimate children in the eyes of the Mormon Church. What have I done?

When order was finally restored, Thomas Henry stood and pointed down at Amos and shouted, "Were you or were you not excommunicated? Answer me!"

Amos shuddered. His eyes burned with hatred as he turned them up toward his accuser. "God has forgiven me! I have chosen to remain in the church, and no man, not even Brigham Young himself, can sever the bonds between me and the teachings of Joseph Smith. I am a saint!"

No one said a word for a moment, and then the opposing attorney was speaking. "Your Honor, my client is a God-fearing man, as are his wives and his children. Are we so blind that we refuse to recognize that this marriage was performed according to our laws with the intentions of the heart in every way faithful to our teachings? This marriage was not only legal in the eyes of our church, but also in the eyes of the laws of this territory. What man would say that Amos Ludlow's wives and children will be denied heaven because of this? Is there no mercy, no moral rule that transcends error? Would we, on this day, before all the world, cast out four decent, God-loving wives and fifteen children so that this one immoral woman should prevail? It would be a mockery! An injustice so foul that it would never be forgiven!"

The judge swallowed and banged his gavel in a distracted manner that left no doubt in anyone's mind as to the level of his agitation. "The court is recessed until tomorrow morning. I need counsel."

"Mrs. Ludlow, you insist you were forced into this marriage in order to protect the life of Bryce Sherman. Is this true?"

"Yes."

"Were you aware that the man stole a pair of horses in order to escape from Temple City?"

"I knew. But he'd worked—"

"Just answer the questions, please. Mrs. Ludlow, was your marriage . . . consummated?"

She had thought herself prepared for this one but she had to try twice before the words were out of her. "By force!"

He smiled. His eyes mocked her, and they slipped to her bosom. "I see. How many times, approximately?"

"Objection! Your Honor, I resent this line of questioning. It is outrageous!"

The judge leaned forward. "Mr. Butler, I'm afraid I also object to this kind of questioning. I will tolerate no more of it. Do you quite understand?"

"Yes, Your Honor. I apologize to the court. It was my intention to establish, without any doubts whatsoever, that this woman fully participated as a wife and member of the Ludlow household. This was not a rape, nor had it been explained that when she came to Temple City, it was to seek help, which was freely given. In return, this woman freely agreed to remain in the household and learn the ways of the Mormon Church. She attended classes and services; she was baptized according to the evidence presented."

He stared accusingly at Rebecca. "Did Amos Ludlow—who took you in, fed and clothed you and your father and your sister, gave you instruction and his charity—did he ever once abuse you?"

She could not bear to tell these people what he had done to her in his bed. Rebecca shook her head.

"And all this while, Bryce Sherman, who would later marry your own sister, was in love with you and you with him and—"

"That is not true!" Rebecca cried. "I never loved him!"

The attorney smiled with pity. "Does it really matter? You have succeeded in ruining the lives of three men whose only crime was that they fell in love with you. Those men are Amos Ludlow, Bryce Sherman, and a captain in the United States Army. How do you feel about that, in addition to the entire Ludlow family, whose lives you have tainted?"

"I never meant to hurt anyone. I tried to save Bryce, not destroy anyone. I am not an immoral woman. All I want is my freedom," she choked.

"For what purpose? To destroy others? No, you are bound by the laws of God and man and you cannot ignore them. Not ever."

"Objection!" Thomas Henry cried.

"Objection sustained," the judge said. He let his gavel fall. "The court will recess until one-thirty P.M., at which time final summations will be made and I will announce my verdict as to the present state of the marriage."

The gavel banged down again, and Rebecca sat immobile while a subdued audience filed out into the hallway.

She didn't remember the recess, nor did Thomas Henry's assurances carry any meaning or conviction. Now she only wanted to be done with this mockery of justice and get on with her own life. They could not make her return to Temple City, but they had smeared her character before the public until there was no sympathy

GARY McCARTHY

either for her or for Amos. Both of them were bloodied by this ordeal. It had been a terrible mistake for her to come here, and now, as she looked at the compassionless face of the judge in his cold black robes, she knew she could not possibly win the verdict.

Amos was wheeled in and once more pushed up beside the witness stand. "Mr. Ludlow," his attorney said loudly enough for everyone to hear. "Our church has just decided, only moments ago, that your marriages are valid."

Once more a number of the reporters dashed outside to race for the telegraph office as the courtroom buzzed with excitement. Thomas Henry moaned; his face assumed a stricken appearance. Rebecca reached out and touched his arm, saying, "You did everything possible. I'm sorry for us both."

"Your Honor, in view of this announcement, and the fact that I have proven that Mrs. Rebecca Ludlow freely chose to enter the marriage, there can be little question of a correct verdict. No one held a gun to that woman's head. She has provided absolutely no evidence to support any of her claims. Her character—let me amend that—her lack of character speaks more eloquently than any words and supports my case. She is an immoral woman."

The judge frowned. "Just stick to the facts, Mr. Butler, and summarize your case as requested."

"Yes, Your Honor. It has given me no pleasure to point out that that woman has lied and cheated. She came to Mr. Ludlow in time of great need and he made the mistake of falling for her beauty and not seeing the corruption within."

"Your Honor!" Thomas Henry roared. "This is no trial! You are purposefully allowing this slander to continue while my client is being assassinated with words."

"Sit down!"

"Why should he?" an ever so well remembered voice thundered from the hallway. "This is a disgrace, a mockery of justice! How dare you judge my wife!"

Rebecca whirled around in her seat. "Devlin!"

Her voice cut through the room like a knife. Everyone

390

swung around to see the disheveled, out of breath doctor. Rebecca jumped erect, but Henry gripped her arm and held her immobile.

"Don't," he begged. "For God's sake, don't go to him now and ruin this one last chance you have to become his legal wife!"

She froze. Her eyes locked with his and she saw him nod. Somehow, she knew, he understood everything. Rebecca sat bolt upright and raised her head, not caring about the tears on her cheeks, not caring what anyone said or thought.

"Your Honor," Henry said loudly. "My client will not call Dr. Devlin Woodson the Second, her true husband, to testify, but it is clear—"

"Damn right I'll testify."

"No!" Rebecca cried, her voice final.

"Then I will," Jude Ludlow said, striding forward to take the chair.

"And who are you!" the judge demanded.

"I am Jude Ludlow. Son of Amos Ludlow."

The courtroom had to be silenced again. Jude took the chair and his oath. Thomas Henry made no attempt to lead him with questions; he let Jude speak.

"My father, Amos Ludlow, forced Miss Rebecca to marry him by swearing he'd have Bryce Sherman killed if she did not."

"That is a lie!" Amos screamed, seeming to rise from his chair. "A lie! Get him out of here. Get him out!"

Now Jude looked at his father. "You had him killed anyway, killed by a hired gunman named Guy Wilson for a thousand dollars."

"Liar!"

"You are going to rot in hell, Father," Jude pronounced.

Amos was thirty feet away, but he lunged at his son, threw himself from the chair with a terrible shriek, and hit the floor, then began to crawl across the stones toward the witness stand. He was babbling insanely, reaching up with his big hands and clenching them, spitting and tearing at the air between them, seeming to pull at it as though it would bring Jude within his grasp.

Men rushed forward to help him back into his chair, and he clawed at them, bellowing like a blind animal. When finally he was removed from the court, no one spoke. Even the judge looked drained. At last he said, "Do you have proof of your accusations?"

"No, sir. Unless you saw what I saw in him now," Jude said.

"Your testimony cannot be considered without proof."

He looked out at Thomas Henry, avoiding Rebecca's eyes. "Do you have anything to add?"

"No, sir."

"Then it *must* be the court's decision," the judge thundered, "that the marriage be held legal and binding."

The courtroom dissolved once again in outrage and confusion.

Rebecca sat still for a moment, too exhausted, too overcome even to think about the decision or beyond the very next second.

She could hear the shouting, feel the room shake as it rocked with wild disorder.

"Rebecca?" Devlin was kneeling beside her. "It doesn't matter what he said. You're my wife. Katie told me what you've been through. I've followed everything in the papers. I believe I know what you want. I'll help you become a doctor. A great doctor. I'll do anything."

"I *would* make a fine doctor." This court was *not* going to beat her. This judge was *not* going to destroy her life. She would never give up. Never! At the touch of Devlin's hand she felt hope flowing back into her.

"Then we must find a way to get you into medical school. I swear that even if we have to go to Europe it shall be done! But for now, all I want to do is make up for all the pain I've caused, the wasted—"

Rebecca pressed her forefinger against his lips to silence the torrent of words. Words. She had heard far too many these past few weeks, and thousands more had been printed about her and Amos Ludlow and polygamy. But all the words meant nothing.

She looked deep into his eyes. "I'm going to fight this

WIND RIVER

court decision. I'll never stop fighting it until I'm free."

She was suddenly so tired. The din of voices, the close, oppressive heat of the packed courtroom, and the shattering court decision given only moments earlier all seemed now to leave her weak and empty. Rebecca laid her head on Devlin's shoulder. "No more words right now, Devlin," she murmured. "Just hold me very, very tightly—as though you will never let me go."

He crushed her in his arms. And, for now, that was all she really needed.

Author's Note

The main characters in *Wind River* are entirely fictional, but Katie Prescott is not so different from Lucy Morrison Moore, the Sheep Queen of Wyoming, who, with her husband, trailed a band of woollies into the Wind River country long before it was inhabited by whites. The Morrisons survived, then prospered, because, like Katie, they had a dream that refused to die. Of special importance to the research of this novel and the development of Katie's character is a book titled *Lady of a Legend*, by Bob Edgar and Jack Turnell, of Wyoming, which was brought to my attention by my editor, Marc Jaffe.

The main character of the novel, Rebecca Prescott, also has a dream, but hers is thwarted by the controversial issue of polygamy. The reader should know that the Mountain Meadows Massacre, and the mass hysteria that caused it, did take place as described. Brigham Young's orders to keep the peace were defied, and those members of his church found guilty were excommunicated. Some twenty years later, the leader of the guilty was executed. Polygamy was the issue that almost destroyed the Mormon Church during its early years, though it is estimated that not more than ten to twenty percent of the married men were involved with the practice. Because polygamy was so hated by the Gentiles, the prophet Joseph Smith was murdered and his people repeatedly driven from their homes in the East until they finally began, with handcarts and starving animals, an epic and courageous ordeal that would carry them via the Mormon Trail to the Great Salt Lake, where Brigham Young founded his State of Deseret.

It was not until 1890 that the LDS Church, facing virtual destruction under an avalanche of antipolygamy laws, finally issued the manifesto that signaled the end of this abhorrent practice. Ironically, although vigorously denounced and outlawed by the Mormon Church itself, polygamy still exists. As *Wind River* was being written, a Magna, Utah, polygamist filed in a federal court the first challenge to the current antipolygamy laws in more than a century.

South Pass City and Fort Bridger are real and are remarkably well preserved today; each has an outstanding historical museum where one can learn about such famous Wyoming pioneers as Judge William Carter and Esther Hobart Morris. Esther Morris is still referred to as the Mother of Woman Suffrage. At South Pass City, a visitor can peer inside a replica of her log cabin to see where many historians believe the seed of equal rights first was sown on an election eve in 1868. Esther Morris went on to become the first female justice of the peace in the world.

James Bridger, the famous mountain man and explorer who claimed to be the first white man ever to see the Great Salt Lake, did found a settlement along Black's Fork of the Green River, where he proved himself to be an able trader and businessman. In time he sold Fort Bridger to the Mormons, who were soon forced to abandon it because of a brewing conflict with the United States Army. It was Judge William A. Carter—sutler, postmaster, Virginia gentleman, and enterpreneur—who had the greatest impact on southwestern Wyoming. He was famed for his hospitality and beloved by his family and friends, who included the great Shoshoni chief, Washakie.

Washakie was leader of the Shoshoni for almost sixty years. He was just as impressive as Rebecca sees him— tall, dignified, and a peacemaker, the only Indian chief ever to choose his own beloved reservation and keep it. To this day, his descendants remain on the Wind River

Reservation, where another famous Shoshoni, Saca-jewea, is buried.

Wind River, then, is a novel heavily laced with real characters forging their actual roles in American history. Such women as Rebecca and Katie and men like Bryce, Amos, and Devlin might well have existed in those turbulent, exciting days when the issues of polygamy and woman suffrage were hotly contested throughout the land. The struggle for women's rights still continues, and I hope that after *Wind River* it will be more widely recognized that Wyoming was the first state to give its women the right to vote and to hold public office. Her residents have every reason to be proud of their state motto: "Equal Rights."

Gary McCarthy
Lake Havasu City, AZ
1998

About the Author

Gary McCarthy was raised in Southern California and very early developed a keen interest in the West and its history. He grew up around horses and old-timers who cherished their gift of storytelling. In his mid-twenties, he began to write Western novels while working as a labor economist in Carson City, Nevada.

Mr. McCarthy is an award-winning author who has written many novels of the American West and who now lives in Arizona.

WILL HENRY

JOURNEY TO SHILOH

While the bloody War Between the States is ripping the country apart, Buck Burnet can only pray that the fighting will last until he can earn himself a share of the glory. Together with a ragtag band of youths who call themselves the Concho County Comanches, Buck sets out to drive the damn Yankees out of his beloved Confederacy. But the trail from the plains of Texas to the killing fields of Tennessee is full of danger. Buck and his comrades must fight the uncontrollable fury of nature and the unfathomable treachery of men. And when the brave Rebels finally meet up with their army, they must face the greatest challenge of all: a merciless battle against the forces of Grant and Sherman that will truly prove that war is hell.

_4203-7 $4.50 US/$5.50 CAN

T. V. OLSEN

Winner of the Golden Spur Award

THE STALKING MOON

Army scout Sam Vetch is finally ready to settle down and start a new life on that quiet New Mexico ranch he's been saving for all these years. He has no way of knowing that his cherished wife had once been the woman of Salvaje, the notorious Apache chieftain known as The Ghost—and that she has borne two sons by him. When Salvaje comes to claim what is his, the duel begins—a deadly contest between two men of strong will, cast-iron courage, and fatal honor—a duel that can only end in tragedy under the stalking moon.

_4180-4 $4.50 US/$5.50 CAN

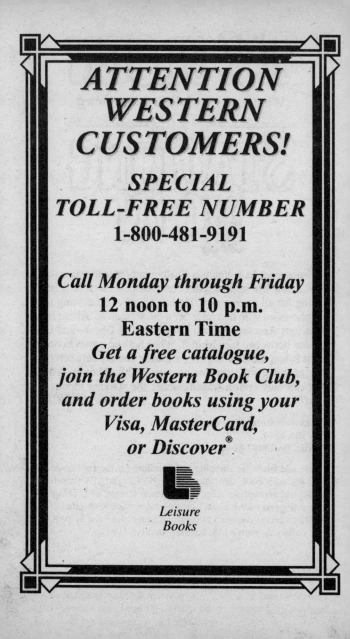